THE MURDER LAWYER

THE COMPLETE SERIAL NOVEL

PIPER PUNCHES

The Murder Lawyer is a work of fiction. Names, characters, places, and incidents either are the product of the author's imagination or are used fictitiously. Any resemblance to actual persons, living or dead, events, or locales is entirely coincidental.

Text copyright © 2018, 2019, 2020 by Piper Punches

All rights reserved.
No part of this book may be reproduced, scanned, or distributed in any printed or electronic form without permission. Please do not participate or encourage piracy of copyrighted materials in violation of the author's rights.

The Complete Serial Novel First Published in the United States in 2020.

ISBN 978-1-7353895-5-4 (hardback)
ISBN 978-1-7353895-3-0 (paperback)
ISBN 978-1-7353895-4-7 (ebook)

For inquiries, please contact the author directly at:
http://piperpunches.com
piper@piperpunches.com

To all who fight for justice.

NOTE TO READER

Two years ago, I had an idea to create an episodic fiction series, a twelve-part novelette similar to a television series in the way that each part would include a primary plot of its own with a continuous story arc weaved throughout the series. From that idea, *The Murder Lawyer* was created and what follows this Note is that concept in its complete serial novel form.

The Murder Lawyer isn't another courtroom drama. It's a novel that pushes the reader to reconsider the idea of justice and how the criminal justice system isn't always black-and-white. It's about a young idealistic criminal defense attorney who believes that everyone deserves a defense, even those people accused of seemingly indefensible crimes. It's also a story about balancing motherhood, marriage, and career success.

The first seven parts of *The Murder Lawyer* were previously available on Amazon and other platforms where ebooks are sold. If you previously purchased any of these stories, find the part where you left off to continue reading or start from the beginning and reacquaint yourself with the story.

Now, without further ado, I invite you to grab a hot drink, get comfortable, and immerse yourself in *The Murder Lawyer*.

PART ONE

WHEN LUCK DIES

1

Cold, shivering, and chilled from the inside and out, Luna Goldwyn stands naked in front of the foggy bathroom mirror taking long, deep breaths. Inhale . . . one, two, three, four, five. Exhale . . . five, four, three, two, one. She repeats the breathing pattern three more times and feels her heart rate start to slow. There's a trickle of blood running down the back of her leg, tickling her calf. That's what she gets for trying to shave with only soap, water, and a month-old razor. Her chestnut-colored hair sticks to her neck, the middle of her back, and between her breasts. She stepped out of the shower forgetting to dry off and stands in a puddle on the vinyl floor.

Over the white noise of the exhaust fan, she hears the muted clang of pots and pans being pulled from kitchen cabinets. She anticipates the smell of maple sausage, scrambled eggs, and strong-brewed coffee. Breakfast is her favorite meal, but managing even a small bite today seems impossible.

She shivers again and slides an oversized, plush brown towel off the rack. It feels so warm and luxurious. It's an expensive sort of towel that belongs in the bathrooms of elegant homes with Ladue or Town and Country zip codes. Not in her little St. Charles fixer-upper. Last Christmas, Mark surprised her and installed a towel warmer in their tiny master bathroom. He took the surprise one step further when he wrapped up Turkish cotton bath towels in ridiculous elf wrapping paper. Some women want diamonds and gold for Christmas. What Luna desires most is warmth, something her husband always gives her.

As she blots her body dry, she hears Ian clip-clopping up and down the hallway like a rambunctious and awkward young show pony, wearing the flea-market cowboy boots her father bought him. For two weeks he's worn those boots, even to bed. The thought of his little feet touching someone else's foot sweat creeps her out, but the way his face lit up when he saw the boots won her over. So she's disinfected them the best she can and made him promise to always wear socks. Now like the exhaust fan, the boots against the hardwood are part of the background noise of her daily life.

Luna wraps another warmed towel around her body. She cracks the bathroom door to release the steam and runs a comb through her hair. It takes her thirty minutes to dry it through, another ten to brush it back into a tight, low bun, and then she spends twenty more minutes applying her makeup. When she leaves the bathroom, she walks to her closet and stands in front of the zip-up bag that reads Nordstrom. Inside the bag is a navy suit jacket and pencil skirt pair, and a white, silk blouse that cost too much money. When she handed over her credit card to make the purchase, her stomach seized. When she purchased the matching nude heels for twice as much as the suit, she threw up a little in her mouth. But inside that fancy bag is a power outfit, one she needs today more than any other.

After dressing, she moves to her dresser and opens the top drawer. Inside a tiny, maroon box is a pair of pearl earrings. Her grandmother's earrings that were a law school graduation gift from her mother. Luna isn't really a pearl earrings sort of person. She rarely wears jewelry, other than her wedding ring and a silver watch with a thin band. Today's the first day she removes the earrings from the box, sliding the posts through her pierced ears and stepping back from the dresser. She turns around to stand in front of the full-length mirror in the corner of the room. A smile starts to tug at her painted, pink lips as she takes in the woman staring back at her, who cleans up well and looks professional and confident. Then she remembers. Her heart races again. She's not playing dress-up. She has a job to do.

Today she gives closing arguments in her first murder case. Today her job is to keep her client alive.

2

One week earlier

The black cat should have been a sign. That's what she'll tell herself as the hours and days pass, but at the moment, it's just another stray lazing about in the middle of her parking spot. Luna honks her horn. The cat lifts its head. It yawns, stretches, and makes a big production of leaving, giving Luna a backward glance, reminding her that she's the problem.

The streets are quiet at seven o'clock in the morning. Although the law office of Mikey George & Associates is squished between the courthouse and the hospital, not much movement happens this early. It's not until after the kids are dropped off at school and the caffeine sets in that the suits and scrubs show up, ready to get to business. Luna loves the calm right after sunrise. She was named for the moon, yet the brilliant sunshine makes her the happiest.

Parked in the next spot is Doris Wall's fancy Cadillac Escalade, a vehicle too big for the Hot Wheel-sized space. Mikey doesn't even drive a Cadillac, and he's practiced law for thirty years. His vehicle is the red Honda Civic with a cracked windshield and a bumper sticker encouraging one to make it legal and do it with a lawyer. Doris drives the Escalade because she won it at the river casino during a promotion. Every day for nine months, during her lunch, she walked half a mile to the casino and entered her name for the monthly drawing.

"Some women wait nine months and get a baby," Doris joked. "Well, my baby weighs a ton and looks good in the McDonald's drive-thru. It also doesn't shit in my arms."

Luna shakes her head at the SUV, smiles, and lets herself into the office through the back door, careful not to spill the two cups of coffee cradled between her forearm and elbow. Doris is sitting hunched over her desk sorting papers.

"Morning, Luna," she says.

"Hey! Had to do the breakfast blend this morning from the gas station. The drive-thru line at Starbucks was twenty deep and the line inside was out the door."

"I'm going to have to tell Mikey to hire another lawyer. One who gets better coffee," she says, teasing.

Luna sets the paper cup on Doris's desk. She nods at the stack of files growing by the day. "Maybe he should hire another you. The case files keep getting higher."

"There is no other me, sweetheart. I'm the best there is. Don't forget that." She winks at Luna, takes a sip of the coffee, and winces. "God, this is horrible. It's going to take at least six Splendas to make this drinkable."

Luna reaches into her purse and pulls out a handful of artificial sweeteners. "I thought ahead."

"Good girl. You're my favorite lawyer." Doris sprinkles the white particles in the cup and reaches for the date book. "Want your schedule for the day?"

"Does it involve anyone who isn't facing a parole violation?"

"Doubtful."

"Let's keep it a mystery a little while longer then. Looks like you could use some help going through those files."

Doris sits back in her chair and sighs. "These are all from the White case. Closing arguments are at the end of the week."

The White case. Talk about an uphill battle. Luna is second-chairing the case with Mikey, but only in the sense that she sits at the defense table taking notes that she then adds to the stack of files on Doris's desk. Mikey George & Associates isn't a big-time criminal defense firm. There's only one associate, and it's her. Between the two of them, they deal by and large with parole violators, a few meth heads, and drunk driving cases. Those cases are farm league, Triple-A.

Tammy White's case is major league, a first-degree murder case deserving of a bigger firm with more resources and a legal team that knows how to argue a capital case. It deserves a Clayton firm like Brysen, Clyde, and Muller, one that bills no less than a grand an hour and exhausts the court system with motion after motion, keeping the case from reaching the jurors for at least three years. Unfortunately, Tammy White's case and Tammy herself aren't Clayton-worthy. With barely two hundred dollars to her name when she was arrested a year ago on suspicion of first-degree murder, two options existed: hand the case over to a public defender or call Mikey, the lawyer who knows her best friend's mother's cousin from his first marriage.

Truth be told, Mikey should have refused the case. Even with thirty years of trial experience, this case required a bigger firm and not one that accepts sliding-scale payments. Luna would have passed off the case. Not Mikey. He salivated at the thought of publicity and a big-time murder case. Who cared if it was at the expense of a client's life? Luna is sure Mikey doesn't see it this way. He doesn't think that far ahead, and that could prove detrimental to his client.

"You get what that woman did, right?" Doris asks, pulling the White case file off the top of the pile and setting it aside. "She point-blank shot that man between the eyes while he slept."

Luna doesn't argue. "Yup. She did it, and you and I know why she did it, don't we?"

Doris nods. "Yeah, I understand."

"The bigger question is, does she deserve a conviction that comes with the possibility of lethal injection attached to it?"

"Mikey's arguing this case in front of a jury in the most Republican county in the state."

"I know, Doris. It's going to be tough. Thank God it's Mikey giving the closing. I don't think I could stomach it. Speaking of the old man, where is he? I saw his car parked out back."

"Doris shrugs. "I assume in his office. His car was here when I got here an hour ago."

"You don't think he slept here last night, do you?"

Doris raises her eyebrow at Luna. "What do you think? My guess is he spent the better part of the evening scribbling notes on his legal pad and tossing back a few too many shots of Wild Turkey." She reaches into the wastebasket by her desk and pulls out an empty pint of the whiskey.

"Good investigative skills, Doris." Luna looks down the hallway. "Still, he doesn't usually stay holed up all night, does he? What about his dogs?"

The two women look at each other.

"I'll go check on him," Doris says. She takes her coffee with her, whistling as she walks down the hall to Mikey's office.

Luna stands up and walks in the opposite direction to her office. Her hand is reaching for the door handle when she hears Doris say something inaudible. Then the screaming follows.

***

The police and paramedics arrive ten minutes after Luna dials 911. The paramedics estimate Mikey's been dead for several hours. When Doris opened the door, she thought, at first, he'd fallen asleep at his desk. His head rested on a stack of papers like a school kid sleeping through math class. But Mikey was a snorer, especially when he pulled a late night and drank himself to sleep. The office was too quiet. So Doris moved closer to the desk, and that's when she noticed the congealed blood on the papers. She focused on his back and waited for it to move, up and down, up and down. It didn't. That's when her grip loosened on the coffee cup and she screamed.

"Probably a heart attack," Tom, the lead paramedic, says.

"Are you sure? What about the blood from his temple?" Doris asks.

"It likely happened fast. He fell forward hard, hitting his

head," he says.

Officer Lee Colton, a middle-aged man who'd done some private investigating for Mikey here and there, says, "I don't see anything to suggest foul play or suicide."

"Mikey would never commit suicide," Doris says, grimacing and crossing her arms in front of her.

Lee puts his hand on her shoulder. "I know. No one ever entertained that thought. Look, Mikey wasn't a healthy guy. We all know that. He drank a lot, inhaled fast food, and—" He looks over his shoulder at his partners who are trying to move the 300-pound man onto the gurney. "Well, he just wasn't healthy. Of course, the coroner will have a cause of death as soon as possible. Has anyone gotten in touch with his wife?"

"She's been living with her sister in Cleveland for the last six months or so," Doris says. "I'll track down her number and let her know."

It happens so fast, Luna thinks. Just like that, someone is living and breathing, and then they're not. Mikey's reputation for being crude and hard to deal with in professional circles was well known, but he always treated Luna with kindness. He was an unexpected mentor who took a chance on her after she graduated from law school when no one else in town would. When Luna applied to law school, she expected to excel to the top of her class, graduate with job offers at the most prestigious law firms in the St. Louis region, and live the glamorous lifestyle as a top-billed attorney. Of course, every law student has this dream. The reality is that law school is hard. Always an A student throughout high school and her undergrad career, she struggled her first year to get Cs. The amount of reading was overwhelming, and learning legal terminology was like learning a different language. Then there was the part-time job she worked at a coffee shop to pay the costs her financial aid package didn't cover. She also had the brilliant idea to get married after that first year and buy a home. It was too much too soon.

Between the wedding, the part-time job, a new house, and the insane amount of work law school required, Luna struggled to stay in the middle of the pack. By graduation, she was a solid C student and owed $100,000 in student loans. For five months, she applied for positions in large firms throughout the St. Louis area with no luck. With less than a month before repayment on her loans started, she needed a job that paid more than $9.50 an hour. So she settled and took the job at Mikey George & Associates.

His practice wasn't horrible; the work was just unfulfilling. Handling probation and parole violations, fixing tickets, and pleading with her clients to at least try to wear something with sleeves when addressing the court was not her vision of being a lawyer. Some days she felt she made a very expensive mistake going to law school. Tammy White's case was the most exciting case that came through the office, and she wasn't even front and center on the case.

Tammy.

What about Tammy?

Closing arguments are this week.

She watches the paramedics zip up the black bag, hears Doris on the phone asking for Cheryl George, and spots the bloodstained legal pad she's certain has Mikey's closing argument outlined on it.

"Lee? When can I get in this office?"

"About an hour, I suppose."

Luna turns on her heel and runs to her office. She texts Mark, telling him she's unavailable for the rest of the morning. She doesn't want to tell him Mikey's dead. She knows if she speaks the words out loud that she'll break down and she won't be able to handle what's waiting for her. After she sends the text, she lies her head on her desk, forehead on her desk calendar, and starts breathing slowly.

She just caught her first big case.

3

Karen Reynolds has served on the bench as a circuit judge in Division II for just over a year. Before her election to the 11th Judicial Circuit Court, she was an associate circuit judge for a small, rural community in Northwest Missouri, where big-city crimes like murder weren't an everyday occurrence. In her twenty-plus years practicing the law and then judging it, only one murder showed up on her docket, an involuntary manslaughter charge when two hunters mistook the other one for a deer. A routine docket included listening to petty disputes between neighbors that started as civil confrontations in front yards to criminal charges argued in her court. Things like petty theft, passing bad checks, trespassing, and disorderly conduct were the usual cases she heard eight hours a day, five days a week. When she was young and had first been appointed to the bench, these cases had excited her. After ten years of hearing the same arguments all day, every day, boredom settled in for an extended stay. So when her husband was offered an administrative position with the Agricultural Farm Bureau Association in the St. Louis area, Karen leaped at the opportunity to leave behind her stale position on the bench and move on to bigger and better things.

After building a law practice in the metro area and

developing personal and professional relationships, Karen built a solid base to run for the open circuit judge position. Unlike the district in northwest Missouri, in St. Charles County, judgeships are decided by election and not appointment. A new face in the county, Karen wasn't sure the election would tip in her favor. Lucky for her, three weeks before polls opened, when she was still trailing by ten points, her opponent, the (dis)Honorable Kent Harrison, was arrested for lewd conduct in a public place and attempted solicitation of a minor.

Two months later she was sworn into office. Then, six months ago, only three weeks into her term, her first murder trial showed up on her docket. Not just any murder trial either—a first-degree murder trial with the prosecutor putting the death penalty on the table. The defendant, a working-class woman, was accused of murdering her sleeping husband. While Karen was excited about getting this case, she never thought it would make it to opening remarks. She fully expected Ms. White's attorney to begin sentence bargaining immediately to get the death penalty out of play. Instead, she found herself refereeing a judicial boxing match of words between prosecuting attorney Wiles Nyler and the always-adrenalized Mikey George.

At the arraignment, Karen asked, "How do you plead, Ms. White?"

She remembers how Tammy looked over at Mikey and rubbed her left thumb with her right thumb. How she took a deep breath when Mikey nodded his head for her to answer.

"Not guilty, Your Honor."

Mikey spoke up quickly after his client. "Your Honor, the defense is requesting a pretrial motion that Ms. White's confession be suppressed from evidence."

Wiles Nyler, as lanky and towering as Mikey was round and thickset, jumped to his feet. "Objection!"

"Mr. George, what is your reason for the motion to suppress?"

"The confession was obtained from Ms. White while she was under emotional distress and not thinking clearly enough to make a reasonable statement of guilt or innocence."

"That's preposterous," Nyler declares. "It's not unusual for a person who just committed murder to be under emotional distress. However, she was of reasonable and sound mind when she made the confession. In fact, I believe she said, 'The bastard deserved it.'"

"Mr. Nyler is right, Mr. George. Confession is allowed. Any other pretrial motions will be heard—"

"Excuse me, Your Honor," Mikey interrupted. "Based on our defense, it would be unlikely that Ms. White's confession was made in a reasonable mindset. You see, Ms. White was a battered woman for fifteen years. She believed on this day that her life was in jeopardy and that—"

"Your Honor," Nyler interjected, "we are not here today to hear the defendant's defense. That's for the jury to hear."

"Wiles, Your Honor, I'm simply laying the foundation for our defense."

Karen put up her hand. "Mr. George, am I correct in assuming you'll be using the battered woman syndrome as a mitigating factor of homicide in your defense?"

"Yes, Your Honor. We will. It's important that the jury understand why Ms. White, a law-abiding citizen without any priors or a hint of malice in her, would be accused of such a crime."

Karen looked out at the defendant. She'd seen many women like her come through her courtroom back in Northwest Missouri. These women stood before her like a deer in headlights. At first, they asked for orders of protection to keep their partners away, but pieces of paper were never ironclad shields against abusers. Truth be told? They were nothing more than kindling, fueling a small fire that eventually became an explosive fireball of fury. When that happened, she often saw these same women, bruised, cut, and otherwise deadened, watching their abusers be tried for assault, unlawful detainment, and other horrific crimes. In these women's eyes, she always saw the struggle between love and hate, relief and fear. Never, though, had she looked into the eyes of a woman accused of having the final say.

"While I'll allow the defense to proceed using the battered woman syndrome as a mitigating factor in the homicide case," Karen began, "the motion to suppress the confession is denied."

That was the beginning of what had proven to be a long trial filled with motion after motion and two contentious attorneys who liked to battle back and forth, each enjoying hearing himself speak more than the other. With only three days to closing arguments, Karen feels the case's noose loosen from her neck. She's ready to move on from this case that's caused her too many sleepless nights.

Now another motion on her desk.

The young lawyer who'd sat at the defense table with her head down looks Karen straight in the eyes today. Wiles Nyler, unusually docile, stands by her side looking as stricken as Karen feels. The air in her chambers pushes down on her shoulders with the same force as a crusher at the junkyard.

"Dead?" she asks.

"Overnight," says the young lawyer, clarifying.

Nyler clears his throat. "Judge, if you'll allow me? While circumstances are tragic, delaying this case any longer isn't favorable to anyone. We have jurors who are tired. They want to get back to their lives. We have other cases that need our full attention."

The young lawyer ignores him. "Your Honor, I've never been a lead on a murder case. I only assisted Mr. George with this case, and only partly. I feel that it's necessary to bring someone onto the team who has the experience my client needs to get a fair trial."

"Excuse me, Your Honor," Nyler says, interrupting, "but her client has gotten a fair trial. Closing arguments are not something we should wait on. We need to move on this. I'm sure Ms. Goldwyn has Mr. George's notes and knows enough of his defense strategy to make a compelling argument for her client to our jury."

Karen nods. "I agree with Mr. Nyler, Ms. Goldwyn. While circumstances are unfortunate, I can't grant a continuance for," she glances at the motion on her desk, "six months. I'll give you three more days to prepare your closing, but that's it. Is this agreeable to both parties?"

Nyler sighs and runs his hand over his shaved head. "I'll agree to three days."

"Ms. Goldwyn?"

The young lawyer sets her lips in a straight line, looks Karen in the eye, and nods. "Three days."

4

Tammy expects Mikey to be sitting at the table by the window overlooking Fourth Street. It's his choice seating in the common area because it allows plenty of opportunities to look elsewhere, anywhere but her eyes. She doesn't take it personally. Some people are just like that. They can't get comfortable looking into another person's soul, especially when that person is a murderer. Tammy, on the other hand, enjoys eye contact. Being married to Ray meant always looking away, making sure she never made eye contact when he was in a mood. *What are you looking at, woman?* Only when he was hurting her did his tune change. That's when he wanted her to look at him, full on. He wanted her to see the anger and disgust in his eyes when he wrapped his calloused hands around her throat, or he dug the heal of his palm into her cheekbone.

Now that he's gone, she enjoys the freedom of looking into everyone's eyes.

Mikey is not at the table though. It's that woman. What's her name? Luna, or something hippie like that. She's sat at the defense table with them but has rarely spoken to Tammy, which suits her just fine. When she does say something to her, it's the same two questions: Is she sleeping well? Does she need water?

When she notices Tammy, she stands up. Usually, the silent

woman is put together and stoic. Today her shirt has come untucked from one side of her pants and red, blotchy spots spread across her pale cheeks. As Tammy moves closer, she realizes the woman is upset. She's been crying.

"Amy?" That's what it must be, she thinks. "Has something happened to Amy?"

Luna shakes her head. "No. She's fine. I didn't mean to startle you. Will you sit?"

Tammy lowers herself into the plastic orange chair, watching Luna guardedly. "What's wrong, then? And, no, I don't need water," she says as Luna attempts to slide the tiny bottle of Evian from the visitor's vending machine toward her.

"I'm not sure how to tell you this."

"Mikey's dropping me? He doesn't want to lose, right?"

"No, Tammy. It's not like that at all."

"Okay. So, what is it?"

"He's dead."

"Who's dead?"

"Mikey."

"Mikey's dead?" The words stick in her throat like peanut butter.

Luna nods. "This morning—or, maybe last night. I don't know. We don't have the full report yet from the coroner. Just an estimate from the EMTs. He passed away at the office. Doris found him this morning."

Tammy looks away. Where does that leave her? "I don't understand."

"I'm sure you have questions," Luna says.

"Does this mean the trial starts over?"

"Not at all. I filed a motion to have closing arguments postponed due to the nature of the emergency. We've been granted a three-day continuance."

"Wait, three more days?"

"That's all the time we were given."

For three more days, Tammy will sit in uncertainty. She gazes out the window, thinking about her options. But what options exist for her? She has none. Motions and jailhouse schedules dictate her days, her movements. She gave up options the day she pulled the trigger.

"Tammy, do you hear me?"

"Yes. What?"

"I know I haven't been lead on this case, but you can trust me to work for your best interest."

"To keep me from facing the death penalty?"

Luna leans forward, closing the gap between them, and reaches out a hand. It's an unexpected gesture that takes Tammy by surprise. She hurriedly slides her hands away from Luna's and places them under her thighs. "We know what's at stake. Your story deserves to be told. The jury needs to hear it one last time. Do you trust me to do that for you?"

"Do I have a choice?"

Luna sits back in her chair and loops a piece of hair behind her ear. Tammy remembers a time, before all the beatings, when she was pretty like that. "Not really."

"Well, then, I guess it's tag. You're it. I just have one question."

"Yes?"

"What the hell kind of name is Luna?"

5

Her coffee tastes like burnt toast. She pokes at the sausage links with the tip of her fork.

"Eat, Mommy," Ian sing-songs his demands from his booster seat.

Luna tries to take a bite to appease her little boy, but the food feels like mud on her tongue. She pushes the plate away from her, gives Mark a small smile, and says, "Mommy's not too hungry this morning."

Mark reaches across the table and takes her hand. "You have this." Not his usual, *Don't worry about it,* or *You're overthinking it.* He doesn't even play the it's-going-to-be-okay card because even her ever-optimistic husband knows canned encouragement won't suffice today. Only twelve jurors know if everything will be okay. Of course, it won't be. How can it? She's prepared a solid closing based on the defense that Mikey created. She's done the work and stayed awake long into the night choosing the right words and practicing her facial expressions. But in a few short hours, everything she's done may not matter at all.

"Do you want me to make you some ginger tea?" Mark asks. "I heard a report on one of those morning talk shows that ginger is supposed to calm the stomach."

"I thought it was mint?"

Mark winks. "I wasn't listening that close."

Luna shakes her head. "I'm fine."

"How late were you up?"

"I don't know. Maybe two o'clock? Finding the right words is hard."

"You've always been good with words," Mark says, back to his usual assuring self.

"It's easy to write a nice birthday card, babe. It's not quite the same when you're defending someone's life. Mark, I'm not ready for this. I'm not the person for this job."

"Yes. You are."

"I'm not. I've practiced law for five years, and I've never given a closing. *Never.* All I do is file motions and other administrative BS. We plea out nearly every case. Mikey should've never taken this case. It's too much for us—for me. There's too much at stake for this woman."

"It doesn't matter anymore, Luna. Woulda, shoulda, coulda doesn't change anything." He strides over to her, taking her hands in his. "You were meant to do this. No one is ever ready for the one thing that's going to change their life. All you can do now is take a deep breath and believe in yourself. I believe in you."

She knows he does. He always has. "I know you do."

"But, I need to tell you something."

"Okay?"

"Today's not about you. It's about Tammy White. It's about getting justice for a woman whom justice has failed. How many times did the cops come to that woman's home and tell her to just give him some space? What did you tell me? Seven times?"

"At least."

"At least. So, I know you're scared. I know this is hard, but today is about Tammy, and, lucky for her, she has the best damn lawyer in the state."

"You always know the right things to say," Luna says, smiling.

Mark rolls his eyes, plucking Ian from his booster seat. "Of course, I do."

"Conceited much?"

"Always. Now, are you going to go do your kick-ass lawyering? Because I have to tell you that the little man and I would like to get on with our day. It's full, you know. We've got blocks to stack, some books to read, and a very long nap scheduled at one."

Luna plants a kiss on her son's sweet, cherub cheeks then buries her head between her husband's chest and her son's chin. "I'm going to kick ass," she says softly.

***

A cluster of microphones, news trucks, and heels and suits create a traffic jam outside the courthouse's front entrance. Luna balances on her new heels and searches for a way around the reporters. A hand on her elbow makes her jump. Wiles Nyler smiles down at her, soft lines etched out around his eyes. He smells like cheap bargain aftershave. "I have a secret entrance."

He pulls sunglasses from his suit pocket and leads her away from the reporters, making their way around to the courthouse's back entrance. Two bailiffs, smoking cigarillos and drinking coffee out of stainless-steel tumblers, nod at them.

"Morning, Wiles," says the shorter one with closely cropped blond hair and a lazy eye.

"Hey, Lars. How'd the championship go last night? You win?"

The man tosses his cigarillo on the ground and opens the door. "Nah, we lost by three spares. I'm not there for the twenty-five-dollar trophy and exercise, though. I only care about the cheap beer."

"Bowling is exercise?" the other bailiff teases. "Even when the bumpers are up?" The three men laugh together.

"Good luck today, Niles," Lars says. He nods at Luna. "Ma'am."

Luna nods back and walks through the door to a single metal detector. An assistant prosecuting attorney Luna's dealt with before is in line in front of her and places her bag on the belt.

She smiles at Luna. The PA is younger and looks like Luna did after she graduated, anxious but excited to play on the big playground. When Luna got her first case, a probation hearing, she puked in the women's restroom right before. She wonders how many times this woman has stared into a rust-stained toilet bowl.

"Nervous?" Wiles asks.

Luna considers bluffing. She chooses honesty. "Yes."

Wiles nods. He grabs his briefcase off the belt and raises his arms for the wand. "Me too."

Luna narrows her eyes. "Really?"

He laughs. "You seem surprised."

"I figured you thought you had this case in the bag."

"Let's take the steps." He opens the door to the staircase. They climb two flights before he says, "Nothing's ever a sure thing, and justice is rarely served no matter what my record states." He stops and winks at Luna. "My record is nearly impeccable."

"Nearly," she repeats. She can't stand ostentatious men.

"Feisty. Hmm." He nods his head. "But sure, I'm nervous. I wouldn't be doing my job if I wasn't."

"And what's that? Your job?"

"To give closure."

"Does that ever happen in these cases? Do people ever really feel complete and whole again?"

Wiles stops at the door to the third floor. Even behind the steel door and concrete walls, she hears the murmuring of the crowd. "Not in my experience. As I said, justice is rarely served. Everyone enters this courtroom broken, and they leave pieced together with jagged edges and gaping holes."

"The defendant too."

"In some cases, I suppose that's true."

"In this case, it's true."

"Ms. Goldwyn, your client murdered that man. It was a calculated, heartless murder. She had choices. There were places she could go. People who would help her. Witnesses testified that they offered a safe haven, a respite from her husband's violent outbursts. She didn't have to resort to killing him."

"That's for the jury to decide. Not us." Luna feels the heat rising in her chest, spreading up her neck and coloring her cheeks.

"I applaud your devotion to this case and to your client, but don't get your hopes up. When this case went to the grand jury, the vote was unanimous. It was the quickest indictment in my fifteen years practicing law. What makes you think this jury is going to feel differently?"

"Because a trial jury is different than a grand jury. You know that. My client had no defense in those proceedings. Those jurors were only presented with evidence of a crime. I'm making a case about why that crime happened and that it might not be as simple as it looks."

Wiles laughs. "To be so young and naive again. Don't think I've forgotten those first few years after law school, getting my first big case. You'll learn soon enough. My advice? Plea bargaining is your strength. Stick with that in the future."

"Can I ask you something?"

"Sure."

Luna looks him straight in his eyes. "Why are you allowing the jury to consider the death penalty in this case?"

"Because the punishment fits the crime."

"Can you sleep at night knowing you may be responsible for the death of another human being?"

Wiles' eyes go dark. "I'm not responsible. Your client is responsible for her own fate."

"What about the jurors?"

"What about them?"

"Do you worry about the burden you're placing on them? Essentially, after today, you have washed your responsibility from this case. You're passing the buck to those twelve men and women, making them play God."

"You're misguided, Ms. Goldwyn. If you want to discuss the moral implications of the death penalty, I suggest you go back to school and sign up for an ethics class. The law has no room for soft-hearted people."

"Maybe that's the problem. There are too many people like you," Luna challenges.

Wiles glares at her and pushes open the door. "Good luck today, Ms. Goldwyn. You're going to need every ounce of it because you don't have a shot in hell of keeping your client off death row."

6

There's a soft knock on the door. Then a second, louder knock, and the clearing of a throat before Karen is aware that she's being summoned.

"Come in," she calls out.

Lars peaks around the door. "You ready for this?"

"Am I?"

The middle-aged bailiff smiles and says. "Temperature is just right. Can't get any readier, I suppose."

"Thanks, Lars."

Karen likes to have her courtroom cooled to sixty-five degrees to keep it from heating up like the Sahara. It's her one "celebrity" request. All judges have them, demands for their courtrooms to keep order and make the time behind the bench comfortable. Judge O'Connell, in Division 1, always asks for a back pillow since his pilonidal cyst surgery, and even though he denies it, Judge Mandell has his coffee cup filled with an ounce of brandy every morning. The temperature is Karen's demand because she knows that when the temperatures rise so do the tempers. Today is not the day that she needs overheated jurors or attorneys, not to mention the other spectators, in her courtroom. She wants to get closing arguments finished and instructions handed to the jury before lunchtime. This trial has dragged on for too long, and the case bothers her.

Impartiality is her chore, but that doesn't mean cases don't keep her awake at night. You're taught that murderers are inherently bad people. How could they be anything else? Anyone who takes another human's life is certainly the devil himself, especially premeditated murder with no apparent remorse. Still, a part of Karen feels sorry for Tammy. An even greater part of her understands why this woman wouldn't have a drop of remorse in her body.

How many years of abuse can a person take before they just snap? Is it better to face lethal injection or be locked away for a lifetime, than to live in the clutches of an abuser for one moment longer? Her heart feels heavy for the twelve jurors faced with this decision.

"What's the galley look like?" she asks.

"Packed like expected."

"You know those reporters don't care one iota about this defendant or the trial. It's gotten scant coverage up until they got wind of Mikey's death."

Lars shrugs. "I don't know. There are a few reporters from a couple of the liberal papers. I saw Sarah Roaden from *The Riverfront Times*. You'd be surprised. White has a following, especially with the women's groups."

"Can I ask you something? How would you feel if that was one of your daughters out there, on trial for murder?"

"I don't think it'd be that way. Someone treated my girls like that man treated her, I'd be the one facing a death sentence."

"I hope we never have to know for sure."

"You and me both."

Karen rises and pulls on her robe. "I always said I wanted something more exciting than trespassing and cow-tipping cases. What the hell was I thinking?"

"Probably that justice needs a champion."

"Now that's funny. I'm just doing my job, trying to follow the letter of the law without dampening the spirit."

Lars puts a hand on her shoulder and squeezes it softly.

"Judge, that's what a champion does."

7

For the last several days, Tammy has sat cross-legged on the cell floor trying not to feel. After meeting with Luna, she lied face down on her bed and contemplated smothering herself with the pillow. Any hope for mercy seemed like a foolish wish. Mikey had stamina and grit. His replacement seemed too unsure of herself to have much fight, a lot like Tammy did every time she convinced herself that the next time Ray raised his fists, she'd leave. Unsureness had never served her well, and now was the time she needed someone in her corner with confidence.

Vess, coming back from a meeting with her psychiatrist, found Tammy lying face down in tears and snot. "You know you're not getting a clean pillowcase."

"It doesn't matter," Tammy said.

"In this place, girl, it's the little things that do matter." She reached under her mattress, finding the slit in the mattress, and pulled out a bleach-discolored pillowcase. "I sneaked it out of the laundry room after laundry duty. Sometimes it's just nice to bury my face in clean laundry more than a few times a month. It feels like being home." She handed the pillowcase to Tammy.

"Thanks."

"You know my mother wasn't nothing too good for me and my brother. She spent most her time whoring and the other days snorting crack until her nose bled for days. That woman taught me how to run my first con, convincing the teachers that she was dying of cancer so they'd put on a fundraiser to raise money for treatment. Got about two thousand dollars before someone at the school started getting suspicious. Luckily, it only took us thirty minutes to pack up all our things and bolt across the county line to a trailer park in Festus. That money lasted us five more days before mom blew it on drugs. To her credit, though, she did spend some of it to fill the freezer with television dinners and a jar on the counter with black licorice."

Tammy had sat up and pulled her legs in close to her chest, wrapping her arms around her knees. She'd learned that Vess's stories always had a point even if they took the long way getting to it.

"Yeah, she didn't teach us much that wouldn't eventually catch up to us, and not in a good way either. But she did teach us how to breathe. When we had a nightmare or weren't feeling well, she'd sit with us and we'd breathe together. After a few deep breaths, we always felt calmer. Sometimes, when times were really bad and mom had been gone for days, I'd sit in my room and try to breathe away everything. If I tried hard enough, I could take myself far away from that grimy life and just float above it all."

Tammy never once in her life thought she had the power to escape, physically or mentally. During the worst beatings, she'd close her eyes and wait for it to end one way or the other. She thought death was her only escape each time Ray's fist connected with her body. The only time she was free from that man was the fifteen minutes it took for the ambulance and police to arrive after she'd called 911.

That day she let Vess teach her how to breathe, to find the place in her mind where everything shut off.

She's sitting on the floor in her cell, her toes numb and her breathing light, when the guard summons her. "Let's go."

The fear she has felt for so long is finally anesthetized. Walking out of the cell, handcuffed at the wrists and ankles, she doesn't feel much like a prisoner anymore. She feels like a woman one step closer to knowing what the rest of her life will look like.

8

Prosecutor Nyler clears his throat. He glances briefly at Luna before turning to his audience, his hands behind his back. He takes his time approaching the jury box. Luna watches him with the alertness of a cheetah in the wild, watching its prey with careful consideration.

"Ladies and gentlemen, let me begin by thanking you for your time. I know it's not easy to put your lives on hold. Nonetheless, I and the 11th Judicial Circuit Court appreciate you, and justice commends your service. This hasn't been an easy case to listen to. It's heartbreaking, the taking of a life, regardless of how unlikable the victim may be. Let there be no misunderstanding: Ray White wasn't a saint. He was flawed at best, reprehensible and culpable at worst. However, it's not your job to assign guilt to the victim. Your job is to weigh the evidence against the defendant, Ms. White, and that evidence is blatant. By Ms. White's own admission, she killed Ray White in cold blood. But why?

"The defense wants you to believe she did this because she thought her life was in imminent danger from a sleeping man. Yes, a sleeping man. How could a sleeping man pose an immediate threat to someone's safety? Let me answer that for you. He can't. No, Ms. White took this opportunity to seek revenge. To get back at her husband. Her words after she was Mirandized were, and I quote, 'That bastard got what he deserved.'

"'Deserved.' That was her summation of the events that led to Ray White being shot dead by a single bullet to the forehead. Did he deserve it? That's not our decision to make. It certainly wasn't Ms. White's decision to make. Nonetheless, she took it upon herself to play judge and jury, and so here we are.

"'Facts are stubborn things; and whatever may be our wishes, our inclinations, or the dictates of our passions, they cannot alter the state of facts and evidence.' Those are the words of our nation's second president, John Adams. Although spoken over two hundred years ago, they ring just as true today.

"The facts, ladies and gentlemen, are your responsibility to uphold. What are these facts? In this case, they are simply this: Ms. White walked to her husband's gun cabinet. She took the box of bullets from the top shelf. She loaded her husband's deer hunting rifle, a Timber Classic Marlin, with those bullets, one at a time. That rifle, by the way, was a tenth-anniversary gift she had purchased for him. After loading the rifle, she walked to the living room and stood in front of her husband, who was fast asleep in his recliner. She raised that rifle to no immediate threat but shot anyway."

Nyler stands in front of juror number five, one of *his* jurors.

"Ms. White was as close to her husband as I am to you when she put her finger on the trigger and fired. One shot and he was dead. There was no resistance. There was no threat of danger from this sleeping man. Those are the facts."

He takes a long pause, looks down at the floor, and then back at the jurors. The corners of his mouth twitch. "It's hard," he begins again. "It's a difficult thing to do to find someone guilty in a first-degree murder case, especially when the consequences are so permanent. Capital punishment isn't something to take lightly. I assure you that my colleagues and I don't seek capital punishments except in extreme cases. This is an extreme case. Ms. White's legal team would like you to consider a lesser charge, one that allows the defendant leniency, but let me ask you this:

What mercy did Ms. White show to the victim? None. Her actions were calculated, reprehensible, and final. By Ms. White's hand, she took a life without regret and certainly without reason.

"Ladies and gentlemen, I thank you once again for the time you've devoted to this case. I simply ask that you give a little more of your time and deliberate with care. Remember John Adams' words, 'Facts are stubborn things; and whatever may be our wishes, our inclinations, or the dictates of our passions, they cannot alter the state of facts and evidence.' Let the facts in this case guide you to return a verdict of guilty of first-degree murder. Thank you."

He backs away from the jury box. Luna keeps her eyes cast downward at her legal pad. During the summation, Tammy had sat stoic and focused. Reading her client has always been difficult for Luna. She's fearful that Tammy's refusal to allow any emotion to crack on her face has already colored the jury's opinion. Now it's her job to show the shades of gray, to color over implied bias. It took Luna a while to understand the different tones of domestic violence. She hopes she's able to help this jury understand today.

She rises slowly from her chair, placing a gentle hand on Tammy's shoulder as she makes her way around the table. She walks with gentle purpose to the jury box, smiling at the group of men and women.

"Good morning," she begins. "Allow me to also extend my sincere gratitude for all you've sacrificed throughout the duration of this trial. Asking you to give up your time, forgoing your family and professional responsibilities, has not gone unnoticed. There are some cases that are particularly hard on jurors. By the stroke of fate, you've participated in one of the hard ones, a case that tears at your heart, challenges long-held beliefs, and creates reasonable doubt.

"Yes, ladies and gentlemen, reasonable doubt, a great feat and the highest burden of proof in criminal proceedings. The prosecution holds tightly to facts, but if I may, could I ask you to consider what hides between the folds in facts' fabric?

"Did Tammy White kill her husband? Yes, she did. Without

any doubt, she killed her husband. We're not disputing these facts because they are what they are. You can't hide from facts, as Mr. Nyler pointed out, but what does allude facts is reason—actions that are driven by assumptions based on past experiences. Today, that's what I ask you to consider. Did my client take action, no matter how permanent and seemingly unprovoked, based on what she knew constituted a threat to her life?"

Luna pauses for a moment. She looks each juror in the eyes before continuing.

"Can I tell you a story? This is a story that you've heard before, not only in this courtroom, but I'm sure you've heard variations of this tale in your own lives. It's a story about a woman who loved a man, a man who seemed to love her until his violent nature darkened their love story. We call this storm domestic violence. It's something that happens every day in all types of relationships: between high school sweethearts, college-educated professionals, families with children, elderly couples, rich families and poor families. Domestic violence doesn't discriminate, and it comes in all forms.

"Tammy White lived for fifteen years with a man who not only abused her with his fists, but he controlled her by keeping her isolated from her family and friends. He allowed her to speak on the phone only when he was able to monitor the conversation. Usually this meant making her sit on his lap while he calmly, but with malicious intent, stroked her throat with his fingers. Tammy White was married to a man who didn't allow her to have her own money. She was married to a man who sent her four-year-old daughter to live with friends of the family because she was another man's child, a man whom she'd been involved with years before she ever met Mr. White. All the while, during their relationship, he carried on affairs with multiple women, infecting Tammy with two sexually transmitted diseases, one of which took her fertility.

"For fifteen years, their relationship was volatile and fueled by rage, insecurity, and control. It was also controlled by these words: 'Today's your lucky day. I think I'll let you live.'

"Every morning before Ray White left the house, he spoke these words to Tammy. He then reminded her that if she disobeyed him, not only would she pay with her life, but he'd go after her daughter too. Day after day, Ray White told Tammy she was lucky."

Luna stops and looks Tammy in the eyes and says, "Until her luck ran out.

"October 15, 2016, started off like any other day. My client woke at six o'clock to make her husband breakfast: two eggs scrambled, three sausage links, and two pieces of whole wheat toast. She worried about the toast because Ray didn't like whole wheat, but she'd run out of white bread and didn't have any money to go to the store. So, she slathered the pieces of toast with butter and hoped for the best. They sat at the table together and ate in silence. Tammy only nibbled at her food because when she ate too quickly, Ray called her Miss Piggy and pinched her upper arms between his fingers. Ms. White was aware the entire time that Ray avoided the toast. When he cleared his plate of the eggs and sausage, he took a long drink of water and then went to the refrigerator, where he filled a flask with vodka. Still, he didn't say anything to her—that is, until he got to the door, ready to leave. That's when he spoke. With his hand on the door, he looked her directly in the eyes and said the words she'd dreaded for fifteen years. 'Today's not your lucky day, Tammy.'"

Luna lets those words settle over the jury like a dense, morning fog.

"An empty threat? My client didn't think so. She believed that was the day she would die. So, even though Ray came home in a better mood, even though he fell asleep in his chair, she knew that he'd make good on his threat. When my client pulled the trigger on that rifle, she did so out of self-defense. Years of threats, years of beatings, and then those words, *'Today's not your lucky day,'* convinced Tammy White that she had to defend herself right then and there. There was no other option.

"It's a hard scenario to imagine, especially if you've never been in a relationship like Tammy and Ray's. I hope you never are because that's not any sort of life. Still, I ask you to try to imagine what a reasonable person would do when faced with a blatant threat against their life. Would Ray have murdered Tammy that night?" Luna shrugs. "We can't know. But based on past actions and Ray's passive threat before he left for work, Tammy believed wholly that he would, and she acted accordingly.

"We are not asking you to ignore the facts in this case. There's no denying that Ms. White pulled the trigger. What we're asking of you is for you to show mercy and consider the lesser charge of second-degree murder. Ms. White lived under Ray's sentence for fifteen years. She lived every day with the threat of violence but also the hope that she'd at least survive the beatings. Every day that Ray told her she was lucky was another day she knew she'd live. Tammy only took extreme measures when Ray made her believe otherwise. Under reasonable circumstances, without the threat of bodily harm, she'd never have taken another person's life. Ms. White was aware of her environment. She knew what constituted a threat. She knew that at five-foot-one, she could not overpower her six-foot-two, two-hundred-fifty-pound husband. She knew that the threat of life-ending violence existed at all times, so she turned the tables in her favor.

"It is not my job, or your job, to forgive Ms. White for her actions. Only she and her greater power can do this. Our job is to seek out justice. As you deliberate, I ask you to consider these words once spoken by Eleanor Roosevelt: 'Justice cannot be for one side alone but must be for both.' What is justice for Tammy White?"

***

Small pods of people cram the atrium of the courthouse waiting for the verdict. It's been four hours since the jury was given instructions to deliberate, and the waiting is beginning to take its shape among the groups. The reporters gather together, speaking to each other in hushed words while staring at their phones and trying to sneak in Facebook live reports before the bailiffs spot them. These men and women, the reporters, fair the best during the waiting game. They're used to it. Besides, they have other things to occupy their minds. The news never sleeps. There's always a story waiting around the corner or on Twitter.

It's the pods of family members that are starting to show the frayed edges of wear and tear, the unraveling of an enduring spirit. High-heeled shoes usually worn only for weddings and funerals have been removed and hang from fingers, some shoved in purses or in empty corners. Ties have loosened, and a musty, barroom odor hangs over the family pods. Too much time allows for too many smoke breaks. Benches and windowsills provide ample room for collections of soda cans, water bottles, and vending machine food wrappers.

No one wants to be here, yet no one wants to leave. Too much is at stake, no matter what pod you belong to.

Luna found a bench on the first floor, away from the crowds gathered above and out of sight from the cluster of reporters. She's sat in the same position for the last hour, afraid to move even though she has to pee and is desperate to get out of the overheated building.

"You know how these things go, sweetie," Doris says. "You sure you don't want to sneak out the back and grab something to eat on Main Street?"

"This imitation Ho-Ho isn't too bad." She holds up the half-eaten vending machine pastry. "Although I prefer Twinkies. Do they still make those? I thought I heard they stopped making them."

"You were great today."

Luna takes a bite of the snack cake. "You know what that felt like in there?"

"Victory."

"Hardly. It felt like playing school or house when you're little. You've set the stage. Everything's in place. You've put on your grown-up, make-believe clothes, and, if you close your eyes, you believe you're not playing a role. You are the role. But the truth is that you're still just a little kid, in clothes that are too big, pretending to know it all when you don't know shit."

"No one ever knows it all. We do the best we can with what

we have and wing it. That's life."

"What do you think the jury's thinking?"

Doris shrugs. "I don't get involved in other people's thoughts. It doesn't do any good. I just trust they make the right decisions with the information they're given. That's all anyone can do." She reaches into her purse and pulls out a pack of spearmint gum. "Want some?"

"And ruin the taste of my lunch?" Luna smiles. "Absolutely."

Doris hands her the stick of gum. "Do you know why Mikey hired you?"

"Because no one else wanted the job?"

"Well, yeah, that's true," she replies, snickering. "Can't pretend that's not true. But it's not the only reason."

"No?"

"He saw a person who embraced the whole idea of the law, all of its nooks and crannies. People like Wiles Nyler, they don't see beyond the scope of their obligation. Their job is to apply the law as written. They don't worry about saving room for reason. Being a prosecuting attorney doesn't require emotion. Any robot could do that job, and trust me, plenty of robots are doing that job. It's defending people, especially when the cases are hard to understand, like this one, that takes a special heart. It's draining, and it's a thankless job because who's going to thank you for defending a drug dealer, a burglar?" Doris pauses and pops the tab on her Coke can. "Who's going to thank you for defending a murderer? Not too many people. But every person deserves to have someone on their side to protect their rights, to tell their story of why, when they can't.

"Mikey knew you had the nature to tell that story when it needed to be told. That man was a lot of things, not all of them always good. Ask Cheryl. He drank too much. He spent too much time shaking hands and making deals that kept him just shy of the straight and narrow, but he knew people. Mikey knew with a little polishing, you'd make one hell of a defense attorney. Now, you just have to believe it too."

"Excuse me." A soft voice interrupts Doris. It belongs to a small-framed young woman who Luna immediately knows belongs to Tammy's daughter, Amy. She saw a picture once during the early stages of the case when Mikey asked Tammy about any children, except that picture was of a three-year-old girl, not a young woman. There is no question that this is Tammy's kid, though. Although she doesn't have the deep grooves formed from years of worry and frustration between her eyes, she's the spitting image of her mother.

"Amy, right?" Luna says.

The girl crosses her arms in front of her, keeping her right hand free to stroke her blond ponytail, long enough to be worn over her shoulder. "You're my mom's lawyer."

"I am." Luna stands, extending her hand. The girl keeps her arms crossed, taking a step to the side.

"Do you think she'll get the death penalty?"

Luna pulls her hand back. "That's getting ahead of ourselves. The jury won't decide that today or whenever they reach a verdict. That's for after, the sentencing phase."

"Yeah, I know. I watch television crime shows. I get it. What I mean is, if the jury says she's guilty of first-degree murder, will she die?"

Despite her best efforts to lie and give Tammy's daughter a little comfort, she frowns and speaks honestly. "I don't know."

Amy looks down at her feet, wrestles with words that want to come but are slow to form on the tongue. "You know," she says quietly, "I hated Ray. I hated that he hurt my mom. I hated that he took her away from me. And I'm glad he's dead. But I hate her too."

"Your mom?"

She shrugs. "I don't call her that. You know she chose him over me, right? I had her for four years. I don't remember much of that time. Just bits and pieces of a story that my brain likes to tell me, but it's not much." Amy wipes tears from her eyes. "To her credit, the people I grew up with, they gave me a nice life. So, props to her and Ray for that."

"I don't think your mom sees it that way. She was probably trying to protect you."

"She should've left him. She should've stayed with me." Amy

rests a hand on her stomach. "I would never do that to my daughter."

Luna frowns. She didn't notice the young woman's small, protruding stomach, but it's obvious now that she knows to look. "Does your mom know?"

Amy shakes her head. "I haven't spoken to my mom in over ten years. For a while, after she sent me away, she'd call on my birthday, at Christmas. Then, the calls stopped. So, no, she doesn't know."

"I don't know what to say," Luna says. Her parents haven't been perfect, but through all the little battles, she can't imagine being in Amy's place. Not speaking to her mom for years or not having or wanting her parents to share the joy with her when she was pregnant with Ian would have been awful.

"There isn't anything to say. I want you to know that I don't want her to die, though. There's not being there, and then there's not being there forever. You know?"

Of course Luna knows. The former means a chance for reconciliation. The latter means a lifetime of not knowing, regret, and what-ifs. She considers giving Amy some unsolicited advice about letting go and moving forward when her phone vibrates on the bench. Doris is looking at her phone too. She looks up sharply at Luna.

"What?" Luna asks.

"Verdict is in."

"Already?"

Amy's eyes dart between the two women. "Wait. Isn't it too soon? I thought we'd be sent home in a few hours and start this all over again tomorrow."

Doris gathers her stuff off the bench. "It doesn't look that way."

"So, is this good news or bad news?" Amy asks.

Luna picks up her tote that is stuffed full of papers and her tablet. She feels an obligation to Tammy's daughter to comfort her, but telling Amy something that she doesn't know to be certain is a disservice. She searches for the middle ground and puts her hand on Amy's upper arm. "Some juries agree quicker than others. It's neither good nor bad. It just is."

"Yeah, but this was fast. Those jurors already had their minds made up."

"Maybe, but it doesn't mean it's not in our favor."

"You think they're going to find her not guilty?"

Luna sighs and shakes her head. "No. Your mom confessed. What we want is for those jurors to stand in your mother's shoes for one second and try to understand."

"And come back with a second-degree murder charge?"

"Exactly."

Amy closes her eyes, placing a hand on her stomach again. When she opens them, she says, "How can twelve strangers do that when I can't?"

Again, Luna wants to give Amy a bit of hope, but she's not sure either. She's not sure she or Mikey did enough to make a convincing argument, but it's been decided. That's the only sure thing right now.

***

Every sound is amplified in the packed yet still courtroom. A cough in the back of the room pings off the walls. A woman, sitting behind the prosecution's table, blows her nose and cracks the silence. Each morsel of sound digs its way into Luna's ear canals to the point that the sound takes on a deafening nature. It's too much. All she wants to do is cover her ears and run away, back to when her job was routine and she didn't hold her clients' actual lives in her hands. Today, she feels the weight of her responsibilities.

Judge Reynolds slowly makes her way up the steps to sit behind the bench. The fabric of her robe swish-swish-swishes against her body. When she sits down in her chair, the aged wood frame groans.

Next, the jurors return to their seats in the galley. The room feels smaller, as if it's taking in a deep breath, holding it, trying to lengthen the moment a bit longer before finally exhaling. Luna tries to read the expression on the jurors' faces, but no one looks up. They study their feet as they shuffle to their seats and then sit still, looking at their hands. One juror, the forewoman, has a piece of paper in her hand. Luna regards the paper. She imagines Tammy is looking too, but she doesn't risk a sideglance. The two women sit without speaking at the defense table.

It's time.

"Ladies and gentlemen of the jury," Judge Reynolds asks, "have you reached a verdict?"

The forewoman, an older woman with caramel-colored skin and sleek, white hair pulled tight at the base of her neck into a ponytail, stands. "We have."

"So say you, Madam Forelady, as to complaint number 2504, wherein the defendant is charged with first-degree murder, what is your verdict?"

"We find the defendant, Tammy White, not guilty."

The courtroom exhales. Tammy drops her head, loses her composure, and leans on Luna for support. Some of the victim's family members begin crying; a low rumble of words among the crowd grows louder and louder as the verdict slithers through the crowd like a snake, wrapping its thick, heavy body around ankles and necks.

"Order!" Judge Reynolds raps her gavel, waiting for the crowd to calm and unwrap itself from the verdict. "Madame Forelady, the jury was instructed to consider the lesser included charge of second-degree murder. As to this charge, what is your verdict?"

"We find the defendant, Tammy White, guilty."

Tammy grabs Luna's hand tightly. She whispers, "Now what?" There isn't time to speak because the courtroom is under command of the legal script, a performance that must be played out.

"Members of the jury, I thank you for your service as do all the members of the 11th Judicial Circuit Court. It is no small sacrifice what you have given to serve the court, your fellow citizens, and justice as a whole. The court accepts your verdict and relinquishes you of your duty to this case. You are officially discharged. The court officer will escort you back to the jury room where you are then free to go. Again, thank you for your service."

The courtroom waits while the jurors are escorted out of the courtroom. Luna remains standing, Tammy's clammy hand clenching hers. Two court officers come to stand behind them. One pries Tammy's hand from Luna's as Judge Reynolds addresses them.

"Ms. White, you've been found guilty of second-degree murder, by a jury of your peers, for the murder of Ray White. The court releases you back to the women's jail, where you'll stay incarcerated until sentencing is complete." She looks down at the calendar on her desk. "Sentencing is scheduled two weeks from today at nine o'clock."

9

Two weeks later

"Red or white?"

Luna wrinkles her nose. "It's boxed wine. Is there a difference?"

Doris turns the red wine box over and squints, reading the small print. "Well, this one's been expired since 2009. So, maybe white?"

"I'm going to miss this," Luna says.

"Bad wine?" Doris fills a plastic cup and hands it to Luna.

"Good company."

"All these years and it's over like that. What am I going to do with my time?"

"At least you don't have to worry about a car payment." Luna winks. She really is going to miss seeing Doris every day. She's going to miss it all: the crappy office that's freezing cold in the summer when the air conditioning runs; the early-morning run-ins with Mikey before he had his first cup of coffee with a splash of bourbon. It isn't until now that she's realized how much this place has shaped her.

"I might have to sell that big baby to pay my mortgage."

The wine goes down smooth, doesn't taste half bad, but the

conversation is leaving a bad taste in her mouth. "Doris, don't say that. I'm still going to need an assistant. I'm just not sure how much work there will be right away."

Doris waves her off. "You're a good girl, Luna, but don't worry about me. I'm being melodramatic. Bob's picked up a new route. Keeps him out on the road longer than I like, but he's bringing home the bacon . . . and some eggs too." She grins. "Everything will be fine. Besides, Cheryl said a nice little parting gift would be in the mail, if you get my drift. Also, I just signed up with Uber."

"You're going to let total strangers in your car?"

"Why not? Can't be any worse than the total strangers who walk through these doors. Besides, I get paid extra if someone pukes. What about you?"

"What about me?" Luna slides her shoes off, rubs her toes, and then pulls her hair back in a ponytail. She's exhausted from an entire day of prepping files for document storage. Once the movers get here and pick up the boxes, she's headed home to sleep for at least eight hours. If she's lucky, maybe eight and a half.

"Did you find a space?"

"Yeah, a co-op on Second Street. Just renting the space a couple hours a week when I need to meet with clients. It's temporary, though. I wanted to wait for Tammy's sentencing before I started approaching other firms."

"Can you believe it? Fifteen years and eligible for parole in eight?"

"It's surprising. But the whole case was a roller coaster, and I'm glad to be done with that ride."

Doris raises her glass. "To better days and fewer roller coasters."

A short series of raps on the front door's window startles the women. Luna glances at the clock on the microwave over the kitchenette. "Maybe we get to get out of here sooner than we thought. Whoever heard of movers being early?"

When Luna looks back on this day, she won't remember her tiredness. She won't recall the flat, boxed wine in plastic cups or even what time the clock read. What she'll remember is the way that sorrow seeped from the tiny Asian woman's body. How it dragged her down, hunched her over, and kept her hostage. Sorrow drenched the woman's body like an afternoon downpour that catches people off guard.

"Please, help me," the woman cries when Luna opens the door. With tears in her eyes and clutching her purse to her chest, she looks from Luna to Doris. "You must help me. You . . . you are the murder lawyer, right?"

"I'm not sure what you mean," Luna says.

The woman digs in her purse and pulls out her phone. She pulls up a news report from Tammy's sentencing, spreads the screen, enlarging Luna's tired face. "This is you. Yes? You. The murder lawyer?"

Luna takes the woman's phone and reads the headline: "St. Louis's Youngest Murder Lawyer Keeps Client off Death Row". Below the headline is a photo of her walking out of court the day Tammy's trial ended. She hasn't seen this story yet, and the moniker, murder lawyer, makes her cringe. She hands the phone back to the worried woman. "It's me. What can I help you with, ma'am?"

The woman taps at her phone again and shows her a picture of an older Asian man, graying at the temples, wearing a blue windbreaker, and hunched against the wind that blows his hair to one side. It's a vacation picture, Luna thinks. The Golden Gate Bridge is in the background. The man is laughing. "My husband." She begins to weep again. "He killed a boy."

"A boy?" Luna asks.

"A teenager. He didn't mean to. He didn't want to, but the boy. Oh, the stupid boy and his stupid pranks. Please, my husband . . . Look." Tap, tap, tap . . . She hands Luna the phone again. Another news article. This headline reads: "Sam the Chandelier Man Charged in Death of Kirkwood Teen." She quickly scans the body of the article.

Long-time Kirkwood business owner, Sam Le, was arrested today for the murder of Logan Rees, 17, a senior at Westgate High School. Police have not released many details about the case, but witnesses say that Le and

Rees had an ongoing feud. The feud, according to police, escalated into a violent showdown last night at Le's lighting business on South Kirkwood Road. Currently, Le is being held in the St. Louis County Jail. Bail has not been set.

Mrs. Le wraps her shaking, petite hands around Luna's hand. "Please, my husband needs you."

PART TWO

SAM THE CHANDELIER MAN

10

The yelling at first distant and garbled gets louder, clearer. He hears the sharp voices shouting his name. They tell him to get down, get on his knees. Put his hands on his head. He remains still, breathing evenly. He fixes his gaze on the playground across the railroad tracks. It's where so long ago he took his children on Sunday mornings. Long before all-inclusive playgrounds and safety regulations changed the landscape. Back when metal slides in the summer were conquered and braved by adventurous five-year-olds. When teeter-totters and roundabouts were a child's delight and parents' nightmares. He recalls the time when Jason, only five or six, had lost his shoe and nearly his foot under the long-gone roundabout. How do thirty years fly by so fast? Wasn't it just yesterday that he watched his children climb the jungle gym wearing their Reebok shoes and Jordache jeans? He recalls the way pride and relief filled his chest, worked its way into his fingertips and his hair follicles. Pride because he worked hard to give them this life. His American children. Relief that he and Linh survived long before Jason and Samantha were even imaginable.

The textbooks and history call people like him Boat People, refugees from Vietnam's ravished cities after Saigon fell. That's the term Samantha used when she did a project on the Vietnam

War for her middle school history project. The images she glued onto poster board took Sam by surprise. To see how his life looked like from someone's camera, a bird's-eye view of horror and retreat. The images were one dimensional, but not his memories. He remembers running away from poverty and death's lingering stench, piling onto over-crowded boats and watching their homeland become a speck in the distance and then disappearing forever. He recalls the pirates and the storms that threatened to capsize the boats every day as they floated toward refugee camps in Southeast Asia. He hates to remember those camps. Weeks spent living in conditions where food, water, and shelter were constantly fought and killed over. Once Sam and Linh were on their way to America, he finally felt the weight of an uncertain destiny fall from his shoulders.

Now what has he done?

His life since fleeing Vietnam had been one of reinvention and newfound joy. Owning a business, buying a home with indoor plumbing and electricity, and watching his children grow into successful people, were his and Linh's greatest achievements. Last month, he'd become a grandpa for the third time. This is the life he envisioned that kept him moving forward. That made him so much more than just another boat person with a sad, tragic past.

The voices are on top of him now.

He looks down at the gun lying next to his feet and raises his arms slowly, placing his palms on either side of the back of his head.

What has he done?

11

No matter where Luna goes, she can't escape the news. Sam's case has dominated the local networks for weeks. Now the national media has picked up the story as opening arguments are set to begin in five days. Doris phoned her at seven o'clock this morning to tell her *Dateline* was calling to request an interview.

"You're famous," Tracey says, removing the bun top from her hamburger. She proceeds to fold her hamburger in half like a taco. The white, gooey mozzarella oozes from the sides.

Luna ignores her best friend's carb-conscious eating habits and picks at her black bean burger. It's tasteless and boring, but she's been trying to eat with a moral conscious to compensate for her client list. The restaurant's televisions are set to the local NBC station. The noon news replays yesterday's press conference on the steps of the St. Louis County courthouse. The prosecutor, Siobhan Finney, flanked by Logan Rees's mom, dad, and 5-year-old sister, promises to bring justice to the family even though justice can't bring their son back from his grave.

"Grim," says Tracey. "How are you doing?"

Luna squirts a mound of ketchup on her burger. "Managing with little resources. Doris and I are working eighty hours a week trying to prepare this case. I slept more when Ian was a newborn."

"Exciting, though. Isn't it?"

"I think excitement's over-rated."

"It's all so *Law & Order.*"

Luna shakes her head. "Not exactly. Television shows wrap everything up in a neat little bow in sixty-minutes -"

"Forty-five," Tracey says, interrupting. "Commercials take up fifteen minutes."

"My point is nothing about these types of cases is neat. Lives have been completely destroyed."

"I hear that kid was an ass."

"That's what I'm learning. Unfortunately, ass or not, he's a kid who was shot dead by a Vietnamese shop owner who doesn't have a McMansion. We're fighting an uphill battle."

"Hey, I don't want to hear that defeatist talk. You rocked the Tammy White case. I mean, hell, that woman was facing the possibility of a death sentence. Now she's going to get out in, what, a blink of the eye? That's some good lawyering."

"Mikey laid the foundation for that case. I didn't do anything but give the closing. He did all the work. This time I have to create the foundation. I have to build the whole freaking house of cards."

Tracey reaches across the table. "You're the smartest person I know, Luna. And, that's saying a lot because I'm pretty much a freaking genius. Did I tell you I took an IQ test on Facebook last week? My results were Stephen Hawking genius level. So I know what I'm talking about. You've got this."

Luna smiles. She can always count on Tracey to cheer her on. When the Whitaker's moved in three years ago, it was Tracey who showed up on Luna's doorstep with a welcome pie and huge smile. The pie was cherry, Luna's favorite, and their friendship grew from that moment. She feels immense gratitude to have this friendship in her life because, except for Doris, Tracey is the only other friend she has. Raising a family and working full time doesn't leave her much room to grow and nurture friendships. She also loves Tracey's bold nature and the way she speaks her mind. Strong women have always found their way into Luna's life, which, if she's being honest with herself, she loves and hates. Sometimes all that confidence that oozes from Tracey, Doris, and even her mom, leaves her feeling inferior. She's strong too. She knows this. She just hasn't found the need to unleash her roar.

"Hey!" The loud, deep voice startles Luna. She jumps and knocks her glass over. The iced tea spills and widens into a small lake across the table. "Are you that lawyer?"

Luna stands and begins blotting the mess with a wad of napkins. She glances at the man standing in front of her, a meaty man, one of those gym types with the tight black shirts and over-developed upper bodies. "I don't know what you mean,"

The man jabs his finger at the television in the corner. "You are. Aren't you? You're defending that gook?"

Luna ignores him. She wads up the napkins and tries to move around him to take them to the trash. Her heart's pounding so fast she can feel her pulse in her temples. "Excuse me."

He doesn't move. "I asked you a question, sweetheart. You like the gooks? You get off on their tiny -"

"Woah! Hey, Thor, back off. What's wrong with you?" Tracey looks at Luna and asks, "You want me to call the police?"

"No, it's fine. Freedom of speech and thought and all those good things, right?" Luna says hoping that the man will just walk away.

The man laughs. "Oh, I get it. Gooks are just a side job. You like the ladies. Whatever," he says, moving aside for Luna to pass but placing a hand on her shoulder. "You better watch your back, though. People like them," he nods at the rich, white family. "They destroy people like you."

Luna narrows her eyes and studies the man's face. She takes a mental snapshot of every detail: the dark, blonde stubble with a hint of red that lines his upper lip, the razor-thin scar above his eyebrow, the silver-blue eyes, and the chipped canine tooth. "Take your hands off of me."

"Lady, don't flatter yourself. Impish dikes aren't my type. I just thought you might appreciate a little warning. Good luck."

"What was that all about?" Tracey asks. Both women watch the man exit the building and disappear into midday crowd on

Main Street.

Luna lets out her breath, not realizing she'd been holding it while he left. Sweat forms between her breasts, but her heart stops racing a little. "I guess that's what happens when you're famous."

***

"More fan mail."

Doris motions to the envelopes splayed all over the table. She spots the ones from the prisons right away, identifiable by the taped flap and block letters. Luna ignores the collection of letters and sits at the conference table that takes up half the area in the rented co-op space. She decides not to tell Doris about the man at lunch just like she frequently decides not to tell Mark about the death threats and lewd propositions found in those letters. It was after Tammy's sentencing that the first batch of letters started arriving. She's since stopped reading them. They disgust her and scare her. They also motivated her to get security cameras installed at her house.

"What's happening here?" Two weeks ago, Mark had come home to find technicians crawling over the roof and porch like life-sized ants.

"Just a little extra protection," Luna had said, holding Ian and watching the men work.

Mark frowned. "Luna, what aren't you telling me?"

"Nothing, babe. I think it's a good idea. Tracey said a couple of people on Jackson were robbed the other day. Got me thinking. That's all."

He'd let it go, but Luna knew he didn't buy her explanation. She'd noticed him watching her check the front and back doors twice over before bedtime. He didn't say anything, but she knew what he was thinking. *Why is my wife, the person most likely to go on a vacation and leave all the windows open, suddenly concerned about window alarms?*

Luna settles into her seat at the conference table and opens her three-ring binder divided into color-coded sections: opening argument, evidence, witnesses, and closing argument. She turns to the witness section and runs her finger down the list. Her character witnesses Linh Le, Jason Le, and Samantha Le-Connor have been interviewed several times and all say the same thing. Sam Le was a gentle man who didn't wish harm on anyone. He is a man who coaxes spiders and insects into Tupperware jars, releasing them back outside rather than stomping them to death. According to Sam's son, Jason, he literally wouldn't kill a fly.

"But he killed a boy," Luna said during the first interview with Jason.

"It was self-defense. He thought he was being robbed."

It's the same story that all three members of the Le family insisted was the truth. Sam Le worked late hours at the family's chandelier and lighting shop on South Kirkwood road. It wasn't unusual for him to stay at the shop hours past closing, sometimes until midnight, cleaning the delicate light fixtures.

"My father took a great deal of pride in his business and those lighting fixtures. I can't even begin to tell you how many Saturday mornings I spent scrubbing invisible smudges from the fixtures," Samantha told Luna. The woman's eyes glistened with fresh tears as she recalled the memory. Her three-month-old son wiggled in her arms, stretching his arms and opening and shutting his mouth like a goldfish.

"My husband is a good man." Linh Le repeatedly said during all her interactions with Luna. "He didn't mean to kill the boy."

All three family members agreed that Sam staying late at the shop that night wasn't unusual. Had Sam had an ongoing feud with the seventeen-year-old victim, Logan Rees? That was the question Luna asked.

Jason dismissed the question with a wave of his hand. "Of course not. That Rees boy was only a teenager. Why would my dad care about arguing with a teenager?"

Luna referred to the police report when she said, "According to witnesses, Rees and your father argued a lot."

"What witnesses?" Samantha had asked. "Friends of that boy? They'll say anything. They were a problem too."

"What do you mean?" Luna asked.

Linh ran her hands over her thighs and shook her head. "That boy came into our shop three, four times a week. We tried to be nice, but he and his friends came in and taunted us. Called us names."

"What type of names?"

"Does it matter?" Jason had asked.

"I'm afraid it does, especially if we want to convince a jury that your father felt threatened."

"Gook, chink, tunnel diggers," Samantha said. "Look up a list of racial slurs on the Internet and he said them all."

"Did you witness these interactions?" Luna had asked.

Samantha had shifted in her seat, "No, but that's what mom told us. I'm not making it up and neither is she."

"I don't think you are," Luna had said, but felt disappointment slide between her shoulder blades. It would have been nice to have another witness to the taunting other than Sam's wife. "What else can you tell me?"

"Well, then there was the bottle of orange Kool-Aid he spilled all over the front of the store."

"Kool-Aid?" Luna asked.

"Tell them, Mom," Jason had said.

"It was supposed to be Agent Orange," Linh said, softly.

"It stained the flooring. Dad had to spend his hard-earned money to hire people to replace the hardwood."

Linh had shaken her head. "Who cares about the floor? Don't they know? No, they couldn't know because they never lived through something like that."

"Through what?" Luna asked.

"War."

"Vietnam?"

Linh nodded. "So much bad. So many memories that a stupid bottle of Kool-Aid stirred up. It made Sam angry."

"How angry?"

"Not enough to kill a stupid teenage boy," Jason argued.

Luna had turned her attention to Linh. "Ms. Le, did your husband ever have memories that made him act out? Become angrier than normal?"

THE MURDER LAWYER

"Stop that!" Jason's voice cracked. "I know what you're getting at."

"I'm just trying to understand your dad, Jason. There can't be any surprises in the courtroom."

"I told you, Ms. Goldwyn. My husband is a gentle person. Does he get sad sometimes from bad memories? Yes. So, do I. We lost so much before we came here. But that was forty years ago. We've embraced this life, a better life. At least it was," Linh had started crying.

Luna shuts the binder and puts her head in her hands. She tries to concentrate on the case, but the startup renting the space across the hall just turned up the afternoon music. That's what she should have done. Instead of getting a law degree she should have spent money on a business management degree where she could have worked for a startup, used a workout ball for an office chair and posted foodie picks all day on her social media accounts. Right now that seems like a better life than worrying about the life and death ramifications of her clients' lies.

Lies.

Everyone lies. Six years working with criminals she's learned how to spot the lies in people's eyes. Her job is to identify them then ignore them. To provide her clients with representation that was bigger than any lies.

Were the Le's lying?

No.

Sam had accidentally killed the kid in a moment of self-defense, they had said. Jason, Samantha, and Linh, they were telling the truth that they knew. They believed that truth.

Did Luna believe that truth?

Would a jury?

12

Every afternoon at one o'clock Sandra Rees dusts the silver-plated frames on her mantle. Before Logan died she wouldn't even consider picking up a duster. That's what she paid Linda to do, but these days she doesn't want anyone else touching the frames. Each afternoon she runs the feathers over the frames, taking her time in front of each photograph to remember.

She remembers the time her son was five and drove his Little Tykes police car up and down the gated driveway; the time when he was ten and he cracked his head on the side of the in-ground pool while chasing their Golden Lab, Boomer. She pauses in front of his senior portrait and she swallows a lump of bile. She'll never see him graduate. She won't have that memory. Never.

"Mrs. Rees?"

Sandra turns around and faces Siobhan, the prosecuting attorney trying the case against her son's murderer. "I'm sorry. What were you saying?"

"I asked how you are doing," she says.

"That's a funny question. Don't you think?"

Siobhan shifts in her seat. Sandra looks at the woman's bargain heels, the backs worn down from too much wear. If Sandra had a choice, she'd have chosen someone better to prosecute her son's murder, but she gets what the county offers.

That won't be the case when she files her wrongful death suit. She has money to buy what she needs, and she'll spend it all if it means watching that family get what they deserve.

"I know how exhausted you must be," Siobhan says.

Sandra laughs. "Do you? Do you really?"

"We need to go over a few things before the trial begins," she says, ignoring Sandra's question. "Will both you and your husband be attending?"

"Why wouldn't we?"

"Sometimes families find it difficult to hear the specifics of the case. Things get," Siobhan pauses, searching for the right phrase. "Things get technical."

"I identified my son in the morgue. Wouldn't you say that's technical?"

"It's best if Allison stays away," Siobhan says.

"I'm not planning on putting my five-year-old daughter in such a position. How dare you?"

"How dare I?"

"Yes. How dare you question my parenting skills."

"Mrs. Rees, I wasn't questioning you."

"Why not?" Sandra sits down on the couch. "Everyone else is. You think I don't hear the commentaries on television or what people are saying on social media? I can't leave my house because of the protesters who show up every few nights, yelling at me for being a privileged white bitch and raising a self-entitled teenager who deserved what he got."

Siobhan reaches across to take Sandra's hand, but she jerks it away. She doesn't want this woman's sympathy. She wants this woman to help her get an eye for an eye. But that's not happening because the evidence the police handed to the PA's office supports a second-degree murder charge. Ten to thirty years in prison, if convicted, is all the justice she'll get.

"Another thing we need to talk about is how to handle the defendant's family. They will be in attendance. You and your husband aren't to speak to them, Mrs. Rees. Do you understand?"

"Chinks," Sandra says, quietly.

"Excuse me?"

"Never mind."

Siobhan studies her, bites her lips and seems to proceed with caution. Everyone is cautious around Sandra these days. "I know the emotional burden of being in the presence of your son's murderer's family," Siobhan says. She holds up her hand when Sandra starts to interrupt. "Please let me finish. I've prosecuted enough murder cases to know that it's hard to sit in a courtroom and hear horrible details about not only a person's death but their life. Mrs. Rees, Le's defense attorney is going to raise questions about your son's intentions. She's going to present witnesses that state your son and his friends continuously verbally assaulted the defendant with racial slurs. She's going to say that your son, who towered over the defendant by a foot, strong-armed him on several occasions and took items from the store."

"That's not true."

"Unfortunately, there is surveillance footage that shows these actions by your son."

"Then get it thrown out."

"I tried during pre-trial motions, but Judge Simpson's allowing it into evidence. My point is that the defense is going to argue that the defendant feared for his life because he was assaulted and robbed by a racist, privileged white boy. So, do not speak to the defendant's family under any circumstances. Do you understand?"

"Fine."

"Even if they approach you, don't engage. Walk away."

"I understand." Sandra begins to cry. She's cried so much since Logan died that some days she wishes she didn't have Allison to care for. She wishes she could climb into bed, dump the entire bottle of Xanax that sits next to her bedside down her throat, and be with Logan again. "I understand."

13

The nighttime sounds chill Sam's blood. After dinner, when time stretches long and merciless is when the mind starts to peel away from reality, allowing memories and fear to seep in. When the lights dim, that's when the muffled wailing begins. Sam thought he'd left the primal sounds of loss behind in the jungles, the refugee camps. For forty years he's worked hard to drown out those cries, especially the ones in his nightmares. He should have known you can't escape. Loss follows you around like a persistent shadow, always waiting for the sun to peek out just to remind you it's still there.

His trial starts in three days. He's anxious, and oddly, excited because he gets to see his family, and wear pants with a belt and shoes with laces.

The men in this place tell him not to get his hopes up. They remind him that he should have taken the plea deal that his lawyer brought to the table.

"Second-degree murder with a 10-year sentence, possibility of parole in four years. That's a good deal, Sam," Luna told him after the pre-trial hearing when the prosecutor wanted to deal.

It wasn't a good deal for Sam. Admitting to second-degree murder meant admitting that he knowingly killed that boy. He didn't. He never saw the boy's face until after he pulled the trigger.

"But you ran," Luna reminded him. "You called and then ran away. That makes you look guilty, Sam."

"Aren't I guilty? I did kill that boy even if it was accidental."

Luna tries again. "It makes it look intentional."

"I was afraid. That's why I ran."

The fear sizzled through his veins like boiling hot water. Once he realized what he'd done and what it meant, the fear gripped him by the shoulders then pushed him out of the shop. The police didn't find him until dawn. He's still unclear about what happened that night and it frustrates his family and his lawyer.

"The more we know, the better for you, Mr. Le," Luna says over and over. What she doesn't understand is that his mind won't allow him to remember.

This is what he knows.

At eight o'clock he flipped the open sign to read closed. He didn't lock the door because he'd forgotten. A habit that Linh fussed about relentlessly.

"Criminals like unlocked doors, Sa'ng." Linh used his birth name affectionately. Sam didn't care for the name anymore. It wasn't who he was. He changed it when he applied for citizenship and hasn't thought of himself as anyone other than Sam Le since.

So at eight o'clock, he closed up but didn't lock up. He remembers going into the back to look for a box that needed to go to the post office in the morning. Inside the box was a rare, 1960's red swag lamp that he'd helped a young woman find for her mother. He'd promised to ship it first thing in the morning so it would get to the San Francisco address in time for the woman's sixtieth birthday.

At first he thought the noise he'd heard was a raccoon in the trash can on the back porch of the shop. The neighboring shop, a trendy cat cafe, tossed kitty food outside for the stray cats that roamed the alleys, which created a raccoon problem. Sam had secured the trash can lid with a metal chain, but the raccoons still tried to pry off the lid. He had peeked out the window, ready to smack the glass and scare the animal, but nothing was there.

The sound came again. This time it didn't sound like an animal at all. Instead, it sounded like shuffling feet. When he heard the obvious sound of tinkling glass, he knew someone was in the shop.

Sam reached for the rifle he kept locked in a gun safe. He didn't want the damn gun, but Jason insisted. He bought it for him as a Christmas present five years ago. With shaky hands, Sam loaded the rifle. He'd never fired the gun, but he had let Jason show him how to load it. As he inserted the ammunition, he feared he was being too loud. Maybe he should say something, he thought. Give the intruder a chance to leave.

That's when he'd heard the crash. And then another and another.

"Why didn't you run out the back door?" Luna asked when Sam told her this. "You could have left."

Sam shook his head. "You don't understand. Have you ever built something from nothing? When I knew someone was destroying my business, I couldn't walk away."

So he turned his back to the wall and slid along it like he'd seen people do in movies. He followed the wall until he reached the door frame and then stuck the rifle out in front of him.

"Did you shoot before you turned all the way or were you facing the victim?" Luna asked.

"I don't know."

"You don't remember?"

"I said I don't know. It's the same, no?"

He doesn't remember. But if he'd seen the intruder's face, he wouldn't have shot. Would he? That's what bothers him the most—the not knowing. Would he have put down the gun?

14

For the first time in weeks, Luna's lying on the couch. She rests her head on a massive mound of pillows that for once aren't littering the living room floor. Ian's nestled against her chest, twirling his finger in her hair, and watching an episode of *Paw Patrol* he's seen at least fifty times. The downtime with her son centers Luna. She feels the tightness in her chest start to ease. Her breathing matches his.

Her eyes get heavy. She thinks she may be able to nap for the next ten minutes before she peels herself off the couch to make dinner. Mark said he left a chicken and broccoli casserole in the fridge for her to warm up. Tonight is his night to work the late shift at the recycling center in St. Peters. Four nights a week, he works from six in the evening to two in the morning then comes home to sleep for a couple of hours before taking care of Ian. It's a blessing for Luna that she married a man not emasculated by her job; one who loves being a dad and goes the extra mile for all of them. But she knows he's just as tired as she is, which is why she's been thinking about finding a day program for Ian. Just two days a week, she tells herself. It would be good for Ian and good for Mark. He won't admit it, but the days after he works overnight, the dark circles under his eyes are more noticeable. Lately, she's noticed his clothes fit looser too. He's a caretaker who doesn't understand the value in taking care of himself.

In her head, she's running through the list of day programs she's looked into as she drifts off. But sleep's short-lived.

She doesn't hear the front door open or the door alarm's ten-second warning beep. What brings her full on her feet is when the alarm shrills, causing Ian to wail out loud. Then she hears fumbling and cursing.

"Bloody hell, what is all this nonsense?" The voice she recognizes.

"Mom?"

"Luna, turn this off. My God, are you trying to deafen me?" Her mom's poking at the illuminated keys.

"Move out of the way," Luna says. She punches in the code to disarm the system and looks for her phone. Already the alarm company is calling. She gives them the safe word and assures the dispatcher everything is fine.

"Mommy?" Ian's standing in the hallway, sniffling and holding his blanket.

Luna scoops him up in her arms. "It's fine, sweetie. Look. It's just Grandma."

"Loud," Ian says.

"Yes, very." Luna turns to her mom. "Very loud. What are you doing?"

"I'm visiting my daughter and grandson. What does it look like I'm doing? Robbing you?" She has a reusable grocery bag hanging from her forearm. "I bought dinner. I didn't want to disturb you, so I let myself in."

"You really should knock first," Luna says.

"Then why did you give me a key?" Her mom says, raising her left eyebrow.

Luna shakes her head. Why did she give her that key? She talks about boundaries all the time with her mom, yet she gave her a stupid key. "We have dinner, Mom. It just needs warming in the stove."

"How about dessert then? Oreos?"

"Sure."

Ian slides down Luna's body and runs ahead of her into the kitchen. She reaches for the grocery bag and peers inside: a couple of single-serve frozen meals, a package of store-brand Oreos, and a bottle of red wine. She smiles and rolls her eyes. This is exactly the type of meal Cindy Thompson would serve up.

"So, are you going to tell me what's up with all the security?" Her mom asks.

"I just want to make sure we're protected."

"From what?"

"People, Mom. What else?"

Cindy pulls out the bottle of wine and starts digging around in drawers looking for a bottle opener. "Remember those two grizzlies when we were living in Idaho? How old were you? Nine, ten? Doesn't matter. Man, remember how they shook the RV, pulling at the handles like they were human? What was the name of that town?"

Luna goes to a cabinet and lifts a small corkscrew, bottle-opener from a hook. "The name of the town was Beer Bottle Crossing. I was eight, and they weren't grizzlies, Mom. They were black bears."

"Does it matter?"

"Well, if you want to be factual, it does."

"Oh Luna, I love you, but can you not be a lawyer for a few minutes. Let's say they were grizzlies, mean sons of bitches."

"Sons of witches!" Ian says, giggling in the corner where he's pulled out Tupperware and a few spoons.

Cindy laughs hard, but Luna doesn't find it funny. "Mom, please."

"Oh, lighten up. He's only two."

"Exactly. I'd prefer my two-year-old not to go to daycare with a potty-mouth like his grandmother."

"Daycare? I thought you and Mark had an arrangement. You bring home the bacon and he changes the diapers."

Luna takes the casserole out of the fridge and peels back the foil. "Mark works, too, Mom. We both work extremely hard. I'm just considering the possibility of daycare for a couple days a week."

"Well, what about me? Why pay a stranger to watch the kid, when his grandma's here?"

"And do it for free?"

Cindy pours herself a generous glass of wine. "How about for a discount?"

"Mom, you're not watching Ian."

"I raised you, but I'm not good enough for my grandson?"

"I didn't say that. I only meant that a positive aspect of a day program is he gets to interact with other children."

"Hmm . . . Well, it would be a generous discount," Cindy says. "I've seen the news about that shop owner in Kirkwood. You look very pretty on television."

"Thanks, Mom. I'll let my stylist know you approve."

"The older you get, the snarkier you become. Just like your dad."

"How is he?"

"Oh, he's good. He's traveling this weekend. There's a gypsy caravan event in Branson that he's headed to."

Russ Thompson, an eccentric and self-taught artist, paints abstract pictures of tropical birds. From the time Luna was one to just before she started middle school, the three of them traveled across the country so her father could sell his weird, overpriced paintings to hippies, celebrities, and the occasional politician. Luna never quite understood the appeal of the birds with triangle heads, octagon bodies, and inverted legs, painted on tea-stained canvas that smelled like patchouli and campfire. But there was a market for strange and her dad figured out how to corner it.

"You're not going with him?"

Her mom shrugs. "I'm working at Randall's this weekend," she says, referring to her part-time job at a mom-and-pop grocery store. "Besides, now that you've beefed up security, I feel like I need to stay here and worry about you. I mean what if the grizzlies come?"

"Mom, you don't need to do that. Go enjoy your life."

"You know what I thought when you told us you wanted to

be a lawyer?"

"That I was selling out to a system that was part of the problem with America?"

Her mom smiles. "Sounds like something I'd say."

"You had a lot to say."

"Some of it wasn't fair."

"Some?"

Luna knew her parents loved her, but she always felt like a disappointment to them, starting on her thirteenth birthday when she declared she didn't want to live on the road anymore. She decided that she wanted a bedroom that wasn't a pull-down bed in a fifth-wheel camper. She wanted a room with privacy, a four-post canopy bed, and pink walls decorated with posters of the celebrities she saw in magazines. She wanted a normal teenage life that wasn't spent moving from state to state and spending weekends at flea markets or state fairs. She wanted to sleep in on the weekends and wake up to the sound of neighbors mowing their lawns, cars driving up and down the street. She wanted to hear trash trucks.

To their credit, Cindy and Russ submitted to her demands and moved back to Missouri. But from that moment on she was a disappointment. Normalcy was a dirty word in their household. Cindy took the job at Randall's and her dad worked construction jobs during the week, but still traveled to fairs on the weekends. When Luna told her parents she wanted to pursue a law degree, they laughed out loud. Once she convinced them she wasn't joking, her dad lit a joint and passed it between him and her mom a few times before Cindy said, "We're not paying for that."

"Luna," her mom says, putting down her glass of wine and coming around the island. She reaches out and pushes a strand of hair behind her daughter's ear. "What I thought when you told us you wanted to be a lawyer was, *That's it. She's finally going to realize she's smarter than us and never want anything to do with us again.*"

"Mom, why would you ever think that?"

"I was pretty high that night if I remember right."

Luna laughs. "True."

"I've always wanted the best for you. But I'm scared."

"Why?"

"Because I've seen the protests on the television. I've seen the threats on social media."

"That's why you need to stay off the Internet. I do."

"Luna, people aren't happy that you're defending that man."

"People like you?"

"Of course, not. How could you even think that? I respect what you're doing. What you did for that woman? Wow, that was amazing. And, this man deserves just as fierce of a defense, if you believe he acted in self-defense."

"But?"

"No buts. Just be careful. Grizzlies attack when you let your guard down."

15

Midmorning light slices through the bedroom, revealing the tiny dust particles floating in the air, waking Mark rather dramatically. He sneezes once. Then three more times before he's fully awake. He sits up in bed, runs his hand through his disheveled hair, the color of watered-down tea that's starting to show signs of graying at the temples. The white down comforter is damp with sweat, but he shivers from the chill that travels from his spine to his toes. He reaches for his cell phone to check the time. It's a few minutes past ten-thirty.

"Shit," he says, unwrapping himself from the sheets. He throws on an old AC/DC T-shirt and slides his feet into the memory foam slippers Luna gave him at Christmas. When he reaches the bottom stair, he smells coffee and hears soft voices coming from the kitchen.

"Luna?"

"In here, babe," she says.

He follows her voice into the kitchen. The table is covered with legal pads, law books, and in the corner between the pantry and the fridge are several white cardboard boxes stacked five high. Doris is at the kitchen sink rinsing out the coffee pot and refilling it with water to make another batch.

"Hey, Mark," she says. She nods at his flannel pajama

bottoms and crazy hair. "Love the lived-in look."

"What's up, D? Where's Ian?" he asks Luna.

"Mom took him to the park for a few hours and I think they're going to the children's museum this afternoon."

"Um, okay," Mark says. "You trust her with him? He's a big ball of energy these days."

"She did raise a kid, Mark."

He takes a mug of coffee from Luna's outstretched hands. "Did she? Seems you raised yourself a lot."

"Be nice," Luna says, kissing Mark on his unshaven cheek. "I thought you might like to sleep."

Mark goes to the pantry and pulls out a box of sugary cereal. "You're not working at the office today?"

"No. We need to get this opening statement written and Doris can't take anymore Justin Timberlake from the start-up peeps."

"Look," Doris says. She pulls out a kitchen chair, sits down, and runs a hand through her hair. "I do love me a little J.T., but I bought sexy back ten years ago. You know?"

"I like this woman," Mark says with a mouthful of cereal. "So, what's the plan?"

"The plan?" Luna asks. "The plan is to win this case."

"But we have a tough jury," Doris says.

"That's what we've been going over this morning. Jury composition. We don't have the most diverse group of jurors I would hope for," says Luna.

"What do you have," Mark asks.

"We're evenly split gender-wise, six women and six men. One woman is a single mom of a five-year-old boy, in her late twenties. Another woman is in her mid-thirties and has a teenage boy. Both women are Caucasian with sons. Not great for our case. Another woman is in her late 60s, close in age to Sam, but she's white also. The only Asian jurors we managed to get are a female college student and a forty-year-old car salesman. We have one Black man, fifty years old and a small business owner. He's my favorite juror."

"Why is that?" asks Mark

"If anyone is going to appreciate the struggles of a minority business owner, it's this man. We can appeal to him."

"Well, don't you just need to convince one juror?" Mark asks.

"If we want a hung jury," Doris says.

"We don't want a hung jury," Luna adds. "A hung jury means we go through this process again. We need to create sympathy for Sam, but we also have to make his actions seem practical. What would these jurors do if they were in his position?"

"We have to convince them that a white, teenage boy is something to fear," Doris says. "If this was the case of a white store owner and a Black or Latino boy causing problems, well, I doubt the PA would have even brought charges. But you know the world we live in. Justice doesn't play well with certain races."

"I thought the shop owner didn't see the victim when he shot?"

"That's what he says, but the PA's going to argue that he did see the boy and took advantage of the situation."

"What makes you think that?"

"When the judge granted our motion to allow the security footage, it meant that the PA has the opportunity to use that footage too."

"Doesn't that work against their case?" Mark asks.

"Not necessarily." Luna glances at Doris before she continues. "It's a double-edged sword for us. The footage does show Logan Rees and his friends vandalizing and physically intimidating Mr. Le on numerous occasions, but it also shows what the security cameras see. The cameras point to the outside of the building and the showroom. There are no cameras in the backroom where Mr. Le says he was when he heard the intruder. What is in that room is a monitor that shows live video footage of the security feed from the outside and floor."

"So, he could have seen who was coming through the door."

"Exactly," Luna says.

"Well shit," Mark says.

"Exactly. Shit."

16

A five-car accident on I-70 backed up the interstate for miles during the morning commute. Even with strategic side-street maneuvering, it still took Luna an extra thirty minutes to get to the courthouse in downtown Clayton. The closest parking garage didn't have any spots available, forcing her to circle back and park at the garage on Shaw three blocks away.

She walks fast, weaving in and out of businesswomen and men on their cell phones, running through her opening statement in her head. Unlike with Tammy's case, she feels prepared for today. Taking on Sam's case from the beginning makes her feel like she has a steady grip on it, a clear understanding of the facts and the objectives. Today the objective is to tell the jury a story that gets her client one step closer to crawling back into his bed with his wife and spending time with his grandchildren.

"How do you sleep at night?" She hears the question but thinks it's someone talking on their cell phone. But then she hears the question repeated; the speaker's breath on her neck. Luna looks to her right. She recognizes the woman as Logan Rees's mother.

"Ms. Rees." She's at a loss for words and says the first ones that come to mind. The words a reasonable person would say.

"I'm so sorry for your loss."

"Bullshit. You're not sorry. Why are you doing this? Why are you representing that man?"

"I can't understand what you're going through, but I empathize. That being so, I can't discuss this case with you, Ms. Rees." She starts to walk away knowing she's made a mistake. She hears Mikey's advice in her head. *Don't speak to the victim's family when you're not in control of the conversation.*

"You have a son. Don't you?"

The question kills the brakes on Luna's fast walking. "Excuse me?"

"A little boy. They're all little boys for a while and then they grow up." Sandra slides her dark glasses onto the top of her head. Luna sees the dark circles and bloodshot eyes. "They grow up and do stupid things. Does that mean they deserve to die?"

Luna turns away from the woman. "Of course not."

"I tried my best with him. I did. He wasn't an angel, but he didn't deserve a bullet in his chest," she yells.

"Sandra!" A tall, lanky man with thinning hair and a suit that fits loosely on his frame stands on the courthouse steps next to the prosecuting attorney.

"He didn't deserve that," Sandra says, her voice slightly louder than a whisper.

"Sandra, come here," her husband says, softer this time. "Come here, please."

He holds out his hand as Sandra walks toward him. She doesn't take it but glides past him up the courthouse steps. Luna waits for the husband and the prosecutor to turn away then gets on her phone.

"Hey, hon, what's wrong?" Mark answers on the third ring.

"How's Ian?"

"Fine. We just came in from playing in the backyard. Luna, what's going on? You sound scared."

She watches Sandra walk through the courthouse doors and lets out her breath. "Nothing. I'm just a ball of nerves. Just scared of the grizzlies, I guess."

Mark laughs. "What? You're not making sense. Are you

okay?"

"I'm not sure I'm cut out for this. Why did I take this case?"

"Because you believe in justice."

"Where's the justice here? What if it were Ian? What if we do everything right by him and he does something stupid? Something that he can't take back."

Mark doesn't say anything for a few seconds. "Luna, stop. You're spiraling. Take a breath. Nothing is going to happen to Ian."

"You don't know that."

"Did something happen you're not telling me about?"

"Of course not. Dammit, never mind. I shouldn't have called. I just -"

"What?"

"I'm just scared. When will this stop? When will I become one of those confident, kick-ass criminal lawyers who doesn't get all sloppy with emotion? When are those nerves of steel going to kick in?"

"You mean like the ones on television?"

Luna laughs. "Yeah. Why can't I be like them?"

"Well, because that's not real life," Mark says. "Life's sloppy. We just do our best."

"God, you're like an after-school special."

"I've got something special for you later," he says, teasing.

"Thanks, babe. I think you talked me back from the ledge."

"One step at a time, right?"

Luna sees Doris standing at the front of the steps waving at her to come on and starts walking to her. "One foot after the other."

17

Linh smells like a field of spring flowers. She rubs the rose-scented moisturizer in between her fingers, over her forearms, and under her chin. It's a nervous habit.

"Mom, stop. It's going to be okay," Samantha says. She takes the lotion from her. The family sits in the galley behind the defense table. Linh keeps glancing toward the side door near the bench waiting for Sam to come in. It's been three weeks since she's seen him. Three weeks since she's heard his voice and even longer since she's touched him.

"Maybe when they transfer me to the prison, we'll get to sit next to each other in one of the community rooms like on television," Sam said during their last visit.

"Don't," Linh pleaded. "Don't say that. You're coming home."

Sam shrugged. "Maybe, but we need to prepare for the worst."

Linh shook her head. "I don't want to."

"I think it's better that we don't talk for a while," Sam said.

"No, Sam. What are you saying this?"

"I need time to prepare, mentally, and you need a break. Why don't you go to that spa in Chicago you've been wanting to visit? Take Samantha."

"You want me to go on a vacation while you're in jail? How

can you ask that? Besides, who's going to watch the store?"

"Linh, we talked about this."

"No. I can't do it."

"Jason said he'd help."

"I'm not closing the store, Sam. That's our life."

"No one is ever going to step foot in our store again. Have you had any customers since I was arrested?" Linh's silence answered for her. "Sell the inventory. Use the money to take care of yourself."

"Sam, we're fine. Money-wise, at least."

Sam had shaken his head. "Even if I get out of here, I don't want the store anymore. Don't you understand?" He started to raise his voice. "I killed someone in that store. Dammit, Linh, just get rid of it. Get rid of everything."

Get rid of everything. The words stuck in her head. Doesn't he know what it means to get rid of everything? It means packing up and selling everything they built together over four decades. It means moving on and Linh fears that Sam wants her to move on without him. How can she do that? They've been together since they were nineteen years old, falling in love during their birth country's most tumultuous times. Linh always believed falling in love during wartime was a whole different type of love, one that lasted and persevered through anything.

"Mom," Jason says. He nods toward the door as the bailiffs bring Sam into the courtroom. She smiles at her husband. He looks briefly at Jason and Samantha then hangs his head. She knows he's ashamed to look at his children.

The courtroom remains quiet with the exception of a few murmurs. Luna leans over and says something to Sam. He nods and adjusts his suit jacket. Linh resists reaching out to touch him. To whisper his name. Doris told the family that court rules prevent anyone but the defense team, the judge, or the sheriff deputies from speaking to Sam.

"It will be hard, but you have to be quiet," she told them, specifically looking at Linh.

So Linh sits watching her husband's back fall and rise with his breath. She closes her eyes and wills him to feel her love.

18

"All rise. The 22nd Judicial Circuit Court is now in session, The Honorable Judge Randall Simpson presiding."

Judge Simpson enters the courtroom. He's a dominating presence, standing nearly six feet, five inches and with a wide berth. Luna hears Sam take a sharp intake of breath.

"Everyone but the jury may sit. Officer Stephenson, please swear the jury in." Judge Simpson waits for the bailiff to swear the jury into service then continues with his opening dialogue. "Members of the jury, thank you in advance for your service and commitment to justice. Your job is to determine if the defendant is guilty or not guilty based on the evidence and facts presented to you by the prosecution and the defense. Please keep in mind that the burden of proof remains on the prosecution during the trial. This means that the prosecution must prove beyond a reasonable doubt that a crime was committed and was committed by the defendant. If after both arguments have been presented, you find that reasonable doubt exists, you must find the defendant not guilty. Furthermore, discussing the specifics of the case with anyone other than your fellow jurors or speaking about the case anywhere other than in the sequestered area, will result in dismissal from the jury.

Before the prosecution presents its opening statement, I

would like to address the courtroom. All cell phones must be silenced during the trial proceedings. Additionally, no video recordings or photographs of these proceedings are allowed without written or verbal consent from me. I ask that you limit coming and going from the courtroom as much as possible. However, should you need to leave please do so in between testimony and do so quietly. Is the prosecution ready to proceed with opening statements?"

Siobhan Finney stands. "Yes, Your Honor. We are ready to proceed."

"Is the defense ready?"

"Yes, Your Honor, "Luna replies, standing.

"Then we shall begin the proceedings," the judge says.

Siobhan walks to the jury box. She's not much older than Luna, but she has a long case history with a good conviction rate. Her presence in the courtroom is polished and to the point. She knows how to win a case, not on technicalities or grandstanding but convincing arguments.

"Before I begin, please allow me a moment to thank you for your service. Being a member of a jury isn't easy, especially when you're faced with a case like the one you'll hear about over the next few days. This trial is about the murder of a young man, just seventeen years old and ready for the rest of his life to begin. Unfortunately, this boy's life ended too soon because of the actions of the defendant, Sam Le. The defendant didn't like Mr. Rees. He made that very clear as our witnesses will tell you under oath. He believed there were certain places in hell for boys like Logan Rees. Again, our witnesses will tell you, under oath, that they heard the defendant say this on numerous occasions.

"What kind of boy was Logan Rees? Well, according to the witnesses you'll hear from, he was a typical teenage boy. Fun, mischievous, and, yes, capable of making bad decisions. On the night of his death, Logan Rees made a bad decision. He entered the shop after hours. This is a fact. The store was closed, but the door was unlocked, according to the defendant's own admission. Why was Mr. Rees there? We'll never know, unfortunately, because speculation has no place in a courtroom, only facts. Remember that. Speculation isn't fact.

"Here are the facts. Mr. Rees entered Le's Lighting at just before eight-thirty. We know this because there is security footage, time and date stamped, which shows the moment Mr. Rees entered the building. Police reports state that the defendant, Sam Le, believed he was being robbed. He stated that he removed a rifle from the gun safe and shot the defendant in self-defense with no malice aforethought. We believe the facts pertaining to the relationship between Logan Rees and the defendant prove otherwise. We believe that the defendant, when presented with the opportunity, decided to murder Mr. Rees.

"Ladies and gentlemen, we intend to prove beyond a reasonable doubt that the defendant, Sam Le, committed what is called an impulsive killing with malice aforethought. What does that mean? It means that Mr. Le decided at that moment to take his revenge on Mr. Rees and deliver him to that place in hell he thought he belonged. It means Sam Le must be found guilty of second-degree murder. Thank you."

Siobhan walks back to the prosecutor's table, smooths the back of her pants, and sits down. She rests her hands on the table in front of her, the fingers interlaced like she's praying.

Luna waits for her to sit down then stands and approaches the jury.

"Ladies and gentlemen, the man sitting at the defense table is Sam Le. His customers and friends call him Sam. His family calls him Dad, Grandpa, and his wife often calls him her funny guy because he loves to tell a good joke. On Halloween, the children who visit the shop call him the Candy Man because he gives out full-size candy bars. At Christmas, some of the kid's call him Santa when he dresses up in the red suit and hat, to help his friend Dan spread Christmas cheer at the Boy Scout's Christmas tree lot. You see, many people call Mr. Le many things. You can too, but you cannot call him a cold-blooded, child murderer.

"The prosecution wants you to believe this. The prosecution wants you to believe that Mr. Le killed Mr. Rees because he could. Because the opportunity presented itself and he took it."

Luna stops in front of juror number seven, the woman who has the teenage son. She counts out her pause in her head, evening out her breath because she feels like she's rushing through the statement. One, two, three, four, five . . . She lets her eyes scan over the heads of the jurors and then returns her gaze to the woman.

"It's hard to imagine a life taken so young. We can't help but think, what if that were my son? It's normal to compare our lives. To count our blessings and condemn the actions of another without knowing the full story. That's the job you have during this trial. You must listen to the whole story.

"During the course of testimony, you'll hear that Mr. Le and Mr. Rees had an ongoing feud. A feud isn't the right word, though. For months, Mr. Le was victimized by Mr. Rees and his friends. Mr. Rees verbally assaulted Mr. Le with racial slurs, vandalized his property, and, on more than one occasion, grabbed him by the arm and threatened him. Did Mr. Le fear Mr. Rees? Absolutely! Did he want Logan Rees dead? Never.

"On the night of Mr. Rees's unfortunate death, Mr. Le heard someone enter his shop after hours. He was not expecting anyone, so he reached for his rifle and went to confront the intruder. At that moment, all he saw was a hooded figure coming toward him and he shot. He reacted the way anyone would in the situation. Only after, did he realize who he shot.

"Mr. Le is a hard-working member of your community. He's a man who cares about human life. A man who's worked hard to provide a stable, loving home for his family, and a man the community supports. The events that happened on that night were tragic. A life was lost, and Mr. Le will live with guilt every single day for the rest of his life. Every. Single. Day. Wouldn't you? But that doesn't mean that his actions were driven by malice or contempt for Mr. Rees. Mr. Le is not a murder. He's a man who was forced to defend his life and property. A man you must find not guilty."

19

He feels untethered to this world. For three days, he's listened to the testimonies of his family, the teenager's family, and the other witnesses put on the stand. He listens closely, but it's like the story being told is about someone else. It's unnatural to hear your life regurgitated in carefully scripted answers, the best and worst parts on display for others to judge. The plan was to let the evidence and the character witnesses tell the story, but he couldn't bear it a second longer. After his lawyer called the last witness, he leaned over and said, "I want to testify."

"That's not a good idea, Mr. Le," Luna whispered back. "Everything's going well."

Was it? Sam didn't think so. He'd seen the way Luna's back tightened every time the prosecutor objected, and the judge allowed the objection to stand. He'd seen the way his family's faces became longer, and the way they held their bodies at the end of each day, rounded and falling in on themselves. He knew that everything wasn't going well. He needed to participate in his defense. The jury needed to hear him.

"Please," he said.

So she relented, standing and asking for a short continuance before the defense rested its case.

"A continuance for what?" Judge Simpson asked.

"My client would like to testify. I need time to prepare him for questioning."

The judge sized Sam up and nodded. "All right. I'll give you one day."

One day for Sam to look everyone in the eye and finally say for himself that he never meant to kill the boy. It was an accident. A sad, sorry accident that he wished he could take back every day.

20

"I don't like this," Jason says on the day Sam's scheduled to testify. He, his sister, and mom stand in the hallway outside of the courtroom huddled together. The three have formed an assemblage excluding Luna, keeping her on the outside of their fear.

Throughout the course of the trial he's shared his dislike with Luna. Some days his objections to how she's handling the trial are so much that it rattles her. Makes her think that he's right. That her defense strategy is going to tank the case. That she's done too little to paint the picture of a man who was simply defending himself.

"They're just scared," Doris told her earlier that morning. "They're powerless. They want to feel like they have something to contribute. In this case, it's criticism. Don't let it rattle you."

"Jason, I know this isn't what you want, but it's what your father wants," she tells him now. "He has a right to speak at his trial."

"The lawyer will twist his words," Samantha says.

"Then on rebuttal we twist them back in place. Give your dad some credit," Luna says. "He's going to do very well."

She's not just saying this. She's prepped Sam hard over the past twenty-four hours. He's ready to tell his story.

At nine o'clock everyone takes their places in the courtroom. Sam arrives wearing the same shirt and pants he's worn the last three days. He sits next to Luna. She reaches into her bag and pulls out a pink tie. It's a tie Linh got him for his fortieth birthday, one he wears for graduations, weddings, and now a murder trial. He wraps the tie around his neck and secures the knot in place.

When he's called to the stand, he walks slowly making sure to keep his gaze forward and his shoulders pulled back. As the bailiff swears him in, he keeps his eyes fixed on the man's forehead. Under no circumstances, does he allow himself to look at his children or Linh. It will undo him.

"Mr. Le," Luna says. She approaches the stand. "You've asked to testify on your own behalf today. Is that correct?"

"That's right."

"You do so willingly and waive your fifth amendment right, correct?"

"Yes."

"You also understand that you waive your right to be silent. You must answer all questions from myself and the prosecution presented to you while you're on the stand under oath."

"Yes."

Luna smiles. "Thank you, Sam. Can you tell us why you wanted to testify today?"

Sam takes a deep breath. "I wanted to tell my story."

"Sam, on the night of the burglary -"

"Objection," Siobhan interrupts. "Speculation, Your Honor. The victim entered through an unlocked door. And the defendant killed him, so we don't know what his intent was that evening."

Judge Simpson raises his hand. "Calm down, Counselor. Your objection is sustained."

"Allow me to rephrase," Luna says. "On the night that Logan Rees entered your shop, were you expecting company?"

"No."

"Were you afraid?"

"Yes."

"Did you have an ongoing feud with Logan Rees?"

"Logan was a teenager. I don't fight with teenagers."

"Did he ever intentionally scare or frighten you?"

Sam frowns. Luna inches closer to the stand, hoping her presence reminds him of their conversation. Sam didn't want to appear weak in front of his family. To admit that a teenage boy scared him. But that's what the jury needed to know. That age didn't matter. Intimidation is intimidation. Logan Reese intimidated Sam.

"He would come into my store after school a couple times a week. He and his friends, they said mean things."

"What type of things did they say to you, Sam?"

"At first, they said things under their breath like gook, ching-ching, and on a couple occasions they played something called K-Pop on their phones."

"Korean pop music?"

"That's what my daughter tells me."

"Mr. Le, are you Korean?"

"No. I was born in Vietnam. But that boy thought every Asian was the same. I think he was rather stupid."

Luna grimaces. "Your Honor, that's a speculative statement by the defendant. Please ask the jury to disregard."

Judge Simpson nods. "Agreed. The jurors will disregard the last statements made by the defendant except for where he was born. Mr. Le, please answer only the questions you're asked."

"Okay," Sam says.

"Did Logan and his friends do anything else while in your shop?"

"A couple of times they damaged some of the inventory."

"How so?"

"In my shop, I have many chandeliers hanging. Logan and his friends would take prisms from some of these lamps."

"Did you ever ask them to stop?"

"Yes. Many times. My wife did too."

"What did they say?"

"They laughed at us. Told us to go cook them some rice. Then they left the store."

"Were there any incidents leading up to the night that you shot Logan Rees?"

"Yes. Two days before, Logan came into the shop. He was playing that dreadful music so loud that it drove away two of my customers. Once the customers left, he started pulling handfuls of prisms off the chandeliers, very expensive chandeliers, putting them in his book bag."

"Did you confront Logan?"

"Yes. I asked him to leave. I told him I would call the police. He told me that his mom and dad were friends with the police. They donated lots of money to some police officer fund and they'd just laugh at me."

"What did you do next?"

"I reached for the bag and tried to take it from him."

"And then what happened?"

Sam looks down at his lap. "He shoved me."

"Shoved you hard?"

"Yes. I fell onto the floor and hit my back on a pole. What do you call those? Um, a supporting pole. Something that holds the ceiling up."

"What happened next?"

"Logan reached down and yanked me up." Sam points to his bicep. "He held me by the upper arm."

"Sam, how tall are you?"

"Five feet, seven inches."

"Was Logan Rees taller than you?"

"Yes, much taller."

"What happened after Logan pulled you to your feet?"

"He got in my face and told me that he'd always take what he wanted. If I didn't like it, I could go back to where I came from."

"Sam, were you afraid of Logan Rees?"

"Yes."

"Did you see who entered your building on the night of the incident."

"No."

"When did you realize the person you shot was Logan Rees?"

"When the person fell and his hood fell back off his head."

"Sam, did you intentionally kill Mr. Rees?"

As Luna instructed him to, Sam turns toward the jury. "No. I never wanted Logan Rees dead."

Luna goes back to the defense table and avoids eye contact with Sam's family. Now comes the hard part, listening to Siobhan try to discredit Sam. Luna believes they did a good job preparing for the cross-examination, but she also knows that emotions make people unpredictable. She's nervous that Siobhan will bring up the security footage. She never considers that the PA has a different approach in mind.

"Mr. Le, may I call you, Sam?" Siobhan asks.

Sam nods, and she reminds him he must answer verbally. "Yes," he says. "Sam is fine."

"So, Sam, you say that you never wanted Logan Rees dead. Correct?"

"That's right."

"Yet, Ryan Boyle, Logan's friend, testified that you told Logan that he deserved to go to hell and that he would get what's coming to him. Do you recall saying those words?"

"Those boys made you say things," Sam says.

"Sam, please answer the question asked of you. Do you recall saying that Logan would get what's coming to him and would go to hell?"

"Yes, but, -"

Siobhan smiles and walks toward the jury box. "Thank you, Sam. No further questions for this witness, Your Honor."

Siobhan's line of questioning was short, but it made its point. Luna stands. "Redirect, Your Honor. Sam," Luna says. "What did you mean when you told Logan he'd get what's coming to him?"

"I only meant that people who do bad things eventually get caught."

"Do you believe Mr. Rees is in hell right now?"

Sam shakes his head. "No. I only said those things because I was angry and scared. Reasoning with the boy didn't work. I hoped to scare him into acting better."

"What do you think of Logan Rees now?"

The tremors in Sam's body start slow and gradually build as he releases a long wail, sobbing hard while tears and snot slide down his face. "I wish he was still alive."

21

Two days pass while the jury deliberates. Since the jury got their instructions on Friday morning, Luna has had the whole weekend to go over Sam's testimony and pick it apart.

"I shouldn't have let him get on the stand. It was stupid," she says, reaching for Mark's hand as they stroll down Main Street. On Sunday, many of the clothing and knick-knack shops open later, so the crowds are fewer. Luna likes to take advantage of Sunday mornings to visit the quaint bakery at the end of Main which has the most delicious raspberry scones and Guatemalan coffee. With baked goods in her hands, she and her little family make their way over to the riverfront park to soak up the goodness of the morning. These happy moments allow her a moment to catch her breath and put the burden of the trial down. Her clients and their families' fates are too heavy to carry at times.

"Let's try something new today," Mark says. "How about we don't talk about the case?"

"Am I starting to be a buzz kill?"

Mark shrugs. "I just think there are some other things to talk about."

Luna raises an eyebrow. "Really? Like what?"

"Well, your mom asked me why I didn't want her watching

Ian."

"What? Why would she ask you that?"

"Apparently, you're considering preschool. Is Ian even old enough for preschool?"

Luna reaches over and takes a piece of grass out of Ian's hand. She hands him a dump truck with wheels the size of her hands. "I did not tell my mom that you don't want her watching Ian. That's what she said because she didn't want to hear the truth. That I just don't want *her* watching him."

"Why does anyone need to watch him?" Mark asks. She hears hurt in his voice.

"First, it's not preschool like five days a week or daycare from six in the morning until six at night. I was only thinking a day or two a week, maybe for three or four hours. Just some time for him to get used to other people. That's all."

"I don't mind staying at home with him, Luna."

She frowns. "Of course, not. I never thought you did. But wouldn't it be nice to have a little break. You work so hard for us too. I've noticed how tired you look these days." She touches the sleeve of his shirt. "You've lost weight."

Mark pulls away from her. She wonders what she's said to upset him. He seems moodier lately, like something is pressing on him. Money is fine, and she hasn't sensed anything off in their relationship, but now she's not so sure. "Mark," she begins, "What's the—"

Her phone rings. She glances at the number and gives Mark an apologetic look.

"It's Doris. I need to answer. Hey," she says into the phone. "What's going on? . . . Okay. I'll be there soon."

She hangs up and starts gathering their belongings. "I have to go."

Mark kisses the top of her head. "Hon, don't worry about me. I'm okay. But, if you think a daycare or preschool program is good for Ian, then let's do it."

"Thanks, we can talk about it later. Nothing needs to be decided now."

She waits for Mark to gather Ian and they walk briskly back

to their house. "I picked your pantsuit up from the dry cleaners on Wednesday. It's in the closet."

Luna reaches out and rubs her hand lightly against his jaw. "I don't know what I'd do without you."

22

Life is a series of before and after. Sam's seen many in his lifetime. The span of life before he met Linh and the time that existed after their love blossomed. The time before war tore his country apart and made it impossible for them to stay. Another time, after he landed in America lost then found in a country with a language and customs he didn't understand. The lonely times before he held his children in his arms and after when his life felt full of meaning and an abundance of love. These series of before and after moments are never-ending in a lifetime. Today is another one of those moments.

Before the verdict is read, he steadies himself, leaning forward against the table and feeling its edge push into his thighs. He knows that a guilty verdict changes everything for his family. It tarnishes their name. It mars the memories of him because they'll have their own before and after memories. Before he was a man with a gun and a rash decision. After, when they took him away in handcuffs.

When the presiding juror speaks, Sam closes his eyes and when he hears the words spoken and his future decided, he falls to his knees.

23

"Are you sure you don't want to go out to dinner with us? We can't thank you enough for all you did for our family." Samantha stands next to Luna outside the courthouse while she waits for her husband to bring the car around.

"It's nice of you to offer, but I think you and your family need this time together. To celebrate. It's been a long time since you've all been together."

Samantha picks at the neckline of her dress and nods. "It's been such an ordeal. You know even though that boy was a menace, I feel bad for him. Things shouldn't have happened that way. If my dad could change everything that happened that night, he would."

"I'm sure if Logan knew how things would have turned out, he would have changed some things too. So, what's next?"

"Well, dad's actually talking about going back to Vietnam. Not permanently, but to visit. He says it's time he and my mom reconcile some things." Samantha's husband pulls up and gets out. He waits by the passenger door. "I should go. Thank you again, Luna. Thank you for saving my father's life."

Luna smiles and allows Samantha to embrace her. She watches the car drive away, and her breath returns, slow and even, for the first time in weeks.

24

It rained hard overnight. Not one of those late afternoon thundershowers fueled by the atmosphere's need for relief from the scorching heat. This was a soaking, steady rain that filled the gutters and produced lightning going off every ten seconds like camera flashes. The rain kept Mark awake all night, but Luna slept soundly. She didn't even wake when Ian began wailing after a loud clap of thunder shook the house. The last few months with one high profile case after another had taken its toll on her. She had lost weight on her petite frame and she rarely slept. When she'd come home after the trial yesterday, she was worn down and not at all celebratory like Mark thought she would be after Sam's not guilty verdict.

"Let's get dinner at one of those swanky Clayton restaurants," Mark had suggested. "Think your mom would like to babysit?"

Luna tossed her shoes in the corner of the foyer and shook her head. "I don't feel like going out for dinner," she said. "Can we just stay in and order pizza?"

"Sure," Mark agreed. "Everything okay?"

Luna reached out and touched his cheek. She ran her fingertips from his temples along his jawline and smiled, a forced smile, he thought. "Why wouldn't it be? We won."

He wanted to believe her, but he'd known Luna since they were fifteen. When you know someone longer than half your life, you know them inside and out. It is harder for them and you to hide the tiny fragments that deception leaves behind. They reveal themselves in body language; how a sentence is phrased, and when a smile hesitates on the lips or reassuring words are spoken a beat too late.

She had moved away from him, but he reached out and wrapped his hand loosely around her wrist. "Luna, I love you."

Her head tilted to the right, her eyes widened and her lips parted in a half-smile, half-frown. "Yeah, babe, I know. I love you too." She giggled, and Mark felt a chill go through his shoulder blades. Luna always giggled when she was masking her feelings. He had let go of her wrist and watched her move into the kitchen, but he knew something was not right. What was it?

Now he lies awake beside her and watches her while she sleeps. The peacefulness on her face and the way her nose twitches when she's dreaming makes him fall in love with her all over again. Luna tells him it's creepy when she finds him watching her. He can't help it. All he wants to do is protect her and the life they've built together. He knows she's a strong woman and doesn't need him to defend her, but he doesn't know what he'd do without her or Ian. What type of man would he be?

Mark's breath catches in his chest, and he turns away from Luna. Getting up from the bed, he walks across the room to his chest of drawers. He glances over his shoulder to make sure she is still sleeping. When he feels confident she isn't waking up, he slowly opens the top drawer and slides his fingers under his T-shirts. When his fingertips touch the metal housing of the handgun, he breathes easier.

PART THREE

DO NO HARM

25

The miracle happened ten years ago on a rainy Sunday morning at the tail end of summer. Cara stood in her apartment's tiny bathroom holding the drugstore pregnancy test between her thumb and forefinger, the blue Spanish tile cool beneath her bare feet. To save money on utilities, she had left the window open overnight and wedged a box fan within the frame to cool the studio apartment. When she listened hard enough, she could hear the muffled sounds of the neighborhood coming alive outside below her apartment. Usually, she drank her morning coffee on the balcony, sitting on a folding chair and watching the children play at the park across the street. Sometimes she read the morning paper, but mostly she closed her eyes and just breathed. She relaxed into her breath and forgot about the patients she couldn't save, the exams she needed to take, and the pressure to find the best surgical residency to jumpstart her medical career.

But not that day. On that Sunday morning, Cara watched the thin blue lines appear on the stick as she held her breath. Of course, the test had to be wrong. Still, the longer she stared at the stick, the darker the blue lines turned. She closed her eyes, convinced she heard her baby's heartbeat pounding alongside her own, strong and determined.

Cara placed the pregnancy test on the edge of the sink and lowered to her knees. The stress of medical school and her recent breakup with this baby's father all fell away from her. At that moment, in the presence of her miracle, she knew everything would be okay.

She would nurture this little one. Make sure her child knew he or she was loved and wanted. She would make any sacrifice to keep her child from feeling pain or fear. She would protect her miracle, no matter the cost. Little did she know then how far she would go to make good on this promise.

26

The two-year-old room is wide open, bright and airy, with pops of color and individual stations for all the things toddlers love to do. A reading nook in the far-right corner has two tot-sized armchairs, a collection of colorful, geometrically patterned beanbags, and board books collected in soft-sided baskets. In another corner, free-standing art easels and whiteboards are attached to the wall at toddler height. Two children, outfitted in vinyl art smocks, paint using large brushes, covering the canvases with squiggly lines. *Abstract art, toddler style,* Luna thinks. She points out the easels to Ian. He kicks his little feet against her hip and squeals with delight then buries his head against her neck. In the middle of the room, rectangular worktables are placed parallel to each other, and a sand table stands ready for little hands to make sandcastles.

"The room smells lovely," Luna comments.

"Thank you," says Belinda, the center's director. "It's lavender and vanilla. We use essential oils because they create soothing effects. Do you use essential oils at home?"

"Nah," Mark answers. "We use Febreze."

Belinda laughs, a boisterous laugh that Luna imagines could get very loud and out of control quickly, but also a laugh that inspires everyone to find the humor around them. "Nothing wrong with that. So, what do you think? Would you like to let Ian hang out in here with Ms. Chrissy while we talk in my office?"

Luna looks to Mark, and he shrugs. Luna hasn't left Ian alone with anyone but her parents. The few times he has interacted with other kids was at story time at the library. They go to the playground often, but he prefers to toddle around the perimeter of the tot area, watching the other children curiously, never engaging. Now Luna fears she is making the wrong decision. Maybe Mark is right. It's worked out fine so far. Does Ian really need socialization with others right now? Maybe he's too young.

"What do you think, buddy?" Mark asks. "Want to hang out here and play while Mommy and I go with this nice lady?"

Ian pulls his head away from Luna and looks up at her. His deep brown eyes search hers, and her heart longs to capture the moment forever because even as he stares into her eyes, he is slipping away, literally. He loosens his arms from around her neck and gravity pulls him to the ground. Luna lowers with him, squatting down. As soon as his feet touch the floor, he lets go of her neck and runs off toward the book nook.

"Looks like we have a reader," Belinda says. She smiles at Luna and Mark. "It's always hard letting them go. Let's go into my office and talk."

They leave the room and walk back up to the reception area. Belinda's office, around the corner from the receiving desk, is decorated in monochromatic shades of blue with windows on three sides so she always has a view of the center's rooms. When they walk past the receiving desk, Luna notices the two young women at the front glance casually her way.

"Don't mind my staff. It's just that we've never had a celebrity's child in our care." Belinda motions for Luna and Mark to sit.

Luna crosses her ankles and shakes her head. "I'm not a celebrity. I'm actually very uncomfortable with people calling me that."

Mark looks over at Luna and winks. "She has been making a name for herself."

"That's all I meant. I hope I didn't offend you," Belinda says. "So, I sent you an email with all the financial information, health releases, and other pertinent enrollment information. I assume you have questions. Most parents do, especially first-time parents. Here at Little Lamb, we want the children and parents to feel comfortable. Ask as many questions as you need to." She leans forward in her chair and waits.

"Well," Luna begins, "Ian's never been in childcare before. How do you handle that?"

"With patience and love, to say the least. We have a child-centered program that's similar to the Montessori style of teaching. We let the child create his or her own experience, so they feel more in control of their space. With our two-year-olds, it's really just about exploring, playing, and socializing. We don't do schoolwork or formal teaching."

"So you're saying my son won't come home with a vocabulary larger than mine?" Mark asks. "Don't get me wrong. I want him to learn, but I also want a few more years of him thinking his parents rock the Casbah."

Belinda smiles. "We want children to be children."

"What about security?" Luna asks. As soon as the word escapes her lips, she notices Mark shift in his seat.

"Well, first and foremost, we never allow anyone to take a child from the premises who isn't listed on the emergency release form. This includes grandparents, aunts, uncles, and even family friends. Only people who have been added to the list by the parents and have a center-issued photo ID are allowed to pick up. The ID must be presented at the time of pickup. Parents are expected to follow these procedures too.

"We also have a two-entry system as you experienced when you arrived. First, you're buzzed into the main foyer, and then you're buzzed in again after you show your ID to the staff at the window. All doors lock automatically behind you upon entry, and we have security cameras throughout the entire center. Additionally, we issue a passcode to all parents. This allows them to view any room of the center at any time throughout the day . . . with the exception of the bathrooms, of course."

Luna nods and looks at Mark. "Sounds good to me. What do you think?"

"Sounds like a kiddie fortress." His lips form into a tense smile.

Luna laughs, but she knows what he's thinking. If she is so concerned about security and someone else being with their child, then why doesn't she let things continue as they have been? What has Mark done wrong? The answer is nothing. He has done nothing wrong, but her reassurances have not been enough to convince him.

"I'm kidding," he says, reaching over and patting Luna's knee. "Seriously, I don't mean any disrespect. It all sounds great."

Belinda swivels around in her seat and points to the monitors behind her. "It looks like Ian's enjoying himself."

Luna leans forward to get a better look at her son cuddled up in the corner reading a book with a giant stuffed bear. Another little boy sits next to him and is also reading. Ian looks happy and content, which soothes Luna's uncertainty just a bit.

"He can start whenever. We have openings right now that fit into your two-day-a-week schedule. How about tomorrow?" Belinda suggests.

"Let's start next week," Marks says.

Luna raises her eyebrows. He looks over at her and gives her a quick smile, but she sees the resolve in his eyes. He is not going to budge on this one.

"Next week works great for us," Luna agrees.

Belinda nods. "Next week."

"Yep," says Mark quietly. "Next week."

27

It's not like how it happens on television or in the movies. The police didn't come bursting through her front door with guns drawn hours after his death. In actuality, it took so long that Cara stopped holding her breath each time she saw a cop car. Two months had passed from the time Harvey Gold died at Mercy Hospital to the time she was arrested for his murder. During the long, agonizing days of waiting and catching bits and pieces of whispered conversations between her colleagues, Cara continued on with her days, treating patients and being a mom. She no longer held surgical hours but instead focused on palliative treatments for her terminal patients, always under the watchful eye of her superiors. After her shift at the hospital ended, she drove to her parents' house to pick up Ellie and tried to keep life as normal as possible. Although, in truth, things hadn't been normal for a long time, even before Harvey Gold showed up as a patient at Mercy Hospital.

Cara hoped the police would never come. She hoped that everyone would realize what happened the day Gold died was a mistake, but she knew better. She knew that life allotted for only one miracle.

The day of her arrest began like every other day. She was startled awake by a nightmare right before her alarm went off.

Her white, sweat-soaked T-shirt clung to her body, and the bed sheets were tangled around her legs. She reached for the water bottle on her nightstand, guzzled half of it, and forced her legs to carry her into the shower. Once dressed and composed, she walked down the hall to wake Ellie. As a toddler, she was a horrible napper, always fighting the sleep that robbed her of exploring life. Then the preteen years came, and all she wanted to do was sleep. Getting her up in the mornings became a struggle. She physically had to drag her from the bed each morning and walk her to the kitchen, plopping her down in a chair at the kitchen table to eat breakfast.

That morning when Cara walked into Ellie's room, her daughter was sitting up in bed staring out the window.

"You're up early," Cara said.

Ellie didn't look at her. "I heard the woodpecker again. He was pecking at the gutters. It woke me up."

Cara leaned in toward Ellie, reaching out her hand to brush a stray hair from her forehead. Ellie flinched and scooted away from her.

"It's okay, baby," Cara said.

"Mom?"

"What is it, sweetie?"

"When am I going to be normal again?"

"You are normal."

"I'm not. I feel scared all the time. I just want everything to be like it used to be."

Cara felt her stomach twist. She swallowed down stomach acid that hiccupped into her mouth. "Baby, it will take time."

Ellie let Cara wrap her arms around her and pull her into a hug. That's when she knew her time was up. No one would believe her. Just like the police didn't believe Ellie. After everything she did to give her daughter a beautiful life, it was all for nothing. The police would come, and Ellie would end up alone and afraid.

***

It's a little after two o'clock in the afternoon when Annie, the charge nurse, finds Cara sitting in the empty doctor's lounge starring out the window and grazing on a salad.

"Cara?"

Cara turns away from the window and smiles. She has always liked Annie because she keeps the med-surg floor in order and always tells the bawdiest jokes. You would never expect such filth to come out of the mouth of someone who sounds like Minnie Mouse on helium. Of course, that is what makes the jokes even funnier. Cara knows that Annie, by nature of her position, has been working behind the scenes with the police and meeting with hospital administrators to piece together the story of what happened the morning of Gold's death. Even though she is on the inside of the investigation, Annie gives her a sympathetic smile because she knows. She understands what happened, and she doesn't hold it against her.

"I would have done it too," she told Cara one night when the two were alone on the med-surg floor.

"I don't know what you're talking about," she had responded.

Annie then touched Cara's shoulder and whispered, "He deserved it."

Now Annie stands in the doorway, transferring her weight from one foot to the other and biting her fingernails. "Dr. Mitchell asked that you come to his office."

Cara pushes the salad away from her, stands, and removes her white coat. "Will you call Dr. Morris in to cover rounds this afternoon?"

"I already did," Annie says.

"Ellie's out of school in an hour. My mom is volunteering at the children's center this afternoon, so my dad will need to get her. His cell number is—"

"Your dad's number is in my phone," Annie interrupts. "You gave it to me last week. Remember?"

Cara does remember because she has prepared for this day for weeks ever since the hospital administration told her the police were investigating. "Thank you. You have the other number I gave you, right?"

"I got it, Cara. I promise."

"It's Friday," Cara says.

"Yeah?"

"I won't be home until Monday at the earliest. That's if they let me post bail. My baby is going to spend the weekend without me. We've never spent more than one night apart." Cara pinches the bridge of her nose with her fingers and takes a deep breath to suffocate the sob that is filling up her chest.

Annie walks toward her, but Cara puts up her hands and backs away. "I can't."

"It will be okay."

"Really? Tell me how any of this is going to be okay?"

Annie opens her mouth to speak but shuts it right away. When she finds her words, they are the truth. "I can't."

"Will you walk with me?"

"Of course."

The walk down the hall and up the flight of steps to the chief medical officer's suite passes too quickly. When she turns the door handle and lays eyes on the room, she has to steady herself against Annie.

"Dr. Weber?" A small-framed man with glasses and a receding hairline addresses her and moves closer to her. "Dr. Cara Weber?"

"Yes. That's me."

"Dr. Weber, you're under arrest for the murder of Harvey Gold."

28

"Bob and I drove down to Taum Sauk Mountain State Park this weekend," Doris tells Luna over coffee and a chocolate donut while sitting at the conference table. It has been weeks since the surface has been clear of files, motions, and other legal papers. Luna can't help but feel that a clean conference table is a sign of a fresh start. "We were supposed to go camping. Instead, we ended up staying at a stinky cabin with a coin-operated vibrating bed."

"So fancy," Luna says.

"Better than the alternative—sleeping in a tent. Good thing I conveniently forgot to pack it."

"Bob is a saint to put up with your antics. When is he going to get wise to you?"

Doris laughs. "Never, honey. That's why I married him. The trip down to southern Missouri was pretty, though. I'd never been. Do you know I counted twenty-two dead armadillos on the side of the road in a five-mile span? What's wrong with those things? Are they stupid or just suicidal? Also, there wasn't a Target anywhere. Who can live in a place that doesn't have a Target?"

"You're quite chatty this morning." Luna raises an eyebrow and pulls apart her donut.

"I'm just well rested. What about you? Did you have a nice relaxing weekend with no major case hanging over your head?"

"It was quiet. Ian started his new school today. He seemed excited to be there. He barely even said goodbye to me when I left."

"Is Mark still acting weird?"

"He seemed fine this morning, but I don't think he's one-hundred percent accepting of the idea yet."

The truth is that Mark spent most of the weekend tinkering around in his workshop, starting one project without finishing another. He was restless and moody, very unlike his usual self. He has been distant since the childcare center visit, but Luna knows whatever is bothering him isn't only about sending Ian to day care. It is something more, but he won't open up to her, and it troubles her. Mark has always been the open one in their relationship. He lays his feelings out and never holds back. This time around, it's different. He is holding something close to his chest that he refuses to give up. He says everything is fine, but for the first time in fifteen years, she doesn't believe him.

"He'll come around. Mark's a good guy. He also grills the best T-bone steaks. When are you guys going to invite Bob and I over again for a free dinner?"

"Free for who?" Luna laughs. She gets up and throws her napkin away in the trash can. The can is filled with Styrofoam coffee cups leftover from the late nights and early mornings. "When was the last time we emptied this thing?"

"Isn't that included in the rent?"

"We don't rent that kind of space in that kind of building. I'll make a dumpster run."

Luna ties up the bag and slings it over her shoulder. Today is the first day she has come to her office not dressed for clients or court. She threw on a pair of old jeans, a black V-neck T-shirt, and pulled her hair up in a topknot before leaving the house to take Ian to the center. She didn't even put on mascara. For the first time in weeks, she feels fresh-faced, relaxed, and not weighed down by a sensationalized trial.

On her way to the dumpster, she passes an older man

wearing a cabbie hat and a Polo shirt. Although she can't see his face well, she pegs him to be in his sixties. She continues to move past him, puts the trash in the dumpster, and makes her way back around the building. When she approaches the front of the building, she finds the man standing on the sidewalk with his head down and shoulders rounded. Luna brings her hand to her back pocket and rubs her fingers over the outline of a pocketknife. She picked it up over the weekend during a Bass Pro trip to buy a kiddie fishing rod for Ian for his fishing date with her dad later this week.

When she steps closer, she sees that the man's shoulders move slightly up and down, a sobbing rhythm.

"Are you okay?" Luna asks. She doesn't move any closer and keeps her hand on her back pocket.

The man turns to her, extracts a wad of tissues from his front pants pocket, and pulls them apart to find a clean tissue. He blows his nose and wipes his eyes then reaches into his back pocket for his wallet and pulls out a piece of paper.

"Am I at the right address? This doesn't look like a lawyer's office."

Luna looks at the address. Under the street name, she reads her own name written in red and underlined twice.

"Come on up," she says.

***

Ellie likes to sit in the plaid rocking chair by the window and watch the squirrels jump from branch to branch. Usually, Dr. Partridge encourages her to talk. She asks her open-ended questions, reaching for the feelings Ellie keeps deep inside. This is one of the reasons she likes sitting by the window. It gives her someplace to look when she talks so she doesn't have to look Dr. Partridge in the eyes. Today's visit is very different though. Today, Dr. Partridge isn't asking her questions. She doesn't try to scoop out the words Ellie wants to keep hidden behind her sealed lips. Instead of asking questions, Dr. Partridge lets her sit and stare out the window while she sits at her desk writing in her blue notebook. Silence fills the space. Ellie's not dumb. She knows today's therapy is really a babysitting session while her grandparents are at court.

"I want to go," Ellie pleaded earlier that morning as her grandma rushed her to get in the back seat of the car. They were running late because her grandma couldn't find her purse, even though it was hanging on the hook in the foyer like always.

"We talked about this last night. You're going to Dr. Partridge's this morning. We'll pick you up after the arraignment." Ellie didn't know what that fancy legal word meant, but she did know words like "arrested" and "murder."

Ellie wasn't surprised that her grandpa picked her up from school on Friday. Sometimes her mom had a surgery that ran late. She didn't think anything was wrong until he took her for frozen custard. While she gobbled up her hot fudge sundae, her grandpa stared out the window, not saying a word. Usually, he ordered a Hawaiian coconut banana concrete and asked her to tell him about her day. *Don't leave one detail out*, he would say, smiling so hard Ellie thought his face might crack around his eyes where the wrinkles were thickest.

When they went back to his house afterward, Ellie got nervous. "Why aren't we going home?"

"It's just for a little bit, sweetie." He turned the radio up a little louder. Taylor Swift's voice came out of the speakers. "You like this music, right?"

Ellie hated when adults did that, not answer your question. Instead, they try to trick you into thinking about something else. She didn't fall for that trick anymore. When her grandma came home, and her eyes were red and puffy, Ellie's heart beat faster and her words tangled in her throat. "What, um, is Mom okay?"

Her grandparents dodged the question and told her not to worry.

"Sweetheart," her grandma said, "why don't you go into the den and watch Netflix?"

Ellie did as she was told but kept the television turned down and put her ear to the door, straining to hear the conversation. Her grandparents' voices shuffled back and forth, hushed and unintelligible. She had started to give up on the conversation when she caught the word murder and her mom's name in the same sentence. Then she heard the word she hated the most. A word that pushed her away from the door and toward the couch where she found her grandpa's fuzzy blanket and pulled it over her head. A word she was too young to hear and know, but she learned about in the last three months.

Rapist.

29

Luna doesn't bother driving to the courthouse. She runs down the narrow sidewalks of Main Street in her canvas slip-on shoes, clutching her bag against her chest. Her T-shirt rides up on her stomach, and her jeans slide down on her hips. A group of older women out for a stroll step aside for her and shake their heads. Luckily, the security line isn't crowded, allowing her to glide right through. She sidesteps a crowd gathered by the elevators and opts to take the stairs.

The heavy wooden doors to Division II are shut tight. When Luna presses her body against the doors to open them, she does so slowly, trying to not disturb the cases being heard. Judge Reynolds likes an orderly courtroom that is quiet, attentive, and punctual. The clock on the wall above the empty jury box reads eleven o'clock. Court has been in session for over an hour, but Cara Weber's arraignment is second to last on the docket, which gives Luna a few minutes to sit in the back row and catch her breath. But not for too long.

"Next: The State versus Dr. Cara Weber," the clerk reads from the docket.

Cara is guided into the courtroom by a female officer. Her left hand grasps the middle of the cuffs, while her right hand stays clamped down on Cara's shoulder as she leads her to the defense table. She stumbles over her feet, and the officer yanks her up like one might yank a rag doll out of a mud puddle, without hesitation and with much disgust.

"Dr. Weber," Judge Reynolds says, "will you please state your full name to the court for the record?"

The woman clears her throat. "Dr. Cara Lynn Weber, Your Honor."

"Thank you, Dr. Weber. You have been charged with second-degree murder. Do you have counsel present in the courtroom today?"

Luna takes the cue. She stands up and makes her way to the bar separating the gallery from the rest of the courtroom. "Your Honor, I'm representing Dr. Weber in this matter."

The judge cocks her head to the side and smiles. "Was today laundry day, Ms. Goldwyn?"

"I apologize for the street clothes, Your Honor. Dr. Weber's case was just brought to my attention this morning when her father hired me. I didn't have time to change. May I?" she asks, motioning to join Cara at the defense table.

"I'll allow it."

"Thank you, Your Honor." Luna opens the gate and walks to the defense table. Cara stands several inches taller than Luna and looks down at her with sad, tired eyes.

"I thought Annie didn't get the message to my dad," she whispers.

"I don't know who Annie is, but she came through just in time," Luna tells her.

"Dr. Weber," Judge Reynolds says, "Ms. Goldwyn has entered her appearance as your defense counsel. Do you accept this?"

Cara nods.

"I need you to answer yes or no, for the court record."

"Yes, Your Honor," she says.

"Let the record show that Ms. Luna Goldwyn is retained by the defendant, Dr. Cara Weber. Now, Dr. Weber, you have been charged with second-degree murder in the death of Harvey Gold. How do you plead?"

"Um," Cara looks to Luna for direction, who nods. "I plead not guilty, Your Honor."

"Let the record state that the defendant has entered a plea of not guilty. Now, on to matters of bail. Prosecutor, what are you looking for here?"

Luna hadn't paid attention to whom the prosecutor was when she walked into court, but it doesn't surprise her to hear Wiles Nyler's voice bouncing off the walls of the courtroom. "Your Honor, given the serious nature of the charge, we ask the defendant be denied bail and be held in the St. Charles County Jail until trial."

Cara mumbles something and grips the table. Luna speaks up quickly so that her new client doesn't say anything to make her situation worse. "Your Honor, my client is a lawful woman. She doesn't have a criminal record. In fact, she's never even received a parking ticket. She is also a single mother with a young child. To deny this woman bail would be a detriment to her daughter and to the cornerstone of justice. We ask that she be released on her own recognizance and be allowed to go home pending trial."

"That's unacceptable, Your Honor," Wiles argues. "The woman used her authority as a doctor to take revenge on a patient and kill him. Our evidence proves that Dr. Weber knew exactly what she was doing when she did it and, therefore, is a potential threat to others."

"Mr. Nyler, as you know, this is an arraignment. Save your evidence for trial," Judge Reynolds says. "That being said, you are correct that these are serious charges. Therefore, I'm setting bail at five hundred thousand dollars, property and ten percent allowed." She strikes her gavel, and the clerk calls out the next name on the docket.

"What now?" Cara asks as the female officer returns to take her back to her cell.

"Your father is waiting downstairs. He's ready to put his property up as collateral. You should be back home for dinner tonight."

30

Her parents have lived in the same house since Cara was born, and even though she hasn't lived there since she left for medical school, she still calls this place home. Today, when her dad opens the front door, the familiar scent of Gain laundry detergent fills her nostrils.

"Your mom went to your place to get a few of your things, some clean clothes, your shampoo and conditioner," her dad says.

"I need to go back home. Ellie and I—" Cara spots Ellie's purple Converse sneakers in the corner of the foyer and starts to cry, unable to finish her sentence.

"Cara, right now, this is home. It's better for you and for Ellie to stay here."

"How is she?"

Her father pulls her into a bear hug, and she feels his back tighten into her embrace. "She has questions, but she's doing okay. Your mom took her to Dr. Partridge's office this morning. They'll be home in a little bit. We thought you'd like some time to shower and clean up before you saw her."

"Thanks, Dad." Cara wipes her eyes and catches a glimpse of herself in the hallway mirror. She hasn't looked in a mirror since the morning she was arrested. The woman staring back at her is a stranger—one who has the same golden-copper hair and green eyes but who looks ragged, tired, and guilty as hell. "I look like a monster."

"A hot shower and you'll feel better." Her dad nudges her toward the interior of the home.

"Will I? I thought I'd feel better when Gold died, but the pain is still right here." She points to her heart and feels the panic rise in her chest. "I don't know what I was thinking. What did I do?"

"Enough," her dad says. His voice is stronger, stern and steady this time. He's mad at her. Of course he is. Why wouldn't he be? One moment ripped her family apart. "Cara, we can't talk about this. Your lawyer asked me what you said to me about what happened at the hospital. I told her you said nothing. She said that's good and to keep it that way. She doesn't want to put us in a position that hurts your case."

Cara understands. She now exists between two shifting realities: her parents' house and the real world. Inside this house, she is Cara Weber, mother and daughter. She is the person who used to run through these halls in tap shoes holding a teddy bear in one hand and a Fisher-Price medical kit in the other. The person who took her dad out to breakfast every Father's Day and bought her mom her favorite fudge—the kind that could only be found at Ozarkland an hour and a half away—every year on her birthday. In this house, she is scarless and merciful.

Outside of these walls, she's the woman responsible for the death of her daughter's rapist.

31

Judge Reynolds set the preliminary hearing for two weeks, which doesn't give Luna much time to come up with a strategy to argue for dismissal of the charges. Yet, with all she has to do, she can't concentrate. Since she has returned to the office, she has picked up her phone every five minutes to check on Ian. Right now, he is sitting with his teacher and working on a puzzle. For the millionth time in weeks, Luna wonders what she would do if someone hurt her child. Before she got pregnant with Ian, she never considered herself overly maternal. While some women had a thirst for motherhood, Luna figured if it happened, great; if it didn't, well, no big deal. She didn't think she needed a child to feel whole. Her world shifted the afternoon Ian was born and she held him for the first time. That was the moment she knew what it was like to want to protect someone so fiercely that you would do anything to spare them pain and suffering.

Anything.

When she invited Edwin Weber into her office that morning, she offered him a chair, which he fell into, sobbing. It took him ten minutes to compose himself. When he did, he pulled out a school photo from his wallet.

"This is my granddaughter, Ellie. She's ten." He handed the photo to Luna.

"She's very pretty. I like the purple streaks in her hair," Luna had said.

Edwin sniffled. "They're clip-in hair pieces. My daughter," he stopped and choked back another sob, "she bought them for her as a compromise. Ellie wanted to dye her hair, and Cara told her no. She's still too little."

"Sure," Luna had agreed, handing the photo back to him. She remembered the first time she colored her hair. It was the summer between freshman and sophomore year. When her mom wouldn't take her to the salon, she bought a box of Clairol from Walgreens and went to her friend Kellie's house. She wanted to dye it sun-kissed blonde but ended up with patches of orange hair. Her mother shook her head, served her a plate of lasagna, and suggested she shave it.

"She's just so little, you know?" he repeated. Luna didn't know, but she had learned to let people talk and tell their stories at their own pace. "Too little for all of this to be happening."

"What happened to her?"

"He hurt her. He hurt her bad. Now my daughter's been arrested for his murder."

32

"He raped my daughter," Cara says.

Her voice is flat, not because she doesn't feel horrified to say those words, but because she has gone into clinical mode. It is an odd place to be, a place where you are suspended between normal human emotion and superhuman resilience. When she allows herself to be human, she falls apart. A broken human can't protect another broken human, so she must stay in one piece. The problem is that you can't deny your humanity its need to breathe, not when you watch your daughter struggle to find some bit of herself again, and so her humanity cracks and her tears spill through and fill the room.

"I'm sorry," Cara says when Luna hands her a box of tissues. She is so tired of saying sorry because, no matter how many times she says the words, it doesn't change anything. Ellie still dreams of that man. She continues to struggle to make it through the school day without an episode of crying or hiding in the bathroom. No matter how many times Cara says she is sorry, it doesn't make an ounce of difference.

"Your father told me a little about what happened. The incident with Ellie, mostly, but I'd like to hear your version of events."

"Where do I start?"

"You said the victim—"

"Can we not call him that?"

Cara sees that this woman still believes there are two halves to the world: right and wrong. She used to be like that, and then Harvey Gold entered her life. Right now, she wants to lean forward and take Luna's face in her hands, bring her forehead to hers, and steal the innocence, the goodness. She wants to have it back so bad, but once it is gone, she fears it is gone forever. That is what makes her heart break into tiny pieces when she imagines how Ellie feels. Will her beautiful miracle ever feel free and innocent again?

"What do you want to call him?"

"I don't care, but he's not a victim."

"Can you tell me how Mr. Gold ended up as a patient under your care?"

"He was brought into the ER by ambulance following a hit-and-run."

"Did they ever find the driver?" Luna asks. She writes something on her notepad.

Cara shrugs. "Not to my knowledge. I didn't ask."

"Did you know it was Mr. Gold when he first arrived?"

"No. When we were working on him, he was just a body that needed mending. I didn't see him in the ER when he first arrived. He was stabilized there before being sent to surgery. That's when I first worked on him."

"When were you alerted to who he was?"

"I wasn't given any information about him until after the surgery was finished."

"What types of injuries did he have?"

"Trauma to internal organs, specifically in the torso area. He also suffered a broken femur, lacerations to the face, and, I believe, a broken wrist."

"How long was the surgery?"

"I'm not sure. A few hours? Time moves fast on the surgical table. What seems like twenty minutes is really five hours. The hospital has that information if you need it."

"So, after the surgery, what happened?"

"He was moved to the med-surg intensive care unit and listed in critical condition. Although Dr. Wilson, the on-call cardiothoracic surgeon, and I were able to stop some of the internal bleeding, we were concerned about the condition of his heart and lungs. He wasn't out of the woods."

"By this time, you knew his name?"

"Yes."

"How did that make you feel?"

Pissed off and sick to her stomach, Cara recalls. Angry that she saved a monster. Can she tell her lawyer that she wishes she let him die on the table? Instead, she decides to take a safer route. "Guilty. That man hurt my daughter and I saved him. I couldn't save her."

"Dr. Weber, I know it's hard, but can you tell me what happened to Ellie?"

She knew the questioning would eventually land here—to that awful day three months ago when her daughter's life had changed forever.

33

The weight of the day follows Luna home, trailing behind her like a heavy bag of stones. She had to pull over once in the Schnucks parking lot because she was crying so hard she couldn't see the road. When she picked Ian up from the center, she held him so tight that he pushed back against her to find a pocket of air.

"No, Mommy," he said. She put him in his car seat, fastened the belt, and drove home with those emotional stones sitting on her chest.

A full day of play at the center wipes Ian out. He barely made it through dinner, his head wobbling back and forth each time he reached for a strawberry on his plate. Now, the dinner dishes sit piled in the sink, Ian naps on the big, comfy chair in the corner, and Luna puts her bare feet on the coffee table. She wishes Mark were home tonight so she could decompress, talk about mindless crap, and watch old '80s sitcom reruns on television. She texted Tracey earlier in the evening to see if she wanted to come over for a glass of wine, but she texted back that her night was filled up with dance and gymnastics classes for her girls.

That leaves Luna alone in the quiet house with nothing but Edwin's words running through her mind: *He hurt her. He hurt her bad.* What immediately follows are Cara's sharp words, the one's chiseled into her brain: *He raped my daughter.* She sits in the silence and lets those words sink into her skin, penetrate her maternal layers, and settle in her heart. Being a parent means making choices. Every day, parents question themselves and the choices they make for their children. *Should I let my child wear socks that don't match? Is it really necessary that he finishes his broccoli? Will staying up one hour past bedtime make that much difference in the morning?* These are low-risk choices. Make a wrong decision and all you get is a cranky kid who doesn't want to get up for school in the morning.

What about the high-risk choices?

"I shouldn't have let her walk home alone," Cara said, weeping and blowing her nose. "But I was running behind at work that day. My parents weren't able to pick her up, and the school is only three blocks from our house. She had been begging me for months to let her walk home like the other kids in her class. I always told her no because it was too risky. What if she didn't look when she crossed the street and got hit by a car? What if someone had broken into the house and she surprised them? But that day, I was stuck at work, out of options, and worn down. I should have said no. Why didn't I say no?"

34

Three months earlier

On the corner, across from the school, she watched her friends climb up into the buses while others slid into the back seats of their parents' cars. Ellie gripped her bookbag's shoulder straps, pulling the bag tight across her back. Before the last bus pulled away, she turned toward Clovis Avenue and started the three-block journey home. As she walked, she went over her mom's instructions in her head: *Go straight home. Do not speak to anyone. Keep your head up and pay close attention to who is around you. The moment you get in the house, text me.*

Ellie had every intention of following the rules exactly as they were spelled out. This was her first trip to grown-up territory. If she proved she could walk home alone this one time, maybe her mom would let her do it more often. Then, maybe, she would let Ellie walk around at her school's summer picnic, alone with her friends.

It was the music that caught her attention first, upbeat and teeming with Latin flavors. It reminded Ellie of the music played at El Maguey, a Mexican restaurant in town that she went to every year for her birthday. She looked forward to the sombrero-wearing waiters clapping and singing "Happy Birthday" to her.

Although she knows it didn't happen this way, it seemed at that moment that the music swirled around her legs and carried her toward the street opposite of her home and down an alley between a cluster of duplexes.

When she got closer to the music, she realized it wasn't a street fair or party, but music playing from someone's back porch. The Latin sounds burst through the speakers of an old CD player like the one her mom keeps in the garage. She turned around to leave, feeling stupid for letting the music distract her and pull her off course. She didn't see the man until he was in front of her.

"Hey! Are you lost?" He smelled like cigarettes, wore a short-sleeved, buttoned-up work shirt, and had a Coke can in his hand. His name was embroidered on the left pocket: Harvey.

Ellie shook her head and tried to move around him. He blocked her way.

"Excuse me," she said. An odd sensation started to work its way through her body, a persistent pounding in her ears and a quickening heartbeat.

"What's the hurry? Want a Coke? I have plenty." The man gestured to a cooler sitting on the ground next to one of the duplexes.

Ellie didn't answer him. Instead, she tried to move around him again. He moved into her path. Now she felt sweat begin to form behind her ears and between her shoulder blades. *These were the people she was warned about,* she thought. *Strangers.*

"You think you could help me with something?"

"No," Ellie said. She tried to make her voice loud and strong, but it came out tiny and soft.

The man shook his head. "You kids are so rude these days."

"Please, my mom is waiting for me across the street."

The man looked over his shoulder toward the empty street and laughed. "Right, of course she is."

At that moment, he moved closer to her and grabbed her backpack. He yanked her toward him, and she gagged from the smell of cigarettes and body odor. Pulling on her backpack even harder, he dragged her toward the porch.

35

These days, Cara views her life like it's a time-lapse video, every moment speeding by on fast forward, pushing her faster and faster toward her trial date and the verdict. The days are swallowed whole by the night too quickly, and the sun rises in the blink of an eye. It's been three weeks since she was released on bail, but it could have just been yesterday. Time is a foe that mocks her, and right now she feels the urge to jump up from her seat, take her daughter in her arms, and run out the front door. Could she do it? How far would she get before they found them? Instead, she raises her mug to her lips, swallows the bitter coffee, and asks Ellie if she's finished her math quiz.

Ellie shrugs and chews on her pencil. She's quieter than usual, but what does Cara expect? Everything she did to protect Ellie from the pain that Gold inflicted on her means nothing now. Because Cara was arrested, and the case is in the public eye, Ellie's been outed by association.

Respected Mercy Hospital Surgeon Arrested for Second-Degree Murder of Daughter's Rapist. Those are what the headlines read online and across the television screen during the nightly news. So much for protecting a victim's identity. Last week, Cara took Ellie out of school for an indeterminate length of time until she can figure out the next best step. The principal didn't argue. She merely nodded, collected a week's work of assignments from Ellie's teacher, and told Cara she could mail in the finished work.

"No need to bring them up personally," she said. "We know you're struggling right now."

Cara nodded, accepted the stack of papers, and walked out of the school with her head held high. She could feel the building sigh with relief when she got in her car and drove away.

"Mom," Ellie asks, still chewing on the pencil. "Can I ask you something?"

"Sure, but quit eating the pencil. Your grandparents have food in the cupboards."

Ellie ignores the joke. The shade of seriousness colors her face. "Why did you do it?"

Cara swallows hard. "Do what?"

"Kill him."

"I didn't kill him, Ellie," Cara says.

"You promised you'd never lie to me."

How she wants to get up from her chair and wrap her arms around her little girl. But she stays put in her seat. Ellie's armor is on today, and she doesn't want her to feel threatened.

"I'm not lying. I didn't kill him."

"Then why did they arrest you? Grandma says I'm not supposed to talk about it. She tells me not to worry and that everything will be okay. I don't believe her. Why should I believe *you*?"

Cara takes a breath, considers her words. "I didn't kill that man. But I didn't do everything I could to save him."

"You let him die?"

"Baby, I want to tell you everything, but I can't."

Ellie throws her pencil across the room and slams her palm on the table. Her cheeks blush crimson. "Stop it! Just tell me what happened. You made me tell you what happened. I didn't want to, but I did. Now you won't talk to me."

There's too much truth in her daughter's cries. It's too heavy for Cara to hold. She feels as if she'll fall to her knees if she stands, but she has to. She has to wrap her daughter in her arms and tell her she's so sorry for it all. What she did do. What she didn't do. Everything in between.

"I'm so sorry for everything that happened to you that day. I wish I could take it all back."

"You can't," Ellie says, her hot mouth against Cara's neck. "No one ever can."

"We're going to get through this. I promise."

"Mom, don't lie to me."

Cara pulls out of the embrace. She looks into her daughter's eyes. "You are going to get through this."

"Can I tell you something?"

"Always."

"It's okay if you killed him. I'm glad he's dead."

***

"I like the new office," Wiles says. He walks over to the shared wall and puts his ear against the drywall. "Is that Coldplay? My wife likes them. Well, she liked them when Gwyneth was married to what's his name."

"Did you take time out of your schedule just to come here and make fun of me?" Luna asks.

Wiles laughs and shakes his head. "I'm not making fun of you. I'd rather listen to that crap any day than the people yapping and complaining in my office all day. You've had quite a run lately, haven't you? Keep it up and you're going to have a nice corner office in a swanky building that serves Starbucks in the lobby and plays soft rock in the elevator. Defense attorneys always get the spoils. It's those of us on the other side who get the public-funded coffee."

"If you hate your job so much, why not quit?"

"And do what? Be a criminal defense attorney? No thank you."

"Are you ready to drop the charges against Dr. Weber?"

"Why would I do that? We have a solid case against the good—or should I say, bad—doctor. I have three witnesses who are willing to testify that when he coded, she did nothing. She stood over his bed and watched him gasp for breath."

"She froze," Luna says.

"Froze? No, you give her too much credit. That woman saw a moment to get even and she took it. Would have been easier for her to get away with it if she'd let him bleed out on the table, but it's my understanding she didn't realize who he was then. That came later. Not that I can blame her." Wiles walks to the window, looks out over the rooftops toward the river. "If a man like him did what he did to one of my kids? Well, he'd be all the way down the Mississippi to the Gulf of Mexico by now. What would you do if someone hurt your son?"

An icy jolt of panic finds its way between Luna's shoulder blades. It is a scenario she doesn't want to consider. She glances at her iPad on the table, the screen black, but she knows with one touch she can see what Ian's doing when he's at day care. What about the times when she won't be able to? She knows those times are going to come too soon. The in-between moments when all the bad has the opportunity to slither in through an exposed crack in the routine. All it takes is one second of taking a breath and relaxing for everything to fall apart.

"At worst, she's negligent for providing proper care," Luna states, refusing to answer Wiles. "That's a civil issue—one that might come up in a wrongful death lawsuit. It doesn't make her actions criminal. You can't prove intent. Why not just drop these charges and let the woman take care of her daughter properly?"

"We all have our roles in this circus, Luna. Mine is to champion justice. What's yours?"

"The same."

"Hmm . . . maybe. Two sides of the same coin, I guess." Wiles gestures to a file he placed on top of the conference table when he arrived. "Sometimes, justice gets a little jumbled though."

"I'm not following you."

"Why don't you take a look at what's in that file there? It's a little folder that I labeled 'New Developments.' Take this to your client and then let's talk. I'm not a heartless man. I just want justice for our victim—all the victims in this case. One way or another, I'm going to get it. It can be harsh, or it can be painless. I know your client doesn't want a public trial. Who'd want to drag their kid through all that shit? But I have a job to do. If I look the other way, what does that do? It promotes vigilantism. The truth is, you and I aren't that different. We both believe in equal justice."

"Justice isn't black and white, Wiles."

"In my role, I have to be color-blind. There's no other option. Otherwise, we'd live in a world of chaos and disorder."

"She's not going to accept a plea."

"Read the file, Luna, and share the information in it with your client. I think it might change her mind."

36

From the Weber's kitchen, Luna hears a neighbor mowing the grass and the exhausting *chug-chug-chug* of the mower running on fumes. She hopes the sound is enough to mask her growling stomach. The last time she remembers putting anything in her body was yesterday afternoon when she sipped a room-temperature vanilla latte while reading the file Wiles left behind. The only other sound in the room comes from a snoring Roxie, the one-year-old German shepherd that Edwin adopted two days ago from Pets-A-Lone Sanctuary.

"Someone abandoned her on the side of the highway. Just opened the door and let her go, I imagine," Edwin told her when he'd opened the door to her that morning. "I thought Ellie and Roxie might be good for each other."

Luna let the dog sniff her feet, and she forced a smile. There was no arguing that Ellie needed everything good in her life, especially now.

The silence at the kitchen table stretches long between her, Cara, and Edwin. Last night when she called the Weber residence to ask about a meeting this morning, she suggested to Cara that it would be best if Ellie weren't present. Cara didn't argue, and Ellie had left to go to Bill's Pancake House with her grandmother for breakfast shortly before Luna arrived.

Now the three of them sit at the table staring at the papers before them.

Cara breaks the silence with one long gasping breath, the kind you take when you realize you can't hold your breath any longer, but you try to contain the fire building behind the breath. Luna stopped believing in fire-breathing dragons when she was eight years old, but she swears if that type of magic were possible, fire would spit from between Cara's lips right now.

"Is this true?"

Cara asks the words out loud but not to anyone in particular. Instead, she lets them hang in the air, waiting to see who will reach out and claim them.

Edwin scoots his chair away from the table, stands, and walks to the window over the kitchen sink. He grips the edge of the sink and lowers his head.

"Dad?"

"I'm sorry," he whispers.

Cara looks to Luna and shakes her head. "I don't understand what any of this means."

"The sheriff's department had an open investigation into the crash that caused Harvey Gold's injuries. That investigation has been ongoing even after you were charged because, as you said, Mr. Gold was a victim of a hit-and-run. During initial police interviews, several of Mr. Gold's neighbors mentioned seeing an early-model, dark blue Mercury Sable parked across the street."

"The car you've been keeping for Ellie someday?" Cara asks her dad.

Edwin doesn't answer, and Luna continues. "The neighbors say they saw it parked across the street from Gold's residence several times throughout the day for three or four days before the accident."

Cara shakes her head and knits her eyebrows together. "The police told our admitting nurse that no one saw anything."

"Right. No witnesses the night of the hit-and-run. No video either, it seems. The intersection where Gold was hit didn't have those red-light cameras or any traffic camera, for that matter."

"Lots of people drive older cars. Are they sure about the make and model?"

"A few of the neighbors interviewed also say that they witnessed Mr. Gold arguing with an older man. Some say late sixties. Other lean closer to early seventies. Regardless, all the neighbors who witnessed the argument agree that the man was around five feet, eleven and wore an old, cabbie-style hat." Luna looks over at Edwin, remembering the day she met him outside her office wearing the same type of cabbie hat.

"Dad? What the hell is happening here?"

Edwin runs his hand over his head. "I only went to speak to him."

"Speak with him? Why?"

He continues to gaze out the window. Breathing evenly until—*thud!* He slams his fist against the window, not hard enough to shatter the glass, but startling enough to make Luna jump. "Because nobody else was making him talk. No one was taking what happened to Ellie seriously. The police weren't moving fast enough. Where were all these so-called neighbors—witnesses—when he grabbed Ellie and dragged her into his home? Huh? Who the hell was looking out for her?"

"Oh my God. What did you do?"

Edwin shrugs. "What do you think I did? The monster laughed in my face. He told me no one would believe a scared little girl because they never had before. He'd done this to other children, Cara. He took away their innocence. He stripped them of their security and peace."

"Dad—"

Edwin holds up his hand. "I'm not sorry about trying to protect the people I love. What I am sorry about is that it didn't work. Not well enough, as it stands. I let my foot off the accelerator too soon because I got scared. That's why the bastard lived. Then, because everything is so twisted and wrong, it was you who was on staff the night he came in. If I'd known how all this would end up, I wouldn't have done it, Cara. I wouldn't have put you in that position. I wanted to end Ellie's suffering, not make it worse. Not take a mother away from her daughter. Ellie needs you right now. I'll confess. That will put an end to this, right?"

"Unfortunately, Edwin, confessing isn't going to put everything in order. The State isn't ready to say that the accident caused Gold's death. Prosecutor Nyler's case is built on the assumption that had Cara responded quicker when he went into cardiac arrest, he'd still be alive. That his injuries from the accident were not responsible for his death.

"For my part in preparing this case for trial, I've spoken with expert witnesses who are willing to testify that this isn't the case—that the injuries Gold sustained were life-threatening, and even with prompt medical intervention, he might not have been able to be resuscitated the day he went into cardiac arrest, that Cara's one-minute delayed reaction wouldn't have made a difference in the long run."

"So, what's the problem?" Edwin asks. He approaches the table and looks between Luna and Cara, who are exchanging knowing glances.

"Dad, if you confess, you go to jail."

"If I don't, *you* go to jail, and you did nothing wrong." His voice trembles. He reaches out and touches his daughter's shoulder. "I didn't want this, Cara. Not this outcome. It was supposed to be different."

Cara shakes her head, runs her finger under her nose. "I know."

Luna looks down at the file. She thinks about all the wrong that could have been righted weeks ago if Edwin had been upfront with her from the beginning. Now it's just one big mess because no one wins. In another file, one that Luna hasn't put on the table yet, is a plea agreement. It's her duty to relay this information to Cara, but she hesitates. Doris told her it's a win for the family, to look at it that way. But, in a case like this, Luna can't see the space where justice exists. Not for Edwin, Cara, and certainly not for Ellie. Winning isn't always justice.

"There's another option: a plea agreement that the prosecution is willing to accept."

"A plea? For Cara?"

Luna nods. "Yes."

"But she didn't do anything wrong."

"Right."

"Why would she agree to a plea if she did nothing wrong?"

"Because the prosecution wants a win, and this is the easiest way to get it without dragging your family through the mud. Gold was a monster. There's no doubt about that, and the prosecution knows this. The prosecution knows that they can't argue this case without exposing what might have motivated Cara to delay care. Cara is a sympathetic defendant, and quite frankly, so are you. Sympathetic or not, the question becomes, do either one of you want to take that chance? If Cara pleads guilty to third-degree assault, the State is offering five years of probation and suspended imposition of sentencing."

"No prison time?" Cara asks.

"None, as long as conditions of the probation are met, which are strict and career-altering."

"What does that mean?" Edwin asks.

"It means, Dad, that I lose my medical license."

"No, no, no! Dammit, Cara, no!"

"Oh, Dad, don't you see? My license was revoked the second those handcuffs clicked around my wrists and they took me out the back door into the squad car. Who'd want to hire a liability like me ever again? My reputation is shot. I'll take the deal as long as I know the investigation into Gold's death is done. I don't want to wake up one morning with the police knocking down the door and taking my father away."

"Those are the terms. As soon as you sign, the investigation is over."

"Do you have a pen?" Cara asks.

37

Luna places her hands on the steering wheel, listens to the hum of the car's motor, and takes several deep breaths. On the passenger's seat in the plain manila folder is the signed plea agreement, ending Cara's legal battles but signaling the start of a life changed forever. Luna doesn't know what Cara was thinking when Gold coded in that hospital room. Did she stand above his bed and count away the seconds necessary to save his life? All she knows for sure is that when she met Cara's eyes after the plea agreement was signed, she saw her own reflection looking back at her. She understood that you do what it takes to protect those you love.

Anything.

PART FOUR

THE BAD DAUGHTER

38

Luna can't believe how many costumes there are for kids. She also can't believe she's standing in a crowded aisle at Party Center on a Saturday morning trying to decide between a brown-and-white dog costume or a Super Mario costume. She turns to her mom and holds the Mario costume out.

"This is cute, but is this cultural appropriation?" she asks.

"Against who? Plumbers?"

"Never mind." She puts the Mario costume back. She should know better than to bring her mother Halloween costume shopping, especially on a crowded morning when there are more people to offend.

Her mom sips from her silver Yeti and says, "Isn't it silly how much people spend on Halloween? Thirty dollars for a unicorn mask? Outrageous. I guess creativity mattered more when you were little."

"Some of us don't have time for creativity, Mom. Would you like to make a costume for Ian?"

Cindy waves her hand. "That wasn't my point. I don't even like Halloween."

"That's not true. You love Halloween. Remember when we were living in that RV park in Utah and you threw a huge Day of the Dead party? Everyone talked about that for weeks. How old was I? Seven? Dad painted our faces, and you made those amazing sugar skulls that you gave to all the kids."

"You were eight, and *Día de los Muertos* is not the same as Halloween, Luna. Halloween is a commercialized event. The Day of the Dead is a cultural event and recognized by UNESCO. It is a celebration of life and death. It has meaning. What meaning is there in a dog costume and kids running from house to house like fools trying to get candy that makes their teeth fall out? Halloween is a dentists' holiday."

Luna shakes her head and holds the dog costume close to her chest. It's the last one and people get a little crazy in these places. "I guess you won't be trick-or-treating with us this year? It's the first time we're taking Ian around the neighborhood."

"Don't be silly. Of course I am. Well, I'll stay and hand out candy at your house. That's more my style. But, let me just say, my grandson is going to be the cutest dog on the block. The cutest, you hear that everyone?" Cindy raises her voice and looks around the crowd, daring them to disagree. No one pays her any attention.

They walk to the checkout line that's at least ten people long. Luna sighs, glances at her phone, and takes a deep breath. There's so much to do today, and standing in this line for the next twenty minutes is not what she had planned. She has case notes to review before her meeting with Janie Thompson tomorrow.

"Hey," Cindy says, tapping Luna's arm. "Do you know those women?"

Luna looks in the direction of the women her mom's pointing at. The women are a couple people ahead of them in line and, dressed in their colorful spandex leggings, look like they came from the gym or possibly Starbucks. Who knows these days? One has a blue streak barely noticeable in her dark hair, the other a purple streak that's very noticeable in her blond hair. The women don't seem familiar, but that doesn't mean anything. With little sleep and even less coffee in her system, Luna's not even sure she'd recognize herself if she looked in the mirror.

"They don't look familiar."

"Then why do they keep glancing back here? It's very rude." Cindy raises her voice again and narrows her eyes at the women.

"Stop it, Mom. Maybe they think I'm someone else. Leave it."

The women lower their heads, and one of them pulls her phone from her purse. Her finger swipes the screen a few times and then the phone disappears behind their heads as they scrunch together to look at the screen. After a couple of seconds, the taller woman with a streak of purple in her blond hair glances at Luna. Her mom doesn't miss the look.

"Hey!" she shouts.

Luna touches her mom's shoulder. "Don't."

Of course, she doesn't listen.

"What are you two yoga-pant, unicorn-streaked hair princesses looking at?"

"I'm sorry?" the blond unicorn says.

"No, you're not," Cindy says.

"Mom," Luna hisses.

"You're Janie's lawyer, aren't you?" the dark-haired woman asks. She looks Luna up and down and shakes her head.

"Who are you?" Luna asks.

"People who know Janie well," she says.

"Well," Luna says, "it's nice to know she has friends."

"Oh, we're not her friends. No one is friends with Janie. You got kids, huh?" the blond-haired woman asks.

Luna doesn't answer. She hugs the costume tighter to her chest and wishes she would've just ordered the cow costume she found on Amazon. Going out in public these days makes her anxious, and being with her not-so-subtle mother worsens the anxiety.

"Why don't you mind your own business and make an appointment with your hairstylist? How old are you, anyway? Like, thirty-eight? You look like a couple of My Little Ponies that weren't taken care of," Cindy says.

The blond woman gasps and turns away.

The dark-haired woman laughs. "Words don't bother me. You know what does? People who think it's okay to kill their mothers." She turns to speak directly to Luna. "Of course, if I had a mom like yours, maybe I'd go all Janie Thompson on her too."

The women turn back around, and Luna stands frozen in place. It takes her a second to realize the line has moved forward. Her mom doesn't say another word until they are out the door and buckled up in the car.

"Honey, does that happen a lot?" she asks.

"All the time."

Luna starts the car. She wonders how long it will be before someone puts a clip of that little interaction on social media. As she's backing up, the navigation screen lights up with a text from Tracey that reads "Yikes", followed by a surprise emoji and two angry, red-faced emojis.

There's her answer.

39

Tara knows it's silly, but she needs something to do with her hands. It's hard to sit still in the visitors' hallway waiting to see Janie. So she sits in the uncomfortable plastic chairs that make her feel like she's back in school and she knits. Today she's knitting a blue-and-gold hat for her grandson, Bryce, who's turning two next Saturday. Her car trunk is also filled with toddler toys that make noise and light up because what two-year-old really wants a hat for his birthday? Truthfully, the hat is really for her daughter, who's a huge St. Louis Blues hockey fan. She asked Tara to make one for Bryce and one for her.

Of course she would, she said, even though she really didn't have the time. She's been taking double shifts at the hospital that leave her tired, physically and emotionally, but what won't a mother do for her children? That's what her friend Sandy used to say. There's nothing in the world a mother wouldn't do for her kids, no amount of love she wouldn't give.

"Who else will do it if we don't?" she had once asked Tara. They were probably sitting on Sandy's front porch drinking mimosas on a Sunday because that's what they did. But she doesn't remember, and it doesn't really matter now.

Hearing her friend's voice in her head makes her drop a stitch. She takes a deep breath and begins again. *Clickety-clack, clickety-clack.* The knitting needles click against each other as she focuses on taking deep breaths.

Yes, Sandy, she thinks, *what won't we do for our children? What won't I do for your child now that you're gone?*

"Tara Collins?" The officer's voice startles her, and she drops her knitting needles. The blue ball of yarn rolls away from her, and she scrambles after it.

"Sorry about that, ma'am," he says.

Tara puts her knitting supplies away and hands her bag to the officer. Knitting is fine in the hallway but not beyond those steel doors. She feels so out of place in this concrete hell. She feels like a criminal herself every time she visits Janie. The first time she came here, shortly after the arraignment, the officer led Tara into a small room and told her to sit at the table. He left and returned with Janie. She wore orange medical scrubs with black numbers scrawled across the back, and her hands were handcuffed in front of her. The officer pushed her down into the seat across from Tara and unhooked one cuff, attaching it to a hook on the table. He told her they had ten minutes, and when the officer left the room, Tara jumped when the doors locked, but she had promised Sandy she'd look out for her children if anything happened to her. How could she have known making that promise would mean this?

"Seems like Miss Thompson isn't up for visitors today," the officer says.

"Did you tell her it was me?"

"I did."

"She's refusing?"

"That's the way it looks. Sorry," the officer turns away.

"Wait! Can she do that?"

"She can refuse any visitor she wants. Don't take it personally."

"That's not the point. I need to talk to her. I promised her mother."

"Her mother?"

"That's right."

"I'm not sure that matters to that girl. If it did, she wouldn't be here, now would she?"

"Sandy loved her children. She asked me to look out for them. Janie knows this. Will you try again?"

The officer sighs. "Listen, I know you mean well. You sure as hell are a better person than me, visiting that girl every week, but if she says she doesn't want to see you, well, that's that."

Tara nods and decides it's not worth the fight. Janie is just having a bad day. She knows she's struggling more than usual. The guilt is weighing her down like one of those heavy anchors her husband uses to keep his boat in one place while duck hunting, and Tara hopes that the guards are watching her closely. She wanted to see her today to remind her she can still do right by her mother. To remind her that Sandy loved her. That even though she's no longer with her on this earth, she's watching over her every step of the way.

Tara's not ready to forgive Janie, but she knows Sandy already has because that's what you do for your children. You forgive them. You love them. You keep showing up for them even when they keep turning away from you. Even when they take your life, you keep loving them, you forgive them.

***

Nineteen-year-old Janie sits on her hands and rocks back and forth on the edge of the metal-framed cot in her holding cell. She closes her eyes and hopes today will be the day she sees nothing but darkness. It's impossible. Every time she shuts her eyes, she sees her mom's face, pleading with her and telling her she loves her. On good days, she sees a happy family, a mom, a dad, and two daughters smiling and laughing, playing basketball in the backyard on the court her dad built when she started playing basketball in the third grade. It's hard for her to understand how they got here from there.

Janie knows Tara will be unhappy that she refused her visit. She just can't do it today. Not right now. Every time she visits, Janie knows she's only doing it because she made her mom a promise to take care of her kids if something happened. Once a week, the woman shows up at the prison and sits across from her asking her stupid questions like, *How are you sleeping? How is the food? How are they treating you?*

Janie always mumbles a few appeasing words, but all she wants to do is laugh in the woman's face. How does *she* think it is in a cage? She knows Tara doesn't want to be in the same room with her. She sees the disgust in the woman's eyes even though Tara tries not to look at her. Janie can't blame the woman after what she's done. Would you?

She wonders how long Tara will keep coming. Will she visit her every week until her sentence runs out? That's a lot to hope for, but even though she doesn't want to admit it, she hopes she does because she is the only person who visits her besides the lawyer. Her sister doesn't come, and she can't speak to her dad anymore.

The more time that passes with her living in this eight-by-eight cell with the exposed toilet, no mirror, and little sunshine, she stops missing things from her old life. She doesn't crave the latte anymore from The Study Hall, a campus coffee shop she and her friends went to each morning before classes. She hasn't missed Anderson Hummel in weeks, and she's sure he's not missing her. Who wants a murderous girlfriend? She does miss how her little sister Amber smelled after showering each morning before school. The Katy Perry body spray she applied from head to toes made Janie happy and hopeful. She knows it's not the smell she misses—it's Amber, a sister who probably won't speak to her again.

Sitting alone in a jail cell, you have long stretches of time to think. That's the point, right? It's not to keep you locked up and society safe, but to make you sit in your thoughts and go crazy. She figures she's to that point. She must be if she's going to walk into that courtroom on Monday and do what she's going to do.

She's noticed the guards coming by her cell more often, collecting her sheets first thing in the morning and giving her finger foods that don't require utensils. They think she will kill herself. It's not that she hasn't considered this possibility. Yes, ending her life would take care of so much, but she won't do it.

If she killed herself, she'd have to face her mom, and she's not ready for that.

But she's also not ready to face her dad.

That's what has everyone so worried. Monday morning is the day of reckoning for Robert Thompson. It's the day that she takes the stand and testifies against the man who killed her mother . . . the man whom *she* let kill her mother.

40

Some people hate waking up each morning knowing what to expect, but not Mark. Routine keeps him steady on his feet. Each morning he takes his coffee the same—two tablespoons of sugar and two tablespoons heavy cream. He prepares a plate of scrambled eggs, a side of bacon, and two slices of wheat toast. It's not that he can't be flexible. He can, and he has, but since he can remember, he's always preferred to have his life planned. He likes knowing what's around the corner with no surprises because he knows not all surprises are good, and lately, there's been too many surprises. The moment Tammy White's case fell into Luna's lap, Mark's carefully planned life shifted, and he can't seem to steady himself. Nothing is routine anymore, especially the conversation he's having with his mother-in-law in his kitchen while Luna's giving Ian his bath.

"She says it happens all the time," Cindy tells him. "Has she told you about the other incidents?"

Mark shakes his head. "She's stopped talking about her cases."

"Well, I'm worried about her, and you should be too."

"Luna's a strong woman. If she felt like something was wrong, she'd tell me."

"You need to tell her to quit taking these ridiculous cases."

"That's not happening. No one tells your daughter what she can and can't do. You of all people should know that. You raised her, didn't you?"

"Oh, please, don't flatter me."

"I wasn't. I'm saying your stubborn genes are in her. Anyway, I'm not telling her to back off these cases."

"What if some lunatic comes after her or Ian?"

Mark sighs and stands up. He walks over to the kitchen window that faces the street. This is one thing in his routine that's changed since Luna has taken these high-profile cases. He used to peer out the window because he liked watching the magnolia tree in the front yard bloom in the spring and the people walking their dogs up and down the sidewalk. Now he walks to the kitchen window several times a day checking for cars he doesn't recognize that are parked too long in front of the house. He doesn't pay attention to the dogs but to the people, memorizing their faces, just in case. Cindy doesn't have to lecture him on what he'd do if someone came for his family. The answer is upstairs in his dresser drawer.

"I'm worried about my daughter. Does she seem happy?"

Mark turns away from the window and faces Cindy. "I think so."

"But you don't know?"

"She's just tired, Cindy. She gives a lot of herself to her clients. You know how she is. When she's in the zone, she's in it. She's focused."

"That's what I'm worried about. What if she lets her guard down? What if she misses something? She needs help."

"She has Doris."

Cindy waves him off and reaches into her purse for her phone. "I mean security, Mark. Here. Look." She hands him her phone. On the screen is the homepage of a private security firm.

"A bodyguard?"

"They're called security consultants."

"You're overreacting, Cindy. Luna's fine. We're fine."

"I want my daughter and her family to be more than fine. I want them safe."

Mark hands the phone back to her. "We are, but to put your mind at ease, I'll talk to her about it."

"Talk to me about what?" Luna asks. She walks into the kitchen holding Ian, both with big grins on their faces and smelling like lavender and rose petal soap. The front of Luna's shirt is soaking wet because giving Ian a bath is always an adventure, especially when it's time to get out. Mark's heart melts.

He gives Cindy a warning look and says to Luna, "We're just trying to decide what time to go trick-or-treating. Do we start early or after dark?"

Luna grins. "No question about it. We go when it's dark. Do we really want to be those parents who show up with their kid at three o'clock?"

Mark laughs. God, he loves his little family. It's all he's ever wanted. He'd do anything to keep them safe. That's his top priority . . . but a bodyguard? Has it come to that?

41

Luna waits for Janie in the common area of the women's state prison along with family members of other inmates. As a rule, she tries not to schedule visits with clients on the weekend for two reasons. The first reason is she needs time with her own family. Not just face time but quality time. Some Sundays, quality time means snuggling with Ian under an afghan on the couch watching cartoons while Mark reads one of the espionage thrillers he loves so much. He has several boxes full of these paperbacks that seem to tell the same story over and over. Sometimes it's sitting out back on the deck sipping a cup of coffee, watching Ian play in his sandbox and listening to her neighbor, Mr. Dennisey, sing off-key while sweeping acorns off his back porch. On Sunday, Luna and her family sleep in, well, as much as you can with a two-year-old, eat slow meals, and recharge. Luna tries not to think about her clients and how one wrong move on her part can send them to jail for the rest of their lives or worse. But no matter how hard she tries, she can't. It's her new normal, sharing her time between her family and her clients.

The other reason she doesn't schedule Sunday visits is that family members get only one visit a week for forty-five minutes, and she knows how important these visits are for families. Even when she represented clients charged with far lesser crimes than murder, she recognized the need for families to have this time together. Adults make bad choices, but that doesn't mean they love their families any less, especially their children. Kids don't understand why their parent can't come home. They don't understand why one moment they were eating breakfast with Mom only to find her gone, arrested and booked, when they get home from school. Luna knows many people behind bars in the women's state prison have been convicted of horrific crimes. But she also recognizes that most of these crimes bear no weight on how much children love their parents.

Today, Luna's breaking her Sunday rule because she has no other choice. Besides, she knows she's not taking family time away from Janie. Each time she visits, she asks to see the visitors' log to see who's visiting her clients. Janie gets one visitor a week, Tara Collins. The woman comes every Saturday to visit the teenager. She's also the one who reached out to Luna and asked her to take the case. Normally, a case like Janie's would be turned over to a public defender, but Tara insisted Janie's mom would want her daughter to have the best defense possible. At first, Luna found that hard to believe, but she gets it now.

A loud buzzer sounds, and the steel door separating the common area from the prison space opens. One by one, the inmates enter the room. Their eyes scan the crowd. Those who find the people they're looking for walk toward them and move to an empty table or bench. The ones who find no one waiting for them in the room stand against the wall, their wrists cuffed in front and their eyes downcast. Hope has drawn them to the room, but hope isn't enough for family members to show up and make small talk.

Janie is the last inmate through the door. She sees Luna and ambles toward her.

"Hey," she says. "Can we sit by the window today?"

Luna nods and leads her to a two-person table in the far right-hand corner of the room. "How are you?"

The girl shrugs. "Not great."

"Did Tara come see you yesterday?"

"I wasn't up for visitors."

"I see." Luna knew this already. Tara called last night to tell her Janie wouldn't see her. She was worried that Janie had decided not to go ahead with her testimony.

"But you know all this," Janie says.

"Tara mentioned something about it."

"Of course she did. You're my lawyer, but we all know you work for her."

Luna frowns. "I work for you, Janie. What's going on?"

"I hate the way she looks at me. I hate the way everyone looks at me. When I get out of here, people will never see me as anyone other than a mommy killer."

Luna wants to tell her that isn't true, but she doesn't. She remembers what happened yesterday at the party store and thinks about all the social commentary she's seen online. It doesn't matter what Janie's reasons were for doing what she did. People don't forget easily when you do bad things.

"Are you having second thoughts about testifying against your dad?"

"Not really, but do I have to do it in front of him?"

"I'm afraid so, Janie."

"Couldn't we do like a video deposition?"

"It doesn't work like that. The prosecutor trying your father's case needs you on the stand, but you don't have to look at your dad."

"His name is Robert."

Luna nods. "You don't have to look at him at all. You look at the prosecutor, and you can look at me if you get nervous or scared."

"After I testify, then what happens?"

"That's it. You come back here and finish your sentence."

"You know I'll be thirty-four when I get out of here? I'll be an old woman." Janie puts her head in her hands, and Luna laughs.

"I'm thirty-one, Janie."

The girl looks up and smiles. "Sorry."

"Listen, I know fifteen years in here seems like a long time.

It's not short, that's true, but it beats the alternative. Without your testimony, your plea deal is void. If you don't testify against your dad, you're looking at a life sentence. Fifteen years is nothing compared to life."

"Yeah, I get it. I know."

"You were in college before all this happened. There are programs to help you continue with your degree. You can make what you want of these fifteen years, Janie."

Janie's hands shake, the metal cuffs clinking against the table. Her bottom lip trembles, and she cries for the first time in front of Luna. The girl's flat affect is one reason she was relieved Janie took the plea deal. Luna did not know how she would have gotten a group of jurors to have sympathy for her. She reaches across the table for Janie's hands. A correction officer standing near the vending machine raises her eyes. Luna moves her hands to her lap.

"What's wrong, Janie?"

"What if it's not enough?" she whispers, leaning toward Luna. "What if I get on the stand and tell the truth, but no one believes me? What if he gets away with it?"

"That will not happen," Luna says firmly. "The evidence against your dad is strong, and your testimony makes it stronger. There's not a jury in this state that wouldn't find your dad guilty after you get on the stand."

"I feel so stupid. I don't know why I didn't try harder to . . . to stop all this."

Luna thinks about this. Janie, along with her father, were arrested six months ago for the murder of forty-five-year-old Sandy Thompson. The state charged her with first-degree murder and sought a sentence of life in prison. When Luna took the case, Tara insisted it couldn't be possible. Janie was a wonderful girl. A girl who had the usual teenage spats with her mother, but not a murderer. There's no way she would have taken part in such a heinous crime. But Janie confirmed otherwise. After she realized the penalty she faced, she told Luna a chilling story.

A mother never wants to think her child is capable of

violence, especially against her own flesh and blood. Yet Janie admitted that she'd helped her father stage her mother's death as a suicide. When Luna listened to Janie's side of the story, her stomach twisted and her heart ached for this mother. What must she have been thinking in those final moments of her life?

"A child shouldn't be put in the position you were in. A father doesn't do that to his child. You didn't have a choice."

Janie scoffs at the suggestion. "I had a choice."

A week after Luna took Janie's case, she hired a forensic child psychologist. Even though the courts didn't recognize her as a minor, Luna knew the trauma Janie suffered had started as a child. If she wanted to mount a plausible defense for her client, she needed to start at the beginning.

The psychologist, Dr. Laura Webb, listened to Janie's account of what led up to that night and was ready to testify that Janie took part in her mother's murder because of years of emotional stress caused by her father convincing his children that their mother was the source of all their problems. The marriage between Robert and Sandy Thompson broke down when Janie was ten and her sister seven. Since the divorce, Robert Thompson did everything he could to turn his daughters against their mother, persuading them that she was conniving, self-serving, and a person hell-bent on destroying his relationship with his daughters. Young minds are impressionable and susceptible to influence and suggestion, Dr. Webb told Luna. Maybe he didn't clinically brainwash Janie, but the manipulation tactics he used on his daughters over nearly ten years were enough to make the case that Janie felt she had no choice but to help her father.

"Your father gave you an impossible choice to make."

"I chose wrong."

"I have other news to tell you. Tara said your sister wants to see you."

"Amber?"

"What do you think about that?"

Janie looks out the window. "I don't know. Is she going to be in the courtroom tomorrow?"

"Not while you're testifying. She's on the prosecution's witness list and scheduled to give her testimony later in the day. So she can't be in the courtroom during your testimony."

"That's good. How is she doing?"

"Well, she's living with your grandma. She started a new school and is making friends."

Janie nods, and it doesn't get past Luna that she doesn't ask about her grandma. Tara told Luna that Sandy's mom is having a hard time forgiving her eldest grandchild for taking away her only child, but she's willing to try for Amber.

The correction officer standing by the vending machine has moved to the middle of the room and, after clearing her throat, states there's five minutes left. The inmates and their families talk louder and faster, making sure everything gets said before visitation ends.

"I'll think about it. Luna," Janie says, "I don't know how to make this right."

Luna has no idea how she can do that either. "Just do the next right thing. You can't change what happened. You can only change what happens next."

Janie smiles. "That sounds like advice off a refrigerator magnet."

"It's where I get my best stuff."

"Sorry I called you old."

"Not a problem. Try to sleep tonight. I know you have a lot on your mind and sleeping isn't easy, but try. You're doing the right thing for you, for Amber, and even for your mom."

Janie stands up and walks away, shoulders hunched, gazing at her feet. Luna waits for the last person to leave the room and then follows suit. She moves down the hallway, trailing far behind the crowd of people in front of her, and notices how quiet it is. No one talks. Instead they leave silently, the weight of their loved ones' crimes heavy on their backs, wondering how the hell they're supposed to live with the burden of loving someone everyone else hates.

42

Porch lights and cigarettes.

Mark stands on the front porch leaning against the porch column and smokes the cigarette slow, letting the bitter flavor coat his tongue. It's seven o'clock in the evening, and the porch lights turn on and off in sync with his neighbors' habits. Graciela Simpson, a forty-something single mom of twin boys across the street, turned on her porch light five minutes ago, and now the pizza delivery car pulls up to the curb. A lanky teenager unfolds himself from the driver's seat, walks around to the passenger door, and opens it. He pulls the pizza from the front seat, slams the door shut with his foot, and walks up the steps to the house holding the insulated pizza bag in front of his body. At the same time he's ringing Ms. Simpson's doorbell, Mr. Dennisey's light comes on next door. It's time for his nightly walk with Sammy, his five-year-old dachshund, who barks at leaves, squirrels, the wind, and everything else imaginable. That dog has been the source of many sleepless nights for Mark.

In a few minutes, the porch light at the Marcelos, his next-door neighbors on the other side, will turn on and Stan Marcelo will walk out onto his porch with two empty glasses and a tall bottle of this month's whiskey-of-the-month selection. The boxes have been delivered by accident a few times to Mark's house. He's always wondered what the appeal was of getting a new box of whiskey each month, but to each his own. At half past seven, Stan's husband Lewis will pull up, fresh off his Sunday shift at the Ramada, dressed in wrinkled khaki pants and a tie that hangs loosely from his neck. He'll sit on the porch next to Stan and accept the drink, a two-finger drink tonight because it's been one of those days. The two men will drink and whisper to each other, but within the hour, their voices will grow louder and they'll start arguing, the whiskey bottle empty. Mark never knows what they argue about because, by that time, he has had enough of the cigarettes, the porch lights, and his neighbors. He goes inside, brushes his teeth, and takes a shower.

The cigarettes are a habit he picked up in high school when things with his sister Maya started to get really bad. He never really liked smoking. It was just a way to calm his mind and find some peace when everyone in his house was at each other's throats. When he'd wake up and hear his mother sobbing in the bathroom, or the front door slamming and his father's car peeling out of the driveway in the middle of the night to go rescue his sister from another bad situation.

When Mark moved out of his parents' house and into his college dorm, he stopped smoking cold turkey. Being away from home, even if it was only a fifteen-minute car ride away, calmed him enough. It also helped when Luna told him she was tired of kissing an ashtray. He hadn't smoked a cigarette in at least twelve years, but three weeks ago, he found himself standing in line at Walgreens and asking the clerk for a pack of Camels.

Now it's become his Sunday night habit, leaning against the porch column, watching his neighbors, out of sight from everyone, standing in the shadows with only the small glow of the cigarette's tip to give him away.

***

He thinks she doesn't know. Or, maybe, he doesn't care. Luna's not sure what Mark thinks these days. But she knows he's out on the porch smoking his secret cigarettes. When she spotted a couple cigarette butts on the ground beneath the porch two weeks ago, she assumed they were from her mother until she borrowed Mark's truck to go to the store. She hated driving his 2005 Ford Ranger. As far as truck sizes go, it's not a huge truck, but it's still a truck, and Luna feels tiny and out of place behind the wheel. But she drove it anyway because it was blocking her car in the driveway and she wanted to let him sleep. He'd worked late the previous night and didn't come to bed right away when he got home. It was when she was loading the bags of groceries into the truck that she noticed the pack of cigarettes. Camels, the same brand Mark smoked in high school.

She had planned to ask him about the cigarettes, but during the short drive back home, she decided to wait. For weeks she'd noticed small changes in him: the slight weight loss, his withdrawn behavior, and the way he stared out the kitchen window several times throughout the day. She and Mark weren't the type of married couple that had problems. Sure, they had small disagreements, but they were as compatible as apple pie and vanilla ice cream. Even though the cigarettes bothered her, she figured it was something she could let him have. Maybe it would help him get through whatever was bothering him because he wasn't opening up to her.

Now, as she watches him from the upstairs window in their bedroom, she wonders if there's another reason why she hasn't pushed him to talk. Maybe she's scared to ask.

43

Janie sits alone in the back of the prisoner's transport van. Each time it stops at a stop sign, she lurches forward and the chain around her waist digs into her flesh. *Who taught this person how to drive*, she thinks. Her dad had taught her to drive.

Stop it!

She squeezes her eyes tight because she doesn't want to think about the good times.

Why did you do it, Janie? Your own mother? That's the question the detective asked her when she was arrested.

Why did she do it?

During the police interview, she had kept her eyes down and her hands under her thighs. She wanted to explain, but she couldn't because she didn't understand how everything turned so bad so fast. It took her a long time to come to the point of understanding she had now, but reaching this point hasn't made her feel any better.

The van hits a bump.

The last time she felt good was two days before her mom died. She had finished writing a ten-page paper for her statistics class. The second she hit send and the paper was on its way to her professor, she felt lighter and decided to go outside for a run, letting go of the stress and soaking up the sunshine. Running through campus, zigzagging in and out of her fellow students, feeling her ponytail swish-swish-swish against her back, the endorphins sparking through her, it all felt so good. She had felt alive and free. *Is it even possible to feel that way again?*

***

Weekend arrests and Monday morning arraignments mean a chaotic courthouse. A line of people has already formed outside the building when Luna arrives a little before nine. It's your usual mix of lawyers carrying their stainless-steel travel coffee mugs and family members sipping their gas station coffee. Luna gets in line behind a teenager in a red skirt, black silk shirt, and black ballet flats. She's leaning against an older woman with white, shoulder-length hair. The older woman rubs the girl's shoulders vigorously.

"You sure you don't want me to go back to the car to get your jacket?" she asks.

The girl shakes her head. "Don't go anywhere."

"I promise I won't, sweetie."

The woman leans in and kisses the top of the girl's head, looking straight at Luna. At first, she thinks the woman doesn't recognize her, but she figures it out soon enough. They all do. Luna looks down at her shoes and waits for what comes next. She expects Janie's grandmother to say something to her, but instead, she and Amber move away to another line.

The line starts to move, and Luna's phone vibrates in her hand. She smiles at the photo on the screen that Mark sent to her. Ian is dressed in his dog costume with his tongue hanging out of his mouth and his eyes closed. *Someone's ready for trick-or-treating NOW. See you at 6.*

She can't wait.

***

"Will you please state your name for the court?"

She clears her throat. "Janine Thompson."

"Miss Thompson, are you here today under your own free

will and ready to enter your testimony?"

"I am."

Janie reaches for the glass of water in front of her. She takes a sip and waits for the prosecutor to continue. He shuffles his papers on top of the podium, writes something on a piece of paper, and then, finally, approaches the witness stand. He's a small man, balding with thin arms and legs but paunchy in the middle. He wears thick glasses that slide down onto the tip of his nose. When he speaks, he looks over the top of the glasses.

"Miss Thompson, you participated in the murder of your mother. Is that correct?"

Janie nods. She knew the questioning would be blunt, but she hadn't expected it to start off that way. She thought they'd ease into the hard part.

"Miss Thompson, please say yes or no."

"Yes, I did."

"Tell us about that day."

"Um, where do you want me to start?"

"It's always good to start from the beginning, don't you think?"

Janie doesn't like this man. No problem. He clearly doesn't like her either.

"I guess. Well, I got a phone call from my dad early that morning. He asked me to meet him at his house. I told him I had a class that morning, a test I couldn't miss, but he told me it was important." The words stick to her tongue. She takes another sip of water.

"So, you skipped class and went to your dad's house?"

"Yes."

"When you got to his house, where was he?"

If you get scared, look at me, Luna had told her, so she searches the gallery for her. She sees her sitting in the first row right behind the prosecutor's table. When their eyes meet, Luna nods, and Janie takes a deep breath.

"In the kitchen."

"What was he doing?"

"Just sitting at the table."

"Was there anything on the table?"

"A half-empty mug of coffee, two envelopes with my name on one and my sister's on the other one. Also, there was a . . ." She feels everyone's eyes on her, and she begins fidgeting in her seat.

"A what, Janie?"

"A gun," she whispers. Then, louder, she says, "A gun."

The prosecutor turns to the jury and repeats, "A gun. Did he say anything to you?"

"Yes."

"What did he say, Miss Thom—Can I call you Janie?"

"Sure."

"So, Janie, what did he say?" He asks this question like they're friends gossiping over coffee.

"He told me that my mom wanted to ruin him. That the child support she got wasn't enough. She wanted everything—his house, his business, his life savings, everything."

"What did you say?"

"I don't know. I don't think I said anything. What was I supposed to say?"

"That's fine, Janie. What happened next?"

"My dad picked up the gun and turned it over and over in his hand. He was stroking it. I think he cried. It was all very weird."

"What did he do next?"

"He said, 'It's her or me. That's the only way it can be. Her or me, Janie girl.' That's what he'd call me sometimes."

"What did that mean to you when he said that, 'Her or me?'"

"Well, he had the gun in his hands, and I saw those envelopes. Like I said, I think he was crying, and I knew he'd been under stress lately. He'd mentioned in past conversations that he was behind on his house payment because my mom had his wages garnished for child support. So I thought it meant he was going to kill himself. I, like, told him to put the gun down. I don't remember exactly how I said it, but I told him I would talk to Mom. I would get her to back off of him."

"What did he think about that?"

"He said he'd already tried talking and couldn't reason with the . . . with the bitch. He said, 'Why would she ever listen to you? Has she ever listened before? You know how she is. We need to do it my way.'" Janie shifts in her seat.

"His way. What happened after he said it was being done 'his way'?"

"We drove to my mom's house."

"Together?"

"Yes."

"Did you tell him no? That you didn't want to go?"

"I really didn't feel like I had a choice. He was upset, and when he's upset, he's hard to reason with. Plus, he still had that gun."

"Was your mom home when you got to the house?"

"She was in the shower. In the mornings, she usually drove my sister Amber to school and then came back home to get ready for work."

"You used your key to enter the house. Is that correct?"

"Yes."

"Your dad went inside with you?"

"Yes."

"What happened when you went inside?"

"He started to go upstairs, but I grabbed his arm."

Janie looks down at her hands. She'd told variations of this story to the police and the complete truth when she made her statement to Luna when accepting her plea deal, but she's never spoken the words out loud to the public. After today, everyone would know her for the monster she had become that day in her mother's bedroom.

"Janie, are you okay?" the prosecutor asks.

"I'm fine."

She knows she shouldn't do it, but she can't stop herself. She turns her head in her father's direction and looks straight at him. It's been months since she's seen him, and jail has aged him. His pale skin sags around the corners of his mouth, and his dark brown hair has grayed unevenly. The left sideburn is completely gray, but the right one is sprinkled with salt and pepper. He's so thin that Janie thinks he's sick. *Has she done this to him?* He doesn't smile at her. He doesn't even acknowledge her. She was his Janie girl, and now he stares blankly over her head.

She takes a deep breath and says, "I grabbed his arm and told him to stop. That he was too upset right now. That I was scared. I told him we shouldn't be here. After Mom and Dad divorced, she didn't want him in her house. But he didn't listen to me. He just said, 'Have I ever done you wrong, Janie? Everything I've ever done is for you and your sister.'"

When she speaks the words aloud, she hears them differently than she had before. Sure, her dad had let her and Amber stay up hours past their bedtime when they were younger. He had let them eat ice cream for dinner and signed them out of school to go to the movies, warning them not to tell their mother. "She wouldn't understand. She'll get angry and then I'll be in trouble." That's what he said over and over. "Your mother *this*. Your mother *that*. She's the one who's causing this family so much pain and breaking us apart." He'd turned them slowly against her, telling them that she didn't care about them and that she only wanted his money and her revenge on him. He widened the usual rift that forms between teenage daughters and their mothers into a canyon with no bridge for crossing or meeting in the middle. *Why hadn't she realized what he was doing to them?*

"Janie?" The prosecutor cocks his head to one side and scratches at a mole on his cheek. "Do you need a break?"

God no, she thinks. *I need to get these words out and finish this day. I need to be done with all of this.*

"No, let's keep going."

"Okay, so you and your father go upstairs?"

"Yes."

"What happens next?"

"We hear my mom humming to herself. She liked to hum show tunes when she was getting ready for work. I think she was singing a song from *Mama Mia* that morning." Why did she say that? Why did that even matter? "She had on this old, ratty terrycloth robe. It used to be a bright lavender color, but it had faded. She wore a bath towel on her head like a turban to dry her hair."

The prosecutor walks back to his table and picks up a plastic bag. Janie hadn't noticed it before, but she already knows what is in it before he brings it to her.

"Is this the robe your mother was wearing?"

"Yes, it is."

"Let the record state that the witness has identified the robe in Exhibit C as that of Mrs. Sandy Thompson. Okay, so she's wearing this robe and singing a song from *Mama Mia*. Tell us what happened next."

"She took off her robe." Janie turns red remembering her mother standing in the room, naked and vulnerable. "Then she turned around to walk to her closet, and that's when she saw us standing in the doorway of her bedroom. She screamed and grabbed the towel off her head and wrapped it around her body. She said something like, 'What are you doing here?' I don't remember exactly."

"Did she ask you to leave?"

"She told my dad to leave or she would call the police. Then she asked me why I had brought him to the house. I tried to explain that he wanted to talk to her. She told me to stop taking his side. She was tired of all his bullshit. After she said that, he went for her."

"What do you mean, 'he went for her'?"

"He ran toward her and picked up the robe off the floor. He pulled the tie or the sash—you know, the thing that ties the robe across your body—he pulled that loose from the robe."

She's talking fast and feels her heart pounding. What happened next in that room happened in less than five minutes, but it felt like five years. Time slowed, and it felt like they were moving through molasses.

"It happened so quick. He grabbed her wrist and pulled her toward him. Somehow, he got behind her and wrapped the robe's sash around her neck. He held her close to him, pulling hard on the sash, until . . . she had her arms out like she was reaching for me and then they went limp. She didn't move again."

Janie stops, shuts her eyes, and takes short, sharp breaths. Her chest feels hollow like all the air is being vacuumed from her lungs. She begins to sob, any future words suffocated by her ugly crying. No one says anything. They wait. Everyone waits for Janie to pull it together and finish her testimony. Her tears and her guilt are too little, too late. No one has time for that now.

"I'm sorry," she says. She wipes her nose with the back of her hand. No one offers a tissue. The prosecutor keeps his distance. The judge looks down at his hands. Her dad whispers something to his attorney.

"Are you ready to continue?" the prosecutor asks.

Janie nods.

"After your dad strangled your mom, what happened next?"

"He said we had to make it look like an accident."

"And how did you do that?"

"We dragged her body to the landing. Dad tied the one end of the sash around her neck and the other end around the rail on the banister."

"What happened next?"

Again, she closes her eyes. You might think that murder is murder and all parts of the killing carry the same gruesome weight. Well, Janie thinks, you'd be wrong because what came next was the worst part of that day. It's something that she'll never forget even if she somehow finds a way to live with what she's done.

"The two of us held up her body and we—" Her throat constricts, and the words get stuck. She feels like she might be sick. "We tossed her over the railing."

Someone gasps in the crowd. There are a few quiet sobs. Janie keeps her head down. She doesn't dare look at her dad.

"Tell us what happened next, Janie."

She wipes her runny nose with the back of her hand. "He told me to drive him home and go back to class and then pick Amber up from school. He didn't want her to walk home and find our mom."

"What did your dad say to do if the police wanted to question you?"

"He told me to cry. To tell them I was too upset. That everything would be okay. It wasn't."

The prosecutor walks in front of the witness stand. He stares at Janie, and she wonders what he sees. Does he see a young woman who was played by her father or a diabolical young woman who didn't do enough to stop her dad from killing her mom? She's pretty sure she knows the answer. After all, it's his job to lock away the diabolical.

"Thank you, Janie. No further questions."

He walks back to the prosecutor's table, and the judge addresses her dad's attorney. "Does the defense want to question this witness?"

The lawyer stands up and buttons the top button of his suit jacket. "Yes, Your Honor, we certainly have some questions for this witness."

Witness. He grimaces when he says this like he's gotten a gnat caught between his teeth that he can't spit out.

"Miss Thompson, why are you here today?"

Janie frowns. "Um, to tell the jury what happened the night my mom died."

"Right, that's true. But let's tell the jury why you're *really* here. You took a deal. Is this true?"

She swallows hard and glances at Luna, who, once again, nods. "Yes. I did."

"So, you were originally charged with first-degree murder. Is this correct?"

"I believe so." She looks at Luna again. "My lawyer could tell you more."

The defense attorney waves his hand and dismisses the suggestion. "That's not necessary. Just so we're all clear, you were facing a first-degree murder trial that would carry a maximum sentence of life in prison or the death penalty. Is that correct?"

"Yes."

"The prosecutor trying your case had enough evidence to support that you knew what your dad had planned before going to your mother's and you were a willing participant. You could have stopped it, but you didn't. You weren't under duress. You didn't have that supposed gun pointed at your head. You always had the choice to say no. Is that correct?"

"I guess. I don't know."

"It doesn't matter, really. What matters to the court today is hearing that you took a deal. Is that correct?"

"I accepted a plea agreement."

"Tell the court today what that deal was."

"I agreed to testify against my dad for a reduced sentence."

The defense attorney raises his eyebrows and looks at the jury. "A reduced sentence indeed! Miss Thompson, is it true that you accepted the deal and pled guilty to one count of second-degree murder?"

"It is."

"And your sentence is what?"

"Fifteen years."

"Say that again, please, so we're one hundred percent clear."

"Fifteen years."

The attorney shakes his head. "Unbelievable. That's some great work by your attorney. Is she here?" He turns around and faces the crowd. "I'd like to applaud her accomplishments."

"Your Honor is this grandstanding necessary?" the prosecutor asks from his seat.

"Counselor, let's get on with your line of questioning. This doesn't have to take all day."

"My apologies. I'll move on to my next question." He pauses for effect before asking, "Miss Thompson, are you a liar?"

"No."

"You're not?"

"I said no." Janie shifts in her seat. Her cuffs are tight on her wrists.

"But you lied to the police, didn't you? When they asked you if you knew why your mother would want to kill herself?"

"That's different."

"Different because you didn't want to get caught? It's okay. You don't have to answer that. But you did lie to the police, right?"

"I guess."

"You guess?"

"Yes, I wasn't honest."

"You lied to your grandmother too, right? She was the one who found her, right?"

"Yes," Janie whispers.

"So to recap, you *lied* to the police. You *lied* about where you were that day. You *lied* to your sister about what had happened to your mother. You lied to your grandmother. You lied so many times. Why should we believe you now?"

"Because I'm telling the truth."

"The truth is that you killed your mother and your dad helped you cover up the crime. Isn't that right?"

"No, that's not what happened."

"Janie, did you love your mother?"

"Objection!" The prosecutor stands. "The witness is not on trial."

"That's true. In fact, this witness never stood trial because she took a plea bargain, and now, here we are. Here we are listening to a murderer tell more lies."

"That's enough, Counselor." The judge points his finger at the attorney. "I don't like theatrics. If I did, I'd go see a Broadway show. The objection is sustained and, Counselor, let's move the questions along."

"Miss Thompson, had you ever said you wanted your mother dead?"

"I don't think so." Janie thinks about all the fights she had with her mom. The last few years, many of the arguments got loud and heated. She said a lot of mean things to her mom during those fights, but had she ever said she wanted to kill her?

Her father's attorney walks over to a table near the court stenographer. He opens the laptop, taps a few keys, and the projector screen lights up. On the screen is a conversation, one Janie had forgotten about but remembers now as the enlarged text is displayed for everyone to read.

"Do you recognize these texts?"

"Yes," she says.

"Can you read me what's inside the second blue bubble from the top?"

"Um, okay, it says, 'I hate her so much. I'm so tired of Mom telling me what to do. I just wish she'd leave us alone. Why can't she be understanding like you? I wish she were dead. It would make everything easier.'"

"Janie, who were you texting?"

"My dad."

"You were texting your dad. Do you mind reading the gray bubble? The one right below your text."

"It says, 'Don't say such awful things. Your mom loves you. She's just trying to get back at me. You'd miss her if she were gone.'"

"That text was sent a week before you claim your dad murdered your mom and forced you to help make it look like an accident. You know what I think, Miss Thompson? I think you'd had enough and went to your mom's house knowing she'd be there alone. I think you two had an argument that got out of hand. You killed your mother and panicked. You asked your dad to come to the house to help you cover up the crime. It was you, not your dad, who was responsible for your mom's murder."

"That's not true. That is not how it happened at all. I told you what happened." Janie looks out at the crowd. She catches Tara's eyes, and the woman looks away quickly. Anger swells up like a fireball in her chest. She looks at her dad. He sits at the table in his suit and tie while she's on the stand in prison orange. "Why are you doing this? Why aren't you helping me? You know what happened. Just tell them," she yells.

The judge raps his gavel three times on the bench. "That's enough, Miss Thompson."

Her dad's attorney approaches the witness stand. Janie looks at him and shakes her head. "That's not what happened."

"Only three people know what happened, and one of them is dead. So, I guess it's just the word of a liar who wished her mom was dead and a father who told her not to wish such awful things. Who should we believe, Miss Thompson?"

44

It's late afternoon by the time Luna leaves the courthouse. She wanted to talk to Janie before she is transported back to the prison, but she gets sidetracked by a phone call from Doris. The neighbors in the apartment next door to the co-op space she's renting have started to complain. They're not sure they like the type of people the *Murder Lawyer* is bringing to the neighborhood. She hates that stupid name, but it sounds good on television, and newspeople quickly grasp on to a catchy name.

"One of the women stopped me when I left for lunch and told me she's not comfortable with all the unsavory people coming and going in the neighborhood. Like our clients and their families are spoiled food," Doris says. Luna imagines Doris's face puckered like she ate a lemon.

"Maybe we should look for another space?" Luna suggests.

"And let them win?"

"Doris, we have so much to do. The Williams case is getting ready to go to trial, and I don't have time to deal with a bunch of angry neighbors. I'm just too tired."

"Ms. Goldwyn!" a man's voice calls out to her. She turns around. The prosecutor handling Robert Thompson's case is speed walking toward her.

"We'll talk about this later, okay? I have to go." She hangs up and waits for the prosecutor to catch up to her.

"I thought you'd like to know that Robert Thompson is going to deal."

"Really?"

"Yep, seems that your client's testimony scared him or at least got him thinking straight. Of course, he wants the same deal as his kid—fifteen years and he'll plead to second-degree murder. Told that bastard and his attorney they're crazy. Can you imagine a father doing that to his child, taking away her mother and in that way? No way is he going to have a chance to ruin those kids' lives again. I told him life in prison or no deal."

"And he took it?"

"I expect to have the deal signed and delivered by the end of the day."

Luna is happy to hear that news. It makes her feel good knowing that perhaps now, Janie could begin to heal and find some way to reshape her life. Of course, she also knows that fifteen years in prison changes people, especially someone so young and impressionable. She hopes that Janie will continue to allow Tara to visit. Maybe even try to repair the relationship with her sister and grandmother because Luna knows if Janie is released without anyone waiting for her to help her reenter life, she won't have much of a chance. That's just how these things went. Comeback stories in the criminal justice system are rare. Maybe Janie will prove her wrong. She hopes so.

45

The temperature dropped fast as gusty northwest winds developed in the early afternoon. What started out as a crisp autumn day turned into a downright chilly evening. The wind picks up the fallen leaves on the sidewalks, and they move in a circular motion, floating up in a tiny leaf tornado. Ian, riding in a vintage, red Radio Flyer wagon, another flea market gift from her dad, reaches out his little hands to catch the leaves as they rise. Last year, they dressed Ian up for Halloween as a pumpkin and stayed home passing out candy. This is the first year they've joined in on the craziness of neighborhood trick-or-treating. Luna had been looking forward to the evening, but after a long day in court listening to Janie's testimony, she realizes she's simply going through the motions.

"Here. It will warm you up," Mark says, handing her a plastic tumbler.

She takes it from him, sips the hot liquid, and smiles. "What's in here?"

"That's called an adult hot chocolate."

"Brandy?"

"You know it. Your mom made it."

Mark pulls the wagon, navigating around the mobs of people standing around talking and watching their children run up and down the street collecting candy from the houses. Luna wonders how many years they get to do this with Ian before he doesn't want them holding his hand and walking him to the doors. She knows he's only two and that time is way off in the future, but she also knows that time moves fast, and kids grow up way too soon.

"You ready, buddy?" Mark asks as he stops the wagon.

Ian grins at him and untangles himself from the blankets on his lap. Luna didn't want him to get cold, but as she watches him try to free himself from the four fleece blankets she piled on him, she realizes maybe she went a tad overboard.

"Here, sweetie, let me help," she says.

Ian puts up his hands and pushes her away. "Me do, Mommy."

She steps back and lets her son extricate himself from the blankets. Once he's free, he scrambles over the side of the wagon and gets down on all fours, crawling across the sidewalk.

Mark laughs. "Let's stand, buddy. This puppy uses two legs, not four."

"Wait!" Luna says. "I need a picture."

Mark turns Ian around, whispers in his ear, and then they both deliver big, toothy smiles for the camera. Luna smiles too and watches them walk up the steps to the house.

"Cute kid," says a woman's voice behind her. Luna turns around. A woman wearing a Mardi Gras mask and a black bodysuit is also watching Ian and Mark walk up the stairs.

"Thanks. Nice costume," Luna says. She's noticed a few of the other parents dressed up and wonders if that is the thing now, dressing up with your kid. God, she hopes not. Does she really want to start that tradition? It's hard enough finding a costume for Ian. She can't imagine trying to come up with clever family costumes each year.

"Which one's your child?" Luna asks.

The woman waves her off. "Oh, I don't have kids."

Luna frowns. The woman smiles, but the mask makes the gesture look sinister rather than inviting.

"Mommy! Looky what I got!" Ian's tugging on her jeans.

He's clutching a fruit roll-up in his tiny fist.

"Sorry to bother you," the masked woman says as she slips away.

"We'll try for something better like a full-size Hershey bar at the next house," Mark tells Luna. He winks at her and helps Ian back in the wagon. "Who was that?"

"I have no idea. Just some random woman with no kids dressed up for Halloween."

"Huh," Mark says. "That's weird. She didn't tell you her name?"

"Nope." Luna puts her phone in her pocket. "I know what you're thinking."

"You do, huh?" Mark raises an eyebrow.

"You're thinking that you'd like for me to pull this wagon for a while." Luna smiles, takes the wagon's handle from him, stands on her tiptoes, and kisses his chin. He gives her a half-smile.

"Hey, what's wrong?" she asks.

"It's strange, isn't it?"

"What? That woman? I don't know. Maybe, but it is Halloween. Lots of strange on this day. On the way to court this morning, I saw two clowns and a Care Bear squeezed into one of those tiny microcars. I wouldn't worry about that woman."

"Luna—" Mark walks toward her with an unfamiliar look on his face that makes Luna's stomach lurch.

"Mark," she says firmly, "nothing is wrong. You're being paranoid. Let's just have fun trick-or-treating with our son."

She moves ahead of him, pulling the wagon behind her, and lets the crowd of people swallow them. She's not going to let some strange woman ruin her night, but when she looks back and sees Mark standing among the crowd straining his neck to find the woman, she wonders if maybe she should be more concerned.

PART FIVE

THE HIDDEN THREAT

46

These are the dark days when the fog lifts and she feels her body crack and something foreign move into her, salty and hostile, firing through her veins and racing through her heart. The days they warned her about—the doctors who prescribe her medication, who talk to her in careful voices. Who probably feel like failures because all these years they were trying to save a misguided woman, but they looked the other way and lost a little boy.

The ache in her body, it's her own fault. She made the mistake of walking through the gardens after breakfast. The hosta plants and coralbells have started to shrink in on themselves, preparing for the coming cold. The potted ornamentals have been brought in to the solarium. Too delicate for the frost. Much like herself. She's not a sturdy perennial. Her soul needs a gentle touch because, like those beautiful, fragile plants, she wasn't created to survive harsh seasons. That's how she knows she won't survive prison. Prison is for the hardy and the resilient, not the tender souls that need the right amount of nurturing to thrive.

It was in the middle of the courtyard behind a row of hostas and hydrangeas that she found him curled in a fetal position. His little body cool to the touch, his breathing too shallow. Mud caked his tiny cherub lips like brown lipstick; specks of dirt lingered on his tongue. She had picked him up, felt his body go slack in her arms. He didn't wrap his arms around her neck like he did when he fell asleep on the couch and she'd take him to his room. He didn't say "Mommy."

He didn't say anything ever again.

These are indeed the dark days when the veil is lifted, and Ruby sees so very clearly what she's done.

47

The living room is trashed, a chaotic mess of photo boxes, scrapbooks, colorful wooden cube blocks, and no fewer than ten dinosaur-themed touch-and-feel books. Ian's crouched over a chunky, orange book, running his palm over a bumpy dinosaur and humming a tune only he knows. On the coffee table, lying flat, is a neon green trifold project display board. In the middle of the board are colorful bubble letters that read "Star of the Month" and a large photo of Ian, presumably taken at school, affixed slightly off-center under the words.

"What's all of this fun and clutter?" Luna asks, putting her briefcase on the couch.

"Oh, this? This is very exciting stuff," Mark says with mock enthusiasm. "This is a school project that's all about Ian. Right, buddy?"

Ian ignores them and starts stacking his blocks on top of the book.

"I thought these kinds of projects weren't supposed to start until second grade at least?" he asks, swiping a stack of photos off the couch to make room for Luna to sit.

"I guess they like to prepare parents early to start doing their children's projects."

She sits beside Mark on the couch and reaches for a

scrapbook labeled "Baby's First Year." The first page contains the fake birth certificate the hospital gave them stamped with Ian's footprint. His tiny baby bracelet is flattened perfectly on the page next to it. Luna runs her finger over the bracelet, caressing it with the gentleness of a mother's memory.

"Can you believe how fast time has flown by?" she asks, raising her eyes and letting them land on her toddler, no longer a tiny, fragile, and wrinkly creature but this little human who is growing more and more apart from her each day than a part of her.

"Remember this day?" Mark points to a photo of the three of them sitting on a bench outside an ice cream shop. Luna's balancing Ian on her knee and trying to hold a double-scoop ice cream cone in her other hand while Mark attempts to take a selfie. Only half of Mark's face shows up in the shot, and Luna's grinning, completely unaware that the chocolate ice cream is dripping on her poor son's head. The caption next to the photo reads "Ian's First Ice Cream Cone."

"He was always such a happy baby," she replies.

Mark gives her a look.

"What?" she asks.

"You forget?"

"Forget what?"

"The colic—weeks of colic. The police pulled me over at one o'clock in the morning because one of our nosy neighbors called the cops thinking someone was canvasing the neighborhood because I was circling the block for over an hour."

"Well, no parents have a perfect baby, right? But we got pretty lucky."

"No arguments there." Mark pulls her close and kisses her on the forehead.

"Do we have to fill the entire board?"

Luna's stomach rumbles. It's been another one of those days when the last thing she ate was a banana at ten o'clock that morning.

"We could be rebels and not," Mark suggests.

"You think? I mean, if we don't fill it, leaving no gaps, how will he ever get into Princeton?"

Mark rises from the couch, stretches his arms over his head, and sighs when his shoulders pop. "How about I grab the bag of leftover Halloween candy, and we'll snack while we wait for Chinese food to arrive?"

Luna glances at her briefcase. There's at the very minimum three hours of work tucked inside. If she waits for dinner to be delivered and helps Mark put this project together, she won't feel the soft, crisp pillowcase against her head until midnight, if she's lucky. You expect all-nighters in law school, but who knew they'd continue indefinitely?

"That sounds fantastic," she agrees.

Mark slides his phone out of his back pocket. "Crab rangoon and egg rolls, too?"

"Yes, please."

Mark leaves the room to call in the order, and Luna removes her heels, rubbing her swollen feet. She pages through the scrapbook to the end, grateful for Facebook and her mom. Every photo in Ian's first-year scrapbook was the direct result of her mother downloading photos Luna posted to Facebook or that she texted to her mom. Never in this lifetime would Luna have had the time, the energy, or—if she's being honest—the motivation to put all these memories together into a scrapbook. They'd stay on social media or her phone's memory forever. She makes a mental note to thank her mom the next time they talk.

When she finishes thumbing through the scrapbook, she picks up the photo box filled with old photos from Mark's childhood. It surprises her that he took it down from their closet shelf. Luna enjoys looking through old family photos, but it's easier for her. Mark's family story is different than hers, a story he likes to keep the book closed on as much as possible.

"Order is placed, and in twenty minutes, we will fill our stomach with three cartons of chicken fried rice, five each of crab rangoon and egg rolls, and some kung pao chicken for yours truly. We'll have leftovers for the rest of the week and heartburn," Mark yells from the kitchen. "Hey, did you take that ten with you this morning that was sitting on the table? I want to give Tony a little extra because he told me he's saving up for his mom to visit from Dayton. She hasn't seen her grandson yet because the train fare is too much. Never mind," he says before Luna answers. "Found it!"

Mark walks back into the living room carrying two wine glasses and a bottle of Dr. Pepper. "Pre-dinner drinks?"

"Why not? That's the good bottle, right?"

"Doesn't expire until next year, so we're good."

Luna giggles like she's tipsy and sits cross-legged on the couch, placing the box of old photos in her lap. "So, are we doing pictures of all of us or just Ian?"

"I say we sprinkle in some photos of us and your parents. Don't want to let too much fame get to the little man. We need to share the spotlight. Right, Ian?"

Ian looks up from his toys, grinning and chewing his fingers. He shoots his legs out in front of him, sending the mound of blocks and books he's collected scattering in different directions. He squeals and jumps up, running around in circles.

"Too late for that," Luna observes. She reaches into the photo box and pulls out a photo of Mark standing next to a fallen tree and holding a make-shift flag constructed from a long stick and a white T-shirt. He looks about five or six in the photo. Standing next to him is Maya, smiling a jagged smile, the kind you get when you've lost a few baby teeth and your adult teeth are still too big for your mouth. She has a similar flag in her hand, but hers is made from a red T-shirt.

"Do you miss her?" Luna asks.

"Miss who?" Mark is helping Ian collect his blocks to rebuild the tower.

"Maya."

He looks up, his eyes drawn to the photo she's holding. "It's been a long time."

"I know, but I just wonder—"

"What?"

"You don't talk about her."

Mark sighs. "There's nothing to talk about Luna. Put the box away, please."

"You don't want any of your family photos on the board?"

"They never met Ian, and he doesn't have a clue who they are. I must have grabbed that box by mistake."

"Mark," Luna coaxes.

"Luna, don't make this a big deal."

"Babe, you know I can help you find her."

"Not necessary, Luna."

"I know, but so much time has passed. Maybe—"

"Maybe what?" Mark sits back on his heels, challenging her.

Maya is a tricky subject. Rarely does her name come up. Luna knows better than to mention her. It's too painful for Mark. "Look, I'm sorry. I didn't mean to upset you. You're right."

Mark runs his hand through his hair and shakes his head. "I know you mean well, hon, but it's complicated. You know this. And you're right. A lot of time has passed. So much time that she's a stranger to me. Hell, who's to say I'd even recognize her if I passed her on the street? It's better this way."

She looks back at the photo of the two smiling siblings, caught on camera enjoying a moment of play. While she'll never tell Mark this, sometimes it makes her angry that he's so casual about his and Maya's relationship—or lack of one. She never had a sibling, someone to fight with, laugh with, or share a mutual parental embarrassment. But she knows that jealousy is stupid. She also knows why Mark hasn't tried to find Maya since the accident. It's too painful, and she's afraid it might break him if he does.

"Luna, you and Ian are all I need. You're my family and that makes me happy. Maya, in our life, would not be good. You know this, right?"

"Of course I do. Just chalk it up to momentary nostalgia and Dr. Pepper inebriation." She smiles and winks at him. "I didn't mean to upset you."

"Don't worry about it," he says. He gets up, sits beside her on the couch, and takes the photo from her hand. "I do remember this day. It was a good day. That tree fell down in a storm the night before. Dad wanted to get it cut up and hauled away right away so it wouldn't kill the grass, but we begged him to let us make a fort. We claimed our own territories and named them Markland and Mayaland. Very original, I must say. We raided the linen closet and then stripped our beds and put every sheet we could find up on that tree and stayed under that tree all night. It's a good memory."

Luna wraps her arms around Mark and kisses away the tear that slides down his cheek. "Sounds magical."

"Yep, it was, but magic isn't real." Mark puts the photo back in the box, places the lid on top, and stands up, untangling himself from Luna's arms. "I'm going to put this away. Can you get the door if Tony rings before I come back down?"

"Sure," she says. "Don't be long, okay? Your fancy drink will go flat."

Mark doesn't laugh. He walks silently out of the room and upstairs. Luna leans back against the couch cushions. There's not much that rattles her calm husband, but when it comes to Maya, all bets are off. She wishes she'd never said anything.

***

He stands in the center of the closet holding the photo between his fingers. Sadness settles between his shoulder blades. Does he miss her? Of course he misses her. Every single day. Every day he misses what's gone and lost, but what good does it do to dwell on the past? Onward and forward, that's his motto. Looking back is only good for historians. He's a man whose one job is to keep the family under this roof safe and loved. There's no room for anything else.

He folds the photo in half and walks over to the dresser. Like he does at least twice a day, he slides his fingers under his T-shirts until they touch the gun. He places the photo under the weapon, and he realizes he's crying again. Dammit! He wipes away the tears with the back of his hand, shuts the drawer, and takes a deep breath. As he moves away from the dresser, he hears the ringing, and it stops him dead in his tracks. He opens the drawer fast, slides his hand to the back of the drawer once again and, this time, finds the phone—a cheap, throw-away phone he bought at Walmart. The kind of phones that drug dealers and cheating husbands use. He answers on the third ring.

"What are you doing calling?" he asks. His heart is racing, and he looks behind him to make sure Luna's still downstairs.

He listens to the caller, runs his hands through his hair, and shakes his head. "I can't. Not tonight." Mark pauses, listening. "Because I'm spending it with my family."

He hears the doorbell ring. Quietly, he tiptoes to the window and looks out at the street. Tony's beat-up, gray-and-silver two-toned car with the Green China topper is parked at the curb. He looks beyond Tony's car, scanning up and down the street, feeling calmer when he doesn't spot anything unusual.

"What?" he whispers into the phone. "Yes, I heard you. Tomorrow is fine. Yes, I know the place. I have to go."

He hangs up and double-checks that he turned the ringer off this time. How could he have been so stupid? That's his first mistake, and he won't make it again.

"Mark," Luna yells up from the stairs, "dinner's here. You okay?"

He quickly puts the phone back in the drawer. "Yup, everything's peachy!"

Where the hell did that word come from? Peachy. Who says that? Not him. Not ever. If it's weird, Luna doesn't seem to notice or give it much thought.

"Okay, but hurry up," she says.

Mark sits on the edge of the bed, puts his elbows on his knees, and clasps his hands on the back of his head. *Ten, nine, eight*... He counts backwards to slow his breathing. There are some things Mark is really good at, but lying to his wife is not one of them.

48

Morning drop-off at Little Lamb takes ten extra minutes that Luna really doesn't have to spare. Ian's Star of the Week collage gets stuck as she maneuvers the second set of doors that close too quickly behind her. Thankfully, one of the front staff workers is right there to help her pull it from the door without damaging it too much.

"Luna!" Belinda's voice makes her jump, and she drops the collage again. "How have you been? Where's Mark this morning?"

"Apparently he's jogging?" Luna said, making a face as she collects the couple of photos that fell off the board.

"For fun? Who does that?"

"Not me, ever. But I guess everyone has their own amount of crazy in them."

"Mine is hot yoga."

"You win," Luna concedes. She hands Belinda the display board. "Our homework."

The woman crouches down, eye level with Ian, and asks, "Is this your family?"

Ian giggles, wraps his little arms around Luna's legs, and cries out, "Mommy!"

Loud unrestrained laughter escapes from Belinda's mouth.

"Will you be joining us on Friday for story hour? I know Friday's not Ian's regular day, but he's welcome to come. We have a special guest who's going to read a book about fire trucks. Really, it's just Rose Marie's husband; he was promoted to fire chief last month," Belinda admits.

"I'll check with Mark. I have a sentencing hearing on Friday."

"Yes, find out if Mark can come." The woman turns her attention to Ian again. "Everyone loves your daddy Ian. He's a funny guy, and he brings Twizzlers sometimes too."

That is news to Luna. What isn't news to her is how much everyone loves her husband. He's a naturally charming guy with a smile that instantly puts you at ease. Apparently, he's the life of the party at Little Lamb. For a brief moment, Luna feels jealous. The times that she's brought Ian to school, everyone has been polite and accommodating, but she gets the sense that she makes people nervous. Not Belinda. She doesn't think anything short of a gang of wild boars breaking down the doors could make her nervous. It's the rest of the staff. The first time they toured the center, the staff treated her like a celebrity. Giggling and whispering behind their hands, ogling her. It's different now. People have come to terms with the company she keeps.

Luna picks up Ian, gives him a kiss above his eyebrow, and tells him to have a good day. Belinda wishes her a good day as well and takes Ian's hand. With her hand on the door, Luna watches her son walk hand in hand with Belinda down the hallway until he disappears into his classroom.

***

She rushes into the office, undercaffeinated and behind schedule, and finds Doris squinting at Luna's notes, scrawled like hieroglyphics across the page, trying to translate the words into a readable document she's typing into the computer. The huge noise-canceling headphones she wears reminds Luna of a helicopter pilot. Luna taps her on the shoulder.

"Good morning, sunshine!" Doris shouts.

"You're going to go deaf," Luna advises.

"What?"

Doris winks at her, sliding the headphones off her ears and placing them on the table in front of her. "Busy morning?"

On the table is a tray with two coffee mugs, a carafe of coffee, and an assortment of croissants, muffins, and a bunch of bananas. Luna tosses her briefcase on a chair in the corner and plucks a banana from the bunch. It's the perfect ripeness, slightly soft but without any mushiness.

"Something like that. Did you know Mark brings Twizzlers to Ian's child center?"

"Candy is always appreciated," Doris notes.

"He's like Mr. Popularity at the center."

Doris laughs, her soft belly moving up and down. "Have you looked at your husband lately? He's not exactly an eyesore."

"Stop it." Luna blushes.

As a teenager, Mark was tall and lanky, with a body type that looked like the wind could knock him over without any trouble at all. His hair fell across his forehead, covering a smattering of pimples. Luna still sees him as the teenage boy she fell in love with in the school cafeteria over French fries and chocolate milk. When other women smile at him while they're out together or when Doris makes comments like that, she sees her husband for who he is today: a naturally slim man with chiseled muscles from his work at the recycling center, an infectious smile, and a deep kindness that draws everyone to him.

"Romero will be here in ten," Luna announces, glancing up at the clock over the front door. "What do you think about her?"

Doris shrugs. "I've heard good things about her. Mikey loved her."

The parents of her client Ruby Williams hired Alyssa Romero, a former probation officer turned private investigator, to create a private presentence report after the court-appointed probation officer recommended a sentence of ten years, the maximum for involuntary manslaughter in Missouri.

"The judges regard her recommendations as fair, legally sound too."

"Of course they're legally sound," a woman's voice

announces. "I didn't spend twenty years as a probation officer only to retire and start littering the streets with filth."

Alyssa Romero stands in the doorway, early to the meeting and grinning from ear to ear. She's not at all what Luna imagined from their few conversations over the phone. She had pictured a woman in her fifties with a no-nonsense haircut and cigarette smoke following her around like a skunk's odor. Instead, when Romero walks toward Luna, hand extended, she smells like jasmine and vanilla. She's older than Luna, but no older than early forties, and her hair is long and wavy, light brown with cherry and chocolate highlights. She has a tiny nose stud in her left nostril.

Luna jumps up from her chair and takes the woman's hand.

"Ms. Romero, thank you for meeting with us this morning. Mikey spoke highly of you, and I'm glad our paths finally crossed." Luna's voice sounds unnatural, flavored with formalness.

"Call me Alyssa." She places her tan leather satchel on the conference table. "Shame about Mikey. That son of a bitch was a hoot. The last time I saw him, we shared a bottle of 10 Year Kentucky Straight Bourbon. The community lost a good one."

Luna has no clue about bourbon, but knowing how much Mikey liked to impress people and knowing that Romero charges four figures an hour for her services, she assumes it's an expensive bottle of bourbon.

"Well, we don't have any bourbon, but please help yourself to some coffee and pastries," Luna says.

Alyssa plops down in a chair, takes a croissant from the tray, and peels off a flaky layer of goodness. Then she pulls right into the fast lane, reaching into her satchel and pulling out a professionally bound report. "I have to be honest. This was a hard one, and I don't have kids. I mean, I feel for this woman, but her negligence is culpable. You can't possibly believe otherwise?"

"As Ms. Williams's attorney, my job, as you know, isn't to assign guilt or innocence. It's to make sure the system treats her fairly within the scope of the law."

The woman smirks and pushes the report across the table to Luna, saying, "Come on, let's be human with each other. Leave that bullshit 'lawyer speak' for the courtroom."

Luna stares down at the thick report. She doesn't have to look inside to know that the words describe her client in short sentences, an abbreviated history that doesn't tell the whole story. Because Ruby pleaded guilty, against Luna's advice and the wishes of her parents, her full story may never be heard. Then again, Ruby's neglect, no matter the medical reasons for it, won't bring her son back into her arms. Ruby knows this, and while ten years in a medium-security prison might seem like too much time or not enough, her client will live, weighed down by the heaviness of her mistakes for the rest of her life.

"It's a big mess," Luna admits.

"Isn't that always the way it is? People make messes and we're expected to clean them up?" Alyssa continues peeling the croissant apart, layer by layer, taking small bites.

"Something like that."

Luna opens the report and skims it.

Ruby Williams, Presentence Summary Report
Prepared by Licensed Investigator Alyssa Romero

Summary of charges: Conviction of involuntary manslaughter, MO Rev Stat § 565.024 (2013)

Version of the criminal act giving rise to the conviction: Ruby Williams caused the unintentional death of her five-year-old son by depriving him of vital nutrients and limiting his caloric intake to unhealthy levels.

Reason for committing the crime: Ms. Williams's strict orthorexia beliefs resulted in the death of her son by proxy.

Prior criminal record, including juvenile record: No known criminal records.

Personal and family history: Ms. Williams resides with her parents at their Huntleigh residence in St. Louis County. Aside from her parents, the defendant reports that she doesn't have any social relationships outside of her family. The child's father is unknown. Ms. Williams has refused to disclose this information, if she has knowledge of paternity.

Education: Ms. Williams holds a high school diploma from a college preparatory school. She attended Washington University in St. Louis for three years as an art major. Mental health issues led her to withdraw from the university before degree completion.

Employment history: No known employment history. Ms. Williams reports that her parents provide her support.

Health: Ms. Williams has been diagnosed with orthorexia, a condition defined by a person's compulsive behavior and rigid ideas about ideal eating. This diagnosis was made following the death of her son Oliver Williams. However, Ms. Williams has been in and out of mental health institutions since her late teens for compulsive behaviors, depression, and anxiety. Her last institutional stay was in January 2010, shortly after discovering she was pregnant.

Alcohol and drug use: No evidence of usage.

Financial status: Ms. Williams is supported by her parents and has access to a $3 million trust.

Military record: None

Likelihood of repeating the crime: High risk without proper mental health treatment.

Sentencing recommendation: After conducting interviews with Ms. Williams, her family, her psychologist, and other involved parties, it is in the professional opinion of this investigator that the minimum sentence of 3 years be served with the requirement that the defendant receive intensive mental health treatment during the term of imprisonment.

***

Luna looks up from the report, surprised. "Not probation? You know the Williamses were expecting a recommendation of supervised probation?"

"As well as you, I suspect, given your reaction. My recommendation is still better than what the court's presentence investigation report recommends."

Luna stands up, walks to the window, and looks out at the people drifting along the street below, going about their day not realizing that they walk among misdirected people, ill people, bad people, and the worst of the bad, murderers.

"Look, when I agree to a private presentence report, I never make promises. I only guarantee that I'll be fair, truthful. With Ruby Williams's case, I have serious concerns, especially after speaking with her parents."

This doesn't surprise Luna. The Williams case *is* concerning. What happened to Oliver Williams is unimaginable, and to think that his mother thought she was caring for him, making the right choices for him. Choices that eventually caused a slow death, dragged out over six months or so. Inside Ruby's case files, there are photos of Oliver: photos of him playing in the sandbox at the park, smiling for the camera in a red-and-gold graduation cap at his preschool graduation. It breaks Luna's heart to look at these photos, partly because she's a mother and the little boy reminds her too much of her own son, but mostly because it makes her want to vomit.

Doris has reminded her gently on several occasions that she's not obligated to accept cases. If a case feels wrong inside her gut, she can say no, and Luna knows this. She doesn't need anyone telling her such, but she struggles with saying no because of her starry-eyed, idealistic view of the law in which someone is needed to make sure justice is applied fairly, and she's had enough victories in the courtroom that the shine hasn't worn off—not quite yet. However, with each new case, the shine dulls a little more.

"What's bothering you?" Luna asks the investigator.

"Ruby Williams is young. She'll turn twenty-eight next month. Her childbearing years are stretched before her. She could have another kid, and history could repeat itself if she doesn't get the right treatment. I don't think her parents fully understand how ill their daughter is. After interviewing them, I am confident that they don't grasp the seriousness of her illness, and they've expressed their desire to gain conservatorship over her. They don't understand what orthorexia is or how it makes it hard for Ruby to manage her life. In prison, she'll have access to mental health care and be able to recover, hopefully."

"Not the same mental health care she could get if she were seeking private psychological services," Luna suggests.

"Probation means returning to the same house without the support she needs to get better . . . the same house where her son died because of her neglect."

"I'm just looking out for my client's best interest. I'm not sure prison is any better for her."

"Prison isn't better for anyone, but that woman needs help. She starved her son slowly to death."

"She didn't mean to. I truly believe she loved that little boy with all her heart. It was the illness, and if she would have let me take this case to trial, I think a jury might have seen that too."

Alyssa shrugs. "Maybe, but you know, half the people that used to sit across from my desk when I was a P&P officer didn't mean to do what they did, but that doesn't mean it didn't happen. Whether she ends up getting three years or the maximum of ten years, we want her to come out healthier."

It's time for Doris to laugh now. "That's not going to happen in the women's state prison. Prison counselors have a full caseload. They can't possibly provide the same level of treatment. Ruby Williams will come out worse than when she goes in."

Alyssa stands up and takes another croissant, wrapping it in a napkin and plopping it in her satchel.

"Present my recommendation to the judge or don't. The final call is yours, obviously, but my professional opinions are not for sale. I make it clear to every defense lawyer I work with that I will give an honest recommendation. That," she points at the report, "is my honest recommendation, and I stand by it."

She extends her hand again to Luna, a firm handshake that punctuates her assertions. Luna knows the woman is right. Even though Ruby's compulsive behaviors and skewed ideas about healthy eating got in the way of caring for her son, Romero can't let that prevent justice from being served. Luna's also done what she can to get Ruby the least amount of prison time, but nothing she does will ever bring Oliver Williams back. That is a sentence Ruby will live with for the rest of her life.

49

The fog that rolled in off the Missouri River overnight still lingers, waiting for the sun to burn it off. The misty morning wraps itself around the old buildings in the Frenchtown neighborhood, giving the empty streets an eerie ambiance. The antique shops and boutiques at the end of the street aren't open yet, but traffic will pick up steadily when they do. Mark pulls his truck around the back of The Tattooed Pig, parking in the alley. He cuts the engine and runs his hand along his jawline; the coarse hairs of his unshaven face tickle his palm. A siren wails in the distance, and a woman jogging with her white Great Pyrenees runs past his truck.

The Tattooed Pig is one of those lazy bars, always open and never questioning. It's the type of place that protects discretion. He'd have been fine meeting at Waffle House or even a commuter parking lot, but he's new at this.

She knows better.

When he opens the bar's front door, grease, smoke, and whiskey create a thick incense that weaves its way into his nostrils and settles at the back of his throat. He likes to have a couple of beers when he's at a baseball game or a glass of wine with Luna at dinner, but he's never been the guy who sits at the bar and throws back shot after shot, not even in college when all his buddies were staying out late and missing early morning classes two or three times a week. He's never been the guy who walks into a bar before night falls, until now.

Behind the bar is a young man, barely old enough to serve an ounce of liquor. He has gauges in his ears, a stud over his shaved eyebrow, and a tattoo of flowers and hearts that weaves its way up the side of his neck, ending at the base of his shaved head. The man smiles, revealing straight white teeth, a trademark of middle-class suburban kids.

"Hey," the man says.

Mark nods and looks around. There's an old man sitting at the end of the bar, reading the newspaper and sipping a short glass of amber liquid. At a table across from the bar, another man is stretched out on the bench, wearing mechanic's overalls and snoring.

"Thirsty or hungry?" the man asks.

"Um, I'm meeting someone."

The man grins. "Of course you're meeting someone. Everyone's meeting someone here. Well, except for Leroy over there. His wife hasn't let him come home in four days. Not quite sure what he did this time," he explains, gesturing toward the sleeping man. "So, redhead or brunette?"

"What?" Mark asks.

The man cocks his head to the side, revealing a tattoo on the other side of his neck. This one is a tiger with its jaw open, incisors pointy and red. He regards Mark for a second and laughs. "Redhead, definitely. Around the corner, past the pinball machines, last table on the right."

"Thanks," Mark mumbles.

He follows the man's directions to the back of the bar. It's dark and musty. If the windows were open, any sunlight that shone into this space would reveal a million dust particles suspended in the air and covering every solid piece in the place. But they don't open the windows here—ever.

The redheaded woman is facing him. Her hair is pulled in a low ponytail and rests over her shoulder. Her lips are painted a pale pink, making her green eyes pop, a bright figure in this dirty, dark place. Mark's intimidated by her stunning features. She's gorgeous. She has her hands out in front of her on the table, folded in a prayer position, a bottle of Evian at her right side and a manila folder to her left. When he approaches the table, she doesn't smile. Neither does he. He sits down and waits for her to speak because he assumes this is how it's meant to go.

The silence stretches long between them for five, ten, twenty seconds, until Mark can't wait any longer.

"So?" he asks.

The woman sighs and nods.

"She's been in town since the end of August, at least."

"Shit!" Mark buries his head in his hands.

"She's living off the radar. Not using credit cards, hasn't opened a bank account. Her social security number hasn't been run for employment purposes or housing or anything like that."

"But she's here?"

The woman opens the manila folder and pulls out a photo. "She's definitely here."

Mark takes the photo, places it on the table. He traces her face with his finger; old but familiar feelings stir in his chest. Love. Fear. Regret. Then he sees it. Behind the woman's head, he sees the street sign. He looks up sharply. The redheaded woman raises an eyebrow and nods.

"My street?"

"I told you. She's definitely here."

"Fuck!" he bangs his fist on the table.

The woman doesn't flinch. This is business as usual for her, he assumes. Emotional clients with so much to lose. She's seen it all.

"Do you want protection for your wife?"

"No. I don't know. Maybe, but not now. When was this photo taken?"

"The day before Halloween."

He remembers the masked woman on the street, the one who spoke to Luna and saw him with Ian. He feels light-headed.

"What do you want me to do?" the woman asks.

"Let me think about it. If you follow Luna, she'll know."

The woman smiles. "I'm good at my job. Don't underestimate me."

"Don't underestimate my wife," Mark replies, looking directly in her eyes.

She shrugs. "Alright, I'll wait for your instructions."

Mark stands up and pulls an envelope of cash from his jacket pocket. He places it on the table, takes the photo, and sticks it in the emptied pocket. "I'll be in touch."

"I know."

He keeps his head low, pausing on the sidewalk just outside the bar, taking a deep breath, and letting the cool morning air clear his lungs. Wrapped up in his guilt and fear, he makes his second mistake. He doesn't see her across the street watching him.

***

She starts to raise her hand and shout out to him, but something stops her. *That's curious,* Cindy thinks. What is Mark doing in this neighborhood at this time of the morning, coming out of a bar, no less? She never knew Mark to be a big drinker. Maybe it wasn't him. It's not like she got that good of a look at the man. He had his head down and was turned slightly away from her. *Mind your own business, Cindy.* She hears her husband's voice in her head. Russ is always telling her to mind her own business, but what's the fun in that? Still, he's right. That probably wasn't Mark anyway.

Or was it?

Right before she turns away to walk into the tea room and antique shop for morning pastries with her dear friend, Nancy, she spies the man speed past her in a late-model Ford Ranger, the same type of truck Mark drives.

50

Ruby Williams is soft-spoken and thin. Very, very thin. She's wearing a cream sweater and black leggings that sag at the knees. The dark circles under her eyes have deepened in color. She knows she's hard to look at. The few times she's allowed herself to look in a mirror, she's been shocked at the pale creature staring back at her. Today, she sits cross-legged on the tan hand-tufted, Chesterfield-style sofa from Restoration Hardware. She tries to slide her finger under the ankle monitor, but it's too tight, molded to her ankle, a permanent appendage tracking her every move.

The lawyer stares at her, expecting her to say something. Everyone expects her to speak, but she has nothing left to say. She's too tired.

Martha, a tall, older woman with a thin nose and sharp cheekbones, enters the room. She's wearing the usual staff uniform: burgundy sweater, black pants, and a crisp white shirt. With her hair pulled back in a tight, low bun, her features are even starker. She appears stern to outsiders, but she's a loving and kind woman. It was Martha who called 911 the day Oliver died, and the only person who was with Ruby when they pronounced him dead at the hospital. Her parents were on a ski trip in the Alps.

"May I offer you water, tea, or coffee?" Martha asks her lawyer.

"Not water from the tap," Ruby speaks up. "And not that bottled stuff from Arkansas. She shouldn't drink anything in this house besides the filtered water in the red jug in the refrigerator."

Martha nods at Ruby. "Of course, Miss Williams. Only the best for your guest."

Ruby scratches at her greasy scalp, watches Martha leave, and says, "Sorry, I'm not supposed to do that. You may have whatever you like, but you do know unfiltered tap water is full of chemicals."

She can't help herself.

"It's okay, Ruby," the lawyer says softly.

Ruby knows her lawyer's name, but she refuses to say it or think it. Keeping everyone at a distance makes all of this seem less real. It tricks her into thinking that Oliver will run into the room at any moment, sliding on the hardwood flooring in his socks like he's ice skating, the only warmth in this cold, expensive home.

"Have you had a chance to read the presentence report that the court-appointed probation officer worked up?" she asks.

Ruby shrugs. "Someone brought it to the house the other day. I glanced at it."

Lie.

She read it several times. Each time she reread the sentencing recommendation, her stomach clenched into a tight knot, and she dry heaved into her lap. Ten years. How would she manage living in a cage, being controlled, for ten years? Then again, how can it not be more? How can it not be a lifetime to make up for the life she took from her son? These conflicting feelings are hard for Ruby. She lives in a constant state of fluctuation, moving in and out of unbearable guilt, but always coming back to her compulsion to do better, be better, eat better, be healthier. There are parts of her that understand how her illness led her to this point, but there's a bigger part that wonders why she couldn't have been stronger.

Orthorexia. That's what the team of mental health professionals named her condition after Oliver died. Ruby often wonders when it started. High school, when she stopped eating pork because of a documentary she watched about how pigs are treated before and up to the slaughter? Maybe it was the first year of college when she was having trouble sleeping and developed a shakiness in her right hand that wouldn't go away. That's when she stopped consuming sugar. She doesn't know when or why her quest for eating better turned into falling into a wormhole where her food choices became so limited that some days she couldn't imagine getting out of bed and planning a meal. There were so many things that could harm her body.

She got better for a while, after she discovered she was pregnant with Oliver. She voluntarily checked herself into a clinic that treated anxiety disorders, eating disorders, and compulsive behaviors. During her pregnancy, she gained weight and provided a nutrient-rich environment in her womb for her little boy. She still avoided eating pork and wouldn't consume any fruit or vegetable that wasn't organic because of pesticide concerns, but her food restrictions weren't extreme.

After Oliver was born, she continued to stay on a good path, but then something happened. She's still not sure what caused the switch to flip in her again, but one morning about six months before Oliver's death, she woke up in a cold sweat and feared every bit of food in the house. Martha found her at three o'clock in the morning throwing everything in the pantry and refrigerator into the trash.

From that point on, she refused to let anyone feed Oliver. She pulled him from school and taught him his kindergarten lessons at home to make it easier for her to make sure only the best foods made it into his precious body. The problem was that there were so few foods he could eat that were pure and healthy. Within a few short months of the switch flipping, her son's daily nutritional needs were mostly fulfilled by supplements, herbal remedies, and probiotics.

The day she found him in the garden unconscious and barely breathing, he had been eating dirt because his iron levels were low, and his belly was hungry. That's what the doctors told her before social services and the police showed up at the hospital with questions and accusations. *Was she trying to get rid of her son?*

No, she loved her son. She wanted him to have goodness and pureness flow through his body, to keep his little body from being poisoned. But somewhere along the journey, she swerved so far off the path of healthy living that she killed her son.

The lawyer told her they could argue mental incompetence to explain her actions, but Ruby wanted nothing to do with any of that. She didn't want to explain or be forgiven. She wanted everything to be over.

The lawyer hands her a different report.

"What's this?" Ruby asks.

"It's the private presentencing report that your parents requested. I'll present this to the judge tomorrow to review prior to your sentencing hearing on Friday."

"Just tell me what it says," Ruby demands.

She's exhausted. How many days has it been since she's slept? The last time she remembers sleeping sound was when her mother found her curled up under the hydrangeas in the garden. She had dreamed of Oliver that night. He had been engulfed in a field of golden sunflowers, giggling and running toward her. Propelling himself through the air, sailing through the clear, blue sky, and falling into her arms.

Each time since that dream, she's closed her eyes and hoped he'd return to her, but only blackness or nightmares found her.

"Three years," Luna says.

"Prison," Ruby says.

"There's still a possibility for probation. Judge Simpson has the final say."

"I have a strict diet. How will that work in prison?"

"We can put in a request that your dietary restrictions be considered, but it's only a request."

"Will they honor it?"

"Probably not."

"Because I'm crazy."

"You're not crazy."

Ruby laughs, although it sounds more like a witch's cackle to her ears. "Let's not lie to each other."

She hands the report back to the lawyer.

"I'm tired. I hope you don't mind seeing yourself out?" Ruby stands up, carefully because she's light-headed.

The lawyer stands too. She's looking at Ruby and wears a furrowed brow. "I'm worried about you."

"Do you have children?" Ruby asks.

The lawyer takes a step back, looks down at her feet, but then lifts her face to meet Ruby's eyes. "I do."

"Boy or girl?"

"Boy."

"How old?"

"Two and a half now."

For the first time in weeks, Ruby smiles.

"That's a sweet age. I'm sure you're a great mom." She turns away from the lawyer, but before she turns the corner to leave the room, she looks back. She can't help herself and says, "Just don't let him drink the tap water."

***

She tastes the snowflakes on her tongue, soft and light. Is she dreaming? Could it be snowing so early in the season? Oliver liked the snow. He liked building snow forts with buckets and sledding on Art Hill, hurtling down the hill below the St. Louis Art Museum and barreling into the hay bales at the end of the run. Laughing hard when the sudden stop lifted his bottom off the sled.

Behind the trees she catches the first glimpse of the sunrise, a lightening of the black sky. The perfect time of morning to reflect and to let go. To release the hold on the night and let the light back in, but she must hurry. The closer she gets to the tree line and the pond behind her parents' property, the more likely it is that the ankle bracelet will give her away and sirens will disturb the peacefulness of this glorious morning.

No more waiting. It's time to go. It's time to see her son again.

51

Snowflakes sprinkle the sidewalk. Not enough snow to cause alarm, but the first real sign that it's November in Missouri. By noon, the sun's warmth will raise the temperatures into the forties and the snowflakes hopefully won't be seen again until December. The snow and the cold surprised her this morning, and she left the house without a heavy coat. She hugs herself with her arms and walks quickly through the parking garage toward the St. Louis County Justice Center. Her head is down to shield her cheeks from the cold wind, so she doesn't see the crowd of news station vans and reporters gathered on the steps of the courthouse, not until Rose Kenney, a reporter for the *St. Louis Post-Dispatch*, sticks a voice recorder in her face.

"Do you have any comments about Ruby Williams?" Kenney asks, so close to Luna's face that she catches the minty scent of freshly brushed teeth.

"Not this morning," Luna responds.

"Her death is tragic, but does it mean justice has finally been served?" Kenney blurts out.

Luna stops so suddenly that she runs straight into the voice recorder, ramming her teeth against it.

"What are you talking about?" She reaches into her bag for her phone and finds the slot empty. She must have left it on the kitchen table because she was distracted by Ian, who was hanging on her legs all morning because he had an earache.

"Your client killed herself early this morning. Just before sunrise is what my sources tell me."

Luna pushes the voice recorder away and shoves past Rose Kenney. The journalist runs after, relentless and desperate for the inside scoop, but Luna ignores her. She spies Doris in a knitted cap and a short coat standing near the courthouse's side entrance and runs toward her. When Luna is almost to the metal door, Doris bangs on it and a bailiff opens it. The two women are ushered into the courthouse, the metal door closing and leaving Rose Kenney behind.

"I tried calling you," Doris explains.

"I left my phone at home. Is it true?"

"Yes, there was a message on the office phone this morning. I wouldn't have gotten it if I hadn't forgotten to bring the case notes home with me last night. I stopped in this morning to pick them up."

Luna lets her briefcase fall to the floor and supports herself against the cinder block wall. "I can't believe this. How?"

Doris shakes her head. "I don't know, but I'm not surprised. Are you?"

Truthfully, she's not. She was worried about Ruby after their last meeting, but did she think she'd hurt herself?

"We need to talk to her parents."

"Yes, but first, we need to breathe because there's a hungry crowd out their waiting to be fed information."

Breathe. Luna closes her eyes and tries to breathe slowly, but when she closes her eyes, all she sees is Ruby's face. The way she smiled when Luna talked about Ian. Is she surprised? No. She's not surprised because all Ruby wanted was to see her son again

52

Tracey clears the table, rinses the dirty dishes with the sprayer, and opens the dishwasher.

"You don't have to that," Luna says, standing up from the table.

Her friend looks at her and shakes her head. "Don't do that."

"Do what?"

"Tell me what to do. Now sit down."

Luna laughs and sits back in the chair. "Maybe you should take your own advice."

"Oh, I'd never do that. I like to tell people what to do. Anyway, you've had a hard day, and I want to help. Mark's at work, so who else is going to cook and clean for you? You deserve full-service catering from your best friend tonight after the day you've had. You looked great on television, by the way."

"Thanks, I'll tell my team of stylists that you approve of my lip gloss and foundation." Luna pushes her chair back and makes room for Ian to climb up on her lap. She smells his clean hair, curling a strand around her finger. Maybe this weekend she can find some time to take him to get his hair cut. She's started calling him her little lion man because it's grown into a wavy mane around his face. He has Mark's thick, fast-growing hair.

"My friend, you are moving up in this world, giving

interviews, holding press conferences." Tracey puts the last dinner plate in the dishwasher, wipes her hands with a kitchen towel, and turns around with a serious look on her.

"I'm so proud of you. You're killing this boss babe, working mom gig. You're my superhero . . . superwoman."

"You're embarrassing me. It's just a job, and today was one of the hardest days. Losing Ruby like that was—"

Crash!

The sound of shattering glass launches Luna to her feet. Ian screams.

"What the hell?" Tracey yells.

Luna hands Ian to Tracey and runs into the living room.

"Call 911!" she shouts.

53

There's this assumption that only a heartless person defends monsters. A person whose heart doesn't quite beat the same as a normal person's heart because a normal person wouldn't be able to defend people like Ruby Williams. Luna once believed this too. To be honest, there are still moments when she's not sure how she ended up here, in the trenches covered in the foul-smelling odor of her clients' crimes. She's been in the habit of keeping her head down, avoiding eye contact with people, and preferring to stay in her house where she feels safe.

Felt safe.

The brick in her hand, the shards of glass scattered about the hardwood floor and all over her son's toys, this is hard evidence that whatever safety home provided is gone.

"Ma'am," says a tall police officer with a wispy blonde mustache, "is there someplace else you could stay tonight. Or someone we can call to stay with you? You said your husband is working? We should call him."

Luna shakes her head. "We're fine. My friend's husband is bringing over some plywood to help me secure the window tonight."

The other officer, an older man who seems closer to retirement, places a hand on her shoulder. "You and your son shouldn't be alone here tonight."

She shrugs off his hand. "I said we're fine."

"Luna! Oh my God! What happened?" Her mom barges through the front door with wet hair and two different slippers on her feet. Her dad follows in right behind her. He's been traveling for weeks selling his paintings at various fall markets, and it's been so long since Luna's seen him that she's startled at how old he looks. He also looks like he was just drug out of bed by his crazy wife. Russ Thompson always does whatever Cindy Thompson asks him to do.

"What are you two doing here?"

"Where's Ian?" Cindy asks.

"He's with Tracey in the kitchen."

"Russ, go check on Ian and make sure my grandbaby is okay. Where's Mark?"

"He's at work."

"He'll be here soon?"

"I didn't call him, Mom."

"Well, why the hell not?" Cindy's voice is getting louder. The younger police officer backs away and writes something in his black notebook.

"Because I don't want to call him when things are like this."

"Like what?"

Luna points at her mom's hair and slippers. "Like this! Chaotic. Why are you here, anyway?"

"My friend Nancy, you know, the one whose husband passed away last fall, she called me and said she heard a call come in on her scanner for a possible break-in at this address."

"The key word in that sentence is *possible*."

Cindy gestures at the broken window and the glass on the floor. "Well, something clearly happened here. I knew something like this would happen. I told Mark."

"Told Mark what?"

"I told him to talk to you. To get you some protection."

"Like a gun?"

"Like a bodyguard."

Luna laughs. "That's ridiculous. I don't need a bodyguard."

"Well, they're actually called security consultants."

"Mom, go home. We're fine here. I know you're concerned, but this comes with the job."

"Now you're being ridiculous," Cindy says. "You're just going to brush this off?"

"Of course not. I'm filing a police report, and the police are going to keep a car out here tonight."

The older officer nods. "That's right, ma'am. We'll be here all night."

Cindy ignores him. "Luna, please come home with your father and me. We'll call Mark on the way and let him know what has happened and where you are."

"No, Mom. Listen, I know you care, and I appreciate you for that, but you can't let this get to you. It happens."

"What do you mean, 'it happens'? Has someone threatened you?"

Luna thinks about the comment by the man in the restaurant during Sam's case and, more recently, the women in the Halloween shop. Those were just words. Nothing threatening like this. Maybe the person throwing the brick only wanted to get her attention. Not harm her, but . . . She glances at the toys covered in broken glass and her heart leaps into her throat. What if Ian had been sitting in that spot, playing with his toys, at the very moment the brick came through the window? Whether the person meant physical harm or not, her son could have been seriously injured or worse tonight.

"No, no one has threatened me, and it won't happen again."

"How can you be sure?"

She can't.

"Mom, you have to trust me. I have a job to do and that's going to make people angry, but—"

"But what?"

"I'm not backing down. This is what I do. I defend bad people. People who make choices that make us cringe and feel dirty and shameful. But you know what? I'm not backing down." She's raising her voice now, but she can't help it. "I'm tired of looking away and feeling guilty for doing my job."

"Honey, come on. Maybe you need to stop taking some of these cases. You could still practice. Maybe at one of those corporate law firms where you fill out paperwork all day. It's safer."

"I don't belong in that job. I belong here, and I will take care of my family. You don't need to worry about me."

"Luna, you're being stubborn. If only you could see how this could have gone differently tonight. You must come home with us. I insist." Cindy reaches down and picks up Luna's tote bag.

"Cindy!" Russ's voice cracks open the room, making Luna jump. Rarely does her dad raise his voice, especially to her mom. "That's enough. We have to respect her decision. Put the bag down and let's go."

"But—"

Her dad comes over and gives Luna a kiss on the cheek. "You're sure you don't need anything?"

Luna nods.

"Okay, but if you do, call us." He turns around and looks at his wife. "We're going."

"Russ—"

"Cindy, we're going."

"Fine, but I stand by what I say. This," she waves her hand around the room, "is no way to live. It's insane. You must know that, and Mark needs to realize it, too, instead of hanging out in bars with his friends early in the morning."

"What are you talking about?"

"Earlier this week. I saw him coming out of some place called The Tattooed Chicken or Pig or some other farm animal."

Luna doesn't have the energy for this conversation tonight. "I don't know what you're talking about. Mark doesn't go to bars."

"Well, Luna, I saw him with my own two eyes. I was visiting Nancy—you know, my friend whose—"

"Yes, Mom, I know who she is," Luna interrupts.

"It was Tuesday. I saw him, but he didn't see me."

Tuesday. That was the morning she took Ian to Little Lamb. The morning Mark told her he was jogging.

"Mom, if you saw him, he was probably just running past the bar. I took Ian to school, and he went for a jog."

"Well, he wasn't running past anything. He was *walking* out of that bar. I'm sure of it."

Luna looks around at the mess in her house and ponders her mother's accusation. If it's true, a brick through the front window isn't the only thing that could destroy her home.

PART SIX

SHATTERED

54

Her head throbs, her body aches. She stands in front of the medicine cabinet in her bathroom, staring at the various medicine bottles and boxes, not sure what will ease her pain. She can't decide if her body aches from Ian's sweaty body pressed against her last night or from the lack of sleep because her mom's words kept replaying in her head.

He was walking out of the bar. I'm sure of it.

She reaches for the aspirin bottle, shakes a couple of tiny white pills into her palm, and swallows them without water. When she shuts the medicine cabinet door, an unrecognizable woman stares back her. This woman's cheekbones are sharp, not rosy and plump like before. She has dark circles under her eyes and deeper lines between her eyebrows. Luna looks away from the mirror and reaches for the tiny tube of moisturizer on the sink. She squeezes a dime-sized amount onto her fingers, closes her eyes, and rubs the lotion over her face. When she opens her eyes, she looks in the mirror again, but she doesn't see her old self. She sees the same tired and thin woman with a headache and lots of unanswered questions.

When Mark got home last night and saw the broken window, he was angry.

"Why didn't you call me?" he shouted.

"I didn't want to worry you," she said, which was the truth. But she also didn't want to admit that things had gotten out of hand. Someone threw a brick through the window of her family's home. It could have been a random act by a stupid teenager, but it was more likely someone who wasn't happy with her.

"Luna, I worry all the time," Mark said. His voice softened, and he pulled Luna and Ian into an embrace. His body trembled as he held them, giving Luna pause. *He was walking out of the bar.* Perhaps Luna wasn't the intended target. Maybe she was making wrong assumptions.

The family of three slept in the king-sized bed in their bedroom last night. Ian fell asleep fast, exhausted from being up past his bedtime and from the excitement of the evening. Luna tried to sleep but instead spent most of the night staring at the ceiling worrying. Each night she's slept less, often forced awake worrying about her clients and how the media attention was affecting her family's safety. But she'd pushed aside the concerns she had about Mark and their relationship.

The tension and distance between them have grown slowly since Ian started Little Lamb. She figured what Mark was going through was something that would pass. Just a little bump in their relationship—growing pains from all the recent change that would eventually subside. Maybe that was another wrong assumption she'd made.

***

When Mark returned home after his shift ended, he didn't see the broken front window right away. It was the police car parked in front of his home that quickened his pace. He took the front steps two at a time and burst through the front door. That's when he saw the plywood in place of the window.

"What the hell happened?" he shouted.

Ian had been curled into a ball next to Luna with his head resting on her lap. When he yelled, he startled Ian awake. Luna had picked their son up, holding him to her chest, rubbing her hand along his back in a circular motion, soothing him and calming his whimpering.

"Mark, stop it. You're scaring him. It's been a long night."

"Obviously. When were you planning to tell me about this?"

When Luna told him about dinner with Tracey and the events that had unfolded, his first thought was of *her*. But would she really do something like this? Who was he kidding? Of course she would, if she was angry enough.

"I know this looks bad, babe, but it was probably just kids," Luna insisted.

"Kids?"

"Yeah, you know, teenagers playing pranks."

"Since when do teenagers throw bricks through windows in this neighborhood. Was anyone else's house hit tonight?"

Luna shook her head. "No, and I know what you're thinking, but I really think it's random. Just bad luck. It has to be."

Now, as the morning sun pushes against the bedroom blinds, he thinks about what all this means. The police had taken the brick away in a plastic bag, collected as evidence. It would be tested for fingerprints, but the police had warned Luna that it was likely no prints would be found. Mark wasn't even sure they'd actually test the brick. After all, no one was hurt. *This time.*

That thought is what kept Mark awake all night. This time no one was hurt, but what about the next time? Would it be another brick or worse—a bullet?

Then there was Luna's reaction to the incident. It wasn't out of her nature to want to handle the problem herself and not bother him, but last night, there was something different about her. She was quiet and seemed cautious around him. Several times he caught her studying him. That's when Mark realized Luna didn't believe it was a teenage prank at all, but something far more serious and calculated. She believed the brick through the window was a message from someone unhappy about one of her cases. That was his chance to tell her that maybe the brick didn't have anything to do with her cases. It was his chance to come clean.

Instead, he had guided her and Ian upstairs away from the

broken window. He tucked his family into bed without another word, letting Luna believe the brick through the window was her fault and hers alone.

55

Most people don't read the paper anymore. At least no one under the age of fifty with a nest egg set aside in a mediocre-performing, company-sponsored 401(k). But Heidi does. Every morning, she lies in bed and waits to hear the truck with the squeaky brakes slow down in front of her driveway and for the dull thud of the newspaper landing on the concrete. She counts to ten, untangles herself from the sheets, slides her feet into her flip-flops, regardless of the weather, and walks to the edge of the driveway to retrieve the paper. Then she brings it inside, leaves it in its red plastic wrapper until she toasts her bagel and makes her coffee. After she's made her breakfast, she slides the newspaper out of its wrapping, unfolds it, and starts reading.

This has been her habit for the last five years since she broke up with Bryan. For five years, she hasn't been able to let her college boyfriend go, but not because she's still in love with him. Actually, with so much time and space between them, she's quite certain she was never in love with him. Fear is what kept her in the relationship. She still fears him even though they haven't had any contact for half a decade. It's this fear that drives her to complete the same ritual every morning, scouring the paper for mention of his arrest.

Today, on page six, her heart stops. She feels her breath catch in her throat, and she has to remind herself to breathe.

"No," she whispers to herself. Who else would she whisper to? There's no one else in the two-bedroom townhouse. There's no room in her life for anyone else.

She traces the newsprint with her forefinger then rubs her finger and thumb together to get rid of the ink, but it leaves both her fingers black. It can't be true, but it is. Not an announcement of an arrest, but of an engagement.

Does she know?

Probably not, but maybe. A part of Heidi wants her to know because she's tired of carrying this secret around by herself. But if she knows, how could she stand beside that man? It's the same question she's asked herself for years. It's also why she's kept quiet. *It's better that way, right?*

Heidi looks around the empty kitchen that's big enough for dinner parties with friends. There's a spot in the corner perfect for a high chair. The backyard is ideal for cookouts and birthday parties, but that's not her life. She hasn't allowed it to be because she doesn't deserve it. Spencer Tyler lost his life. So why should she have one? True, she didn't take his life, but she knows who did and she continues to say nothing. Her silence continues the agony for a family who lost a son, a brother, and an uncle.

She studies the engagement photo closer. He looks the same only five years older, heavier in the face, broader across the chest, but he has the same eyes, a shade of blue that's almost violet. When she first met him, his eyes were her favorite part about him. After that night on the bar's patio, when he confessed his horrible sin, she only saw evil in those eyes.

What does *she* see?

Heidi reaches for a pair of scissors in a cup on the counter, and in a fit of fury and frustration, she cuts the newspaper into tiny pieces. She brushes the pieces of newspaper into the sink, uses a spoon to shove as much of it into the garbage disposal, then flips the switch. The paper begins to disappear into the black hole, consumed by the blades, but then the disposal stops, jammed.

She can't get rid of him.

Does he think of her? Does he remember what he confessed? Does he live with the guilt like she does? Probably not, because murderers don't care.

Heidi has done everything imaginable to not care too. For months following her breakup with Bryan, she drank herself to sleep each night, hoping the whiskey, wine, and cheap, tall cans of Stag Light would numb the guilt. When that didn't work, she took a job as a pharmacy tech at a small family-owned pharmacy and skimmed pills from customers' painkiller prescriptions until she passed out one night and woke up the next morning with vomit all over her chest. She didn't want to die. She just wanted the guilt to die.

She picked herself off the floor that morning, quit her job at the pharmacy, went to an AA meeting in the basement of a church, and tried to accept the things she could not change.

Now, as Heidi stares at the chunks of shredded paper in the kitchen sink, she knows she can't change what happened to Spencer Tyler, but she can give his family some closure. She can answer their questions. She can stop living a half-life and get rid of the guilt. She opens a drawer in her kitchen that could contain sippy cup lids and pacifiers but instead is filled with take-out menus and newspaper clippings. She pulls out the stack of papers and flips through them until she finds the clipping she saved several months ago: *St. Louis's Youngest Murder Lawyer Keeps Client Off Death Row.*

Heidi has thought about going to the police a million times, but the details she knows about Spencer Tyler's murder could make her a suspect. The only thing she knows about police investigations is from television shows like *Law and Order* and *Dateline*, and even if they didn't think she had anything to do with the college kid's murder, why would they believe her story anyway?

If she's going to do this after all this time, she needs a lawyer.

56

She had to get out of the house.

"Where are you going?" Mark asked when he caught her unfolding the stroller in the front foyer.

"I need air," she told him.

"Okay, let me get my coat, and I'll come with you."

"Actually, would you stay here and call the insurance company? I want to get that window fixed right away."

Mark reached out to her, but she backed away, focusing her attention on the stroller, struggling with the tight opening mechanism.

"Hey, are you mad at me?"

"Of course not," she said, pushing her hair off her face and out of her eyes. She looked around the foyer for Ian's stuffed dog and found it facing the corner like it had been placed in time-out. She reached down, picked it up, and shoved it in her shoulder bag.

"Really?"

Luna sighed. Was she? She didn't know. All she knew was she couldn't sit in this house a moment longer looking at the boarded-up window and ruminating over the distance between them and her mom's insinuations.

"I'm just feeling suffocated in this house. We'll be back in an hour or two."

"Luna, after what happened last night, don't you think we should be careful? How about if Ian stays with me?"

Luna ignored Mark's question and called for Ian. He ran to her, propelling his body at hers, full force, nearly knocking her off her feet. There was no way she was leaving her son. Not today. She couldn't imagine something happening and her not being there to protect him. She had already called Doris and told her she wouldn't be coming in today. There weren't any cases on her schedule that couldn't wait another day.

"Luna, don't be unreasonable," Mark said.

"I'm not. We'll be back soon. Don't forget to call the insurance company," she reminded him as she dragged the stroller down the front steps and carried Ian on her hip.

She had waved to the police officer in the cruiser that was still parked outside her house and walked faster. She'd be lying if she said she wasn't scared walking to the coffee shop. It was only a few blocks away, but when you didn't know why someone threw a brick through your window, every inch of the world became scarier overnight.

Now she sits in the corner of the Picasso's Coffee House on Main Street watching people walk in and out and past the windows. She's positioned herself next to the exit so she can leave fast if she has to. She tells herself she's overreacting. But is she?

The caramel latte she ordered has gone cold, and the leaf drawn into the foam has disappeared. She smiles at Ian, who's happily humming to himself while he looks at one of his train books. He seems to have forgotten about last night's drama.

"Well, look who's here!" The loud voice startles her. She jumps in her seat, her foot flying out in front of her and kicking Ian's stroller. He drops his book on the floor.

"Sorry, that was my bad. I shouldn't have snuck up on you like that," Wiles Nyler says. He picks Ian's book up and hands it to him. "Here you go, little guy."

Luna's never seen Wiles without his courtroom suit. Usually, he's put together like a fashion plate. His suit pressed just so, his necktie tied so the pointed bottom hits just below the upper edge of his belt, and black dress shoes probably spit-shined. Today he's dressed down in black, nylon gym pants, a bright purple, long-sleeved shirt that stretches against his athletic chest and torso, and black gym shoes with the laces undone.

"You think Judge Reynolds will let you in her courtroom dressed like that?"

"I'm taking a couple of days off."

"What a relief for your staff."

Wiles laughs and looks over his shoulder. The line at the counter is growing at a steady pace. "Looks like it might be a while. Mind if I sit?"

"Oh, well, I guess. Just let me—" Luna grabs her bag from the extra chair, places it at her feet, and moves Ian's stroller closer to her to make room. She does mind, but she's being polite.

"Thanks," he says. "Ran uphill for two miles and my legs need a break."

"Bragging is bad manners," Luna says, already regretting letting him have a seat.

"I only brag about courtroom victories. Don't let this smile fool you. My wife, Sarah, convinced me to train for a 10K New Year's Day race with her in Chicago."

"A race in Chicago in January? You're crazier than I imagined."

"No objection here. So, I heard you had a rough night last night?"

Luna tears off a piece of the untouched bagel on the plate in front of her. She hands it to Ian, who grabs it and shoves it into his mouth with the grace of a Tasmanian devil.

"Can't have any secrets in this town, I guess," she says.

"The joke is that lawyers listen to the scanner to chase ambulances, but really we just do it for the latest gossip. But, really, how are you?" he asks, glancing at Ian.

"I'm doing okay. I just had to get out of the house. I couldn't stare at that broken window any longer. I'm driving myself crazy thinking about who would do such a thing."

"People get upset about a lot of things, and they misdirect their anger. It could have just been some kids playing a prank."

"That's what I told Mark."

"But you don't believe that?"

"I don't know what I think," she confesses.

Wiles is silent for a moment. When he speaks again, he says, "Practicing law in the public eye is a lot like being a celebrity but without the perks and with all the hassle. We can't hide from the publicity, but no one is rolling out the red carpet for us. Instead, we're constantly being attacked. I've never had a brick thrown through my window, but I've had my tires slashed, a bottle of Corona thrown at me while walking out of the courthouse, and hundreds of threats on social media. And, supposedly, I'm the good guy putting away the bad guys. You're a whole different species of lawyer—the kind people love to hate."

"My mother thinks I need a bodyguard."

"That's not such a bad idea."

"I have an alarm system."

"How did that work for you last night?"

Luna knows he's right, and if she'd stuck around long enough this morning, Mark would've brought up the same point. Maybe that's why she was so desperate to get out of the house. She didn't want to have that conversation with him, or the conversation about what he was really doing the morning her mother saw him coming out of that bar.

"It seems over the top," she tells him. "I can't imagine having someone following me around twenty-four hours a day. It's weird as it is having the police surveilling my house."

"If it makes you feel any better, they're not surveilling. They're playing Candy Crush on their phones."

"It doesn't," she says.

"Look, I work in a courthouse surrounded by armed guards eight, ten hours a day. Who's protecting you when you're at your office, walking to the courthouse, or eating dinner with your family at night?"

"I'm not going to surrender to lunatics."

"I can't tell you what to do, but I don't think of it as

surrendering. It's about protecting what matters most to you."

Thankfully, the barista calls out Wiles' name. He stands up and raises his hands in a mock defensive posture. "That's only my opinion though. You know, Friday nights are open mic nights here. Sarah and I like to bring the kids for something different that doesn't involve electronics. Maybe you, your husband, and this little guy would like to join us sometime?"

Luna doesn't say anything. When Wiles is out the door, she takes Ian out of his stroller and places him on her lap. He reaches across for the bagel and tries to shove it in his little mouth but concedes to sucking on it instead. Luna smells his hair and closes her eyes. She wants to stay in this moment as long as possible because in this moment she trusts her instincts and knows what's true. When she opens her eyes, the world is blurry and so are her instincts.

57

The floor-to-ceiling windows run the entire length of the outer wall, facing the interstate. Luna's heels tap-tap-tap on the concrete floor, echoing in the empty space. The woman from the leasing office who had walked her through the building earlier that morning assured her that once the space was filled with furniture and some area rugs, the echo would go away. *But you can't beat the tall ceilings*, the woman said. *Look at the exposed ductwork. It's gorgeous, isn't it?*

"It's huge," Doris says to Luna, who's showing her the new offices.

"I rented the entire floor. Three additional offices are down the hall," she motions with her hand to the right, "and a bathroom we don't have to share with a tech start-up or the landlord. We also have a proper reception area."

Standing in the center of the conference room next to Doris, Luna takes in the enormity of the space. Pride swells in her chest and electrifies her nerve endings, temporarily replacing the fear that has been a constant pressure in her body since the brick went through her window over a week ago. She had been contemplating making a move for a while, long before the locals started complaining. It was clear she couldn't do her job well when her clients had to decide between climbing two flights of squeaky stairs or taking an elevator that lurched and heaved. It was also clear she needed a place with better security.

Luna leads Doris to the reception desk and points to a panel of buttons. "These buttons keep us safe. Before anyone gets in the elevator, they have to be buzzed up by security in the lobby. The elevator isn't shared. It leads straight into this space, but we can lock it anytime we need to with this button, and this button," Luna reaches across Doris and points to a blue button, "turns the cameras on in the elevator. We can view the feed on any computer. I ordered new computers this morning, which will be delivered this afternoon. There's also a panic button in each office and the conference room. It's silent and connects straight to the police. Security cameras record everything that goes on inside and outside the building."

Doris runs her hand over the security buttons. "This is certainly an upgrade."

"It's nice, isn't it? You can pick any office you want."

Luna smiles at Doris, waiting for her to pat her on the back and tell her what a good job she's done. Instead, she walks around the empty space. Luna feels the smile slide from her lips.

"What's wrong?" she asks. "You don't like it?"

"I'm worried about you."

"Well, you don't need to be. I'm fine."

"Is that why you've moved us into a fortress?"

"This was a natural move. We're getting busier. I've been tossing around hiring another attorney to assist with some of the smaller cases. That person will need their own legal staff because I don't want to share you. We needed the space."

Doris narrows her eyes at her and says, "That's bullshit."

"I thought you'd be happy," Luna says, although she knew Doris would read between the lines of her thin explanation. Nonetheless, it's true. They've outgrown their space, and this is an option that ticks all the boxes, but mostly, it makes her feel safer. "We even have two dedicated parking spaces. You don't have to try to find street parking for that monstrosity you drive."

"Luna, be straight with me. Tell me what's really going on," Doris says. "I know that brick incident scared you. You're still scared; otherwise, we wouldn't be standing here locked in like prisoners. It's okay to be scared. You know that, right? Maybe you have to put on this brave front for Mark and Ian, but you don't have to with me. I'm in the trenches with you. I know the insanity that surrounds the job we do."

"Do you?" Luna asks. The words leave her lips and land like a blow across Doris's face.

Doris takes a step back. "What the hell is that supposed to mean?"

Luna's cheeks burn hot. One of her proudest qualities is her ability to stay calm and think with a level head, but the past few days, she's morphed into a different person. The fear, the anger, and all the uncertainty are hot oil bubbling under her skin that eventually is going to erupt.

"It's not your face splashed across the ten o'clock news," Luna says. "You're not the one on public display, standing in front of cameras giving interviews and press conferences. *You're* not the target."

"You're right," Doris agrees. "I'm not, but I think there's more going on here than that. I've seen a change for a while now. You barely eat. You spend hours with your head buried in files. Your edges are sharpened."

Luna sighs and turns away from Doris. Why is she always defending herself for doing her job? She's quite certain Doris never talked to Mikey this way. He had a job to do, and he wasn't questioned. How many times had he fell asleep at the office with a half-drunk bottle of whiskey? Did anyone warn him that he was burning the candle at both ends? She knows her friend's concern is genuine, but it's unnecessary and unwelcomed today.

Luna steps toward Doris. Her friend steps back, confused by Luna's sudden aggression.

"Do you want to work with me, Doris?"

"What kind of question is that?"

"One I need you to answer."

"Luna, of course, I do. I'm just worried—"

"Good, then go pick out your office."

Luna turns away from Doris's shocked expression, picks her

purse up off the floor, and presses the green button to open the elevators. She should apologize for her tone, but instead, she boards the elevator and waits for the doors to close, punctuating the silence.

***

The insurance adjuster lets out a long, low whistle. He taps at his phone, looks back up at the boarded window, and shakes his head.

"Shame, isn't it? Not even the nice areas are safe from this crap," he says. "Do they know who did it?"

"Not yet, but I'm not holding my breath," Mark says. He looks over his shoulder at the cruiser parked in front of his house. It's a different one than earlier. There's a female cop in the driver's seat. She nods at him, and he looks away. The patrol cars make him feel watched. Luna told him they'd be gone in a few days, but he's sure that feeling won't go away when they're gone.

"Yeah, broken windows don't promote patrol cops to detectives, I guess. Anyway, to replace with double-pane glass, you're probably looking at two thousand dollars. The way these old windows are set, you have to hire special installers to make sure everything fits just right. You'll probably have to remove the brick too and reset it. The good news is you'll have a sturdier window in case something like this happens again. Anyway, I'll run some numbers and get back to you by tomorrow."

"Sounds good. Thanks," Mark says.

"You bet. Hopefully, whoever is mad at you got this out their system." The adjuster shakes Mark's hand.

Mark nods, but if the person who did this is the person he thinks it is, he's quite certain this is only the beginning.

58

Each time she dials the lawyer's number, it goes straight to voice mail. Heidi checks the time on her phone. It's early afternoon; maybe she's in court. Maybe she's on vacation. Maybe, she thinks, this is a sign that she should leave well enough alone. Why would anyone believe her anyway?

Stop it, she scolds herself.

When the meeting in the basement of the Presbyterian church ended fifteen minutes ago, she snuck out quickly to avoid the small talk. She's always hated those after-meeting conversations—people making plans to meet up later, going on with their lives. She knows she's not the only one with a secret, but she holds it tighter to her chest, allowing it to suffocate her.

What would she feel like if she finally let it go?

She tries the number one more time. This time a woman answers.

***

"Goldwyn Law Offices," Doris says into the phone.

Silence.

"Hello? Is anyone there?"

These damn phones, Doris says under her breath. It's been a full week since they've been in this new building and only a quarter of the phone calls coming in are getting answered because the new system is jacked up.

"I need to make an appointment," says a quiet female voice on the other end of the line.

"What's your name?" Doris asks.

"I'd rather not say," the woman tells her.

Doris rolls her eyes and looks at the stack of paperwork she has on her desk. Nothing about this move has gone smoothly. The new computer system lost half of the old client information, which means she's spent the last week entering client files manually. She's still not used to all the buttons that are supposed to keep them safe and make life convenient. She's locked herself out of her corner office twice, set off the silent alarm once, and was an hour late yesterday because she forgot her security badge and couldn't get into the garage. The last thing she has time for is theatrics from some woman on the phone.

"Are you a celebrity?" Doris mocks the caller. "Are you a head of state or a mass murderer? If yes, press one. Otherwise, please state your name."

The woman is undeterred. "I haven't committed a crime. I have information about a crime."

"Then you need to go to the police," Doris tells her. She chews on the end of a pencil and looks out her window. She hates to admit it, but she does love her corner office.

"I can't. Not right now," she says.

What the hell, Doris thinks. She'll bite. She needs a break anyway.

"Why not?"

"Because I'm afraid."

"Of being arrested?"

The woman doesn't respond right away. Doris thinks she might have hung up, but then the woman says, "No, I'm afraid of being killed."

"Then you really need to go to the police."

"You don't understand." The woman goes quiet again. "Someone is getting away with murder."

"That's not all that uncommon. Trust me," Doris tells her.

"Have you heard of Spencer Tyler?" she asks. "He drowned in the Missouri River five years ago."

Doris recalls the name. The details of the case are blurry, but if she remembers correctly, it was ruled a tragic suicide. She recalls hearing about the search parties sent out on the river, scanning the water for signs of the young man's body. It took them five days to find the body caught in a tangle of downed trees five miles downstream from the Boone Bridge where he had jumped. Doris relays these little details back to the caller.

"It wasn't suicide. Please, I need . . ." the woman whimpers, "I need to tell someone."

This isn't the type of client they'd typically take, but Doris considers how rocky the last few months have been for Luna. Maybe a simple consult is what Luna needs to catch her breath. A quick sit-down with a woman who needs a little reassurance that she doesn't know a killer, just a liar.

"Ms. Goldwyn has availability in her schedule next week. Can you come in Monday at one o'clock?"

"I'll be there."

Doris gives the woman the address and adds her to the new computerized scheduling system. The woman still refuses to give her name, so she enters *new client* into the name field.

After she hangs up, she stares at her computer screen. She's second-guessing herself, something she rarely does, but since Mikey's death in April, so much has changed so fast. Bob has suggested on more than one occasion that she quit and come on the road with him. She wouldn't mind seeing the country beyond the Missouri borders, riding shotgun with Bob, singing along to bad country music while his big rig climbs closer to the clouds as they travel through the Smokies, or maybe the Rockies, but now isn't the time for adventure on the open road. There'll be plenty of time to inhale exhaust fumes and get fat eating gas station food later. Right now, she likes her work, and this is where she wants to be.

Besides, she feels protective of Luna, like a much older sister. Luna's knowledge of the law and her lawyering abilities are exceptional, but Doris has seen firsthand what practicing criminal law does to a person. It changes them. She saw the changes in Mikey. None were good. By the time Mikey dropped dead at his desk, he'd lost his marriage and was on the verge of losing his legal license. Luna didn't know this last little tidbit of information. Mikey had sworn Doris to secrecy. He was being investigated for washing funds for some of his wealthier clients. Was it true? Mikey never confessed, but Doris didn't do the books. Mikey handled all the financials, so if he was washing money, she wouldn't have known. He made sure her hands or Luna's were never dirty.

She doesn't want to imagine Luna like Mikey—bitter, alone, and compromised—but it's not out of the question that it could happen. Doris knows if Luna isn't careful, she could lose the family she loves with all her heart.

59

The wind howling and pelting the house wakes her from a stale sleep. The kind of sleep that keeps you on the edge of peacefulness, always pulling you out right when you're about to fall into the soft, warm embrace of deep slumber. She rolls over and feels for Mark, but the bedsheets are tight and undisturbed. Sitting up, she reaches for her phone and checks the time. It's a couple minutes after four in the morning. She gets up and peeks out the window. His truck is parked out front, and no police cruiser is in sight. Apparently, the expiration date on their fear has come and gone.

Luna picks up her robe from the foot of the bed and slides her arms into it as she walks down the hall to Ian's room. She stands over his crib and watches him sleep, so peaceful with a tiny smile on his lips. His eyes twitch, and she wonders what he's dreaming about. Her little boy will be three in January. *Where has the time gone?* All the parenting books and blogs warn you that time moves faster when you have children, but her logical mind never believed that. Time is time. It moves at the same rate whether you have children or you don't, but these last couple years have proved her wrong. Time takes pleasure in speeding up from the moment your child sips their first breath of air. She leans into the crib and kisses him on his forehead. *Soon he'll be in a toddler bed*, she thinks. *It's all too much too soon.*

She walks quietly out of the room, sidestepping the section of hardwood by the door that creaks, and creeps down the steps. Light from the kitchen casts a soft glow near the broken window. Insurance approved the claim, and a crew is supposed to be at the house tomorrow, which Luna realizes is now today. She's happy to be having the window fixed because the plywood is a constant reminder of what happened, but the new window won't erase their memories entirely. She wonders how long it will be before she's able to be in her home and not remember the horrifying sounds of shattering glass followed by Ian's cries.

Mark's sitting at the kitchen table, a bag of Oreos and a jug of milk in front of him. It's been his favorite snack since they were teenagers. She remembers the first time he came to her house after school and her mom had offered him Oreos. She was pleased and appalled when he thanked her for the snack and then washed the cookies down with milk, drinking it right from the jug instead of pouring it into the glass she had placed in front of him. "I thought we left the animals in the wilderness," her mom had muttered.

"Hey," Luna says. "Can't sleep?"

Mark shakes his head.

"Me neither," she says and reaches for a cookie. "The wind is loud tonight, but Ian's sleeping right through it."

"He's always been a good sleeper," says Mark.

They sit at the table without talking for a few minutes. Luna's been calculating how to ask Mark about what her mom told her. She's tossed around a million different ideas of how to start the conversation and now, sitting across from this man she's known since he was a teenage boy, seems like the best time to ask. What is she so scared of anyway? Is she afraid Mark's cheating on her? The thought that he would do something like that has never crossed her mind, but he's been acting so unlike himself lately. No, even though he's been distant, that doesn't mean he's being unfaithful. It has to be something else.

"Can I ask you about something?"

"Sure, but there's no milk left, if that's your question." He holds up the jug and gives it a shake.

"You've always been a milk hog."

Mark shrugs. "I'm a growing man."

"What I wanted to ask you has to do with something my mom told me."

"Oh?"

"Yeah, well, it's funny, actually, and probably she didn't see what she thought she saw, but she told me you were coming out of a bar that morning you couldn't take Ian to Little Lamb."

"A bar? I think your mom saw someone else."

"It was called The Tattooed Pig, I think." Although she doesn't think, she knows. She looked it up and found a bar by that name near her mom's friend Nancy's shop.

"Hmm," Mark gets up and puts the bag of Oreos away in the pantry. "Yeah, maybe I ran by it? I didn't see your mom, though."

"Right, but she said you weren't wearing running clothes."

Mark leans against the counter and crosses his arms. "I think your mom saw someone else. Why would I be at a bar that early in the morning? Why would I be at a bar, period? You don't believe her, do you?"

Luna frowns. "I don't *not* believe her."

"So, you don't believe me."

"I didn't say that."

"You know your mom. She likes to create drama. She also mixes up names and mistakes people for other people all the time."

"I'm not trying to argue with you, Mark. Look, if you were in that bar, I'm sure there's a reason. You can tell me. I know things have been stressful for us these past couple weeks."

Mark shakes his head. "So, you're going to take your mom's word over mine?"

"No, I just want to know what's going on with you. Ever since I suggested Ian go to Little Lamb a couple days a week, you haven't been yourself."

"And how have I been?"

This is not how Luna expected this conversation to go.

"Distant, moody. You asked me the other day if I was angry with you, but I feel like you're mad at me. What did I do?"

"You really want to know?"

"I do, because I'm worried about you, about us. Am I working too much?"

Mark runs his hands through his hair and lets out his breath. "It's not about how much you're working, Luna. I know you're trying to build a practice and follow your ambition."

"Then what is it?"

"You're not being careful."

"What do you mean?"

"The people you're defending, your clients. They're not people writing bad checks or driving and getting caught after they've had too many drinks at an office party. These people have killed people."

"I am aware of the crimes my clients are accused of committing, Mark. How does that translate into my being careless?"

"You think what you do stays at the office, but it doesn't. I can't protect you all the time!" he shouts, gesturing to the boarded window.

"Lower your voice," Luna hisses. "I know the risks my job carries, and I am careful. I have also never expected you to protect me. I'm a big girl who knows how to handle her business. I've installed an alarm system here. I moved into an office building that's costing me three times the monthly rent as the co-op space to get better security for myself and Doris. And what happened here—how do we even know it had anything to do with me?"

"What are you saying?"

"I'm saying anyone could have broken that window. It doesn't have to be someone angry at me. Maybe you've made someone mad."

Mark throws his hands up in the air. "You asked me what was wrong, and I told you."

"Mark," she pleads, "I love you, and I know you. We've been 'us' since we were teenagers. Something is going on with you.

Whatever it is, just tell me. We'll get through it."

"You're seeing things that just aren't there."

"That's not what's happening here."

"Then what's happening here?" Mark asks.

Luna studies him. He's tightened his posture, standing tall and rigid. Mark's one of the most laid-back guys you could ever meet, but not right now. His jaw is set, his arms are crossed in front of his body, and he's slowly moving farther from her, creating a physical and emotional distance.

She stands up, walks to her husband, puts her hand on his chest, and looks into the same eyes she's looked into for over fifteen years and says, "I know exactly what's happening here. You're not being honest."

PART SEVEN

WHAT IF

60

The forceful powering on of the heating system breaks the silence in the room and makes the woman seated in the chair across from Luna jump. With shaky hands, the woman reaches for the glass of water Doris had given her shortly after she arrived and was seated at the conference table. Luna studies the younger woman, although not much younger than herself, and deduces she's a woman who startles easily. She's a tall woman, probably five feet eight inches, maybe nine. Her long brown hair is brushed straight but begins to wave just below her shoulders. Behind the glasses she wears, the woman's eyes are dark, but Luna can't discern the actual color other than they're darkish. She's perched on the edge of the chair. *Prepared to bolt if she needs to*, Luna surmises.

This woman may or may not need Luna's help, but she needs something. So Luna lets the woman take her time getting to the point of her visit. She knows from the briefing Doris forwarded to her that the woman is afraid of someone and that someone may have been involved in the death of a man five years ago.

"Can you believe this weather?" the woman asks, gazing out the large windows. "I didn't even need my coat this morning. How can it be Thanksgiving in a couple of weeks?"

Luna smiles, hoping to put her at ease and move her closer

to explaining the reason for her meeting. Before the woman arrived this afternoon, Luna spent some time browsing the Internet searching for information about Spencer Tyler. He was twenty-three when he died, a recent graduate of the University of Missouri-Columbia where he studied finance. There were several news articles online detailing the search for the man after his vehicle was found abandoned on the Daniel Boone Bridge. It took the search and recovery team hired by friends and family five days to recover his body five miles downstream from the bridge. After his body was retrieved, there were a handful of obligatory articles detailing the tragic details of his death. Most contained speculation because no one knew for sure if he jumped on purpose or fell over the bridge. A suicide note wasn't left behind, but it's what most of the news articles led the reader to conclude.

On social media and a few community forums, the conversation and controversy surrounding Tyler's death continued for several more weeks. Most of the online conversation suggested that something wasn't right—that it wasn't conceivable that the young man had killed himself. Everything in his life seemed to be moving in the right direction. He had a new job lined up at the end of the month, and someone who claimed to be his best friend stated he planned to ask his girlfriend of three years to marry him. Why would he have jumped off the bridge and taken his own life?

Why does this woman in Luna's office think he was murdered?

Luna knows there are people who peruse forums and follow cases, making up accusations to get attention. Is that what she's doing? Making up stories? Luna doesn't know, but clearly the woman is in distress. Or, maybe, she's just a damn good actress.

"My assistant says you have information about a suicide?" Luna asks, beginning her line of questioning.

"It wasn't a suicide."

"What makes you think so?"

The woman shifts in her seat, reaches out for the glass of water again, but changes her mind and slides her shaking hand under her thigh. "Because the person who did it confessed to me."

"When was this?"

"Five years ago. A couple of months after it happened."

"I see, and you're here because . . ." Luna lets the question hang and waits for the woman to fill in the blank.

"Because it's time to tell the truth, and because I'm afraid."

"You told my assistant you were afraid of being killed? Have you been threatened by the person you say murdered Spencer Tyler?"

The woman shakes her head. "Not directly. I haven't had contact with him in years, but sometimes I feel like I'm being watched. I've come home to find things moved in my house, and I live alone. I would know if I moved something. I'm not crazy. Also, when we were together, after he confessed, there were times I feared for my life. There were little incidents."

"Incidents?"

"Like once when I helped him remodel a house. I was helping him change out a couple of light switches. I didn't know he hadn't cut the electricity, and when I touched the wires, I got shocked pretty badly. So bad that I had a headache for two days. He didn't seem too concerned. He just laughed and said I should be more careful. I could have died."

Luna glances over at Doris. She shrugs her shoulders and goes back to typing on her laptop.

"I know what you're thinking," the woman says.

"You do?"

"I know it doesn't sound like much. That accidents can happen, but there's no accidents when he's involved. He was making a point."

"What's that?"

"That he can hurt me if he wants."

The woman runs her other hand, the one not trapped under her leg, along her outer thigh. She rubs it vigorously, so much so Luna's convinced she'll rub the fabric away. It's hard to watch, but Luna's used to people's signs of distress.

"Okay, how about we start from the beginning? Let me catch up. Can we do that?" Luna asks.

The woman nods.

"Great, so let's start by you telling us your name."

The woman seals her lips into a tight line.

"It's okay," Luna assures her. "Your identity is safe here."

"Heidi," she whispers.

"Here's what I need you to do, Heidi. I need you to tell me exactly what your ex-boyfriend confessed to you. Do you think you can do that?"

Luna watches the woman inhale a deep breath and waits for her to exhale her story.

61

What if?

What if she hadn't left her debit card at home that day? What if she hadn't had to ask the gorgeous, totally-out-of-her-league man parked at the gas pump behind her car for five dollars? What if she hadn't insisted on paying him back even when he told her not to worry about it? Would she be here now?

A life is made up of so many what-ifs. Tiny decisions that don't seem like a big deal at the time but end up dramatically changing the trajectory of your life. Some for the better. Others for the worse.

He had written his number on the back of the gas station receipt then winked when handing it back to her. When their fingertips touched, her heart flip-flopped in her chest and her cheeks burned.

"I really don't want the money back, but I hope you'll call," he told her. He walked backward to his Jeep, gave her a little wave, revved the engine, and drove away.

She waited two days before texting him. Hours after that first text, they sat in a large booth at a chain Mexican restaurant sharing appetizers and drinking jumbo-sized margaritas.

He was the most beautiful man she'd ever dated. Not gorgeous or strikingly handsome, but downright beautiful. He had a soft face that wasn't fat, but his features had an airbrushed quality to them. When he stayed over, she liked to caress his face in the morning, touching the soft, fine stubble gracing his chin. It was nothing like the prickly hairs on her legs that took two passes of a razor to remove.

His blue violet eyes were striking but sometimes cold and unsettling. That should have been her first clue he was dangerous. But how could she have really known?

Life with Bryan was good until it wasn't.

He confessed his dark secret to her three months into their relationship when she had already begun to name their future children like a lovestruck middle schooler. She'll never know why he told her. Was it because the guilt was too much for one person to live with? Did he suspect the moment he met her that she was a vessel he could pour his deceit into and keep it contained, relieving himself of the burden while transferring it to her?

They were eating at a new downtown hotspot where it was nearly impossible to get a reservation. Seatings were booked six months in advance, but Bryan told her a client had secured the reservation for him as a thank you for negotiating $20,000 off the price of a swanky new bachelor pad in the Loft District.

For Heidi, a graduate student studying early childhood development, anything more expensive than McDonald's was a luxury, but this restaurant, like Bryan, was out of her league. Old money, new money, and local celebrities were seated at the tables. The host pulled out her chair, and Bryan waited to sit until she sat. It made her giggle because she wasn't used to these old-fashioned manners. The feminist in her thought it was stupid, but the young, very-much-in-love twenty-three-year-old loved the attention.

"Order anything you want," Bryan told her. "I love treating you."

Heidi blushed and picked up the menu. Not only was Bryan more handsome than the other men she had dated, he was also older. He turned thirty last month. She told people he was her college boyfriend, but that didn't really describe the relationship accurately. He was someone she met while she was in college, but it's not like they were on the same paths. The age difference didn't usually bother her except in situations like these where it was clear he had more experience than her and a lot more money. If she wanted to treat him to anything on this menu, she'd have to save the money from her job at the campus day care center for three months at least.

The dinner was delicious and the red wine absolutely divine. They were on their third bottle when Bryan suggested they go to the bar next door. The bar had a back porch with hanging outdoor lights and an intimate setting, quiet and away from the noisy main bar area. They found a quiet nook under a cluster of faux palm trees alongside a cascading waterfall. Bryan filled her wine glass and grazed her lips with his, a soft, brief kiss. Heidi lost her breath and leaned into him for more, but he pulled away.

"What's wrong?" she asked.

Bryan picked up the drink menu and avoided her gaze. He sat back in his chair, ran his hand through his chestnut brown hair, and gazed down at his feet.

Shit, Heidi thought. *He's breaking up with me. Of course, this couldn't last. Look at him.*

Instead, he said, "Heidi, I really like you. Actually, well, I . . . I love you."

Taken aback, she didn't know what to say. That was the other thing about being with Bryan, who had probably been in love before, but she wasn't sure she had. She wasn't even sure she was in love with him right now. She liked him. She enjoyed their physical relationship and his company, and damn, he looked good standing next to her, but was that love? The type of love her parents had? Unconditional and long-lasting? She didn't know, and all the wine she'd consumed that evening wasn't helping her figure it out.

Luckily, she didn't have to respond because Bryan kept talking.

"There's something I have to tell you because I don't want there to be any secrets between us. Okay?"

"You're married, aren't you?" Heidi knew it. Of course, he

was. Beautiful men cheat with young, clueless women like herself.

"What? No, of course not. Why would you think that? Never mind, it doesn't matter. No, what I need to tell you is far worse."

This time Heidi laughed. It was the wine. Yes, it had to be, because why would she laugh when someone she liked, maybe loved, wanted to tell her something so important?

"What? Did you murder someone?" she teased between giggles.

She expected Bryan to laugh too, but he stared at her, a weary expression on his face. He shrugged.

Heidi stared at him. Was this a joke?

"What are you talking about? This isn't funny, Bryan."

"I know."

"So, what are you saying?"

Bryan leaned in and pulled her closer to him. His hands squeezed her upper arms. He probably didn't touch her any differently than before, but at that moment, those hands felt menacing and tight.

"I'm not that person anymore, but I need to tell you. No one, well," he cleared his throat, "no one else knows."

Had he planned this all along? Did he know the moment he saw her at the gas station that she was the one who'd carry this secret with him? That she'd let it consume her until she was only a shell of the woman she once was?

"Do you know the name Spencer Tyler?" he asked.

"Maybe. I don't know." She thought the name sounded familiar, but she wasn't someone who watched the news often back then.

"Well, we were friends, and he stole from me."

"Stole from you? Was it a lot?"

Bryan's eyes had grown dark. "Does it matter?"

Heidi thought it kind of did. There's snagging a twenty out of a friend's purse and then there's stealing a fortune and all amounts in between. But she figured the money wasn't the issue. She sensed it was the betrayal of friendship, which was infinitely worse. Still, did any of that justify murdering someone?

"I'm sorry," she stammered. They were the only words she could manage to squeak out. The slight drunkenness that had taken over her body when they first walked out onto the porch had disappeared. The fine hairs on her forearms tingled and goosebumps formed.

"You really didn't hear what happened to him? It was all over the news."

Heidi shrugged. "I don't watch the news much."

Bryan grew quiet and leaned back in his chair. He traced the rim of his wine glass and seemed to be weighing what he would say next. She hoped he'd tell her he was joking and that he was sorry for scaring her. Instead, he picked up the wine bottle, poured more of the liquid into his glass, and slammed the contents back like he was taking a shot.

"He could have had a life like this." Bryan gestured to the area around them. "If only he'd been patient, but he was an entitled brat who thought I wouldn't find out."

"Find out what?" Heidi asked.

"That he was stealing clients from me."

"Clients?"

"Yeah, steering them away from me and delivering them to my competitor, the father of one of those frat brothers he was so loyal to. What did that loyalty get him? Nothing," Bryan hissed.

"He worked for you?"

"An intern, but he was good, and I would've hired him in a heartbeat after graduation, but . . . well, it didn't go that way."

Bryan sighed and ran his hands through his hair. "Dammit," he mumbled.

Heidi looked down at her feet and tried to understand the words tumbling from his mouth. *How did the night take such a turn? And why would someone kill another person over a client? Even if it cost Bryan money from a lost sale, it wasn't exactly stealing. Slimy? Sure, but didn't that happen all the time in the real estate business?*

There were so many questions Heidi wanted to ask, but there was only one that came out of her mouth.

"How?"

Bryan regarded her, cocking his head to the side, a slight smiled forming on his lips. His eyes turned icy blue. It made Heidi's blood turn cold, but it also turned her on. God, he was even more beautiful when he looked at her that way. She had been ashamed at how it excited her.

"You really want to know?"

Heidi took a sip from her wine glass and nodded. "I do."

"His car broke down on the Boone Bridge. He called me for help. Of course, he wouldn't have called if he suspected I knew. He didn't have that big of balls. He thought we were still friends. It was so dark that night. I think it was a new moon, and there weren't many cars on the road. I pulled up behind his broken-down Camry, and there he was, pacing back and forth along the side of the bridge. When I got out of my car, he said, 'What took you so long?' The nerve, you know? To complain to me after he stole my clients, which I said to him. He told me I was crazy. Said that isn't what happened and asked if we could talk about it in the car. He didn't like being on the bridge. So, I told him to get in the car." Bryan stopped talking for a moment. He had reached out to Heidi, touched her hair, and that's when she saw tears in his eyes. His vulnerability tamped down her fear, momentarily, but then, cold and unfeeling, he said, "Then, when he turned around and started walking toward my car, I shoved him."

Heidi recoiled from him. "You shoved him?"

"I pushed him hard against the bridge's railing. He stumbled. I think he said something like, 'What the hell, man?' He tried to get his balance back. That's when I rushed him, using all my body strength. That's all it took. He went right over."

Heidi didn't know what to say. She stared at him and realized she'd been holding her breath.

"You know what the weirdest thing about that night was?" he asked her.

Heidi shook her head.

"He didn't make a big sound when he hit the water. You'd think that there'd be a big splash when a body hits the water from so high, but that's not what happened at all. It was barely noticeable. One minute he was there, and the next, he wasn't. The river and the darkness swallowed him just like that." He snapped his fingers and Heidi jumped. Several quiet seconds widened between them before Bryan finally asked, "What are you thinking, my dear?"

She never answered him because she knew if she spoke, she'd vomit, but that didn't mean she didn't have any thoughts. She knew exactly what she was thinking. She invited a monster into her life, and he had just secured the chains around her body to keep her his forever.

***

"What do you think?" Doris whispers to Luna.

The two women huddle together outside the conference room. After listening to Heidi's chilling tale, they excused themselves to converse. Luna glances over Doris's shoulder and spies on the young woman through the conference room's glass door. She's dabbing at her eyes with a crumpled tissue.

"I don't know. She seems fairly credible. What about the supposed murderer? What do we know about him other than what Heidi's told us?" Luna asks, turning her face away from the door and leaning into Doris like they're two teenagers gossiping about the poor, lonely girl at the lunch table.

"Well, if he really did this, then he's hiding in plain sight. He has an impressive professional career as a high-level real estate broker and investor. Thirty-five years old, lives in Webster Groves, and has an impressive LinkedIn profile. From what I can tell, he's entirely self-made. Comes from humble beginnings. Real estate tax records show his parents are Harold and Susan Boyd of Steelville. They own a meat market in town and a small house on five acres. Have lived in that house since they were married in 1977. Bryan Boyd is their second and only living child. Their firstborn died before her first birthday. Oh, and he's engaged to a first-grade teacher. Her name is Erin."

Luna raises her eyebrows. "Wow! You researched all this on your laptop while she told her story?"

Doris shrugs. "It's not a big deal. I'm comfortable with my superwoman status."

"So, let's puzzle this out. Bryan Boyd hires a college student—"

"No," Doris interrupts, "not hired. He was an intern."

"Right, an intern doing work for free for Boyd during his last year of college. He gets an inside look at Boyd's business and decides he has valuable information to sell to someone who'll pay him for it. So, Boyd finds out and feels duped. He gets a call for help from Tyler and . . . what? He realizes he has an opportunity to get rid of him right then and there? Or does the thought not cross his mind until they argue on the bridge?"

"Your guess is as good as mine. There's only one person who knows the answer. Or two, if you believe what our witness claims to know."

"Alright," Luna says, "what do we know about Heidi?"

"Absolutely nothing. You know what I know. We don't even know if Heidi is her real name. Want me to dig through her purse for an ID while you distract her?"

Luna laughs. "I don't think that's very ethical."

"We work in criminal defense. How ethical do we need to be?"

"Doris—"

"Come on, you know I'm kidding. You want this one or should we refer it out?"

"It's not much of a case. It's speculation, at best. Still—"

Luna pauses and peeks over her shoulder. The young woman is hunched forward in the chair, her left leg thumping up and down again, and she's wrapped her arms around her waist like Ian does when he has a stomachache. Luna tries to imagine the young woman she was five years ago before holding onto a murderous secret caused her innocence to fall away. Secrets certainly have a way of changing and shrinking people.

"Which police department investigated the drowning?" Luna asked.

"Chesterfield police, I believe."

"That means St. Louis County would have jurisdiction over

the case," Luna states. She checks the time on her phone. "I have to be somewhere, but let's do this. Let's make sure we have a good way to get in touch with her. Don't let her leave here without getting a contact phone number. Also, double-check that the Chesterfield police investigated the drowning. Then, call over to the St. Louis County Prosecutor's office, let them know the information we've been given, and see if we can get a meeting on the books."

"Sure," Doris agrees. "Everything alright?"

"What do you mean?"

"I'm just checking in. I schedule your appointments too, you know."

"Not all of them. Anyway, it's just a late lunch with my mom," Luna lies. "Feel free to leave whenever you want."

"You don't have to worry. I'll take care of little Miss Heidi-has-a-secret and get a meeting set up."

Luna places a hand on Doris's shoulder. "I never worry when I put you in charge." She looks back at Heidi and shakes her head. "She's a different story."

62

Some guys lie to their wives all the time. They think nothing about these mistruths, especially the white lies—the ones that don't reshape the relationship but protect it from hurtful barbs that never do anyone any good. But that's not what he's doing. Is it?

Mark's not telling white lies. He's keeping a secret that will reshape their relationship into an unrecognizable blob if he doesn't come clean soon.

Even if he does come clean, will it be enough? Will Luna be able to understand where he was coming from in keeping the truth from her?

The other night when she placed her hand on his chest and told him he wasn't being truthful, he didn't argue. He didn't continue to lie. He merely hung his head and let her walk away. Since that night, they haven't spoken much, and the distance between them is killing him because he loves her and wants to protect her. It's why he's lying in the first place.

He doesn't want to be one of those guys, a lying sack of shit that doesn't care how bad he destroys his relationship. Luna is his one and only. She always has been and that will never change, no matter what happens.

There's a short knock on the front door that jolts Mark away from his spiraling thoughts.

"Door, Daddy," Ian says, pointing over Mark's shoulder.

The door opens and Mark hears the alarm being disabled. He hands Ian an animal cookie.

"Here, take this, buddy. I'll be right back."

He marches into the living room and finds his mother-in-law struggling to untangle herself from her winter parka. She calls it her Chicago coat because no one who doesn't live in the Windy City should ever have to wear such a heavy, cumbersome thing. Even though, Mark notes, it's not that cold outside today.

"Cindy? What are you doing here?"

"Oh, don't mind me," she says as she dumps her coat and bag on the foyer floor.

"Do you have the code to the alarm?"

"Of course! After that ridiculous incident a few months ago when I came over with dinner, Luna gave it to me. Where's my grandson?"

Mark stands dumbfounded as Cindy brushes past him and helps herself to his home and his son. *What the hell?* He's used to Cindy's eccentric, overbearing ways and often defends her when Luna's at her wit's end, but this is too much today. He's not in the mood.

"Cindy," he says following her into the kitchen, "you can't just walk in the house whenever you feel like it."

"Well, I told Luna I was going to stop by today and take Ian to a story time at the library since he's home today."

"She didn't tell me anything about story time."

"Huh, seems to be a lot of that going on in this household."

"What's that supposed to mean?"

Cindy looks away from Mark, snatches a cookie from the bag, and pops it in her mouth. "The elephants are my favorite. What's your favorite, Ian?"

"Cindy," Marks says louder, "I asked you a question. What did you mean?"

"Oh, don't be so sensitive, dear. Nothing, nothing, I didn't mean anything. I'm just tired. Russ kept me up all night with his snoring. I do wish he'd head back out on the road soon to sell his paintings. I sleep much better when he's gone."

"Listen, Cindy, I think we need to talk."

She makes a silly face at Ian and avoids eye contact with Mark. "What do you want to talk about?"

"Luna told me that you think you saw me outside of some bar the other morning."

"I don't think, dear." She looks directly at him and says, "I know."

"You don't know, and you need to quit meddling in our relationship."

"My daughter and grandson are my business too."

"You're stirring up trouble where trouble doesn't exist, Cindy."

"I'm not so sure that's true. Look, you know I love you. I think of you like my own son. How could I not? You went through so much with your parents dying so tragically, and then your sister . . . Geesh, it's a wonder you're as stable as you are. But—" She traces Ian's eyebrow with her pinky finger and lets the thought hang.

"But what?" Mark asks, taking the bait.

"You're due. Aren't you?"

"Due? What are you talking about? Are you high? Because you know our rule, Cindy."

"Oh, stop it. What do you think I am? Someone who walks around stoned all the time? Do I smoke weed? Yeah, I do, but I don't do it 24/7. I mostly do it because it helps with my arthritis, and what I mean is that you're due for a crisis."

"Like a midlife crisis?"

"Please, you're a baby. Unless you only plan to live to sixty-four, you're not having a midlife crisis. No, what I mean is, you're due for the past to finally catch up to you."

Mark rests his backside against the kitchen counter and crosses his arms. Luna's mother has always been intuitive, mostly from being nosy and good at guessing, but still. He can't deny that she has the ability to read people.

"The past is in the past where it should stay."

"That's the thing about the past, Mark. It's a bitch. It doesn't care that you've tucked it away and tried to forget about it. It's always lurking over your shoulder. You can't ignore it forever."

"You need to leave this alone."

"I can't because I care too much about my family. I don't want to see Luna or Ian hurt. Or you, Mark. So, whatever's going on, figure it out and do it soon because this family deserves better."

***

She runs her hand over the pockmarked table, polished smooth from years of other hands doing the same thing. Luna wonders how many people have sat at this table in The Tattooed Pig contemplating all the what-ifs in their lives. What if they hadn't said no to a date with the stable guy who didn't thrill them but would prove to be a sturdy rock? Would their life be better or worse for it? What if they hadn't canceled dinner plans with their mom? Would they have gotten to tell her they loved her one last time? What if their boss hadn't dropped dead at his desk and created the opportunity for a young lawyer to become a local celebrity, admired and loathed all at once? Would her relationship with Mark have taken this turn down a path of lies and mistrust? Or would it have happened anyway?

Luna reaches for the water on the table in front of her, no ice and lukewarm, takes a sip, and closes her eyes. There's no smoking allowed inside these walls anymore due to city ordinance, but that doesn't mean the layers of smoke in the walls, the ceiling, the floor, and the furniture from years before don't still give off a musty, smoky smell. It's jarring to the senses, and Luna feels queasy.

She needs to stop thinking about the what-ifs, but after her meeting with Heidi earlier, it's hard not to.

What if I hadn't insisted on returning the gas money? What if I hadn't stayed with him for so long? Would it have made a difference? Would I have had the courage to turn him in? What if I was stronger and was able to let his confession role off my back?

Those were Heidi's questions, and Luna didn't have the answers. All she knew is the what-ifs were a waste of time because they didn't change the past. They merely held you hostage, if you didn't move past them, keeping you from a future.

"I hope that's vodka," Alyssa Romero declares as she slides into the booth across from Luna. Her long hair is pulled back into a tight ponytail. The kind that gives you an instant face lift and, eventually, a massive headache. When she slides out of her light jacket, she's wearing a bright white muscle tee and a pair of neon pink and orange leggings. Her upper arms are chiseled and remind Luna of Linda Hamilton's arms in that *Terminator* movie Mark loves so much.

"Sorry to disappoint you. You're a bright spot in this dark place," Luna says, gesturing toward her colorful workout clothes.

"It's today's costume. Just came from a CycleBar class, tailing a woman whose husband thinks she is banging the instructor."

"Is she?"

"Of course. God, I feel like one of those colorful swirly suckers at the candy shop. Right now, I need to feel like me. Mind if I order a drink?" she asks.

"Not at all."

"Hey," she shouts across the aisle to the man behind the bar. "What kind of whiskey do you have that doesn't taste like piss?"

The bartender laughs. "Not a one."

"Fine, just give me something decent," Alyssa demands. She turns her attention back to Luna. "You sure you don't want something?"

"Yeah, I'm good. I've never been too keen on the taste of alcohol. Wine is about all I enjoy."

"Wish I could say the same. It keeps me sane, which may or may not be a problem. Depends on the day. So, I was surprised to hear from you. I'm sorry to hear about Ruby Williams, but I can't say I didn't see it coming. She was fragile."

"Yeah, I guess it shouldn't have been too surprising," Luna

agrees.

"People are like that," Alyssa says. "I've been in the business of the good, the bad, and the ugly for a long time. After a while, you're surprised when things go well. You'll understand eventually."

Luna studies Alyssa and wonders if it's true. Will she turn into a woman who can't see the good in anyone? Are Mark and Doris right? Has the transformation already begun?

"That's not my goal. That's not the person I am," Luna tells her.

"Fuck! No one wants to get to that point, but with the clientele you represent, that's the only direction to go that makes sense, in my opinion." Alyssa grips the short glass of whiskey the bartender put in front of her and swallows half of it. "So, what can I help you with? I take it this meeting is for another case?"

Luna swallows hard. "Actually, it's personal."

"For you?"

"I need some information."

Alyssa narrows her eyes. "Go on."

"I had an uncomfortable conversation with my mom the other day. She insists she saw my husband come out of this bar one morning when he was supposed to be running. Supposed to be somewhere else. Not here."

"Did you ask him about it?"

"Of course."

"Let me guess. He denied it."

"He said he might have ran past it, but he wasn't inside this place."

"But?"

"But my mom said he wasn't wearing running clothes."

"In my line of work, I find men run to bars a lot, and it's not for any sort of physical fitness . . . Well, not the kind you're thinking of, anyway," Alyssa proclaims.

Luna sighs. She doesn't want to be here, sitting across from a private investigator, divulging her suspicions. It feels deceitful and shameful. Unfortunately, it also feels necessary. She needs to figure out what's going on with Mark.

"I've tried talking to him," she tells Alyssa. "We used to be able to talk about anything, but lately he's shut down."

"How long has he been like this?"

"Really since Mikey died and the Tammy White trial."

"That trial changed a lot for you."

Luna nods. "Yeah, it did. It changed a lot for my family. I feel like we're always being watched. There was this strange woman at Halloween who approached me, and Mark seemed overly concerned about it, and then there was the brick incident—"

"Brick incident?"

"You didn't hear? Someone threw a brick through my front window. If my son had been playing with his toys in that room, he would have been hit. The other night, Mark and I argued. He said I'm not being careful given the type of people I represent."

"What type of work does your husband do?"

"He works part-time at a recycling center. Overnights, couple times a week."

"Not exactly a dangerous line of work."

"Mostly he takes care of our son."

Alyssa finishes off the whiskey and signals to the bartender to bring her another. "Men don't always like it when their wives have both the ovaries and the balls in the relationship."

"It's not like that with Mark. That's not how we are. He's always been very supportive of my career, my passions."

"People change or they show their true colors when the pressure's on."

Luna shakes her head. She knows that's not what's going on here. "It's something else."

"Another woman?"

"No."

"A man?"

Luna waves her off. "No, it's not another person at all."

"How can you be so sure?"

"Because Mark's not that type of person!"

"All types of people are cheaters, just like all types of people are murderers. Sometimes you don't know the person who's been sleeping next to you at all."

"I've known him since we were fifteen."

Alyssa shrugs. "That doesn't matter. In fact, it makes it even more likely he's changed, and you haven't noticed. Or, you've ignored the change. You're not the same person you were when you were fifteen. Are you?"

Of course she's changed. Luna's not arguing the fact that the years change people, but do they transform a person into someone unrecognizable to their loved ones? Never in a million years did Luna believe she'd be sitting in a dark, stale bar on a November afternoon meeting with a private investigator because she suspects her husband's keeping something from her.

"Listen, so he came to this bar and didn't tell you. It doesn't have to mean anything. People look for private places to figure things out."

"Mark's not like that. Besides, when you know someone as well as I know my husband, you know when something's off. Don't you?"

"I guess."

"Are you married?"

"God, no!" Alyssa guffaws in disgust. "I dodged that bullet. Sorry, I don't mean to be rude. I mean, marriage is great for the masses, but I prefer to go at life on my own terms. So, let me ask you something, and it's something I ask all my clients. Are you ready to hear what I find? And, not even that, but are you willing to break the trust between you and your husband by having me follow him? That's what you're asking me to do, right?"

"I suppose that's right. How else would we do it?"

"Now, let's say he finds out what's happening, and he's innocent. How do you see that scenario playing out?"

"Would he? Find out, I mean. Isn't part of the job to stay hidden?"

"I'm good at my job, Luna, but some people have a way of figuring these things out. Are you prepared to deal with the aftermath?"

"Are any of your clients ever prepared?"

"Not as well as they like to think they are."

Luna considers the warning. She knows she's gambling with her marriage, but given the circumstances, she doesn't feel there's any other choice. She's tried talking to Mark, but he's clammed up. His wall is high and impenetrable.

"How much for a week? Just to see what transpires?"

"Nothing. Consider it a favor."

"I don't want to owe you anything. I want to be perfectly clear about that. I know Mikey was cool with under-the-table dealings, but that's not how I work."

Alyssa smiles and rolls her eyes. "You really are a naive little kitten, aren't you? Ruby's case and the others have started to toughen your skin, but you're still a long way from playing the game like Mikey did."

"Some of us still believe in people and doing things the right way, I guess."

Alyssa throws back the remaining whiskey, places her glass on the table, and stands. "Don't get me wrong. It's not a bad thing. It seems to work for you, for now. Time will tell if it continues to do so, but this isn't a professional favor."

She pulls her coat on then places a hand on Luna's shoulder. "Women in this business have enough going against them. We have to stick together. I really do hope you're wrong about your husband because you're a good person, Luna, and you deserve better. I'll be in touch."

Luna never thought she could ever do better than Mark. He's a kind and gentle man and an exceptional husband, but could he also be an exceptional liar?

Her phone vibrates on the table like an annoying restaurant pager. It's a text message from Doris.

Meeting set for 9:00 a.m. P.A. is very interested

63

The county courthouse isn't what Heidi expected it to be. For starters, it's old and dark, and the narrow hallways with their peeling vinyl floors remind her of being at college, except her college didn't have metal detectors and police officers. It also didn't have crowded hallways stuffed full of black and gray suits, frustrated parents trying to control their bored and overtired children, and the lingering smell of cigarette smoke wafting in from the designated smoking areas near the entrance.

She almost didn't come.

When the lawyer's assistant called to tell her the prosecuting attorney wanted to meet with her in person, she hesitated. Could she, *should she*, go through with this? Was she strong enough to face the consequences of holding onto this secret for so long?

This morning she was surprised she made it out the front door and into her car. Something propelled her forward, giving her the nudge she needed to slide behind the wheel, turn the ignition, and back out of her driveway.

"Thank you for agreeing to meet with us. My name is Marjorie Bell." A tall, Black woman, slightly taller than Heidi, introduces herself to Heidi when she and Luna enter a room on the third floor. The prosecuting attorney wears the usual black lawyering suit apart from her shoes, which are red, yet sensible, flats. The woman thrusts her hand out toward Heidi.

Heidi takes the woman's hand, trying to match her strong handshake, but she comes up short, which only makes her feel weak and defeated. She takes a step back and waits for the round of pleasantries to end between the lawyers.

"This is my assistant prosecutor, Siobhan Finney. She'll be taking the lead on this case should we decide to obtain an indictment. Ms. Goldwyn, I believe you've had the pleasure of working together on the Sam Le case?"

"That's correct," Luna responds.

"Please, everyone have a seat," Marjorie says, gesturing to the empty chairs tucked under the round conference table.

Heidi lowers herself into the chair as the door to the conference room opens again. A man and a woman enter with badges attached to their belt buckles, their guns in plain sight. Heidi squirms. The female detective is older, mid-fifties, and doesn't acknowledge anyone in the room. She merely pulls out a chair and seats herself at the table. The male detective is quite a few years younger. Before he takes his seat, he pulls his phone from his sports coat pocket and places it on the table.

Marjorie sends her smile around the table, letting it settle on Heidi. "Standard procedure to record our meetings. Keeps everyone on the same page. Are there any objections?"

"We're fine with it," Luna asserts.

"Wonderful." Marjorie nods at the male detective, and he leans forward to begin the recording. "Also joining us today is Detective Allison Pierce and Detective Joe Whitney. They were assigned to the case when Spencer Tyler first went missing and throughout the investigation after his body was discovered and, ultimately, as you know, ruled a suicide. But, we're here today because we're very interested in hearing from you, Ms.—?"

Heidi bites her bottom lip and waits for the lawyer—*her* lawyer—to speak for her.

"At this time, my client would prefer to have her name not on record," Luna says.

Siobhan speaks up. "You have advised your client that if this case proceeds and eventually goes to trial, she will be required to give her full name under testimony?"

"My client is aware of what is required of her. However, at such an early stage of the game, my client prefers to only provide her first name on record."

The prosecuting attorney seems to ignore the interchange between her assistant prosecutor and Luna. Instead, she's studying Heidi. Her stare reminds her of a lioness sizing up the prey in the field that might come too close to her cubs. She pulls her lips into a smile that seems friendly and frightening all at once.

"How about off the record then? For now?" she offers.

"Sure, that's okay, I guess. Is that fine?" Heidi asks Luna.

"It's your call."

"I'll give my name off the record."

Marjorie nods to Detective Whitney, who leans forward and pauses the recording. Everyone waits for her to speak. Heidi clears her throat.

"My name is Heidi May."

Detective Pierce writes something on a notepad, and Heidi knows the minute she leaves this room, the detective is going to dig up as much information about her as possible.

"Thank you, Ms. May. I will now instruct Detective Whitney to begin the recording again, but we'll only use your first name from here on out."

"Thank you," Heidi says.

After Detective Whitney turns the phone's recorder back on, Marjorie prompts Heidi for her story. "Tell me how long you and Mr. Boyd were in a relationship."

"For about a year."

"And that relationship ended when?"

"About five years ago."

Marjorie leans back in her chair, puts a finger to her lips, and asks, "Why now?"

"Why now what?" Heidi asks.

"Why come forward with this information now?" Marjorie reaches for her reading glasses resting on top of a file folder. She opens the file folder then pauses to read something inside, not bothering to put the spectacles on but merely peering through the lenses.

"It says here in my notes that the person in question confessed only a few months into the relationship. You say you were together for a year?"

"That's correct." Uncomfortable, Heidi feels like she's on trial. She looks to Luna for guidance, but the woman only nods at her, a visual pat on the back for answering the lady's questions.

"So, back to my previous question, why now? What's in it for you?"

"Nothing."

"Nothing?" Marjorie asks.

Assistant Prosecutor Finney scoffs then clears her throat to cover.

"I just want my life back. Living with this secret has been hard. It's robbed me of more than you know, and it's important that Spencer Tyler's family knows what really happened."

"Unfortunately, we don't have any other evidence that supports your statement. That being said, this office has never been opposed to investigating Mr. Tyler's death further. During our initial investigation, there were a few things that piqued the investigators' interest, but curiosity doesn't make a case. Neither does a cock-and-bull confession. Let me ask you something? Are you angry at this Boyd person?"

"I . . . I don't know," Heidi stammers.

"Jealous? He's getting married, isn't he? What about you? Are you in a relationship?"

"I'm not, but that's not what this is about." The truth is that Heidi hasn't had a relationship, not a meaningful one, since she broke up with Bryan. She can't bring herself to get close to another person, to expose herself to their past. She knows her reasoning for avoiding intimacy isn't rational, but it's how she keeps moving through each day without losing any more pieces of herself.

"Isn't it, though?" Marjorie asks. "This handsome man you claimed to have loved isn't yours anymore. He's asked another woman to marry him, and you have no one. Am I right?"

"That's enough," Luna warns the prosecutor. "We came here today to help you bring a young man's murderer to justice, not to have my client's personal life questioned."

"First, as you know, Ms. Goldwyn, there must be evidence of a murder. As we already stated, that evidence doesn't exist. All we have to go on is the word of your client, and frankly, that's not enough."

"That can't be right," Heidi says.

Marjorie leans forward, placing her elbows on the table, and looks into Heidi's eyes. "It's called hearsay, my dear, and it's frowned upon in criminal proceedings. Ask your lawyer, if you don't believe me. Hearsay statements aren't admissible. Of course, there are exceptions like dying declarations, but since Mr. Boyd is alive and healthy, I'm assuming that's not relative to these circumstances."

"No," Heidi whispers, defeated and angry. She knew this was a bad idea.

"However," Marjorie continued, "there is another way. Detective Pierce, would you like to explain?"

The detective nods and turns her attention to Heidi and Luna. "We're very interested in hearing what Mr. Boyd has to say about his involvement with Mr. Tyler's sudden death. During our investigation, there were some things that didn't sit well with me and Detective Whitney about the circumstances that led to Mr. Tyler ending up in the river."

"Like what?" Heidi asks.

"I can't tell you that. It could compromise any investigation going forward. All I can say is that the possibility of Spencer Tyler's death being something other than a suicide isn't entirely unthinkable."

"Why don't you question Bryan then?"

"We could bring Mr. Boyd in for questioning, but that's where things get complicated."

"How?"

"For starters, we have no evidence aside from your statement of a supposed confession that Mr. Boyd was ever with Spencer

Tyler that night. Second, guilty people do one of two things: They get nervous and start spinning stories that end up trapping them in their own web of lies, or they lawyer up immediately," Detective Pierce explains.

Detective Whitney takes his turn to speak. "We don't want to give Mr. Boyd the chance to get any further ahead of us in this case if it's true that he played a role in Mr. Tyler's death."

"So, we need to turn the odds in our favor before we start fishing for suspects. We want to make sure we snag him on the line before we make an arrest. We need a confession straight from Mr. Boyd's mouth," Detective Pierce says, and then she drops the bomb, "and we want you to help us get it."

64

"Absolutely not! That's absurd," Luna declares. "My client lives in constant fear of that man. You can't expect this sort of involvement to make your case."

"I don't understand," Heidi says, looking back and forth between the detectives, the prosecutors, and Luna.

But Luna does.

She knows exactly what they want from that poor woman, and there's no way they're going to get it. It's too dangerous.

"The risk is minimal," Detective Whitney insists.

"Minimal, but not nonexistent," Luna reminds him.

He shrugs and reclines in his chair, placing his hands behind his head and stretches. "It's our best shot."

Luna knows this isn't true. Before meeting Heidi in the hallway, Luna had spoken briefly with Prosecutor Bell, who told her the only reason they were entertaining this meeting with Heidi is because there was a bruise found on Spencer Tyler's left shoulder blade after the body was recovered. While it was probable that the bruising was the result of debris in the water hitting the body or even from the fall itself, something about the wound didn't sit right with the detectives. They always believed the bruise came from being pushed by someone much stronger and bigger. If what Heidi says is true, it's a step in the right direction toward proving the detectives' theory.

But Luna can't tell Heidi this. If she utters one word, it compromises the investigation and taints Bryan Boyd's confession to Heidi, especially if her client agrees to the detectives' plan.

Heidi looks sharply at Luna. "Is someone going to explain what's happening here?"

"We'd like you to get Mr. Boyd's confession on record, on tape, so we have probable cause to make an arrest," Siobhan explains.

"Like going undercover?" Heidi asks.

Marjorie shakes her head and sheds light on the plan. "Not undercover, because obviously Mr. Boyd is well aware of who you are. What we want is for you to wear a wire and engage in conversation with him about the details of his confession."

"I can't do that. I haven't spoken to him since we broke up. I . . . I don't even have his phone number."

"Don't worry about that little detail," Detective Pierce says.

"He'd be suspicious," Heidi says. "I don't even know what I'd say to him."

"We'd help you with that part," Pierce assures her.

Heidi frowns and looks to Luna. "What do you think?"

She turns to Marjorie and says, "Can my client and I have the room for a few minutes?"

Marjorie nods. "We'll wait outside."

When they're alone, Luna turns to Heidi and asks, "How badly do you want to put this behind you?"

Heidi rubs at her eyes. "I want life to be like it was before I ever met Bryan, but that's not possible. Is it?"

"You don't have to do this. This isn't the only way. You can say no and walk out of here and work toward putting all of this in your rearview mirror."

"You mean ignore it? I've tried that and it hasn't worked."

"I understand."

"I don't think you do."

"Heidi, if you agree to this plan, it won't be over and done once an arrest is made. You'll be a witness in a murder trial.

Someone whom the prosecution and the defense will use as leverage to make their cases. You'll have to testify on the stand. Your full name will be in court records. You won't be able to hide."

"You think I shouldn't do it?"

"I'm explaining what your options will mean for you. Only you can decide the right path."

Heidi stands up and paces the room. "So, I'll wear a wire? Like in the movies?"

"Something like that."

"And where will we meet? My house? His office?"

Luna shakes her head. "You'll meet in a public place like a restaurant. Somewhere safe and secure."

"Will you be there?"

"I'll insist on being with the detectives, but you'll likely be on your own in the restaurant."

"Then what happens? What happens if I get him to confess again?"

"We'll discuss those details with the detectives, but if he confesses in his own words right then and there, they'll probably arrest him as he leaves."

"He'll be able to bond out," Heidi forewarns. "Then what?"

"We'll get a protective order in place and make sure you have around-the-clock protection."

"It's that simple, huh?"

"It's not simple at all." Luna rises from her seat and strides over to Heidi, who's looking out the window onto the empty alley below. "That's why this decision has to be yours to make, weighed against all the possibilities. No one will blame you if you decide you don't want to do this."

"They won't be too happy," Heidi says, cocking her head toward the door where the prosecutors and detectives wait on the other side.

"They'll get over it. They're professionals. If they want to continue to make a case, then they'll work harder. This is about you and how you want to proceed." Luna places a hand on Heidi's shoulder. "Take all the time you need to make your decision."

Heidi glances at Luna's hand, turns back to the window, and says, "Tell them I'll do it."

"You don't have to make a decision today. Don't be rash."

"It's not rash. I've been trying to decide what to do for a long time. Nothing else has worked, so here we are. I can't move forward without moving back. I'll get the confession from him, but promise me one thing."

Heidi holds Luna's gaze. The woman's eyes have grown dark, the pupils and irises seemingly one color.

"What is it you want, Heidi?"

"Promise me I'll get to watch when they slap those cuffs over his wrists."

PART EIGHT

DO TELL

65

The first sound that drags Mark out of his dreamless sleep is Luna's gentle snoring. He rolls over to face her, feels her warm breath on his face, and begins to fall back into his quiet slumber, an easy, familiar place. He has no idea how long he's been asleep when a crash startles him awake. Unlike Luna's snoring, this sound yanks him from sleep like someone grabbing him by the throat. Was it breaking glass that woke him? Something heavy falling? He sits up in bed and listens for the sound to repeat, but his beating heart is the only one he hears.

"Luna, did you hear that?" he stage-whispers, reaching out to shake her awake.

She's gone.

He shoots out of bed, scoops his jeans off the floor, and struggles to get one leg in at a time without losing his balance.

Downstairs he finds her by the kitchen sink kneeling over a broken mug. When he draws nearer to her, he sees a thin line of blood across her palm. She smiles up at him, strands of hair falling loose from the ponytail she wore to bed.

"What happened?" Mark asks.

"It looks worse than it is," she says as she gets up and tiptoes around the pieces of the shattered mug. "Could you grab the broom and dustpan?"

Mark glances at the microwave clock. It's a few minutes past four o'clock. "What are you doing up this early?"

"A noise woke me."

"What kind of noise?"

Luna shrugs and turns on the water at the kitchen sink. "I don't know. It sounded like something banging against the house. Probably just the wind. The weather report said the temperature would drop overnight because of northern winds. Anyway, I thought I'd make a cup of hot tea to help me fall back asleep, and I freaked myself out."

"What do you mean?"

She reaches for a clean kitchen towel, wraps it around the angry mark on her palm, and manages a slight laugh. "It was silly. I looked out the window and thought I saw someone staring back at me, jumped and dropped the mug. I'm sorry I woke you."

Mark touches her shoulder and kisses her forehead. He feels uneasy about the uncertainty in the space between them the last few weeks, accusations and distrust hanging in the air. Luna hasn't let her guard down, but at this early-morning hour, she softens and lets him comfort her, giving him a bit of hope that they'll find their way back to each other eventually.

"Do you think you could clean this mess up for me while I go bandage my hand? Then I think I'll start the pumpkin pies and get ahead of the cooking."

Mark had forgotten that tomorrow—well, now today—was Thanksgiving. "Let me take care of the pies."

Luna shakes her head. "It's okay. Go back to sleep. I want to enjoy the quiet alone."

"Sure," he says, the previous moment's hope deflating in his chest.

He watches Luna leave the room, and then he turns to the window above the kitchen sink—the same window he's peered out of anxiously since he's known she was back. There's nothing to see but his reflection staring back at him. Luna was right. She must have freaked herself out. No one is outside. Still, after he finishes sweeping up the ceramic pieces, he opens the front door, switches on the porch light, and steps over the threshold onto the concrete porch. Luna was right about the weather. The wind is gusty, and the temperatures have dropped considerably throughout the overnight hours.

Mark runs his hand through his disheveled hair and starts to turn back to the door when something catches his eye on the edge of the porch by the top step: a large pumpkin. He crouches down to get a closer look at the pumpkin and finds a sheet of paper secured in place under it. He slides the paper out from under the pumpkin and traces the words, *Please talk to me,* with his fingertip. An address is written below the words.

He rises slowly, directing his gaze across the street. Under the single streetlight, he sees her. She looks both the same and completely different. She raises her hand, a hesitant gesture. What does she expect him to do? Maybe it would be different if he didn't have a family to think about, but he does. He folds the paper in half twice, puts it in his back pocket, and turns away from her.

He doesn't look back, but if he did, he would see her rooted firmly in place on the sidewalk, the chilled November air enveloping her, waiting for him to love her again.

***

Luna mashes the boiled potatoes by hand while her mother looks on, scrutinizing her too closely.

"You look tired," she states.

"I'm fine, Mom."

"Have you been sleeping well? We should have had this meal catered. You're way too busy to do all this."

"Who caters Thanksgiving dinner?" Tracey laughs. She's sprinkling French onions over the green bean casserole she and her family bring to Luna's every Thanksgiving.

"Mom, you're more than welcome to pitch in if you think it's too much work," Luna suggests.

Cindy waves her hand, dismissing the outrageous idea. "Oh, sweetie, you know my culinary skills don't match yours. I guess

I could pop in the dinner rolls, though."

Tracey raises her eyebrows at Luna. She shrugs and continues to mash the potatoes.

"That would be wonderful," Luna says. Tracey nudges her and nods toward the two cans of shoestring fries and a container of liquid cheese placed in the middle of the kitchen table. Luna snickers. "Mom, don't forget your special dish."

"Oh, don't worry. I know it's your favorite, honey."

Luna's childhood never included a proper Thanksgiving meal, not like the meals described in books or celebrated on television shows. When she was a little girl, the Thanksgiving meal was prepared on a three-burner stove in their cramped RV at whatever campground they happened to be at. Instead of pumpkin pie, they had store-bought packaged cookies, and instead of sweet potatoes with the marshmallow topping, they had shoestring fries from a can covered with gooey hot cheese. Her dad deep-fried the turkey, and the meal was shared with whatever strangers were parked within their radius. Luna played with the kids at the campground and ate the weird conglomeration of food without complaint. After all, she didn't know better. She didn't experience a real Thanksgiving meal until her freshman year of high school when their new neighbors invited them over to celebrate the holiday with them. Cindy complained they were only invited because their grown children got stuck in Minnesota thanks to a massive winter system that dumped a couple feet of snow on the upper Midwest, but Luna didn't care what the reason was. She was in food heaven. The level of deliciousness served from her neighbors' table was indescribable. She sampled everything and ended up with a massive stomachache later that evening, but it was worth it.

Since that Thanksgiving meal, Luna vowed that one day, when she had her own house, she would open it up to friends and family as her neighbors did. She'd incorporate some of her parents' traditions, including the deep-fried turkey and canned shoestring fries, but also start her own holiday customs like creating festive table centerpieces from an assortment of gourds carefully selected from the neighborhood pumpkin patch.

Although this year, the gourds came from the bin at the grocery store because her schedule didn't leave room for a trip to the pumpkin patch. How the centerpieces came together didn't matter. What mattered was having this time to spend with her loved ones. She wipes the back of her hand across her forehead and peers out the kitchen window to see how Mark and Ian are getting along with her father.

"Are you really okay?" Tracey whispers.

"A sound woke me up this morning, and I never went back to bed."

"You don't think it was someone messing around the house again, do you?"

"It was probably just the wind," Luna assures her, although she has her doubts.

"Not to gang up on you, but I agree with Cindy. You look extra tired lately."

"It's just a case I'm working on, but everything will work itself out. It always does, right?"

"That's what my yoga teacher says, that and a bunch of other namaste bullshit."

The startling clang of a glass baking dish shattering on the floor interrupts their laughter. Cindy stands over the mess, her hands in her hair and a horrified expression pulling at her face. Shoestring fries, bits of cheese, and shards of glass cover the floor in front of the stove.

Luna nudges Tracey and smiles. "I could use a little zen right now."

***

Outside, on the patio, Mark supervises his father-in-law, who's attempting to set up his new turkey fryer. Ian's playing in his turtle-shaped sandbox using a stick to dig shallow lines through the sand while kicking his heels up and down in front of him. Granules of sand detonate around him then shower down onto his coat, in his hair, and in his mouth.

"Yuck!" Ian cries, wiping sandy hands across his mouth,

worsening his condition.

"Come here, buddy," Mark coaxes him to his side. He cleans him up with the edge of his T-shirt while watching Russ out of the corner of his eye.

His father-in-law scratches his chin and squints at the instruction booklet's fine print.

"That's quite an upgrade from your old fryer," Mark says.

"The other one worked just fine," Russ says grumpily. He tosses the instruction manual onto the patio's surface and glares at the shiny and new stainless-steel fryer. "By the time I figure out this one, it'll be Christmas."

"It looks really nice."

"Yeah, it's fine. I just wish Cindy would've asked before she bought me this and threw the old one away. That woman, she's all about upgrading lately. Out with the old; the new is better. Before you know it, she'll be upgrading me."

Mark laughs. "I doubt that."

Russ tinkers with the gas regulator and says, "She's not the easiest woman to live with, but she's the love of my life. The older you get, the more you realize how rare that kind of relationship is. You know? To find someone who you can love even when they annoy the snot out of you."

Mark nods and sends Ian on his way back to the sandbox, knowing the sand eruption will repeat itself in a few minutes. He shoves his hands into his back pockets, and his right fingertips touch the note she left him.

"I know Cindy has been hard on you lately, Mark," Russ confesses as he pours the oil into the fryer.

Mark shrugs. "It doesn't bother me."

"She loves you like a son. We both do, and we've had the joy of watching you and our daughter grow from lovestruck teenagers into amazing partners and parents."

"Did Cindy ask you to talk to me?"

Russ shakes his head. He smiles and puts his hand on Mark's shoulder. "That woman thinks she has a remote control to my thoughts, but it's not true. No, I'm not her mouthpiece. This is me talking, Mark. I'm talking to you straight because I've known you a long time. I know you're a good person. You've had some bad things happen to you when you were young, and you persevered. Not many people come back from losing their parents at such a young age, and then, well, that sister of yours didn't make it any better. You're a good man, but that doesn't mean everything is good right now. You've lost weight and you seem drained. I know my daughter's career is taking her in a direction where things are changing fast, but don't let those changes change your relationship. You two love each other, always. Remember that, and if you're keeping something from her, you need to talk to her. She deserves that. Your family deserves you to be honest."

"Russ, I don't know what you want me to say," Mark says.

Russ removes his hand from his shoulder and turns back to the fryer. "Sometimes words aren't necessary. I just needed you to hear me. Now, let's get this turkey fried up. Otherwise, we'll be going to Denny's for Thanksgiving, and that, my son, is way overrated. Trust me."

66

She followed him to the grocery store yesterday, to his gym last week, and now Heidi waits inside her car outside of a bakery on Second Street, tapping her fingertips on the steering wheel trying to get the courage to face Bryan for the first time in half a decade. When Detective Pierce told Heidi they needed her help to get Bryan's confession, she imagined it playing out as it does in the movies. She'd set up a meeting with him, the police would wire her up, and after a little small talk and a few drinks, she'd bring up their conversation and get him to confess. But that's not what the detective had in mind.

"If you show up out of the blue after all these years and start asking questions, how will that look?" Detective Pierce asked.

Heidi, wide-eyed and out of her element, shrugged.

"He'll be suspicious," Detective Whitney explained. "We only get one shot at this."

They told her to accidentally run into him, make it seem completely coincidental. She'd have established a nugget of trust with him.

Heidi didn't want to draw out the process. She couldn't imagine being in the same space with Bryan again, much less making small talk about the weather. Still, she knew what the detectives told her was the truth. Bryan was a smart man. He'd figure out something was up, and then what? He'd either lawyer up like the detectives suggested or run and make sure the only other person who knew his secret never had a chance to tell it. Heidi knew he was a man not to be underestimated.

That's why she'd gone along with the detectives' plan, to draw him out slowly. They supplied his address, and she became an amateur private eye, following him around town waiting for the exact right time to bump into him. That time is now.

Heidi takes a deep breath and exits her vehicle. She forgets to look for cars when she opens the driver's door into the street, and a black two-door coupe nearly takes off her door. She slams the driver's door and flattens herself against it, takes a deep breath, and closes her eyes. She can do this, but she has to calm down. She has to be careful.

She collects herself and opens the bakery's door, spotting Bryan right away waiting off to the side of a small line. He's jabbing at his phone's screen, biting his lower lip, and swaying his body side to side like a pendulum. To her left is a table stacked tall with premade pies. With her gaze lowered, she selects a rhubarb pie and gets in line. Even if she chickens out now and lets Bryan leave without approaching him, at least she won't come to her AA group's Thanksgiving dinner empty-handed.

"Order for Boyd," a woman yells from behind the counter.

With her gaze still lowered, Heidi watches Bryan carefully. He puts the phone in his coat pocket and walks toward the counter. The woman, young and attractive, hands him a large brown bag, the fancy kind with the handles.

"Happy Thanksgiving," she says.

"You too." Bryan's voice seems deeper, thicker since she last talked to him. It doesn't go unnoticed to Heidi that he holds the young woman's gaze just long enough that she giggles. She remembers his charm all too well and shivers.

Bryan opens the bag and peers inside as he walks toward her at the back of the line. It's the perfect setup, and she surprises herself by not hesitating. When he's about to slide behind her, she turns as if to put the pie back on the table and collides into him. The pie tumbles out of her hands and the packaging splits open. The pinkish-purple filling bleeds out across the top of Bryan's expensive shoes and onto the concrete floor.

"Shit! I'm so sorry," Heidi exclaims.

Bryan lifts his foot out of the mess, and for a split second, a flicker of irritation crosses his face. When he looks up, the scowl slides from his face, replaced with surprise.

"Heidi?"

"Oh my gosh, Bryan?" She giggles like the girl behind the counter. "What are you doing here? It's been—"

"So long," he finishes her sentence. He always did that when they were together. At first, it was cute, but Heidi eventually came to see it as his way to control the conversation like he controlled everything else. He finished her thoughts, and he'd finish her if she wasn't careful.

Heidi pushes her hair behind her ear and nods. She squats down and starts picking up pieces of the pie. Bryan wraps his hand around her upper arm and guides her to stand up. His touch makes her shiver, and she has to try hard to resist the urge to shake him off.

"There are people to do this," he tells her. She watches him raise his free hand and motion to someone behind the counter. Within a minute, the young woman he flirted with behind the counter comes out to the floor with one of those commercial mop and pail combos.

With his other hand still wrapped around her arm, he leads her away from the mess. The brown bag rests in the crook of his elbow and bangs up against her hip. When they're out of the way, he lets go and smiles. She exhales, not realizing she'd been holding her breath the whole time.

"It's nice to see you. How are you?" he asks.

"I'm good."

"The family good? Is your dad still working at the GM plant? He was a supervisor, right? Probably has a sweet retirement plan waiting for him."

"Yeah, something like that." The truth was that Heidi has no clue what her dad is up to. The booze and pills destroyed her relationship with her family. She hasn't had a conversation with them in years. One more thing that Bryan took from her.

"What about you? Do you have a family?"

"Family? You mean like kids?"

"Well, that's a lot of pies for one person." She nods at the bag.

"Oh, no, these are for a shelter in the area."

"No good deed goes unpunished," Heidi says.

"What do you mean?"

"Nothing. Don't worry about it. I always say awkward things."

"You're still so beautiful, Heidi."

He reaches out and takes her left hand. "What about you? Kids? A husband?"

"Not just yet."

"Yeah, me neither," he lies.

"No one? I find that hard to believe."

"It's not easy to be with someone when you keep thinking of what you lost. Can I ask you something?"

"Okay?"

"Would you like to get a drink with me?"

"I don't drink anymore," she says.

"Do you eat?"

Heidi laughs. "That I still do."

"My buddy just opened a restaurant. It's called Swag. It's in the Central West End. How about we meet for dinner Sunday night? Eightish?"

"I don't know," Heidi says, not wanting to appear too eager.

"Just to catch up. It doesn't have to be anything more. What's your number? I'll text you the address."

Heidi hesitates.

"It's just a quick dinner, Heidi."

"Nothing more?"

"Not unless you want it to be."

She gives him her phone number and says, "Sunday it is."

67

Black Friday brings out the worst in people, Luna decides as she watches a brawl erupt four cars away from hers. Three women are fighting over a tall red Kate Spade bag. A woman clothed in llama-printed pajamas wearing a blue knit cap on her head is lying on the ground of the parking garage holding onto the bag's handles with all her might. Another woman, who appears the youngest of the three with black, silver-highlighted hair hanging to her waist, has her arms wrapped around the third woman's upper body, hands locked in front of the woman like she's attempting abdominal thrusts to dislodge something from the woman's air pipe. The women are yelling at each other, but Luna can't decipher the words. All she hears are screeches and grunts until, finally, the woman on the ground loses her grip on the bag and her head hits the pavement. The third woman clutches the mangled bag to her chest, throws her head back in victory, and runs away, hollering and laughing, from the woman struggling to pull herself up off the ground.

Alyssa knocks on the passenger side door, startling her.
Luna unlocks the door to let her in. "Did you see that?"
"Amusing, isn't it?" Alyssa says, sliding into the seat.
"What makes people behave like that?"
"People are crazy, especially when saving money is

involved."

"I think what those two were doing would count as stealing."

"You ever do that?"

"Knock someone down for a designer bag?"

"Go Black Friday shopping. You seem like the type."

"Not ever. Well, once, actually, with my mom. But it wasn't fun. I was nineteen, maybe twenty? My mom had eaten several pot-laced brownies earlier in the evening and then dragged me out of bed at midnight to be her shopping buddy. We showed up at Bed, Bath, and Beyond, or some store like it, and stood in the cold for hours waiting for the store to open at five that morning. Turns out we were standing at the wrong entrance most of the night, and once my mom realized it, we ended up being one of the last people in the store. But Cindy Thompson doesn't admit defeat. She found the best deal in the place she could, and we walked out of there with our arms loaded down with two-dollar bath towels."

"I think that sounds fun. My brothers and I spent most Black Fridays eating dry turkey leftovers and staying out of the way of our dad's hangover. I bet you still have some of those towels."

Luna smiles. "Maybe one or two."

"But we're not here to talk about messed-up Black Friday memories, are we?"

"You tell me. I was a little surprised to get your text. Thought you might need more time."

"You have a choice right now. It's not too late for me to take your money and keep what I learned to myself."

"I know."

It's tempting; to ask Alyssa to leave and let her take what she knows with her. But what good does that do? Could she really put all this aside? How could she swallow her suspicions and it not affect her marriage? How could it not separate her and Mark even further until one day she wakes up and doesn't recognize what they've become? That isn't any sort of marriage Luna wants. She's scared to know the truth, but she knows she's strong enough to handle it. Even if it's worse than she imagines, maybe learning the truth now will give them a chance to find their way back to a place that feels familiar. She loves Mark, and although she recognizes this as a pivotal moment, a point in time with immense power to throw her marriage off track, she's come too far to not know the truth and give their relationship a chance.

"Just tell me," she says.

"It's interesting," Alyssa begins, reaching into her coat pocket and retrieving a flash drive. "I tracked Mark's truck with a stick-it-and-forget GPS device, and he hasn't been anywhere unusual. It's all on the flash drive. You can see it for yourself. He's gone to work, to home, and your son's preschool. Nothing out of the ordinary."

Luna's heart rate slows. This information so far is digestible and expected. She's feeling foolish when Alyssa says, "But I did discover something of interest."

"Okay?"

"I passed Mark's photo around to the bartenders at The Tattooed Pig. One remembered him from that morning, and he told me that Mark met with this woman that morning."

Alyssa pulls up a photo on her phone. The image is of a striking, unsmiling woman with red hair and catlike green eyes. "Her name is Quinn Snow."

"She's beautiful," Luna whispers.

"I guess if you like women that look like they just stepped out of a comic book. You know what I mean? Sharp lines, overinflated boobs, teeny-tiny waistlines."

"Alyssa, please, you're not making me feel like a winner here."

Alyssa shakes her head. "It's not what you think. He's not screwing her."

"What makes you so sure?"

"Didn't you say your husband wasn't a cheater?"

"Didn't you think I was delusional?"

"Well, I know she's not screwing him because I went to her and her wife's wedding six months ago."

"Wait, you know her?"

"She's a private investigator. We run in the same circles."

"What does all this mean?"

"It means you have to ask yourself a question: Why would Mark hire a private investigator?"

"I have no idea. Maybe you're wrong."

"I'm not. Also, there's this." She swipes to another image.

Luna takes Alyssa's phone and pinches the image to zoom in. The image isn't clear. It's pixelated and hard to make out the person's features because they're turned away from the camera.

"What's this?"

"It's the sidewalk in front of your house. I took this photo yesterday morning."

"What time yesterday?"

"Early, a little before four o'clock in the morning."

"Four o'clock?" Luna's pulse quickens.

"I work around-the-clock for my favorite clients."

"A noise woke me up around that time yesterday, and I let my imagination get the best of me."

"What do you mean?"

"I thought I saw someone looking into my kitchen window. But it couldn't have been anything."

"Or maybe it was something. I took this photo a few minutes after the first."

Alyssa takes her phone from Luna and swipes to another photo. This image isn't as dark or pixelated and clearly shows a female figure standing on the steps of Luna's home.

"Oh my God!"

"Do you recognize her?"

"Of course not! You couldn't get a better image?" Luna accuses.

"What would you like me to do next time? Ask her to pose for the camera? This is how these things go."

Luna rolls her eyes and cradles her head in her hands. "I wanted a better understanding of what's going on with my husband. All this is just confusing me even more."

"Again, that's how these things go. Things get murkier sometimes before they get clearer. But what's clear to me are two things. One, Mark's got a secret, and two, related to that secret or not, you have a serious problem." Alyssa jabs her finger at the last photo. "I don't think this is the first time this woman's been to your home. Call it professional instinct. Give me the rest of the weekend. I can get a better shot."

"What if you don't?"

Alyssa scoffs. "Are you doubting me?"

Luna raises her head sharply and looks Alyssa dead in the eyes. "I'm doubting everything."

68

"We'll be hiding in plain sight," Detective Pierce assures Heidi. She holds up a small, one-inch piece of plastic between her thumb and forefinger. "Technology makes these operations much easier. No more sitting in cars parked around the corner listening to bad audio transmissions."

"Great," Heidi says. She looks over at Luna, who nods and gives her a reassuring smile.

"It's all going to work out fine," Luna assures her even though she is far from onboard with this ludicrous plan.

"Cute boots." The detective points at Heidi's black knee-high stiletto boots. "Are you wearing socks with those boots or just the stockings?"

"Just the stockings," she replied.

"Roll them down, and we'll tape the transmitter to your lower calf."

The detective turns away to give Heidi the notion of privacy and inserts a tiny SIM card into the plastic device. Luna turns away too and wonders if it's not too late to talk her client out of this plan. Is all this worth it just to reopen new wounds for the Tyler family? Luna's not suggesting that Bryan Boyd get away with murder because if he killed before, she knows he could easily do it again, but Heidi's a wild card. She's vulnerable.

"Trust us," Detective Pierce says as much to Luna as she does to Heidi. "We do this all the time. We've never had a problem."

"You send civilians to get confessions from murderers?" Luna asks.

"We use informants all the time."

"Criminal informants," Luna corrects her. "People who know their way around a dangerous situation."

Detective Pierce finishes adhering the transmitter and then turns to Luna.

"All she needs to do is get him to talk. You can do that, honey, right? Just get him to talk? Play catch-up and talk about good times?"

"Sure," Heidi says as she tugs her stockings back into place. "It'll be fine, Luna. I want to do this."

"See," Pierce opens her palms to the ceiling and smiles, "it's all fine. Now, let's go catch us a bad guy."

***

The restaurant is louder and more crowded than Heidi expected. The crush of people and the cacophony of conversation makes her nervous. With all these people, Bryan wouldn't dare do anything to her. Someone would see it, or would they? She surveys the room, everyone enmeshed in their conversations, heads together, eyes locked. She doubts anyone would notice.

She has to keep her guard up. One wrong move and the plan goes to shit. Then what? She's accomplished nothing and she goes back to fearing the shadows in the corner of her home, waiting for them to take her in her sleep. So, she lets the hostess lead her to a high-top table in the far corner of the restaurant next to the bathroom and way too far from the nearest exit. Bryan's hunched over his phone, scrolling with one finger while he throws back a shot with his free hand.

"Hey," Heidi says, but an explosion of laughter from a conversation at a nearby table carries her words away. To get his attention, she touches his forearm as she struggles to climb up onto the barstool.

He grins that lopsided smile she remembers so well. She returns his smile and notices his eyes are already glassy. She inventories the collection of glasses on the table, drawing in her breath sharply. She knows from past experiences that he's not as guarded when he has liquor on his breath.

"Heidi, wow, you look stunning!" Bryan exclaims, sizing her up and making her stomach turn over.

"Thanks," she says. She shrugs off the purple wool coat, slides her knitted hat off her head, and shoves it into one of the coat's arms. She smooths her hair, focuses her attention on Bryan, and tamps down the urge to scope out the detectives.

"Have you been here long?" Heidi points to the empty whiskey glasses, crosses her ankles, and settles in. The transmitter is incredibly lightweight, so much so that she can almost forget she's wearing it. What she can't forget is how goose bumps formed on her naked flesh standing in Luna's office with her stockings around her ankles, her bare legs exposed. She shivers thinking about the humiliation.

"It's been a long day," Bryan says.

"Same here."

"You sure you don't want something to drink? I can order us a bottle of wine."

"Like old times?" Heidi can't help but ask.

"What do you mean?"

"Nothing. I didn't mean anything by it. Like I said, I don't drink anymore, but I'll take a glass of water."

She waits for Bryan to flag down the waitress, a brunette in her mid-thirties with an angled bob and heavy, black eyeliner. The woman hurries to their table, gives Heidi a brief look, and inches closer to Bryan. How is it that women fall in love with him instantaneously? The woman in the bakery, this woman—it's as if he's a magnetic force that no female can resist. Don't they know the danger of powerful forces?

"I'm surprised you wanted to have dinner," Heidi says.

"Are you?" Bryan tilts his head to one side and considers the statement. "I guess it's been a minute or two since we talked."

"You could say that."

Bryan reclines against the back of the barstool, crossing his arms in front of his chest. "It *was* weird bumping into you at the bakery."

"Was it? It was Thanksgiving. Who bakes their own desserts anymore?" Heidi forces a smile.

"It felt like fate is what I mean. You know? Like we were meant to find each other again."

He uncrosses his arms and leans into the table, sliding his arms across the smooth surface and offers her his hands. Repulsion and regret ricochet through her body like a tiny ball in a pinball machine. Why is she here? What business is this of hers? Why couldn't she just forget and let karma catch up to Bryan?

But those hands.

How could those same hands, once gentle and smooth on her bare flesh, be responsible for taking another person's life? She doesn't want to touch him. If she does, she's terrified he'll draw her back in. Is that why she's really here? Maybe justice was only a cover. Was the prosecutor right? Did she want justice or revenge? Because if she's being honest, the morning she opened the newspaper and learned of Bryan's engagement, a flicker of jealousy tapped at her lonely heart.

Heidi feels the force of his manipulation tug at her hands, drawing them out of her lap and across the table. Before her palms meet his, the waitress returns and slams the water glass on the table. It's enough to break the moment.

"I think that's true," she agrees.

Bryan's hands remain palm-side up, waiting for her to submit to his perverse game. When she doesn't yield to him, he pulls his hands back and studies her.

"You do, huh?"

"I've been thinking about a few things since we bumped into each other."

"Thinking is overrated," he says. "Remember how much fun we had together when thinking was off the table? The time we went to the Skyview Drive-in? You remember, right? The way I slid my finger between—"

"Bryan, stop it!" Heidi commands. She can't imagine anyone listening to the intimate parts of her time with Bryan.

He laughs and raises his hands. "Sorry, babe, I thought tonight was headed in that direction. Thought I'd get it started early."

She can't do this. The detectives had coached her a little about how to draw him out, directing her to use their sexual history and chemistry to loosen him up and get him to talk. She thought she could do it, but she can't bring herself to show any bit of affection toward this disgusting excuse of a human. She doesn't have to be the ball anymore, moving in whatever direction the players take her. She's the player, and a good pinball player knows their power. They know how to manipulate the ball down a certain path without tripping the sensors.

"I'm not here to have sex with you, Bryan. Let's be clear about that right now. Also, I know you're engaged. You didn't think I'd do a little research about you before I showed up here tonight?"

Bryan smirks and studies her. Without breaking eye contact, he reaches for his drink glass and takes a sip. "You're full of surprises this evening, Miss Heidi."

"Don't call me that."

He puts the glass down on the table, and the smirk disappears. "Then what do you want?"

"I've been thinking about something, and after bumping into you the other day, I thought it might be a good time to ask."

"Ask away, then."

Heidi clears her throat and looks down at her hands. She peers through her lashes, spotting Detectives Whitney and Pierce at the bar pretending to be two other patrons enjoying a Sunday night out. She doesn't see Luna. She promised she wouldn't leave her tonight. Where is she?

"Heidi? You were saying?"

She looks up and meets his gaze. "Right, so, was that story you told me real?"

"What story?"

"The one about Spencer Tyler."

"What are you talking about?"

"You know what I'm talking about, Bryan."

"You must be confused. I never told you anything about that prick."

"I recall you telling me that you murdered him."

"What does it matter? Why are you here asking me about old shit?"

Heidi doesn't answer right away. She's in deep waters. She wishes she could excuse herself to go use the bathroom and find Luna. Ask her what to do next, but she knows the second she leaves the table, Bryan will bolt.

"Oh, I get it," Bryan slaps his hand on the table. Heidi jumps. "You found out about that sweet deal I made with the Cortex developers, and you're broke."

"I'm not broke, and this isn't about money."

"Sure it is. You need a little cash in your pocket. So, what? You're blackmailing me?"

"Blackmail?" Heidi forces a laugh. "That's not a game I play, Bryan. That's not who I am. No, I'm not here to blackmail you. I'm scared."

Bryan pulls a surprised face. "Scared of what?"

"That you'll murder me like you did Spencer Tyler." She hates using such forceful words, but the detectives and prosecutor told her not to use vague language.

"Why would I want to kill you?"

"Because I carry your secret."

"Wow! I don't remember you being so dramatic."

"Bryan, I just need to know if that story was real. You don't understand what my life has been like since we broke up. I can't sleep. I have zero substantial relationships. I jump at the slightest sound, and I feel like I'm constantly being watched."

"Maybe you are," Bryan says, the smirk returning to his lips. "But it's not by me."

"Were you messing with me the whole time? Was everything you said to me that night a lie?"

"You want it to be a lie?"

Of course she does. She wants nothing more than for Bryan to admit he made up a stupid story, but she knows it wasn't a lie. His retelling of the events to her about what happened on that bridge were the absolute truth. She knows this like she knows the sky is blue and hell is real because she's been living through hell.

"I just want to know why you told me that you killed him," she says.

"Why do you keep saying that?"

"Are you afraid someone will hear you, Bryan? Scared someone will find out your secret?"

"I told you about Spencer Tyler because I was drunk. That's it."

"Are you drunk now?" Heidi asks.

"I was up until about ten minutes ago. Nothing sobers up a man and shrivels his dick faster than a nagging bitch."

There it is. The Bryan she knew always existed, hiding under layers of charm and manipulation.

"Don't you think you owe it to his family to come clean?"

"Why would I do that?"

"It's the right thing to do."

"People get away with murder because they don't want to do the right thing."

"You let his family think he committed suicide."

"I didn't make them think anything. The police came to that conclusion."

"Lucky you," Heidi says.

Bryan leans across the table. "You should stop while you're ahead."

"Or what? I'm dead?"

"Don't put words—or thoughts—into my head, Heidi."

"Did you just threaten me?"

"Take my words however you want to take them. We're done here."

Bryan stands up to leave, and Heidi surprises herself. She grabs his wrist, digging her nails into his flesh. "We're done when you give me what I want. Did you kill Spencer Tyler?"

She expects him to pull away from her, but he shocks her by leaning into her like he's going to kiss her. But he puts his lips against her ear and confesses, "Of course I did. People who steal from me and people who betray me always get what they deserve. Always."

Then the lights go out.

A few patrons scream, but mostly the conversations cease. Blackness and an eerie quiet fall over the restaurant. A voice in the distant says something about a tripped breaker.

In the darkness, Bryan yanks his hand from Heidi's grip. His hot breath on her neck is no more, and when the lights flicker back on, he's gone.

69

Luna hears the commotion coming from inside Swag, but she's distracted. She had come outside a moment before the lights went out. She figured Heidi was safe, the detectives were hovering nearby, and the restaurant was packed. Besides, she had to take this call.

"I have a better photo," Alyssa tells her.

"When was it taken?"

"Last night. Earlier this time, maybe after midnight. It confirms my suspicion that she's making a habit of hanging out around your house."

"Damn it," Luna mutters. She leans against the restaurant's brick exterior and tries to make sense of what's happening when voices flood out of the restaurant when the entrance door opens. Heidi emerges, closely followed by the detectives; all three appear panicked.

"I have to go. Text me the image, and I'll be in touch." Luna hangs up quickly and runs to Heidi. "What happened?"

"He confessed!" she cries.

"That's wonderful," Luna says, but the concerned expression on Heidi's and the detectives' faces suggest otherwise.

Heidi shakes her head and bursts out into sobs. Detective Whitney is on his phone shouting commands at whomever is on the other end. Luna looks to Detective Pierce for answers.

"What's happening here?"

"The goddamn circuit breaker tripped, and all hell broke loose."

"But did you get the confession on tape?" Luna asks.

"I don't know," Detective Pierce admits. "It was loud, and he whispered it, but he was close to her when he said it. So, hopefully, the device picked it up. We'll have to take it back to the station and filter out the background noise to see what we have. But that's not the problem."

"What's the problem, then?"

"When the lights went out, he fled," Detective Pierce explains.

"He got away," Heidi wails. She's leaning against the building now, trying to catch her breath.

"What do we do now?" Luna asks.

"I have a unit on the way to his home to pick him up. We'll have him in custody soon," Detective Whitney promises.

"No," Heidi whispers. "You won't."

"Heidi, it's okay." Luna puts her hand on the young woman's shoulder and wipes the tears from her cheeks.

"He won't be there."

"We're good at our job, and the bad guys don't slip away that easily. This isn't a television crime show. It's real life," Detective Pierce tells her.

Heidi pushes Luna away and looks to the detectives. "Then go get him now. Because he's right there."

Luna and the detectives follow Heidi's gaze, and on the corner across the street, Bryan is staring at all four of them. A black sedan pulls up to the curb, and before he gets in the car, he wags his finger at them, as if scolding them for their childish behavior.

"Fuck!" Detective Whitney yells. He gets back on his phone and runs toward the vehicle speeding away.

Heidi falls to her knees and moans like a wounded animal.

"It's going to be okay," Luna reassures her, kneeling on the ground next to Heid's crumpled body. "You'll be okay. We're going to take care of you."

Luna's phone vibrates in her hand, reminding her of the message waiting for her. She places her forefinger on the phone's sensor, and the photo Alyssa sent fills the screen. It's the image of the woman who's been lurking outside her home. She recognizes the woman immediately, and dread settles into the pit of her stomach.

It's Maya.

PART NINE

TRUTH & LIES

70

She's not sure how long she's sat at her desk starring out the window. Long enough for the night sky to fade away and the pale pink sunrise to wash across the sky, promising a new day filled with possibilities. The morning sun peeking over the distant riparian forest's treetops slowly illuminates Luna's office, highlighting the dusty areas the cleaning crew overlooked. She should be at home, warm under her covers, awakening gradually against Mark, but instead, she's here.

After last night's unexpected events, Luna had found it difficult to sleep once she returned home. She'd stayed with Heidi at the police station until the detectives took her to the safe house, and then she went home. Mark was asleep on the couch still wearing his shoes, seemingly ready to jump up and come to her if she needed him. Before last night, the gesture would have made her smile. She would have gently put her lips against Mark's forehead, whispered a thank you, and covered him with the afghan on the back of the couch. But Luna was furious with her husband. All this time that Mark had been accusing her of not being careful, it was him keeping a dangerous secret from her. She left Mark alone on the couch and went upstairs to check on Ian, took a shower, and crawled into bed, but she couldn't fall asleep. So she got dressed, sent

Mark a brief text that she was going to her office, and then sat at her desk gazing out the window until the sun rose.

Maya.

How could he keep this from her?

Luna picks up her phone and pulls up the image. The photo isn't the best quality, but there's no mistaking the woman lurking outside their home is Maya. She's older and wearier, but it's her. It's the eyes. They're exactly like Mark's eyes.

Mark and Maya.

Maya and Mark.

They were often mistaken for twins, but Maya was fifteen months older. When they were children, they were inseparable, one never too far from the other. That was, until their teenage years. That's when Maya changed, and their relationship slowly unraveled.

The elevator chimes. Luna blinks, pulling herself back to the present. She hears the elevator doors slide open, followed by Doris's telltale shuffle. It isn't long before Doris peeks her head around the door.

"I thought I saw your car in the parking garage. How long have you been here?" she asks, concern spreading across her face.

"A while."

Doris lowers herself into the chair across from Luna, placing her worn, black leather purse between her feet.

"How did last night go with Heidi?"

"To call it a disaster is a gross understatement."

"Did he not show up?"

"Actually, he showed up, and he confessed right before a fuse blew and the whole place went dark. By the time the lights came on, he had bolted."

"Shit."

"Hold on, I haven't gotten to the worst part. He saw us."

"He saw you?"

"All of us. Me, Heidi, the detectives, and if he wasn't already suspicious of Heidi's motives, he is now."

"Where's Heidi now?"

"Detective Pierce took her to a safe house last night."

"Now what?"

"They want her to stay out of sight and under 24-hour security at the safe house for the few days. A couple of undercover units will take turns watching her place to see if Boyd tries to contact her. Obviously, they'll send officers to his residence, his office, and check the fiancée's home, but he's not stupid. He's on the run now, and that's bad news for Heidi."

"Very bad news," Doris agrees.

Luna gets up from her chair and paces back and forth. "I never should have let her agree to do this. It was stupid—a long shot that's put her in a lot of danger."

"You can't blame yourself. She wanted to do this, and she was going to do it whether you consented or not."

"Maybe."

"I have an idea," Doris says, slapping her thighs. "Let's get breakfast. Some hot coffee, a stack of pancakes, and a few slices of greasy bacon are in order."

"I'm not hungry."

"Well, I am. So, humor me, huh?" Doris retrieves her purse from between her feet and stands up. "You can watch me eat and tell me what's really going on."

71

The safe house wasn't a house at all. Instead, it was an old brown-and-white two-story motel where all the rooms were accessible from exterior corridors. The windows were scratched up and dulled from years of being exposed to harsh sunlight, and they did a poor job of blocking out the interstate noise. Not that Heidi had been able to sleep. She'd stayed awake all night, sitting in the pale blue upholstered lounge chair with the ugly brown curtains drawn tight, biting her fingernails, eyeing the mold stain creeping up from the vinyl baseboard and wondering what happens next. The detective assured her that the accommodations were safe, and Bryan wouldn't find her, but she wasn't so sure.

A knock on the door startles her. She rises quickly from the chair, rushes to the door, and stands on her tiptoes to look through the peephole.

"It's just me," Pierce says through the door.

Heidi unlocks the heavy door and backs away, letting the female detective let herself in. She looks like she had as rough a night as Heidi. The detective's hair, usually pulled back in a tight bun, is tousled and falls messily around her face. Day-old mascara smudges accentuate the dark circles under her eyes. She wonders if the detective had stayed at the police station all night.

"Here," she says, handing Heidi a brown paper bag. "I found some clothes in the lost and found at the station. Nothing fabulous, but it will get you by for a few days."

Heidi takes the bag from Pierce and puts it on the unslept-in bed. She pulls out a pair of grey sweatpants that looks two sizes too big, a pair of black yoga pants with fraying hems, a couple of tank tops in various colors, and a red-and-white man's flannel shirt. At the bottom of the bag is a plastic shopping bag containing deodorant, toothpaste, a toothbrush, a hairbrush, and trial-size shampoo and conditioner bottles.

"Thanks," Heidi says, holding onto the flannel shirt and the leggings.

"Did you write out a list of snacks and drinks you'd like?"

Heidi nods and walks over to the round table next to the lounge chair. She snatches the pad of paper off the table and rips the top sheet off. She hands it to Pierce, who gives a quick glance.

"You want any magazines or books?"

"Whatever is fine. I like the newspaper."

Pierce chuckles. "Who reads the newspaper?"

Heidi doesn't return the smile.

"I'll see what I can do."

"When can I go home?" Heidi asks. Her voice cracks and her bottom lip starts to tremble. She bites the inside of her cheek to stop the trembling. She's not going to break down in front of Pierce again.

"Hopefully, we'll make an arrest soon. You're safer here until then." Pierce studies her. "You haven't contacted him, have you?"

"Why would I?"

Pierce shrugs.

"I've been in law enforcement for more than twenty-five years. People do all kinds of things I don't understand. All I know is that we're spending a lot of time and resources on this case. What happened last night has made everything more complicated."

"Obviously," Heidi says.

Her frustration is building. Bryan is the criminal, yet she's the one who feels like a prisoner. She can't go home. Her motives are being questioned, and she's stuck in a dank motel room with room-darkening curtains she's not allowed to open.

"I want this to end as quickly as you do," she assures Pierce.

"Okay, well, rules are the same," Pierce says, folding Heidi's list and placing it in the back pocket of her jeans. "Stay in. Don't go out. If you need something, call me or Detective Whitney, and we'll get it for you when we can. And, if Boyd contacts you, tell us immediately."

Heidi nods, thanks her for the clothes, and waits until Pierce leaves before she sits on the bed and pulls out her phone.

The notification flashes blue in the left-hand corner. Heidi clicks it and rereads Bryan's short, to-the-point message.

Someone's been a bad girl.

72

Luna and Doris seat themselves in a back booth with cracked red vinyl that makes embarrassing sounds every time one of them shifts in their seat. The two women stare at the sticky plastic menus without speaking. Luna hasn't been inside a Waffle House since she was a kid, but not much has changed on the menu except now there's calorie information to let you know exactly how bad the cheesesteak omelet is for you, and the prices aren't as cheap.

The waitress approaches their table, weary with wisps of blond-gray hair falling from her unkempt bun. The deep purple circles under her eyes suggest she's the night waitress, and her brusque manner suggests she's ready for her relief to arrive.

"What you need this morning?" she asks without looking up from her notepad.

"I'll start with a bowl of grits, a large side of bacon, and the blackest coffee you have," Doris orders.

"Just coffee with cream and sugar for me," says Luna.

The women wait to speak until after the frosty waitress returns with their drinks. Luna raises the mug to her lips and winces.

"That bad, huh?" Doris asks.

"Exactly what I expected." Luna puts the mug down and

pushes it off to the side.

"So how do you want to start this conversation? You want to play twenty questions, or do you just want to spill it?"

Luna puts her hands in her hair and closes her eyes. She's so tired, but her body refuses to let her rest.

"Where do I even begin?"

"Anywhere you want. I'll catch up."

Luna removes her phone from her purse and pulls up Maya's image.

"Who's this?" Doris asks

"Maya. She's Mark's sister."

"I didn't know Mark had a sister."

"He doesn't talk about her much—at all, really."

"Bad blood?"

"You could say so. She's the reason Mark's parents are dead."

The waitress returns with Doris's order, placing it with a heavy hand in front of her. The plate clatters against the table. If the waitress heard what Luna said it doesn't faze her. She's probably heard her fair share of late night and early morning confessions. It's part of the job description.

"You're joking, right?" Doris asks, stabbing at a slice of bacon with her fork and nibbling on its end.

It happened the winter of their freshman year of college, a few weeks into the new year. A winter storm warning had been issued for all counties within a one-hundred-mile radius of the St. Louis metro area. Temperatures dropped fast, and a thick gray sky settled over the region. Long-term Midwesterners didn't have to check a radar to know snow was on its way. Mark had gotten a phone call from his mom, Debra, earlier in the day. She'd been upset. Maya had checked herself out of the rehab facility, her fifth one in less than two years, and had disappeared. The facility had told Debra that even if Maya showed back up, they'd have to give her bed away. The list to get into the facility was nearly a year long.

Debra was beside herself. She called Mark at college. Had he heard from her? Had she maybe shown up at his dorm room when he was out and left a message? When he told her he hadn't seen or heard from her, she began to cry. What if Maya had nowhere to go and she ended up in the storm, cold and alone. But worse, what if she went back to those friends of hers? The ones who didn't think twice about giving her drugs. Nowhere was safe for Maya.

Mark tried to console his mom. Maya would be fine, he told her, but it was without much conviction. The truth was that Maya hadn't been fine since she was fourteen, and Mark and his parents knew as much. That was the year when the short-tempered outbursts began, and the darkness smothered her for days. But lying to themselves, only accepting tiny fragments of truth one at a time, was all the Goldwyn family could handle. They weren't quite ready to accept that Maya had spiraled far from their desperate reach.

Shortly after Debra had called Mark, his father, Tom, received a troublesome phone call from a man who called himself Vic. He explained that Maya had shown up at his place, demanding that he call their dealer and get her something to make the voices stop. When he told her she had the wrong house, she'd tried calling Tom, but her hands were shaking so bad she couldn't dial the number. She gave the phone to the stranger and asked him to make the call.

"I'd let her stay until the storm passes," Vic had told Tom, "but my kids are here for the week, and I don't want to give my ex one more thing to hold against me in court."

Tom had said he understood. He and his wife would be there shortly.

They never arrived.

"The storm arrived faster than predicted. All the major highways became snow packed within an hour of the first snowflakes falling from the sky. Mark's parents drove a front-wheel drive, two-door sedan that couldn't handle the treacherous winter conditions. The snow came down fast and thick, creating whiteout conditions within minutes. The accident report summarized that Tom, who was driving, couldn't see the white line and crossed into oncoming traffic, hitting the late-model pickup truck head-on."

"How horrible," Doris says softly.

"It was, and still is really. Mark lost his whole family that night. The funeral arrangements, settling his parents' estate, all of it fell on him. My parents helped the best they could, but they could only manage the bullet points: help Mark figure out the life insurance policies, find a realtor, pack up the house, pay off debtors with what money was left after the funeral expenses and the mortgage was paid off. But Mark's grief was something none of us managed well. He wouldn't let us. He kept it all to himself, and he refused to speak of or to Maya."

"He hasn't spoken to her? Not even at the funeral?"

"She didn't show up. My dad called her and left her a message to call him back, but she never did. I'm not sure when or how she found out about her parents."

"Wow, and you have no clue where she's been all these years?"

Luna ran her finger along the edge of the table, working her nail under the plastic table edging.

"Luna?"

"A few times," Luna confesses, "I tried to find her. It was shortly after I started working for Mikey. A woman I went to law school with, her husband is a police officer, and I asked her for a favor. He ran her name through the system and came back with what I expected. A lot of arrests for minor drug-related crimes, possession, trespassing, a handful of solicitation charges. She spent some time in and out of jail."

"You never told Mark?"

"He never wanted to talk about Maya. He still doesn't. I find it sad that these two people who were once so close are so far apart, but it's the way he wants it. Or, so I thought. Anyway, once I found out I was pregnant with Ian, I stopped keeping track of her, but—" Luna gazes out the window.

"What is it?"

"She was just dealt a bad hand. When Mark's parents started having trouble with Maya, they assumed it was teenage hormones, a rough patch they'd get through. But Maya would have these episodes where she'd be superfocused on a project. Not that it was anything too out of the ordinary. She always had an art project, a sewing project, or something she was working on. The first time I went to Mark's house, she was working on a giant soda can sculpture that took up half of their backyard. Maya loved to create, but there would be days when she'd refuse to walk away from a project. She'd stay up with no sleep for two or three days, refuse to go to school, and then crash and burn. She'd sleep for twice as many days as she stayed up and would often destroy the projects she had been so passionate about just days prior. This went on for a year, a year and a half, before the doctors diagnosed her with bipolar disorder. By then, though, it didn't matter. She had started popping pills, drinking, and using anything she could find to manage the mixed episodes, the extreme highs and debilitating lows."

"Sounds awful for her and for the whole family," Doris says. "What about medication? Bob has a cousin who's bipolar, and the medication seems to help her."

"Maya wouldn't take it. Or, if she did, it was sporadic. She couldn't handle the side effects. Mark always said it was like she didn't want to get better. Who knows? I know it's more complicated than that.

"You know, when I hired Alyssa, she pretty much told me to be ready for anything, and I was. I steeled myself to get the news that Mark might be cheating even though it seemed unlike him. He's not that kind of guy."

"No, he's not," Doris agrees.

"But I almost wish that was what Alyssa had uncovered."

"That Mark was having an affair?"

"It would've been awful, but I knew I could handle it if that were true. This? Mark hiring his own PI and finding Maya? I don't know how to handle this at all."

"What do you think she wants?"

"I have no idea, but she's been in town for a while. I'm convinced she was the masked woman who approached me Halloween night and commented about Ian."

"You don't think she was the person who threw that brick

through your window, do you?"

"At this point, it could be anyone, including Maya. All I know for sure is Mark's always said that when Maya's around, trouble follows. I can't imagine this time is any different."

"I'm sorry, Luna. Truly, I am, but it sounds like you need to take all this to Mark. Obviously, he's worried too if he hired a PI to find her. Maybe he has some answers. You don't have to take all this on alone."

Luna knows Doris is right. She needs to talk to Mark, but she wants to wait until she's not so angry.

"We should get the check," Luna suggests.

"Yeah, but first I have to visit the bathroom." Doris slides out of the booth and adds, "It's a good thing you didn't finish that coffee."

Luna manages a tiny smile. An upset stomach is the last thing she needs today. When Doris leaves, she looks out the window and notices the silver Ford sedan with tinted windows too dark to be legal. It's the same one that pulled into the parking lot a few seconds after Doris and Luna arrived at the restaurant. Luna had watched the vehicle pull into a space near the light pole far from the front door but hadn't thought it was odd until the driver didn't get out and come inside. She shrugged off the uneasy feeling, chalking it up to paranoia brought on by the events of the last twenty-four hours. She'd even managed to forget about the sedan until now.

She looks at the time on her phone. They'd been inside the restaurant for close to an hour. She tries to make out if there's anyone in the driver's seat, but the front window is tinted dark like the door windows. It's possible the driver parked the car in the parking lot, met up with someone else, and left the car behind. She hadn't been looking out the window often. There had been plenty of opportunity for the driver to leave without her noticing. Still, something feels wrong.

Doris returns from the bathroom, plops her purse on the table, and pulls out a fistful of cash. "This one's on me. Don't argue."

Luna doesn't. She's still staring at the sedan. Since that brick came through her front window, she's tried to be more aware of who's around her. But this car . . . has she seen it before?

"What's wrong?"

"See that car parked by the light pole?"

Doris looks out the window in the direction of the light pole. "Yeah, I see it. So?"

"It followed us into the parking lot, and it's been here the whole time."

"Waffle House parking lots attract all sorts of weird. Kind of like truck stops. Just ask Bob. He has a lot of stories."

"Maybe, but have you seen that car before?"

Doris squints to get a better look at the car through the window.

"I don't know. Are you worried it's Maya?"

"Her license is expired and there aren't any vehicle registration records under her name."

After Alyssa had forward Maya's image to Luna's phone, she asked her to do a quick records search. She was grateful for Alyssa's around-the-clock work ethic because, before Doris dragged her out of the office, she'd learned that Maya's license had been expired since 2012 and had no property registered under her name. Her social security number didn't return any job information either. It seemed Maya lived on the fringes of society, keeping a low profile until something landed her in jail. But even that hadn't happened in the last two years.

"Come on," Doris says. "Let's get out of here."

Doris leaves the cash on the table, and the women walk out the front door. Instead of getting into Doris's Cadillac, Luna walks toward the parked sedan.

"What are you doing?" Doris shouts.

Whether it's a smart move or not, she's going to find out who's in the vehicle. But she doesn't get the chance. When she's halfway to the car, its engine starts. Luna struggles to pull up her phone's camera to get a photo of the vehicle and the license plate, but the driver's too fast. By the time she holds up the phone to take a picture, the car has sped away.

73

Bryan Boyd had not intended to kill Spencer Tyler.

Not at first. When he pulled up behind Spencer's car, his intention was to scare him. Maybe rough him up a bit and leave him bloodied and stranded on the bridge. But Bryan's temper had always gotten the better of him. He'd been a short-fuse ready to blow since childhood. It didn't take a lot to set him off: a distracted driver cutting him off, getting shortchanged at the gas station, a friend disagreeing with him over a play when watching Sunday night football together at the bar. Little things bugged Bryan and made him angry, and so it wasn't surprising that when he found out Spencer was poaching clients, he was livid. When Bryan confronted him about his disloyalty, that ungrateful punk told him he was crazy, and in that second, he decided the young man had to die.

He took a chance that night when he shoved Spencer off the bridge. The area was well traveled, and a car could've come upon the scene at any time. Yet no car did, and no one saw a thing. Bryan held his breath for weeks, waiting for a police officer to show up at his place asking questions. But no one seemed to question the young man's death. Everyone accepted it as a suicide.

And that made Bryan even angrier.

Spencer Tyler deserved what he got for double-crossing Bryan, so why hadn't he felt satisfied? He had a sick craving for recognition, but he knew that telling the police would send him to prison. Still, the urge to tell someone what he'd done had continued to build.

Then he met Heidi.

She was sweet and young. Her innocence intrigued him, and that made it even more satisfying when he took it. He remembers how her jaw loosened and her mouth fell open when he described how he shoved Tyler over the railing. Instead of her eyes widening, she narrowed them, and she'd stared at him like she couldn't quite see him clearly anymore. Now, five years later, the police have finally come for him, and it's all her fault.

Bryan isn't a believer of coincidence. When Heidi started questioning him about Spencer's death after they had *accidentally* bumped into each other at the bakery, he knew she was up to something. At first, he really did think it was about the money. Of course, she wanted a little cash for her silence. He was surprised it had taken her this long to play her hand. He might have even given the money to her if she'd asked nicely and been more accommodating. Instead, her unflinching attitude infuriated him. Maybe it was time he reminded her of what he was capable of, but he made a mistake. He underestimated her.

Just a split second before the restaurant's power failed, after he confessed a second time to Heidi, he saw her look over his shoulder like she was looking for someone. When the restaurant went dark, he took the opportunity to leave. He waited across the street for her to leave, and that's when he confirmed that she wasn't alone. They weren't wearing uniforms, but he knew the man and woman who followed her out of the restaurant were cops, and he recognized the other woman too. She was someone the news had nicknamed "The Murder Lawyer." He was sure his entire conversation with Heidi had been recorded. The police never had anything tying him to Spencer Tyler's murder until now.

Heidi was a loose end. She was a problem he created, and now for the second time in his life, he was going to take care of an unpleasant problem. There was no doubt he had to get rid of her. But how?

Sitting behind the wheel of the stolen silver Ford Focus, Bryan watches Luna leave Waffle House with an older heavyset woman. He'd been following her since last night, figuring most of the police's attention would be on Heidi. The lawyer would be easier to get to, and it was her he needed the most right now.

74

The midday sun does little to take the chill out of the air. When Mark gets out of his truck, he rubs his hands together to generate a little heat before shoving them in the pockets of his hooded lightweight parka. He stands alongside the truck and surveys the area. The rural setting is not what he expected. Harvested soybean fields stretch for acres on either side of the two-lane country road before reaching dense forest. Mark hears another vehicle approaching and turns around to see a flatbed truck with tires and an assortment of tools. As the truck passes by, the driver raises his hand, the customary gesture of rural residents. The truck continues on for a few yards before the driver backs it up and pulls up parallel to Mark's truck.

"Got car trouble?" the older man asks. He's wearing tan Carhartt overalls, a denim button-down shirt, and a classic Vietnam veterans hat that's a smidge too small for the man's sizable head.

"I'm looking for this address."

Mark approaches the man's truck and hands him the slip of paper with the address Maya left for him. The man pulls a pair of reading glasses from the bib pocket and holds them to his eyes without putting them on. He breathes in sharply before handing the slip of paper back to Mark.

"That's Tucker's property."

"Tucker?" Mark asks.

"How'd you say you knew him?"

"I didn't."

The man huffs and puts his glasses back in his pocket.

"At least once a week, someone's standing right where you are looking for Tucker's place. GPS isn't all that accurate out here."

"Apparently."

"His place is about a quarter of a mile north of here. There's a dirt road on your left. Take that and stay on it until you reach the trees. You'll see the trailer, but you'll probably smell the place first."

"Thanks a lot."

Mark walks around the front of the truck toward his vehicle. The truck driver hollers to him.

"You have protection?"

"What do you mean?"

"I mean, do you have a gun? If you're showing up on Tucker's property unannounced, you better have a gun."

Mark shivers under his warm coat.

"I'm good."

The older man shrugs. "Suit yourself, but consider yourself warned."

Mark waits for the truck to drive out of sight before he reaches into the glove compartment and retrieves his gun. He makes sure the safety is on then secures it in his waistband.

He puts his truck in drive and heads north, following the man's directions. The dirt road is exactly where he was told it would be. But instead of turning onto it, he lets the truck idle, the cold steel gun pressed against his bare stomach. He reads Maya's message again. From seemingly out of nowhere, all the pain and anger he's tried to suppress since his parents' death wells up in his chest, and he begins to weep.

He sits behind the wheel of his truck for what seems like hours, but it's really only a few minutes. Once he composes himself, he removes the gun from his waistband and lays it on the seat next to him.

Whatever Maya's messed up with this time, he can't be a part of it. There's too much to lose. He couldn't save his parents, but he can keep Luna and Ian safe. He whips a quick U-turn and speeds down the deserted rural highway, leaving Maya behind.

75

Luna guides her car around the potholes on Main Street to Jefferson, moving slower than she prefers. On her way home at the end of a very long day, she's excited to see Ian and get in as many snuggles with him as possible before she conks out. She's not as eager to see Mark. The last twenty-four hours have been nothing short of exhausting, and Luna knows it's going to get worse before it gets better.

After breakfast, Luna went back to the office and phoned Detective Pierce. The news was disheartening. Bryan Boyd had yet to be apprehended.

"He can't hide forever," Pierce had assured her.

Luna didn't feel the least bit comforted, especially when she told her about the suspicious silver sedan she'd seen that morning.

"Did you get a plate number?"

"The car sped off too fast."

"I wouldn't worry too much. The description doesn't match any of Boyd's cars, and besides, it could be anyone, right? I can't imagine you haven't made a few enemies with your recent cases."

Luna's blood had boiled at the detective's flippant attitude and made her even less convinced she'd take Heidi's safety seriously. She was angry that the prosecutor and the detectives had put her client in this position. But what leg did she have to stand on? She promised Heidi she'd be hiding in plain sight, supporting her when she confronted Bryan, and what had she been doing? Standing outside checking text messages from Alyssa.

She held her tongue and told Pierce to keep her updated.

"I want to know the minute you get him," Luna demanded.

Luna turns onto her street but doesn't go straight home. She circles the block a few times, scanning for the suspicious silver car and also for Maya. When she's satisfied the perimeter is clear, she turns into her driveway and parks her car alongside her mother's.

Mark called her earlier that afternoon while she was on the phone with Pierce. He left her a short voice mail saying he promised to help a coworker from the recycling center move into his new apartment today. She shouldn't worry about Ian. He'd called her mom, who agreed to come over and stay with him until one of them got home. From the looks of things, Luna's made it home before Mark. With the information she has now, she doubts his absence has anything to do with a needy coworker.

Luna approaches the back door. It's slightly ajar. She sighs. Old houses in her neighborhood ooze charm, but they constantly need work. The back door had been finicky lately. Luna would need to remind her mom to double-check that the door shuts completely behind her.

The first thing Luna notices is how quiet the house is. Late afternoon and early evening are the times of the day when Ian is most rambunctious. It's not unusual for him to be tearing through the house like a tornado, leaving cars, stuffed animals, and Duplo Legos in his path of destruction. But tonight, there isn't a mess of toys that she needs to navigate around.

"Mom," Luna shouts.

"In here, sweetheart."

Luna tosses her bag on the kitchen counter and completes a few slow neck rolls before going into the living room. Her head aches at the base of her skull like something has her in a vice grip.

"Hey," Cindy says. She's lounging on the couch, reading a romance novel with a cover that makes Luna blush.

"Where's Ian?"

"Don't be angry," Cindy begs.

Luna sighs. "I hate it when you say those words to me."

"He was really tired, so I put him down for a nap."

"When was that?"

Cindy looks at her watch and frowns. "About two hours ago."

"Mom!"

"I know. I'm sorry. I should've kept a better eye on the time. But this book—" Cindy gushes.

"Really? He's going to be up all night now." Luna shakes her head and heads for the stairs. "Also, you smell like smoke," she yells over her shoulder.

"I only had two cigarettes. Check the flowerpot on the front porch if you want to count the butts," Cindy calls after her.

Luna ascends the steps, angry with her mom but worried too. Ian's not the best napper. If he's slept longer than an hour, he's probably coming down with something.

Ian's room is the first room to the left of the stairs. The first thing that quickens Luna's pulse when her feet step onto the second floor is the closed door. She never closes Ian's door, not all the way because she's paranoid about fire. Her heart beats faster when she spies a clump of dirt in front of the door. She quickly opens the door and cries out.

Ian is gone.

PART TEN

MISSING

76

The questions come fast.

What was Ian wearing? Could he be hiding somewhere in the house? Had she or her mom seen anything suspicious? Luna tries to answer the responding officer's questions with as many details as she can, but all she can think about is that Ian is gone.

Her son is missing.

It was fairly dark in Ian's bedroom when Luna had opened the door. The blinds were closed and the last bit of afternoon sunlight cast shadows throughout the room. When she didn't see him in his toddler bed, she thought he had gotten up and was playing in a dark corner of the room. But when she flipped the light switch to the left of the bedroom door on, she discovered he wasn't playing with his toys and she saw the same clumps of dirt like that had been outside his door. He wasn't anywhere in the room—only his faint scent.

From the living room, where she is pacing back and forth while the officer questions her, she hears her mom blubbering in the kitchen, trying to answer the same questions being asked of her. Luna knows she has to stay calm and think straight to make sure she doesn't miss a detail that will bring her baby home safe. Still, she shakes, and when she tries to speak, her jaw quivers. She knows all the questions are necessary to find Ian, but why hasn't the officer called for backup to canvas the neighborhood? Why is the officer, the same older man who came to her house when the brick shattered her front window, standing in front of her asking her questions and writing them down on a notepad like he's taking her dinner order? She interrupts his questioning and asks him as much.

"We've already got officers knocking on the neighbors' doors, Ms. Goldwyn. We're going to find your son," he assures her.

She chooses to believe him because, *what's the alternative?* She can't even fathom the alternative.

"You called Detectives Pierce and Whitney too?"

"Yes, ma'am. We've called them, and they're on the way. Now, you said you noticed the back door was open when you arrived home?" he asks.

"Not all the way, only slightly. I assumed my mom didn't shut it all the way."

"And you said the alarm system wasn't turned on?"

"My husband must have forgotten to turn it on when he left."

"And where is your husband right now?"

That's exactly what she wants to know, but she doesn't say this to the officer. She tells him what she's been told, "He said he was helping a friend move. I called him several times, but all my calls went straight to voice mail."

"I'll need that number," the officer tells her.

She rattles off Mark's cell number to the officer all the while thinking, *how can this be happening? It must be a nightmare.* Her phone's alarm will sound and wake her soon from this agony. She'll run to Ian's room and find him safe and warm in his bed. That's how it has to be because this can't be her reality now.

The front door bursts open and Luna jumps, clutching Ian's blanket to her chest tighter when she sees it's only Detective Pierce.

"Detective Pierce," Luna says breathlessly, "where is my son?"

The detective, usually reserved and indelicate, regards Luna with compassion. "We're going to find him. That's a promise."

"Have you arrested Boyd?" Luna asks.

"Not yet."

"He took my son."

Pierce glances at the responding officer, who puts his notepad away and goes to find his partner. When they're alone in the living room, she tells Luna, "Let's not jump to conclusions."

"Not even twenty-four hours ago, your little sting operation went horribly wrong, and this morning I'm being followed—"

"Allegedly," Pierce interrupts.

Luna steps close to Pierce and puts her finger in her face. "Don't tell me not to jump to conclusions."

Pierce sighs. "Luna, sit down."

Luna glares at the detective and stands in place. "Why aren't you taking this seriously? My child is gone. He's God knows where with God knows who. He could be hurt. He's probably so scared and confused. Don't you get it? Jesus, I never wanted this. How did this happen?"

"Listen, we're going to find your son, but let's not be shortsighted here. Like I told you this morning, you've made a few enemies. It comes with the territory when you do the work you do, and to focus on one person this early in the game is reckless. We could miss something essential."

Luna hears her. On an investigative level, she knows procedures must be followed so nothing is overlooked. But as a mother? Standing in her living room, clutching her son's blanket, not being able to go back into his room because it's a potential crime scene, she's desperate and frantic for a resolution.

"I want you to know that, as we speak, my team is gathering camera footage from your neighbors on this street and the surrounding streets. We'll get the footage from your security cameras too. Are there cameras in the house?"

Luna shakes her head. "No, only on the outside."

"Where's your husband?"

"I don't know."

"But you called him?"

"Yes, I called him, and like I told the officer, it went straight to voice mail."

"Is that usual?"

"What do you mean?"

"That his phone is off?"

"It's probably dead."

"Maybe," the detective surmises. She glances around the room before her eyes land on Luna again and asks, "Have you been having any problems?"

Luna scoffs. "You're wasting time asking me these questions. Go find my son!"

"These kinds of questions, they're delicate, I know. But they have to be asked..." the detective pauses and holds Luna's gaze, "and answered."

"Mark didn't take Ian." Luna sighs and buries her face in Ian's blanket.

"But what if he did?"

The question isn't asked by Detective Pierce but by her mother, who's standing at the edge of the living room. She walks with careful measure across the room, her arms outstretched and her eyes raw and puffy from sobbing.

"Mom, stop it. You know Mark wouldn't do something like that."

"He's been different lately."

"It's not what you think," Luna tells her, moving away from her mother's needy embrace. *If only she wouldn't have been so absorbed in that stupid book, this wouldn't have happened,* she rationalizes. Luna needs someone to blame right now.

"He's been hiding things from her," Cindy tells the detective.

"This isn't helping," Luna says to her mom. "Detective Pierce, have you called Doris? She can give you a list of people we've worked with—people who've left threats or had grievances."

"Detective Whitney is handling that part of the investigation, but now isn't the time to keep personal matters private, Luna."

"Mark would never take our son and not tell me."

"Okay, but—" Detective Pierce lets her words hang in the

air between them.

"But what?"

"Where is he now? You left a message that his son is gone, and he doesn't respond? You don't find that unusual?"

"Luna, please," Cindy begs, placing her hands on Luna's shoulders, "if you think Mark could be involved, we have to find him. We have to get Ian back."

"Mom, stop it!" She shakes her mom's hand off her. "I have no clue where Mark is, but he's not involved in this. He can't be. At least not directly."

Detective Pierce steps between Luna and her mother. "What do you mean 'not directly'?"

"It's Maya. That's the secret, Mom. She's been hanging around our place, and Mark's been keeping it from me."

"Who the hell is Maya?" Pierce asks.

Cindy gasps and puts her hands to her mouth. "No, she wouldn't. But how?"

Luna ignores them both and pushes past Pierce, making her way to the front door. She yanks a coat from the coat rack and looks around for her bag. She remembers she laid it on the kitchen counter when she'd returned home and runs through the living room to the kitchen. The uniformed officers reach for her and she pushes them away.

"Luna!" Pierce shouts.

With her bag in hand, she shoves Ian's blanket inside. Detective Pierce and her mom stand in the doorway between the kitchen and the living room.

"Where are you going?" her mom asks.

"To find my son," Luna yells.

"That's not a good idea, Luna," Pierce argues.

Luna stares pointedly at Detective Pierce. "You need to find Boyd, and if you won't do it, then I will."

"Honey, wait!" Her mother yells after her as she slams the door behind her.

Luna rushes to her car and starts the engine before shutting the driver's door. Ian is out there somewhere, and nothing is going to stop her from bringing him home.

77

The moment Mark's truck tires hit the interstate's pavement, his phone starts to vibrate persistently. Without taking his eyes off the road, he leans over and snatches the phone from the passenger seat. There are three missed calls from Luna and one from a number he doesn't recognize. He hadn't realized he didn't have service when he was driving the rural roads.

The blinking blue light in the corner of his phone indicating he has missed calls is another reminder of all the mistakes he's made over the last few months, and it's his family that has suffered. But that's all behind him now. He's leaving Maya behind and moving forward. No more sneaking around and looking over his shoulder. He loves his sister, but with Maya, there's always collateral damage. He won't put his family at risk.

Mark presses the voice mail icon on his phone's home screen and puts the phone to his ear. Luna's first message is garbled. He can't make out two words. The second message that comes through is clearer: *Mark, where are you? Call me back now!*

He glances at the time on his truck's display. The second message was left an hour ago. His pulse quickens as he waits for the third message to play, but already he knows something is terribly wrong. Luna's voice is strange, frightful and emergent.

The next words Luna speaks hit his ears like a bomb.

Gone.
Ian.
GET HOME!

Instead of heading home, Mark accelerates the truck, zooms across three lanes of traffic, and takes the next exit, crossing over the overpass and back onto the interstate in the opposite direction.

He underestimated her. How stupid and reckless to think he could ignore her and she'd leave him and his family alone. When he hired that private investigator, he only did it as a precaution, a safeguard because Luna's job had put her in the spotlight and brought more attention to the family he tried to hide. He didn't want to get blindsided and have Maya show up at his door unannounced. When the investigator told him she was in town, he didn't act fast enough. He thought he could handle the situation and keep Ian and Luna safe.

Stupid!

He slams his open palm against the steering wheel two, three, four times. He pushes his foot harder on the gas pedal, the truck's tires squealing as he races through the yellow light at the intersection and turns onto the two-lane highway that leads him back to his sister.

***

From the mobile home's back porch, she hears the truck's engine and the crunch of gravel under its tires as the truck speeds down the private drive. Much louder than the piece of crap Tucker drives, the full-throttled engine jolts Tucker's prized pit bulls, Maisy and Lucifer, from their slumber. The dogs leap to their paws and strain against their leashes. They bark out of curiosity, not as a precursor to an attack. Tucker's dogs are gentle. Besides, he doesn't need attack dogs. He has an arsenal of weapons in his shed that will get the job done if necessary.

"Shush now," Maya whispers to the dogs. They obey her command and rest on their haunches, panting and waiting patiently for the truck's engine to turn off and the visitor to make themselves known.

Maya wraps herself in the thin coat she bought for two dollars at the Salvation Army thrift store and waits too. All sorts of people show up on Tucker's property throughout the day; most are up to no good, but she knows her way around a firearm. So far, she hasn't had to prove her skill, but she always has a small handgun strapped to her waist when she's at Tucker's. She can't be too careful.

The truck's driver doesn't kill the engine, but she hears the door open and then slam shut. The driver's voice yells over the roaring engine.

"Ian!" a man's voice shouts. "Ian! Where are you?"

Maya frowns. She stands up from her smoking stool, puts out the cigarette she had just lit before the man arrived, and slides her right hand under her coat, ready to show her weapon, if it comes to that.

"Ian!" the man yells louder.

He stops shouting and begins banging hard on the trailer's front door, and Maya decides it's time to remove her weapon. Maisy and Lucifer begin to whine. With practiced stealth, she tiptoes around the creaky boards and slowly steps off the porch. Like people do in the movies, she puts her back against the trailer and slides along its backside, holding the gun close to her chest.

"Open this door now!" the man screams as he continues to pound his fists against the flimsy door.

Maya pauses for a second and knits her brows together, concentrating on the voice. Her heart pounds in her chest and her skin is abuzz with fear, but that voice. It's familiar but not recently heard. It's a voice that exists in the recesses of her mind.

The hammering on the front door stops. She hopes he's given up his search for this Ian person and is leaving, but if there's one thing Maya has learned over the years, it's that angry men never give up and leave without a fight. She releases the gun's safety mechanism and waits for the enraged man to come around the corner.

The moments seem to drag on for hours, but it's only a few

seconds before he rounds the corner and comes face-to-face with Maya and her pointed gun. The man knows her before she recognizes him, and ignoring the gun pointed at his face, he takes her by the shoulders.

"Where is he?" he yells, shaking her hard. The dogs' whining turns into a long, low synchronized growl.

Maya blinks several times, unbelieving that Mark is here. After all these years, he's standing in front of her, furious and accusing, but he's here.

"Mark," she gasps and tosses the gun to the side. She tries to wrench free from his grip to hug him, but his fingers dig mercilessly into her shoulders.

"Where is he, Maya?"

She shakes her head, confused. "Where's who?"

"Where's my son?"

78

Behind the wheel of her car, she drives for hours searching for her son, looking up and down the streets around her neighborhood for the silver sedan, pulling over only when her tears make it hard to see the road. She ignores the texts and phone calls from her mom, the detectives, and Doris. They all say the same thing.

Come home.
Let the police do their job.
You're not thinking straight.

She answers the private numbers, dreading each time she answers that she'll hear an ominous voice on the other end of the line demanding ransom or else. But the private callers are all reporters who've been listening to the police scanner and want an exclusive interview.

Not one phone call is from Mark.

Luna has no idea what she's doing, but she knows she can't sit in her house waiting for someone to find Ian. Each second that passes is another second that he's somewhere without her, scared and alone. She's played every scenario over and over again in her head, and she's come to the conclusion that there are only two people who could have her son. It's Boyd or Maya, and she has no clue where either one of them are.

Let's not be shortsighted here.

Detective Pierce's words are on repeat inside her head as she drives the streets looking for Ian. Hasn't she been shortsighted from the beginning? Since Mikey's death, she's downplayed or downright ignored the danger following her around each day. Right now, she hates Mark for keeping Maya's return a secret, but she's not without fault. She failed to fully understand the danger of her own choices. Mark was right. The people she represents aren't saints, and many people have every right to be angry at Luna for her role in the verdicts rendered. Her sanctimonious views of the law and what it means to provide fair, unbiased representation to ensure impartial justice were shortsighted. The second Tammy White's case fell into her lap, she should have known there was no turning back. Avoiding public scrutiny wasn't something that would be so easy to do, as she'd naively thought. She wasn't defending people who wrote bad checks or committed other petty crimes. Her role in emotionally charged and very public cases didn't only put her at risk, it put her family at risk. The brick through her window. The man at the restaurant during Sam Le's trial. Bryan Boyd leering at her from across the street. All of these were threats created because of her choices.

So, yes, she's furious with Mark, but she's mostly angry at herself. If she doesn't find Ian, she won't survive.

Three hours after reporting Ian missing, she turns onto Calibre Drive, the street address listed in Heidi's file. She's already driven up and down her street several times. Heidi's house is dark and certainly being surveilled, but she doesn't see any suspicious vehicles, including the silver car from Waffle House. As she makes a left turn at the end of the street and continues her patrol of the neighborhood, the squad car's lights flash on and the siren blips.

She considers ignoring the signal to stop but yields to the squad car and pulls over to the side of the street. The officer approaches her window, one hand on his revolver and the other shining a flashlight in her car.

"Luna Goldwyn?" he asks.

"Yes," she says.

The officer looks over his shoulder and a second set of headlights turns on. A shadow emerges from the unmarked vehicle, and as it approaches her car, Luna recognizes Detective Whitney.

"He's at the station."

Luna's heart misses a beat, and she cries out, "Ian!?"

"No. It's Boyd. We have him."

79

She tries to wriggle free of his grip.

"Mark, you're hurting me. Stop it!" she cries out.

"You have my attention, Maya. Now give him back."

She glares at him and shoves him hard, breaking free of his grasp when he stumbles backward.

"What the hell is wrong with you?" she shouts.

"I swear to God, if you hurt my son—"

"Your son? Jesus Christ, Mark, why would I do that? Are you mad?"

The wicked laugh that escapes from his lips surprises him. There's nothing funny about Ian missing, but he can't help himself. Is he mad? He must be because there's no other explanation for what he's doing here and the downward spiral he's taken his family on.

"I can't believe you came," Maya whispers, reaching out for him.

"Stay away from me, Maya. Tell me where Ian is. I know you have him. I know you've been stalking my family."

Maya shakes her head. "No, it's not like that at all."

"Where is he?" Marks screams at her, the words ripping at his throat like shards of glass.

"I don't know. I don't have him. He's missing?"

Maya is sobbing now, and so is Mark. *If Maya doesn't have Ian, then who does?*

"I only wanted to talk to you and didn't know how, but, my God, I would never take your son. You think I would really do that?"

Mark ignores her question and begins spinning in circles. He shoves his hand into his back pocket for his phone before remembering that he doesn't have service out here.

"Let me inside the trailer," he demands, pushing past Maya toward the back door. "I have to call Luna."

"Tucker doesn't have a landline."

"Then give me your phone."

"We try to stay off the grid out here, Mark," she says apologetically.

"I have to go," he shoves past her.

"Mark, wait, let me help. I'll help you find him."

"You've done enough as it is," Mark tells her.

She stares up at him and shakes her head. "I'm so sorry. For everything. Please, Mark."

"I don't have time for this. I have to find my son. I have to get home to Luna."

"Mark, what can I do then?"

"Stay away. That's what you can do. And if I find out you took him, so help me God, I'll—" Mark glowers at Maya but doesn't finish his sentence.

"You'll what?" she asks meekly.

He jabs his finger at her face. "Just stay away from my family."

80

Luna watches from the interrogation viewing room with her bare hands placed flat against the two-way mirror and her forehead resting against the glass. Boyd is in the interrogation room, sitting opposite her with his legs sprawled out in front of him and sipping from a plastic water bottle. He avoids looking at the mirror, knowing full well he's being watched from the other side, but does he know it's her? She wishes the walls would dissolve and allow her a moment to slip through so she could wrap her hands around his neck and strangle the information about her son's whereabouts from him.

"Stay here," Detective Pierce warned her when they brought her into the viewing room. "I know it's difficult, but you have to stay calm. It's the only way to bring Ian home sooner."

They had told Luna that they'd picked Boyd up a few streets away from her home. Preliminary security camera footage they reviewed from the neighbors' cameras had caught him driving the same model of vehicle Luna had reported seeing in the Waffle House parking lot. It was clear he'd been surveilling and driving by Luna's home, but her own security cameras failed to place him at the scene outside her back door. Somehow, he had evaded the camera and snuck in undetected.

"Was Ian in the car with him at any point?" Luna asked when

the detective caught her up at the station.

Detective Whitney shook his head. "Not that we can tell. We're working on getting clearer images of his vehicle during the time we believe the abduction occurred, but the windows are heavily tinted. We probably won't be able to see into the car."

Luna's stomach flipped over at that word—abduction.

"He has to tell us where Ian is," Luna cried.

"We'll get him to break," Whitney promised her.

Forty-five minutes. That's how long they've let Boyd sit in the tiny interrogation room alone with his thoughts before they begin questioning him. Detective Pierce goes first.

"Let's make this easy," she says. "Just tell us where the boy is."

Boyd shrugs and tugs at his shirt sleeve, fingering a loose thread. "I don't know what you're talking about."

"You took a little boy from his mother tonight."

Boyd smirks. "Um, no, I most certainly did not."

"But you were driving through Luna Goldwyn's neighborhood this evening, were you not?" Detective Whitney asked.

"I suppose you already know if I was or not. Why ask the question?"

Detective Pierce grins. "You like to play games, don't you, Bryan?"

"Only if I know I'll win."

"Tell us about Heidi May," Pierce asks.

"What about her?"

"You must be pretty angry with her."

"Why's that?"

Detective Pierce leans back in her chair and crosses her arms in front of her chest. "Let's level with each other, Bryan. We all know what happened at Swag last night. We have your confession on tape. You've been running from us like a coward for the last twenty-four hours, and here's what I think. I think you want revenge. I don't think you meant to hurt the boy. I don't even think you meant to take him, not at first, but you wanted leverage. You wanted something to negotiate with to help you find Heidi. You take her lawyer's kid, the lawyer will be desperate to have her son back safe and sound and will give up Heidi's location, and then you take care of Heidi the way you took care of that Tyler kid five years ago. Pretty basic, if you ask me."

"Here's the thing, though," Detective Whitney interjects. "Taking a little kid is next-level evilness. What happened with you and Tyler—listen, between you and me, I get it. The little asshole had what was coming to him, but a little boy? What did he ever do to you?"

Boyd leans forward in his chair and runs his hands through his hair. "I didn't take the boy," he says again.

"But you were in the neighborhood. So, what did you want?"

"To talk to her. That's all."

"Talk to who?" Detective Pierce asks.

"That lawyer bitch," he shouts

"Why did you want to talk to her?" Detective Whitney probes.

Boyd looks between the two detectives and shakes his head. "It doesn't matter."

"Come on, Bryan. Help us out here," Pierce says.

The man laughs and slams his hand on the table. Luna jumps back from the two-way mirror. "I should have tied up loose ends years ago."

"What do you mean?"

He shrugs. "You know what I think?"

"What's that, Bryan?" Whitney asks like they're old friends.

"I think I want a lawyer."

Pierce stands up and walks behind Boyd, and Whitney shakes his head. "Come on, man. Don't be like that. Let's handle this between us."

Luna's heart clinches. The interrogation is over, and Ian's still missing, but the detectives aren't giving up.

"Tell us where the boy is."

"I didn't take the kid," Boyd yells. "Maybe it was that woman."

"What woman?"

"How the hell am I supposed to know? All I planned to do was grab that bitch lawyer. Scare her a little, you know? Tell her to tell Heidi to back off. I couldn't get to her at her office, so I waited for her to get home."

"How'd you know where she lived?"

Bryan laughs. "I work in real estate. I know my way around property records. Anyway, she took forever to get home and I had to take a piss. I ran up to the gas station on Elm, and when I came back about thirty minutes later, the whole house was lit up with cop cars."

"Tell us about the woman," Whitney says.

"Not much to tell. Just some lady hanging across the street for a while until she walked in front of my car and around to the back of the house. That was right before I left to go take a leak."

"Convenient," Whitney suggests.

"Was this the woman?" Pierce puts her phone in front of Boyd, presumably showing him the photo of Maya that Luna had forwarded to her when she got to the station.

Bryan shakes his head. "No, the woman I saw was older."

"Older?"

"Yeah, mid to late forties. Thinner and taller." Boyd reaches for his water bottle and finishes off the remaining liquid. "Alright, guys, it's been fun, but that's it for me. Looks like you got a kid to find, so why don't you get me that lawyer and leave me the fuck alone?"

Pierce takes her phone back and looks up at the two-way mirror, focusing on where Luna stands. The same question resides in both their eyes: *What other woman?*

81

He finally cried himself to sleep in the car seat. Stubborn like her own boy had been, she remembers. She couldn't soothe him or comfort him with lullabies or bedtime stories. He had to cry out his frustration and fall asleep on his own. She can already tell that this little boy is the same, but she'll do better by him. She'll keep him safe and won't let anything bad ever happen. Not like what happened to her boy.

But first she has to get him to the cabin.

She'd spent the last few weeks getting it ready for his arrival. She had cleared the cobwebs from the ceiling and light fixtures, wiped down the dusty windows, and swept away the rodent feces that had collected in the rooms' corners over the years. Little by little, she decorated the child's room, the convertible crib in the far corner away from the drafty windows, an Amish-crafted hickory rocking chair on the opposite wall, the four walls painted a soothing pale blue and decorated with framed animal prints that spelled out her son's name: I-A-N. This is only their temporary home, but she wants to make it comfortable while they're here. In a few weeks, when their new passports get delivered, they'll travel 900 miles to the property she's secured in Parry Sound, a town two hours north of Toronto and on the sound's eastern shore. When she was a child, she spent her summers on the sound at her grandmother's home, exploring the Georgian Bay waterfront and the town's hidden nooks and crannies. It's an idyllic place to raise a child.

The drive to the cabin took a little over two hours, and exhaustion is creeping up on her. She's drank two energy drinks and opened the windows to let in cool blasts of air, but her eyes keep wanting to close. Finally, when she's certain she'll have to pull off to the side of the road for a short nap, the cabin's driveway is in sight, and relief washes over her—not because she can finally shut her eyes and curl up in bed and rest. The relief she feels is more monumental because she and her son are finally home.

PART ELEVEN

STOLEN JUSTICE

82

Luna pushes the white foam coffee cup off to the side of the table in the lawyer-client meeting room. She refuses Detective Pierce's offers of snacks from the vending machine, and the scratchy blanket a young uniformed officer brought lays untouched on the floor next to her chair. Any offers of comfort are repudiated. Until Ian is found, Luna can't think about eating, drinking, or, God forbid, sleeping. On the other side of the meeting room's wall, Boyd is being booked, but she's still no closer to finding her son.

Doris sits across from Luna, a bleak, concerned expression on her face. "You really should try to eat something. You need—"

"I need my son, and I need my goddamn husband to call me!" Luna snaps.

"Oh, Luna . . ."

"I also don't need your pitying looks. That's getting us nowhere. Did you call Alyssa?"

Doris nods. "She's says she never saw a woman matching Boyd's description near your home when she was tailing Mark."

"Fuck!"

"She said she'd contact Quinn Snow right away, see if she'll do her a professional courtesy and share any information she has about a woman matching that description when she was surveilling for Mark."

"And the list?"

"I've given the detectives the name of every client since Mikey hired you."

"Do you have your laptop with you?"

Doris reaches for her bag on the floor next to her chair and pulls out her laptop. "What do you need?"

Luna closes her eyes, concentrating, and pinches the bridge of her nose. Her stomach has been doing somersaults since she got to the station. Stuck in the police station feeling helpless and scared out of her mind, she fluctuates between feeling like she's going to throw up and wanting to punch the wall. She places her hands on the table in front of her and steadies her breath. She has to focus. It's the only thing she can do right now to find her son and bring him home.

"Boyd said there was a woman at my house before he left to go to the gas station. My mom confirmed with the detectives that she didn't have any visitors over to the house while she was watching Ian. If what Boyd says is true, we need to narrow the list. Let's identify the names of any woman—client or family member of a client—who fits the description: approximately fifty to sixty years old, tall and thin. I know it's like finding a needle in the haystack, but we have to start somewhere, right?" Luna's unable to keep her voice from quivering.

Doris reaches across the table and takes both of Luna's hands in hers, squeezing them gently. "It's a good place to start."

Before Luna can tell her she hopes they're not looking in the wrong direction, the meeting room door opens.

"Mark!" Luna cries out. She leaps to her feet and runs into his arms, momentarily forgetting her anger. She sobs against his chest then pulls away from him abruptly.

"Where have you been?" she demands.

"Oh Luna, I'm so sorry. I should have been honest with you months ago," he cries.

Luna gazes up into his tearful eyes and asks, "Does Maya have Ian?"

A sob that sounds like a hiccup catches in his throat. "You know about Maya?"

"Mark, does Maya have our son?" she asks again with more urgency. She doesn't have time for apologies and regret. That's for later when Ian is home, in her arms, warm and safe in their home.

"No. I don't think so."

"What do you mean, you don't think so? Do you know where she is, Mark? We have to tell the detectives now."

He nods. "I already did, and that's where I was when you left me those messages."

"You talked to her?"

"Not at first. I was going to, and then I realized she can't take back the damage she's done, and it is best to ignore her. I turned my truck around to come home, but then I got your messages, and—I was so scared, Luna. I didn't want to believe she'd take him, but she'd been around the house, and I don't know, I thought *maybe*? Maybe she did it to get my attention. So, I went back to the property where she's staying and confronted her. I was so angry. Luna, I didn't know I had that kind of anger in me. But—"

"Ian wasn't there," she finishes.

Mark shakes his head, and Luna groans. A little bit of her still held out hope that Ian was with Maya because, as messy as her relationship was with Mark, Luna couldn't imagine she'd physically harm his son, her nephew. But if Maya didn't have him, then all bets were off, and Ian could be in real danger.

"I should've called you back right away. The detectives will go out to double-check her story—and mine—but she doesn't have him, Luna. I'm sure of it."

Tears spring to her eyes again. She hates feeling helpless, stuck in this bleak, overheated room with no answers. She pushes past Mark, on her way to demand the detectives do more. *Why aren't they doing more?* She's almost to the door when the floor begins undulating under her feet, tipping up and down, moving side to side like a fun house floor. She hears Mark say her name, but she ignores him, concentrating instead on the door that, little by little, is getting smaller until it's no bigger than a keyhole, and then everything goes dark.

83

She lies in the darkness on the twin-size bed in the cabin's second bedroom trying to soothe the distressed little boy. Once she got Ian out of his car seat and inside the cabin, he'd woken up immediately and had alternated between howling cries and soft whimpering for at least two hours, maybe more. She can't say for certain because, between the boy's crying and her exhaustion, time had eluded her. All she knows for certain is, at present, he's curled in a fetal position facing away from her in the bed sniffling and sucking this thumb while she rubs his back and tells him not to worry.

"Mommy's here," she reassures him.

He whimpers again, and she sighs. *It will be a transition*, she tells herself. It will take time for them to get to know each other and find a rhythm, but he's young, and soon enough, he'll know her as Mommy. It's how it was meant to be. She has to be patient.

Her body is spent, worn-out from weeks of planning and months of grief. She'd been certain that once she was here at the cabin with the boy that she'd finally rest and sleep sound again without worry or sorrow, but each time she closes her eyes, she sees her firstborn. Behind her closed eyes, his short life plays out in drawn-out sequences that clench her heart and threaten to smother her with misery.

The pain will subside, eventually. It has to because she has *this* little boy to care for now, and no one will take him away from her. That she knows for sure. But right now, she needs to get some rest. She turns on her side, opens the nightstand's single draw, and takes out the bottle of Xanax she had refilled before she left and taps out one pill. *Not two*, she reminds herself. When the sun rises, she must be alert and not even a little bit groggy. One pill it is then, placed at the back of her tongue and swallowed without water. She closes her eyes and waits for the warm feeling to fall upon her and bring her a little peace.

84

"Try just a bit," Mark pleads. He tries to give Luna one of the bite-sized candy bars that came from a plastic bowl on Pierce's desk filled with an assortment of leftover Halloween candy.

She sips orange juice from a plastic bottle and says, "This is fine. I'm feeling much better. How long was I out?"

"Just a few minutes." The voice belongs to Tom, one of the paramedics who responded to the 911 call when Mikey keeled over at his desk. He's kneeling in front of her and studying her like she's an interesting exhibit at the art museum, an abstract piece he can't quite figure out.

"How did you get here so fast?" she asks.

"I was bringing my wife a late dinner. We're both working doubles tonight." He gestures to a thirty-something slender and blond uniformed police officer standing in the hallway outside of the meeting room. Detectives Pierce and Whitney are in the hallway too. It seems her fainting episode brought out a crowd of spectators.

"Oh," Luna says. Her throat feels scratchy, and she still feels a little woozy.

"You really do need to eat something," Tom advises. "With all you're going through right now, eating and drinking is important. You need every ounce of energy you can ingest to get through this."

Luna nods and accepts the candy from Mark. She removes the wrapper, puts the candy to her lips and grimaces. It tastes like bark, but she chews and swallows it anyway.

"Luna, I think you should go home," Detective Pierce speaks up. "There's nothing you can do here. We're working every angle. There's a team of officers heading out to speak with your sister-in-law right now, and we're meticulously going through the list you gave us of past clients. Right now, the best thing to do is to go home. Keep the television off, avoid social media, and get some rest. We have officers patrolling the area around the clock in case the person who took Ian had a change of heart and decides to bring him home."

"Does that really happen?" A sliver of hope rushes through her body, or perhaps it's only the sugar from the orange juice and candy. Is the likelihood of that even plausible? Detective Whitney looks down at his feet, avoiding Luna's gaze.

"Let's stay positive," Pierce answers.

"I'll stay here and answer any questions they have," Doris assures her, placing a delicate hand on Luna's shoulder.

"Come on, Luna," Mark slides his forearms under her armpits and helps her to her feet. "Do you feel steady?"

She leans against him for a moment to ensure her balance is sound and that the floor won't start tipping side to side again. "It's okay. I can walk by myself."

Pierce and Whitney lead the group down the hall, away from the interview rooms and back into the main office space that smells of weed, burnt coffee, and body odor. Whitney directs Doris to an unoccupied desk in the far corner of the room.

"I'll call you soon," Doris promises before crossing the room to the desk.

"It's better if you and Mark leave through the side entrance," Pierce suggests. "It's a secured, gated entrance. You'll avoid the reporters and looky-loos that way. It's this way," she says, pointing to a door adjacent to a door with a frosted window that leads to the reception area.

Before they reach the side door, the reception door opens

and a short, overweight, and balding uniformed officer appears. His cheeks are flushed, and he's agitated.

"There's some guy out here insisting he speak with someone important immediately," the officer huffs. "Says his wife's missing."

Pierce shakes her head. "I don't have time for this tonight. Can't you just take his statement?"

The officer shakes his head. "I'm training the new hire in dispatch because Colson's home with the shits, and we're short-staffed tonight looking for that boy."

That boy. Is that all Ian is to these people? That boy? Luna narrows her eyes at the officer, and Mark slides his hand into hers.

"Landry, just find someone to do it!" Pierce barks at him.

Officer Landry looks around Pierce, his eyes falling on Luna and Mark. His cheeks turn a deeper shade of crimson. "I'll take care of it," he says apologetically.

Luna glares at him and watches him leave, but when he opens the door, a tall male figure catches her eye. He's standing at the reception counter, tapping the fingers of his left hand on the counter like he's playing the same four notes over and over again on a piano and rubbing his jaw with his other hand. He looks vaguely familiar to her.

"Wait!" she calls out. "Is that the man whose wife is missing?"

Landry nods. "Yeah, but she's probably some hot young thing who's tired of dealing with some rich prick and is out having a little fun. You know what I mean?"

Pierce gives him a stern look before addressing Luna, "What's wrong?"

"I've seen him somewhere before."

"You have? Where?"

Luna closes her eyes and tries to remember. What comes to mind first are a set of courtroom steps, a poorly fitted suit, an outstretched hand, and then—

She gasps and puts her hand to her mouth.

"What is it?" Marks asks.

"It's Logan Rees's father."

***

Adam Rees wears a gray suit and a black button-down shirt, open at the neck, but nonetheless, too formal an outfit for a visit to the police station in the middle of the night. His weedy frame fits awkwardly in the steel, armless chair, his hands clasped tightly in a fist between his outstretched legs that extend into the narrow space between the rows of desks, the tips of his black leather Oxford shoes touching an unoccupied desk's leg.

"How long has your wife been missing?" Pierce asks from behind her desk.

"I'm not sure, but she didn't pick up Allison from school this afternoon. So, at least since three o'clock," he says.

"And Allison is?"

"She's our daughter. She's five, a kindergartener. My assistant received a call from the school when they couldn't reach my wife."

"And one more time for me, what's your wife's name?"

"Sandra."

"Same last name?"

He nods.

Pierce looks down at her notepad and writes something before resuming her questioning. "Is it unusual for your wife to forget to pick up Allison?"

"No. Well, not usually, but since our son died—was murdered—," he looks directly at Luna, "she's been different. She sits in his room for hours, loses track of time, and won't speak to anyone. So, at first, that's what I thought might have happened. That she had one of her moments and lost track of time."

"But that's not what happened?" Pierce prompts.

He shakes his head. "No."

"Is it possible your wife met up with a friend and communications were crossed?"

"No, my assistant is very good at managing our schedules."

Pierce smiles. "Or, perhaps she left town and didn't want you to know? Have you been having marital problems?"

"I've called all her friends, our mutual friends, and her sister, Carol. No one has heard from her. I found her phone lying on the kitchen table."

"Could she have another phone?"

He shrugs. "I don't know."

Pierce narrows her eyes at Adam. "What aren't you telling me?"

Before answering, he peers at Luna again. His face is sorrowful, colored with regret. His doleful gaze makes her body tingle with alarm.

"I think Sandra might have had something to do with your son's disappearance."

"Oh my God!" Luna whispers.

In a flash, she remembers her interaction with Logan's mom in front of the courthouse the day of opening statements at Sam Le's murder trial. Luna had been running late because of an accident on the interstate and was rushing to get inside the courtroom to have time to prepare when Sandra had surprised her from behind.

How do you sleep at night?

Those were the first words out of her mouth. Then she said: *You have a son, don't you?*

You have a son.

I have a son, Luna thinks, and *she has him. Oh my God, that woman has my son.* Elation and fear rush through her body. This is a solid lead. One that makes sense, but Pierce doesn't pounce on the idea as fast. She edges around the possibility carefully.

"Why is that, Mr. Rees?"

"When the man got away with our son's murder—"

"He was found not guilty," Luna interrupts. Pierce shoots her a silencing look, and Mark squeezes her hand.

Adam Rees ignores her outburst and continues, "When Sam Le was set free, that's when she became more and more withdrawn and more interested in her." He points at Luna.

"How so?"

"She started following her."

Luna gasps. This is news to her. Except for Boyd's silver sedan following her to Waffle House, she hadn't noticed any other unusual vehicles following her since Sam's trial, and Alyssa hadn't seen anyone other than Maya around the house either.

"How do you know this?" Pierce asks.

"Several weeks after the trial, I suggested we go out to dinner. We'd been held hostage in our home and our grief for months. Logan's death—how do I say this?—it tore us apart into tiny pieces. I don't know how to describe the loss in any other way except than it's this blinding, searing pain that never goes away." Luna swallows hard. She doesn't want to imagine how that might feel but she can't help to think about what life would be like without Ian. It would break her. She knows this without any doubt. "But after the trial," Adam continues. "I thought maybe we could start to rebuild our life. At dinner, I planned to tell Sandra that we should sell the house, leave the area, and go somewhere new to make a fresh start and give Allison the normal childhood she deserves. Anywhere she wanted. It didn't matter. But we never made it to dinner. Instead, she asked me to drive across the river. She said she wanted to show me something.

"So, I drove, and I didn't ask questions. She seemed happier, excited about something. It made me feel hopeful that maybe the dark cloud she'd been under was starting to disappear. She directed me to park in front of a two-story brick home in this quaint, tree-lined neighborhood and said, 'This is it.' 'This is what?' I asked. She told me this was the house of the woman who stole justice for her son, who helped free his murderer. I asked her how she knew this, and she said she'd been following her for weeks. She'd even met her son."

"What?!" Luna cries out. "When?"

Adam turns to her and says, "It was Halloween. She said she talked to you and your son was in a dog costume. I think that's what she said."

"She was the masked woman!" Luna exclaims. She gazes up at Mark and shakes her head. "I remember she said she didn't have children, but -oh my God- I can't believe this. It can't be."

"I remember," Mark says. "I thought it was Maya trying to get close to us."

"What happened when you were parked in front of Ms. Goldwyn's house?" Pierce asks him.

Adam makes a long face and looks up at the ceiling. Seconds drag on before he speaks, and when he does, he confirms what Luna has already begun to suspect, "She reaches into the back seat and retrieves this brick. I don't even know where it came from or how it got into the car in the first place, but all of a sudden, she's holding this brick. She tells me to be ready to drive as soon as she gets in the car, don't wait for her to shut the door—just drive. Before I could even comprehend fully the gist of what's about to happen, she opens the car door, climbs out of the passenger seat, stands on the sidewalk, and throws that brick straight at the front window."

"And then what?" Pierce prods.

"She ran back to the car, jumped in, and I drove away."

"Seems to me that makes you an accessory after the fact. Can we assume you don't only suspect she took Ms. Goldwyn's son, but that you know exactly where she took him?"

"No," Adam insists, unclenching his fists and sitting up straighter. "It's a hunch. That's all. After that night, I tried to get her help. I arranged for her to stay at one of those wellness rehabilitation retreat centers. The kind that celebrities go to when they're having mental breakdowns, but she wouldn't have it. She was spiraling out of control. Not eating, barely speaking to me, and becoming increasingly agitated with Allison. God, poor Allison. Not only did she lose her brother, but Sandra's seemed to have forgotten about her in all this."

Pierce narrows her eyes. "What do you mean *agitated*?"

Adam lowers his head and rubs at his jaw like he'd been doing earlier in the lobby. "Sandra had made Logan's room into a shrine. She refused to let anyone go in it, even me. It was a space only she could enter. But one day Allison had a friend over, and they were playing hide and seek, and Allison decided to hide in Logan's bedroom, under his bedcovers. When Allison's friend couldn't find her, she came to Sandra and me for help. We were calling for her and heard giggling coming from Logan's room. Sandra was enraged. I implored her to wait outside the room, calm down, and let me handle it, but she ignored me. She burst through the door, flung back the covers, dragged Allison out of the bed, stood her upright, and smacked her hard across the face. It was horrible."

Luna puts her head in her hands. Sandra's violent, irrational tendencies make her fear for Ian's well-being even more.

"There's also the credit card charges," Adam continues.

"What kind of charges?"

"She's been purchasing items from baby boutiques. One purchase was roughly five hundred dollars."

"Was anything delivered to the house?"

"No, not that I ever saw. But that five-hundred-dollar purchase was for a crib. I called to find out where it was delivered, and the shop gave me the address for a storage facility in south St. Louis."

"I'm going to need a copy of your credit card statements right away, Mr. Rees, and the address to the storage facility."

"Of course, I'll do that—"

"Now," Pierce says. "Also, do you and your wife own any vacation homes or other properties other than your primary home?"

"We have a second home at the Lake of the Ozarks and another smaller property in Colorado Springs, but that's an investment property."

"What about your wife? Does she own properties separate from the ones you share?"

"I don't think so."

Pierce snaps her fingers in front of the ragged man's face. "Think harder. Do her parents own properties? Her siblings?"

"Sandra's parents are dead, and they didn't leave anything behind for her. They died poorer than when they came into this world, but her sister had a cabin. Sandra would take Logan when he was little, and I was out of town. She enjoyed spending time with her sister, and Logan liked playing in the woods, catching frogs and turtles in summer and hearing the leaves crunch under his feet in the fall." His voice shakes, and he clears his throat before saying, "But that was years ago. Carol got divorced, moved to Connecticut with her new lover, and, for all I know, the cabin was sold."

"Well, we have ways of finding things out, including if you're lying to us and buying your wife more time to make her escape."

"I swear on my son's grave that I'm not lying. I'm worried about my wife, and I'm worried that if she has that child," he looks directly at Luna and Mark, "if she has your son, she'll disappear, and we'll never see either of them again."

Luna fears the same thing.

85

Morning arrives quicker than she anticipated, and to Sandra's surprise, when she opens her eyes, Ian is sitting up in bed staring at her with dry eyes and a curious look. She lifts her head from the pillow and sits up slowly, taking care not to startle the boy. The last thing she needs is for him to start crying again.

"Good morning, sweet boy. Are you hungry?" she asks.

Ian sticks his fingers in his mouth and sucks on them enthusiastically, saliva dribbling down his chin and onto the front of his shirt. The suckling sounds make her stomach turn. *We're going to have to break that habit.* But first things first. The boy needs breakfast, and Sandra needs coffee to absorb the lingering effects of the Xanax.

She manages to get Ian into the high chair at the breakfast table with relative ease, and to her delight, he eats a few bites of the oatmeal she made before he pushes the bowl away. Yes, all they need is a little time to get to know one another. By the time they get to Parry Sound, they'll be a happy little duo.

After breakfast, Sandra changes Ian's clothes, dressing him in a warm red sweater with a reindeer on the front and light-washed, cuffed jeans. She's pleased at how well the outfit fits him. It was one of her favorite outfits she had dressed Logan in when he was Ian's age. She kisses Ian's forehead and then pulls out a basket of toys from behind the sofa in the living room.

"Look what Mommy has for you?" She pulls out a toddler-sized fire truck with a removable hose, a firefighter figure, and a fire dog, places it on the floor in front of Ian, and makes a *vroom-vroom* sound. "Do you like it?"

Ian grabs the fire truck with both hands and stands up. He takes it under the kitchen table and pushes it back and forth on the hardwood floor, making the same sounds Sandra had made.

"That's a good boy," she tells him. "Stay here and play while I run outside for a moment."

While Ian plays with the fire truck, she gathers his old clothes and a box of matches. She walks outside to a rusted barrel that she and her sister used to make fires in. The last time they made a fire in this barrel was the last time they'd come to the cabin together. Carol had dumped a boxful of wedding photos into it and they toasted to new beginnings while the once-happy memories went up in flames.

Sandra fills the barrel with small sticks and branches and then retrieves a bottle of lighter fluid from her car's trunk. She douses the kindling with the fluid, strikes a match, and tosses it into the barrel. The fire erupts and warms Sandra's cheeks. Bits of charred leaves float out of the barrel and drift away for a second before they pendulate to the ground. In one swift motion, she steps closer to the barrel and tosses Ian's clothing into the blaze. The flame and smoke work quickly destroying the fibers, and Sandra expels a sigh of relief.

PART TWELVE

MOTHERS AND SONS

86

Within an hour of learning that Sandra Rees might be responsible for Ian Goldwyn's disappearance, the police station is crawling with detectives and uniformed cops working on verifying Adam Rees's story. Pierce has a bottle of ibuprofen opened on her desk, a tall tumbler of bitter coffee in her left hand, and she is wearing an exasperated expression while cradling her phone between her right ear and shoulder.

"Louie, let's not drag this out," she grumbles.

Louie, Luna has learned, is the owner of the storage facility where Sandra had the suspicious credit card purchases sent to. She can't hear what he's saying, but given Pierce's frustration, she deduces he's not keen on cooperating with her request to let the uniforms waiting at the storage facility into the unit to search it.

"There's a little boy missing. Is your renter's privacy worth a child being harmed?"

Pierce is quiet for a few seconds, listening to Louie on the other end. Without warning, she leans forward in her chair and bangs the stainless steel tumbler on the table, startling Luna.

"You have two choices," she yells into the phone. "Cooperate and let my officers in the storage unit now, or I'll call the judge and get a warrant. And you know what, Louie?

That warrant won't just be for searching Ms. Rees's storage unit. It will also include the full search and seizure of your offices."

She pauses, letting Louie consider the deal. A few seconds later, she smiles and says, "See, I knew we could work something out."

She ends the call and turns to Luna and Mark. "As soon as my officers get into the unit, we'll find out what's in there, if anything. But, really, that's more for evidence collection for later when—"

"Ian is safe at home and Sandra's in custody," Luna interrupts.

"That's the goal. Right now, our top priority is figuring out the location of the cabin. Whitney," she shouts across the room, "have you gotten a hold of Sandra's sister?"

Whitney nods and yells back, "I just texted you the GPS coordinates. It's in a rural, heavily wooded area about two hours north of here."

"Neighbors?"

"The nearest ones she's aware of are about twenty minutes west of the cabin. There's a stream nearby that sometimes attracts fishermen who are backcountry camping, but other than that, it's isolated. I'm pulling up a topographic map right now to get a better idea of the area."

"That's good. Also, let local law enforcement know we're headed up. Get a meeting spot secured."

"As we speak!"

"When do we leave?" Luna asks.

"*We*," Pierce gestures at Mark and Luna then points to herself, "aren't going anywhere. You two need to go home and let us do our jobs."

"We're not going home without our son," Marks insists, putting his arm around Luna and pulling her close to him.

"He's right," Luna says. "We don't go home until Ian comes home with us."

Pierce leans forward in her chair and surprises Luna by taking her hands. She holds her gaze for an uncomfortable moment before saying, "I'm not a parent, so I can't begin to understand the depth of the pain you feel right now. I do have nieces and nephews, and I know if they were missing, you couldn't stop me from wanting to do everything I could to find them. But, Luna, here's what I know because it's part of the job: These situations can turn on a dime. What seems like an easy hostage rescue and suspect apprehension sometimes doesn't end the way we hoped it would."

Luna shakes her head and snatches her hands away from Pierce's loose grip. "Sandra wouldn't hurt Ian."

"Are you sure? When people get cornered, they get desperate. They do things they normally wouldn't think twice about doing."

Luna cringes. She knows Logan's death has caused Sandra to snap, but she can't bring herself to believe that she would hurt Ian. Then again, hadn't Adam said that Sandra had lost her temper with Allison, dragging her from Logan's bed and slapping her across the face?

"You're scaring me," Luna says.

"It's better to go home and wait," Pierce tells her.

"Wait for what?" Marks asks.

Pierce looks up at him. "For us to do our jobs, and to bring your son home."

Luna looks up at her husband and he nods. His eyes are fearful and wide, angry and dark, and completely telling. They're both scared, but she also knows that there's not a chance in hell of them going home and waiting.

"I'm sorry, Detective, but whether it's with you or by our own accord, we're going to that cabin one way or another."

87

Luna's heart pounds as the detective's unmarked vehicle bounces along the narrow dirt road. Naked tree limbs brush against the sides of the car and strike the windows every so often. The road's potholes have filled from a drenching overnight rain, and every couple of minutes, the car's tires hit the deep depressions, causing it to rock forcefully from the impact. The journey to the remote cabin seems never-ending, and Luna worries that the longer it takes to get to it, the greater the likelihood of Sandra deciding to leave it and flee with Ian. They can't afford a blown tire, but they can't afford to amble along the road either. They have no time to lose.

"How much longer?" Luna asks Pierce from the back seat.

She doesn't answer. Instead, Whitney turns around in his seat to look her in the eyes. "It shouldn't be much longer. The maps show a turnoff about five hundred feet from the driveway to the cabin."

They ride in silence for several more minutes until Pierce slows the car to a crawl and turns off the road into a heavily wooded area. She puts her car in park and waits for the other vehicles in the procession to pull off the road. Within seconds, a cluster of law enforcement officials emerge from the entourage and assemble at the front of the car. Luna stifles a gasp at the site of the officers, all dressed head to toe in black, wearing bulletproof vests and sporting guns on their hips.

"You're not going into that cabin with guns drawn, are you?" Luna asks. Unease slithers up her spine, cold and serpentine. Next to her, Mark's unshaven jaw trembles with notable concern.

"We know how to handle situations like this," Pierce says impatiently.

"Putting our son in the middle of a shoot-out is not handling it," Mark says, his voice rising with each annunciation. The detectives ignore Mark's remarks and unbuckle their seatbelts. "Hey," he shouts, smacking his open palms against Whitney's seat back. "Are you listening to me? Walking into that cabin with guns drawn is a mistake."

Whitney sighs, opens his door, and exits the vehicle. Pierce turns around in her seat, nostrils flared, and glares at Luna and Mark. "This is why I told you to go home. I should have never let you come."

"Can't you try reasoning with her?" Luna begs.

"What makes you think we can reason with a woman who's been stalking you and throwing bricks through your window, huh? She broke into your house last night and kidnapped your child. The time for reasoning has long past, Luna."

"But Ian will be so scared. There's got to be a better way," Luna argues.

"No doubt he's already scared. That's certain. But you want him home, right? We know how to do our jobs. Taking Sandra by surprise works in our favor. Detective Whitney and I, along with our team, will do everything in our power to get Ian out of that cabin safely."

Pierce gets out of the car but before shutting the door, she adds, "You have to trust us, and under no circumstances are you to leave this vehicle. That was our deal. Understood?"

Luna takes Mark's hand and nods. The reason Pierce had relented and let them ride along was because they had agreed to stay in the car and out of the officers' way. They'd be nearby and ready to receive Ian as soon as the rescue mission was complete.

It was a reasonable request that Luna had been willing to comply with at the station, but not anymore. There's no way she's going to put Ian in the line of fire. She just has to get to him before the detectives do.

***

The forest air smells damp and musty and imbued with a bonfire scent. Although the forest floor is soggy, the leaves still rustle underfoot and force Luna and Mark to slow their strides. The last thing they want is to bring attention to themselves, to spook Sandra or alert Pierce and her team that they've gone rogue. They waited to exit Pierce's car until the group of detectives and officers were out of sight, and then they ran to the main road, walking just inside the tree line, following the blue arrow on Luna's phone. She had peeked at the GPS coordinates Whitney had entered into Pierce's dashboard navigation system when they left the station and put them into her own phone's GPS app. With each step she takes, she prays she doesn't lose service, but her map shows that the cabin's location is just off the main road and only about a quarter of a mile from where they are now. Luna's confident she can get there without the map's guidance, if necessary.

"Luna, wait!" Mark says in a hushed tone. She stops as he places a hand on her shoulder. "I think you should go back."

Luna gives him a quizzical look before shrugging off his hand and trudging forward. "That's not happening."

"Stop for a minute, won't you? Look, Pierce is right. We're not going to be able to reason with that woman. I—I can't lose you both."

"Don't say that," Luna whisper-shouts without slowing her pace. "Ian is coming home. We're all going home together—today. Do you hear me?"

Marks sighs loud. "Pierce and her team have a lot of firepower. We don't want to get caught in the crossfire. Just be careful. That's all I'm saying."

Luna nods and continues to walk in the direction of the

cabin's driveway, swatting away the tree limbs that block her path and stepping around stumps and underbrush. The midmorning sun has risen higher above the horizon and is now shining between the trees, blinding her periodically. She knows she has no business being in the woods, but there's no way she can sit back and wait. What mother could do that? Even though she knows she's not responsible for Ian's kidnapping, it's a result of her job that put him in this situation.

After a few more minutes of plodding through the forest, Luna spies the cabin's driveway, and with most of the trees stripped bare of their leaves, she's able to see the outline of the small cabin, set back several yards from the driveway's turnoff. Before crossing the road, she scans the area around the cabin looking for Pierce and her team. She doesn't see them, but that doesn't mean they aren't around. She says a quick prayer to God, the Universe, Buddha, and any other entity listening to help her get inside the cabin and grab Ian without being noticed.

88

Except for the *vroom-vroom* sounds Ian makes while playing with his new fire truck, he's been quiet most of the morning. Sandra catches him staring at her curiously every once and a while, but then he goes back to playing. She tries not to make comparisons, but he's not at all like Logan at his age. When Logan was little, he rarely sat still. He was a bundle of constant energy, always overstimulated and reactive. Movies, story time at the library, even sitting in the cart at the grocery store were impossible for him to get through without him throwing a temper tantrum because he was antsy and bored.

Logan's behaviors bothered Adam, and he told Sandra as much on several occasions, especially when Logan started school and the notes from teachers about his bullying behaviors toward other students became a weekly occurrence. *Don't you see there's a problem?* Adam had asked her. *Leanne has recommended a wonderful counselor who specializes in behavioral problems in children.* Sandra dismissed his concerns. After all, he wasn't home much. What did he really know? And the last thing she was going to do was take a recommendation from the assistant he was screwing. Logan was a spirited child, highly intelligent, and sensitive, much like she had been as a child. The teachers never understood her, and they didn't understand her baby.

The teachers weren't the only ones hell-bent on bad-mouthing her son. After Logan was murdered, the media turned against him too, spreading lies and falsehoods about him on the nightly news, in the newspapers, and online. The comments on the online boards were the worse. People hiding behind their computers and anonymity condemned her son, writing how he had been harassing Black students at the school, calling them horrible names, and even defacing their cars in the school parking lot. The commenters weren't surprised by what happened in Sam Le's lighting store. In fact, many of them supported Le and, in very clear terms, said her son had it coming to him.

The assistant prosecutor hadn't done much to dispel these untruths. She'd been unable to get the video and audio evidence of Logan and his friends in Sam Le's shop thrown out. Sandra doesn't like to think about that though. The evidence didn't paint Logan in the best light. She'll admit that, but he wasn't the only one calling Sam Le names. Names that, if she were being honest, were names she had called Asian people from time to time herself, especially growing up. Kids say stupid things, but that doesn't mean they deserve to die, does it?

But really, the person most responsible for not getting her son justice isn't the prosecutor or the media. It's Sam Le's lawyer. Every time she thinks of that woman, she remembers her fake pity. The words she spoke to her outside the courthouse: *I'm so sorry for your loss.*

No, she wasn't sorry for Sandra's loss. She could've cared less. Those were empty words spoken by a woman who had no idea what loss was. How losing a child gutted you, leaving you swollen and bleeding, dying a slow, unmerciful death.

Sandra's eyelids grow heavy. The bright light shining through the window and the lingering effects of last night's restless sleep make her sleepy. *A short nap won't hurt,* she thinks as she walks over to the love seat in the corner of the room.

"Mommy's going to close her eyes just for a second. Okay, baby? Play nicely with your new toys," she tells Ian. He continues to play with the truck in front of the cabin's large picture window and ignores her.

Sandra sighs, pulls a throw blanket from the back of the love seat, and curls up on the short sofa, tucking her sockless feet under her and wrapping the blanket around her shoulders. As she lies her head on the love seat's arm, she's lulled to sleep with one thought.

The woman who freed my son's murderer will know loss now.

89

Luna and Mark managed to cross the main road to the cabin's driveway unseen, and now they crouch low with their backs against the trunk of a thick oak tree. The woods surrounding the cabin has fewer trees, and the thorns from the thick prickly undergrowth dig into Luna's shins. At first glance, the cabin looks undisturbed and uninhabited. She doesn't see a car, but she notices fresh tire tracks leading to a side of the cabin she can't see well. There's an old steel burn barrel not far from what she assumes is the cabin's back door. Smoke plumes rise from it. Someone's unquestionably been at the cabin, and Luna hopes if it's Ian and Sandra, that they're still here.

"Which way do we go?" Mark whispers.

Luna shakes her head. "I don't know."

Adrenaline brought her to this place, but now that she's here, she hesitates. She closes her eyes, and although she wills herself not to, she thinks about everything that could go wrong. What happens if she gains entry in the cabin and no one's there? Worse, what if—*No!* She can't even think about the worst-case scenario. She won't.

"Luna, look!" Mark points to one of the cabin's windows.

"Oh my God, Ian!"

From where she crouches, she sees movement pass by a

sizable window. At the distance she's at from the cabin, it's impossible to see clearly, but she's certain the figure moving back and forth in front of the window is Ian. Who else could it be? She starts to take off toward the cabin when Mark grabs her upper arm and pulls her back down.

"Wait," he says. "We can't run in there. We have to have a plan."

Luna looks back to the window, and the child-sized figure she assumes is Ian has disappeared. She surveys the area around the cabin and notices a small window with a removable screen on the right side of the back door. If she can get to that window, maybe she can get a better view of who's inside. But then what? She can remove the screen, but what if the window's locked? She'll have to cross that bridge when she gets to it. The objective now is to make it to the cabin.

"I should do it," Mark says when she explains her plan.

Luna shakes her head. "It's better if I go. I'm smaller and can move quicker. I won't be spotted as easily." At this point, she's no longer worried about Detective Pierce and her team. There's nothing they can do now, but if Sandra sees her, there's no telling what she'll do. "Stay here and be the lookout. If Sandra runs, go after her. We can't let her get away with Ian."

Mark takes Luna's hand in his and uses his free hand to brush away a stray hair. "Be careful. I love you."

Luna squeezes his hand. "I love you too."

She drops his hand and stays low to the ground, shuffling through the undergrowth as she positions herself so she has a clear shot to run from the woods, across the yard, and to the cabin's back door. When she's in position, she takes a deep breath and runs as low and fast as she can to get to the window without being seen. She pauses under the window, her back against the wall, and takes a moment to catch her breath. Once her breathing has evened out, she turns around and slowly rises to look through the window. She sees a small eat-in kitchen that appears to open up into a large great room, but she can't tell for sure. There's a high chair next to the kitchen table, and under the table is a grouping of small toys. Luna's heart quickens. She's surer than ever that Ian's inside, and she needs to get to him now.

Before trying the window, she slides along the cabin's exterior and soundlessly checks the door to see if it's locked. Predictably, it is.

Returning to the window, she carefully runs her fingers along the edges of the screen, looking for a mechanism to pop it loose, but the screens are old, and she can't figure out how to work them. She tries tearing the screen, clawing at it with her fingernails, but the mesh material won't give. Desperate to get inside, she looks for anything on the ground or nearby that she can use to rip the screen. A crumbling terra-cotta pot next to the back door catches her eye. She palms one of the bigger clay shards, careful not to cut herself, and uses it like a knife to saw through the screen. With each cut she makes, she cringes, fearful that the slightest sound will alert Sandra.

Once she has cut the screen cut, she tries the window, and to her surprise, it opens with ease. Luna removes her shoes and leaves them on the soft ground beneath the window. She has to be as stealthy as possible when she enters the cabin. She can't take the chance of a squeaky shoe giving her away.

Luna hoists herself over the window's ledge and enters the eerily quiet cabin. The second her feet hit the kitchen floor, any doubts she had about Ian being inside disappear. A mother knows her child's scent, and her nose tells her Ian is nearby. She has to act fast to find him.

90

"Mommy!"

The boy's high-pitched squeal startles Sandra from her dreamless nap. She blinks her eyes open and feels a cool breeze on her bare feet.

"Ian?"

She calls out to him, but he doesn't answer. Rising from the love seat, she looks toward the window where Ian had been playing before she fell asleep. The fire truck lays on its side, but the boy isn't in the room. She walks into the kitchen and her gaze immediately falls on the opened window. She doesn't remember opening the window.

"Ian!"

She shouts his name this time and runs to the window, concern intensifying like a tidal wave throughout her body. The window isn't high, and if she had left it open and he climbed out, she doubted he would've hurt himself. The real danger lies in the woods with the stream nearby. Now at the window, her gaze sweeps over the yard. The boy isn't outside.

How long had she been asleep? Not long, she surmises, but it doesn't take long for little boys to find trouble.

Damn it! She smacks her hands against the sides of the window and looks down. That's when she sees the shoes.

Sandra backs away from the window and considers her next move. After a few seconds, she calls out to him again.

"Ian, honey, where are you?"

She holds her breath and listens.

Nothing.

But she knows it's not nothing. Someone is inside the cabin, and that someone has her son.

91

"Shh, shh. We have to be quiet like mice," Luna whispers into her son's ear.

"Mice," Ian repeats and giggles. He tries to wriggle out of her grip, but she holds him against her body in a tight bear hug.

"Shh, shh," she repeats. They're squeezed together in the small laundry closet in the kitchen.

After Luna had gained entry into the cabin and walked through the kitchen into the great room, she hadn't spotted Ian right away. It was Sandra whom she saw, sleeping on the short couch, low, intermittent snoring sounds escaping her slightly parted lips. She'd been awestruck at how such a person could sleep so peacefully after committing such an unspeakable act, and it was Luna's watchfulness of Sandra that made her unaware of Ian's sudden notice of her. His unbridled joy of seeing her resulted in an ear-piercing scream.

"Mommy!" he shrieked, running to her, knocking the truck over onto the hardwood floor with a loud bang.

Luna caught him in her arms just as Sandra stirred and called out his name. She had tried to escape through the back door, but she slid running across the kitchen floor and lost her footing, stumbling past the door and falling onto her backside. By the time she and Ian had gotten back on their feet, there was no time to backtrack to the door. Sandra would intercept them. Her only option was to hide in the laundry closet and wait for Sandra to leave.

92

From the laundry closet, Luna watches Sandra. The woman backs away from the window and turns around slowly. Luna draws back further into the laundry closet. After several long seconds, Sandra turns back to the window, shuts it, and locks it. She stands in the middle of the kitchen, fingertips against her lips, and then leaves the room hastily.

With no time to waste, Luna shoots out of the laundry closet like a high-powered missile with one mission—to get the hell out of this cabin. But Ian's heaviness slows her down, and she doesn't move as fast as she needs to. She's only inches away from the back door when she hears the unmistakable sound of a gun's safety lever being disengaged and Sandra's low, raspy voice telling her to stop or she'll shoot.

"Turn around."

Luna complies with Sandra's demand, turning slowly to face her.

"Sandra," she whispers.

"Give him to me," Sandra commands, keeping the handgun pointed at Luna and Ian.

"Let's talk about this, okay?" Luna's voice trembles. She doesn't sound nearly as confident as she did that day in the courtroom when she disparaged Logan and defended Le. Right now, she sounds scared and that makes Sandra feel powerful.

"There's nothing to talk about. You took something from me and now it's my turn to take something from you."

"Sandra, I know you're hurting—"

"You know nothing!" she screams, shaking the gun at Luna. "What do you know? Do you know what it's like to wake up every morning wanting just one more day—one more moment— to hold your child? But you can't because someone took his life, and nothing you do will bring him back?"

"The pain you feel is real, and it's unbearable. I understand, but this isn't the way to feel better. Sandra, please put down the gun. You're scaring him."

The little boy, dressed in Logan's clothes, nuzzles Luna's neck and whimpers. Sandra knows this has gone too far, but she can't stop now. Everything was in place for her and Ian to start anew together. It was Sandra's chance to have her son back and to do things better this time. Maybe Adam was right about Logan, and maybe she should've listened. Maybe, just maybe, Sandra *is* partly to blame for Logan's death because she'd been too dismissive of everyone's concerns about his behaviors. Sandra's guilt consumes her and is almost harder to bear than the loss of her son.

She can't carry the weight of the guilt all by herself. Luna has to carry some of it too.

"Put him down—NOW!"

Luna jumps, and Ian cries out. The primal shriek that escaped her lips startled her too, and the gun begins to shake in her hands.

"Sandra, think about Allison," Luna begs.

"What?"

"Allison. Your daughter. She needs you too."

Sandra frowns and shakes her head. "No, Adam will take care of her. You don't know what you're talking about."

"A child needs their mother, especially one as young as Allison."

"Stop talking."

"But Allison—"

"Stop saying her name."

But Luna doesn't stop. "A child needs their mother. My child needs his mother. Allison needs her mother. Come on, Sandra, put the gun down."

"I can't."

"Yes, you can. Put the gun down."

"You don't know," Sandra mutters.

"Sandra, please."

Sandra shakes her head and begins to weep. She raises the gun higher, the muzzle pointed between Luna's eyebrows. No, she can't. She can't put down the gun, and she can't move on. Her life ended the moment Logan took his last breath, and someone has to pay. Her son deserves justice.

Sobbing and with her finger on the trigger, Sandra mumbles, "I'm so sorry."

The gunshot explodes and cracks the air in the room into a tiny million pieces, falling in slow motion to the ground.

The moment is thundering, terrifying, and dreamlike.

And then silence.

EPILOGUE

Two weeks later

Pierce is waiting at a small table inside Picasso's Coffee House, two mugs of steaming hot coffee in front of her and a tall, thin Christmas tree decorated with an assortment of coffee cup ornaments behind her. The coffee shop isn't too crowded; the late afternoon crowd of freelancers, writers, and other usual coffee shop patrons has gone home.

"Sorry if I kept you waiting," Luna tells her, settling into the wooden chair across from her. "I was at Ian's childcare center all afternoon cleaning out his cubby and saying goodbye to the staff."

Pierce pushes one of the mugs across the table toward Luna. "Hope you don't mind that I went ahead and ordered. You seem like the caffè mocha type."

Luna smiles and wraps her palms around the large mug. "I am. Thanks for this."

"How is Ian?" Pierce asks, raising her own mug to her lips.

"Loud noises bother him, and he has some separation anxiety. The trauma counselor tells us that's normal, but in time, he'll be back to his old self. Aside from those two things, he's doing surprisingly well. We've decided to keep him home for a while and give him time to heal."

"Children are unbelievably resilient," Pierce says, then shrugs. "At least, that's what I'm told."

Luna nods and sips from her cup. "That's what the counselor says. I'm choosing to believe that's true."

"How are you?"

Luna considers the questions. The truth is that she's not sure. "It depends on the day," she admits.

"You know, I told you to stay in the car," Pierce scolds.

"Yeah, but I couldn't do that."

"I probably wouldn't have been able to do that either. You were surprisingly stealth. We didn't catch sight of you until you started messing with the window. If you ever decide lawyering isn't your thing, maybe consider being a cop? We'll have to work on your entry methods though."

Luna chuckles. "Yeah, I don't think I could deal with that much excitement every day. How's Sandra doing?"

Pierce shakes her head and smiles. "Only you would ask about the woman who kidnapped your son and tried to kill you. Lucky for you, she was a bad shot."

Luna touches her right ear. The bullet that fired from Sandra's gun had missed her head by only a couple of inches, instead whizzing over her right shoulder and lodging into the wall behind her. The doctor told her he didn't foresee any permanent hearing loss in her right ear, but she might experience occasional ringing in her ears for a while.

"Luckily," Luna agrees.

"The judge denied bail at her arraignment. I hear she's hired Scott Hill to represent her."

"He's good."

Pierce shifts in her chair. "Hopefully, she'll take a plea. Save you from having to testify and reliving everything."

"She's just a grieving mother. I can't blame her."

Pierce scoffs. "You're a much better person that I am. That woman is a raving lunatic."

"I guess you could argue that, but she lost her son in a horrific way. A loss like that changes you. It can turn you into the worse version of yourself and then some. And then there's

Sam. Even though Sam Le was within his rights to defend himself, it doesn't change the fact that a teenage boy is dead. Sam lives with that every day. His son, Jason, called me a couple days after Sandra's arrest to tell me how sorry Sam was. He feels responsible for Sandra's actions toward me."

"Luna, Sandra—and only Sandra—is to blame for the hell your family went through, and her son's actions resulted in his death. That's the end of that story."

"I know. Really, I know, but that doesn't mean I don't understand where Sam's coming from or even Sandra. We all live with the consequences of our choices. Wouldn't you agree?"

Pierce sighs because it's true. "I do."

"Speaking of taking a plea deal," Luna says, changing the subject, "I hear Bryan Boyd pleaded guilty."

"He did, much to my surprise. God, he's an arrogant asshole, little prick."

Luna laughs. "Don't hold back your feelings."

"Trust me. I'm not."

"Well, now Heidi won't have to testify."

"That's good news. She made me nervous."

Luna narrows her eyes at Pierce. "That's not fair. Boyd had a hold over her for years. She was scared, but she's stronger than you think. She put herself in danger to get you and Whitney that confession."

A reluctant smile pulls at the corners of Pierce's lips, and she regards Luna for several seconds before saying, "You really are an advocate for your clients. So, what's next?"

Luna looks over Pierce's shoulder at the Christmas tree, it's white lights blinking on and off, steady and hypnotic. She hasn't returned to her offices since bringing Ian home. Doris has stepped up big time and has been handling not only client-related issues, but also dealing with the never-ending requests from the media for interviews.

"Everyone wants the exclusive interview with 'The Murder Lawyer,'" Doris had told her over the phone two nights ago. They can wait an eternity or until a bigger news story erupts, for all she cares. She has no interest in discussing *her* case with the media.

"I'm not sure," Luna confesses. "Right now, I'm focusing on my family. By the way, thanks for the referral to the transitional housing program for Maya. I think it's going to work out well."

"Sure, no problem. I have a brother who's bipolar, and he's a lot like Maya. There's a lot of people in the system like her too, and they rarely get the help they need. It's sad."

Luna tilts her head, and grins at Pierce. "Sounds like you're a bit of an advocate too."

"Stop it. I have an image to maintain," she jokes.

"Well, we're grateful for the help. Maya has a job interview next Monday for a housekeeping position at a hotel, and she's coming over for dinner tonight. Mark's excited to introduce her to Ian."

"That's wonderful."

Luna raises her mug and says, "To new beginnings."

"To new beginnings," Pierce repeats. "Well, I have to get out of here. Got a perp to interview. I think I let him stew just the right amount of time to feel like talking. Luna, you're a fierce mother and an unrelenting attorney. I expect our paths to cross again."

She stands up and extends her hand across the table. Luna shakes it and says, "You can count on it."

***

The sun is beginning to set when Luna reaches the courthouse steps. The ice-cold breeze coming off the river stirs up the leaves around her feet. She looks up at the building where so many people's lives are judged and fates decided and thinks about all the unimaginable ways her life has changed since Mikey's death. Although she has no way of knowing what the future holds for her, she knows one thing for sure. Justice isn't black and white. It's not good versus evil, but instead, a force that drives people to become their best or, often, the worst versions of themselves. Justice doesn't always prevail, but Luna will never stop making sure both stories are told in the courtroom and that the right people are punished fairly for their actions.

Luna pulls her coat tighter across her chest, breathes in the icy air, and walks home to her family.

ACKNOWLEDGMENTS

Often, the more we do things, the easier it gets. In my experience, that is not the case when writing a book. Certain things get easier over time, but the storytelling process isn't a straight shot from beginning to end. It's an incredibly emotional pilgrimage through imaginary worlds existing only within the author's mind, and there are numerous unforeseen obstacles that make completing that journey seem uncertain at times. Although the storytelling journey is mostly a solitary experience, it is by no means a journey I walk alone.

Writers need the support and encouragement from their family, and I am incredibly grateful to my family for standing by me and always allowing me to dream big. Twenty-six years ago, I had my first date with my now-husband. We went to Applebee's, and at some point during that first date, we started talking about dreams and ambitions. At seventeen, I didn't know much, but I knew that I wanted to be a published writer. From that moment, my husband has never stopped encouraging me to continue to tell my stories and share them with the world. Thank you, Tom, for being my biggest champion.

To my daughters, who have grown up with a mom whose line of work sometimes overshadows their own amazing talents, I love and appreciate your gifts. Go out and forge a path that's yours and no one else's. The world is out there waiting to receive all the goodness and mightiness you have to share.

A finished novel is the sum of numerous parts, and one of

the largest elements of writing a novel is the editing process. I could not have created a book I am proud to share without the tireless efforts of my editor, Karen Tucker of Comma Queen Editing. Karen, you challenge me to dig deeper, you put up with my missed deadlines, and without a shred of doubt, you make me a better writer.

Shelly, you are really one of the few people in my life that understand what it's like to swim in the turbulent waters of the creative life. I can't wait for all our champagne dreams to come true!

I'd also like to acknowledge the early readers of *The Murder Lawyer*, Jenny C. and Carrie P. Your editorial input early in the writing process was invaluable, and I thank you from the bottom of my heart.

To Tracey Whitaker, you placed a bid to have your name as a character in a book and waited a long time for that to happen. Four years to be exact. The wheels of publishing move slowly, and I move even slower. From the bottom of my heart, I thank you for your donation and your patience.

Allow me a moment to acknowledge St. Louis City Public Safety Director, Judge Jimmie Edwards. Over twenty years ago, I took a Law & Society class at Saint Louis University with Judge Edwards. It was in this class that Judge Edwards told us that everyone deserves a defense. Without a proper defense, our criminal justice system doesn't work. Judge Edwards, you probably don't remember me, but those words have stuck with me for two decades, and they ring truer than ever in today's climate. Those words planted a seed and, twenty years later, were the inspiration for *The Murder Lawyer*.

Every book I write I have to give a shout-out to the parentals. They encouraged my imagination and put up with all my dramatic antics that usually resulted in a phone call from worried parents or school officials. Remember the time when I decided to write and direct the third-grade, recess version of the mini-series "North and South?" Hopefully, I've made you proud and embarrassed you less!

OTHER TITLES BY PIPER PUNCHES

Adult Fiction
The Waiting Room
Missing Girl, a novella
60 Days (Missing Girl Series – Book 1)

Children's Fiction
Brave Hearts (The Lavender Fairies, #1)
Fixing Christmas (The Lavender Fairies, #2)

Journals
You Are Magical, Children's Journal

ABOUT PIPER PUNCHES

Piper Punches is the author of the Amazon bestselling books, *The Waiting Room* and *60 Days (Missing Girl Series - Book 1)*, and the companion novella, *Missing Girl*.

When she's not writing books, enjoys hiking, traveling, practicing yoga headstands, coffee, and connecting with her readers.

CONNECT WITH PIPER
Medium: @piperpunches
Instagram: @piperpunches
Twitter: @piperpunches
Facebook: /piperpunches
Goodreads:/piperpunches
Email: piper@piperpunches.com
Website: piperpunches.com

SIGN UP TO RECEIVE WEEKLY EMAILS FROM PIPER

https://bit.ly/signuppiper

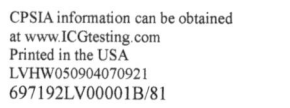